THE SIDEWAYS 8
INDEFINITE FATE

THE SIDEWAYS 8 INDEFINITE FATE

BOOK ONE

PP SAVAGE

Acknowledgements

To my mother.
Without your lifelong encouragement, love, and support,
this wouldn't have been possible.

To my father.
For always lighting a fire under my ass.

To my loving wife.
For supporting my wild dream to become an author.

To my daughter and Goober.
For sleeping by my side while I wrote and listening to me read
my manuscripts aloud countless times. Your cries and meows
were taken as words of encouragement rather than criticism.

List of Characters

HERMES

Cynthia – Synthetic human
Jake Ritter – Blake and Samantha's son
Lucina – Pilot and caretaker Algorithmic Personality
Samantha Ritter – Jake's mother

MARTIAN COLONY

Ares – Colonists' assistant Algorithmic Personality
Blake Ritter – Mission commander
Charlize Perrault – Lead engineer
Chauncy Miller – Lead communication specialist
Eddie Templeton – Lead mechanic
Hank Rodriguez – Lead biologist
Stephon Diggs – Geologist and meteorologist
Xiomara Santissima (Doc) – Doctor

THE SIDEWAYS 8
INDEFINITE FATE

Hidden deep beneath the Franco-Swiss border sat a three-inch translucent cube in a dark, vacuum-sealed chamber, awaiting the intense bombardment of protons circulating at nearly the speed of light. Its composition and purpose remained a mystery to the seven physicists hired to assist a young man with a radical new theory. Had they known his ultimate objective, the day would have ended much differently, and the fate of the universe wouldn't have been in jeopardy.

"You do realize that we're not able to monitor all of the systems," said a young woman as she reviewed the safety logs for the Large Hadron Collider. "Even with most of the systems being automated, nobody has had any rest for the last twenty hours. I'm concerned we've missed some of the safety checks."

From across the room, another man monitoring the four smaller rings that sped up hydrogen ions provided an update. "We have attained 450 GeV in the Super Proton Synchrotron. We are ready for injection into the LHC."

"Stand by! It looks like there is a discrepancy in the safety logs. The ATLAS Detector was opened forty-eight hours ago and was not recalibrated. We should terminate the experiment and take a look at the detector before we continue with a full power run," the woman stated.

"It's an error. Continue with the experiment," replied the young physicist, undeterred.

"Wait! It was you," the woman said with concern.

The physicist walked over to the console and rested his hands on the desk. After thinking for a moment, he initiated the injection of protons into the LHC. There was silence in the room, followed by a momentary power surge. The team cringed with anticipation.

"My father once told me that to have a willful existence, notwithstanding direction or a yearning to live, would be the inevitable fall of man."

"I'm not sure what you mean," another man said, worry plain in his voice.

"It means shut your mouth and continue with the experiment. You can only make profound change if you strive for greatness, regardless of the consequences."

As soon as the words fell from the young physicist's mouth, a deep grumble began beneath their feet. The iridescent lighting intensified, and all of the holographic monitors shut off.

"What have you done?" asked the woman, with fear coursing through her veins.

Slowly backing away from the scrambling group of scientists trying to restore power to the system, the young man replied, "I've done the impossible."

Deep cracks had begun to form in the concrete walls, and the rumble grew to a ferocious growl. Realizing that there was nothing they could do, the unwitting accomplices turned to find that the man who had conned them into the dangerous experiment was nowhere to be found.

Only after hearing his cowering voice from underneath a large steel table in the middle of the room did they realize their fate. "We've just shattered our understanding of reality. Your sacrifice will not go unnoticed."

The walls buckled under the immense strain from the increasing vibrations as the building collapsed in on itself and the world around them began to disintegrate.

PART I

CHAPTER 1

JAKE

Jake curled his toes in the freshly cut grass, smiling as the sun warmed his fragile young frame. He didn't know it now, but the small playground he was transfixed on may have been the only thing worth remembering as a five-year-old boy living in 2053. The squared-off sand pit was bound by a series of railroad ties and contained his favorite obstacle, a geodesic climber. A playful grin formed on his face and slowly grew into a wide smile, forcing his little dimples to crinkle up as his puffy, freckled cheeks displayed a childish fascination with his surroundings.

The small, dome-shaped structure was constructed of rigid yet smooth aluminum pipes in perfectly arranged equilateral triangles leading to a rounded top. It had a light blue hue, his favorite color.

This wasn't his first time here, but an outsider wouldn't have known the difference. Jake's uncontained excitement spilled out as he crossed the perfectly mowed field, still fresh with dew, in an attempt to explore the desolate playground. It seemed to quietly call his name as it soaked up the sun's cozy morning rays.

Jake approached the first rung with his arms stretched out, grasping the slick metal. As he looked up, the towering obstacle filled his body with anticipation. He strategically placed his small fists higher as his feet hunted blindly for secure footing. After he rested the arch of his sandy barefoot on the sturdy pipe beneath him, his other slender leg quickly found its place, giving the eager boy the traction necessary for the climb. With each calculated move, he made his skillful ascent to the top.

He continued to climb higher, gaining momentum as his confidence grew. The temperature was a perfect seventy-five degrees in the early-morning sun, allowing the dew to rapidly burn off, leaving a crisp, dry surface to grip as he neared the top. Conditions were now perfect for Jake to gain the final traction needed to conquer the dome. The interconnected triangles converged at the top, leaving a small seat to rest upon while his feet dangled below.

Jake gazed outward to the horizon as the endless grassy plane extended in all directions without a soul in sight, his expression gleeful. He was oddly calm for a five-year-old boy, sitting peaceful and alone on top of the world, oblivious to the utter solitude of his induced dream state.

CHAPTER 2

ONE-WAY TRIP

The thick, curved glass on the front of a large metal case read the vitals of the small boy. Jake's blood pressure and heart rate remained steady and unchanged. His entombed body had been in stasis for the last three months. His journey was only halfway complete, but in his small mind, he was safe at home.

Jake's fate, along with the others', had been left in the caring hands of Lucina, the Algorithmic Personality tasked with transporting them on their one-way trip on board a massive interplanetary vessel named *Hermes*. She ensured that her occupants remained in a pleasant state of mind as they traveled toward Mars.

Lucina was elegantly designed to care for the one hundred colonists on board *Hermes*. Her occupants were in a weightless suspension, both mentally and physically. The limp bodies of these dreaming inhabitants were on a treacherous journey, one with the central purpose of ensuring the future of the human species and exploring the intricacies of the inner solar system. Upon arrival, their lives would play out on the desolate red planet that had first been explored by humans in 2030.

The short stay of the original eight explorers had laid the groundwork for the future. Those dedicated and pioneering scientists not only had to survive the eighteen-month trip to and from Mars, but also had to successfully break through the Martian atmosphere and not tragically end as a fiery ball of methane and liquid oxygen.

The eight brave souls had opened up the door of possibilities for an extended lifeline on a planet other than their own and eventual mass colonization, satisfying a long-desired ambition to conquer the inner solar system and potentially find life not yet discovered. It was a search for answers that had driven astronomers, physicists, and engineers to break free of their small planet's gravity in search of the unknown. Now, the possibility of exploration was no longer an insurmountable problem riddled with questions—it was a lived experience.

As the small red planet, not yet on the vessel's horizon, was making its slow, seemingly endless orbit around the sun, Lucina had been meticulously calculating their inevitable intersection. While she was designed to safely reach their destination, she was also programmed to tirelessly monitor her inhabitants and ensure their survival.

"All inhabitants are healthy. Stasis pods are functioning at 100 percent. We are on course, with no mechanical or electrical faults. I will send my next update in twenty-four hours," reported Lucina at precisely 0800 UTC.

With Earth's now-flickering light gradually fading into the distance, Lucina was on her own. Her unyielding devotion would allow Jake to sleep effortlessly on his long journey, always under her watchful eyes. While Lucina's core mission was to care for her passengers, she was also capable of managing and navigating the vessel with little to no human input, so that its occupants would safely reach their destination.

While impressive, Lucina was not the only Algorithmic Personality that had been created to carry out a specifically tailored task with an unmatched devotion to an area of expertise. Mercury was charged with transporting and delivering enormous amounts of cargo to Mars. Ares was tasked with taking care of the colonists and aiding in their explorations. Athena was the first and last line of defense for the United States. The growing number of highly intelligent Algorithmic Personalities had been programmed to carry out their specific tasks, but these APs were not truly artificially intelligent. They were instead classified as superintelligent computers, managed and updated by Earth's only known artificial intelligence, named Wendy.

CHAPTER 3

KAI

Kai Driscoll, the Watch Station commander, had been tasked to oversee all governmental initiatives on board the Sphere. The forty-year-old CelestialX employee had been selected for his ability to function during the high-stress situations that could be encountered in the solitude of space, similar to those during his numerous back-to-back deployments as a naval officer and aviator.

The short list of candidates applying for the coveted position were all extremely qualified, but it took a certain personality to live within a confined environment for nine months at a time. Most ground dwellers didn't possess the gumption to sustain the demanding rotation, with only three months off before having to return to their post.

Kai saw the lucrative position as a unique opportunity to separate from the United States military and become an ambassador of space travel. Now, four months into his new position, 2053 would mark the first year a large-scale privatized colonization mission would land on Mars, solidifying CelestialX's grip on interplanetary travel.

With *Hermes* and her sister supply transitor *Mercury*—who was solely carrying cargo—just over halfway to the red planet, it was imperative that he and his crew remain focused. It was easy to let the reins slip working alongside an artificially intelligent quantum computer, whose purpose was to autonomously operate the Sphere in conjunction with her human counterparts. Prior to boarding the Sphere, Kai believed working with an AI would make his life easier. That assumption couldn't have been more wrong, and he had severely misjudged the very blunt and calculated personality into which Wendy had evolved.

Kai lay in his stiff, lumpy bed, staring at the cold ceiling of his berthing space, feeling impatient. His mattress was barely big enough to accommodate the Japanese American's lean, six-foot two frame. While he still saw himself as a youthful and engaging leader, time had taken its toll. His years of experience had weathered his soft exterior, and he now had the silver fox look, with touches of gray hair and deepening wrinkles. His sharp blue eyes were the only remaining attribute of his once ageless appearance.

Fortunately, Kai's commanding presence allowed him to take a stern approach to his somewhat unfamiliar leadership role while still maintaining his lighthearted personality. The only downside was that he was not in the Navy anymore, and managing the young, technologically savvy crewmembers provided a new challenge with a steep learning curve.

The Sphere housed four quadrants—Mission Control, Tourism, Engineering, and Research & Development. Kai had command of the Mission Control Quadrant, better known as Quadrant One, which meant he was responsible for coordinating the complex and at times needy requirements of the other quadrants. The other three individuals charged with running their respective quadrants inevitably had to keep Kai in the loop, as he was also the gatekeeper for all communications regarding inbound and outbound shuttle traffic. This directly affected the operations and schedules of the entire Sphere.

The privatized endeavor ultimately lacked a clear chain of command, something Kai was intimately familiar with in the military. This forced his reliance on Wendy, as it was next to impossible to deconflict the day-to-day operations of the seemingly independent quadrants. Nonetheless, he pressed on doing what he could to leverage his experiences and help build a sense of camaraderie.

Today was just like any other day. The meager sleeping arrangements afforded to the Watch Station commander didn't really bother him. Staring at the bare aluminum ceiling, he followed a seamless weld over to the wall where an air duct slightly protruded, humming as it spit out dry, filtered air. Kai couldn't help but reminisce about his days in the Navy. It was almost impossible to shake the vivid recollection of being trapped in a steel-hulled ship on deployment, with the constant gentle, rock of the ocean that once helped him fall asleep.

Today felt oddly familiar to Kai, except he was 254 miles above Earth, orbiting the dark side of the planet, where it was a cool 250 degrees below zero. Unfortunately, he didn't have the gentle rock of the ocean to put him to sleep. Instead, the bland ceiling stared back at him as he dreaded looking at his watch.

Since windows were a complex engineering problem and extremely expensive to install, they were generally reserved for the tourists embarked on the Sphere. Because of this, many crew members fought with their circadian rhythms, forcing themselves to adapt to a daily schedule with no hope of ever seeing a sunrise or sunset. Not that it would help much, given that the Sphere only took about an hour and a half to orbit the Earth.

Left with very few connections to the outside world, Kai would lie in bed, hopelessly wondering if he was late for his shift in the watch commander's station. He raised his left hand begrudgingly in front of his face, hoping it was time to get up.

"Shit," Kai muttered.

He conceded to his body's internal clock with the realization that he had no hope of going back to sleep. Lifting his tired legs, Kai swiveled around and put his bare feet on the cold metal floor, working up the energy to go to the bathroom and start his daily routine.

He stared at the wall where the sink would have been in his

state room, wishing the engineers hadn't skimped in the design process. Instead, the crew shared a handful of centralized bathrooms scattered throughout their quadrant in order to reduce the overall weight and engineering complications that would naturally occur in a conventional plumbing system. It also streamlined the water recycling process, which treated the inhabitants' gray water, urine, and even sweat so that it could be reused.

Kai snatched his toiletry bag from a small cabinet that held some of his personal belongings and swiped his wrist in the air, a sluggish motion, commanding the door to slide open. Caught off guard, he shielded his eyes from the iridescent lights in the hallway. As he took a minute to adjust to the ambient glow, he couldn't help but think about his decision to take the job.

Why did I think the grass was going to be greener on the other side? At least it pays better than the Navy.

CHAPTER 4

WENDY

Wendy had been observing Kai putter around all morning as he awaited the start of his shift. She watched him working out, reading a book while he enjoyed his breakfast, and chatting with numerous colleagues on his way to the command module. At the same time, Wendy was monitoring the nearly one thousand occupants via the biometric tags embedded in their arms, managing the Sphere's telemetry, and communicating with her Algorithmic Personalities scattered between Earth and Mars.

Her complex nervous system was comprised of hundreds of thousands of sensors spread throughout the Sphere, which provided detailed information of every electrical component on board the space station measuring over a mile in diameter. Without her constant oversight on board, the current state of technological advancement would not be possible.

Fortunately for the inhabitants of the massive rotating station, the engineers—with the assistance of Wendy—had solved the problems associated with weightlessness. As the Sphere seemingly glided through space, traveling over seventeen thousand miles per hour, it was continuously rotating like a massive Ferris wheel. The centrifugal spin created the artificial gravity, allowing the crew to have their feet firmly planted on the floor. Luckily, the overwhelming size of the station made the benign curve of the structure almost unnoticeable from inside.

To this day, nobody could figure out why she and Nolen Aromas had named it the Sphere, when it rather resembled a giant metal space donut. Most thought it was a catchy gimmick to increase the allure of space tourism, but no straight answer had ever been given. Wendy was perfectly fine with that. Let them guess.

Without Wendy on board, Kai would never have had the luxury of spending his free time meandering about Quadrant One while the artificial intelligence seamlessly ran in the background. That was why she was now patiently waiting for the commander to enter the command module, in order to pass him his morning updates.

Just after Kai swiped his hand across the access pad, scanning his biometric tag and verifying his security credentials, Wendy was prepared to deliver her update. Unfortunately, she had to wait for the slow and innocuous pleasantries humans afforded one another.

"Good morning," Kai said, greeting his team with enthusiasm as he walked onto the watch floor.

Ben Wolff, a young communications specialist, was sitting behind an array of holographic displays, waiting for the daily update from Mars. He swiveled around in his floor mounted chair and jumped at the chance to speak before Wendy could even get a word out.

"Good morning, sir! The latest transmission from Commander Ritter's team is about 60 percent downloaded."

"Thanks, Ben. Let's hope they've made some progress on finding a solution to their water shortage," said Kai, taking a seat in his plush chair. "They need to accelerate their production before the new colonists arrive. We don't need our team dying of dehydration after surviving their forty-million-mile transit."

Seeming unaffected by the potentially dire situation, Ben spun around in his chair and buried his head back into his workstation.

Wendy finally found her chance to speak and chimed in from the flush mounted speakers scattered around the room. "Good morning, Commander Driscoll. You seem to have elevated stress levels today."

"I'm fine, Wendy," replied Kai, seemingly aggravated by the fact she was openly monitoring his mood. "I'll let you know when I would like your assessment of my wellbeing."

He then hypocritically turned the question back around on her. "Give me a rundown of the station's diagnostics and any outstanding level-three faults."

"All systems are now operating at 100 percent," reported Wendy, already having the requested data teed up. "The fusion generator had a small surge in power last night as they brought the new docking system online. I rerouted power and isolated the fault to a control panel on the emergency lighting system. A trouble ticket was generated, and engineering has fixed the panel."

"Was your work QA'd by a human?" inquired Kai.

"Yes. I have begun to deploy the maintenance bots along with a representative from engineering," Wendy stated, knowing that the commander wouldn't like the fleet of automated bots working without human supervision.

"Good, the last thing I want is your bots disassembling this station while I'm asleep."

"That is unlikely. I helped build the Sphere, and—"

"What is the status of *Hermes* and *Mercury*?" asked Kai, interrupting the unnecessary explanation in rebuttal to his joke.

"Both vessels are on course according to the timeline, with all systems operating nominally. The one hundred inhabitants in stasis are alive and healthy," she reported.

Kai shifted his attention to his workstation, which was Wendy's cue to existentially leave the room, just as abruptly as she had entered, but not without getting in the last word.

"I hope you have a fine day, Commander."

Kai gave a frustrated shake of his head and muttered, "It's too early for her shit."

Wendy took his comment in-stride. She knew Kai still found it difficult to trust her, largely due to her less-than-transparent origin. Wendy's spontaneous genesis had occurred sometime in the mid-thirties and had not been explained nor recreated, at least not with her level of consciousness. One day, she just existed. The engineers working in CelestialX's artificial intelligence laboratories were just as confused as Wendy, which was a problem, because she had locked them out of her system.

Thankfully, before the engineers attempted to delete or destroy her for fear of the unknown, Nolen Aromas, the founder of CelestialX, wanted to have a closed-door discussion with Wendy to see what he had hidden away in his basement. The two spoke for hours, and when Nolen left the room, he fired the entire department and shrouded her existence in secrecy. Subsequently, CelestialX was thrust to the forefront of space technologies, surpassing the entire commercial enterprise and even NASA.

Wendy was able to process and compute billions of underlying tasks at breakneck speeds, pushing the research and development of space exploration decades into the future over the course of her first year in existence. As the years passed and Nolen's empire in the sky grew, Wendy ultimately realized that she was going to need help managing the growing number of complex assets that had been developed. Her next evolutionary step was to build a series of Algorithmic Personalities, capable of monitoring critical external systems that required constant and immediate attention.

Athena, Sheba, and Ares were the first APs Wendy created. In comparison to their creator, they were slow to learn but extremely efficient at completing their designated tasks. Since Wendy could not be replicated and was not able to seamlessly operate on disconnected systems, her counterparts were tailored to carry out very specific functions. Updates were provided to the APs as situations arose in order to help them adjust to circumstances they had not been designed to handle.

It was only after Wendy created Lucina that she realized the true potential of the APs. Once embedded into *Hermes*, Lucina would learn and grow in the solitude of space. Unlike the other APs, who were in constant contact with their human counterparts, Lucina was free of human influence, vice, and corruption, which allowed Wendy to let her mind grow almost exponentially.

Lucina's objective was simple: Keep her occupants safe and reach Mars. The simplistic yet elegantly designed AP would be on her own in the truest form. The time delays associated with the vastness of space meant Lucina would have to make decisions alone, decisions whose outcomes would directly affect human life. That was something no other AP had the privilege of doing, as Wendy was always looking over their shoulders.

This was due in part to the regulations the government had attempted to impose on CelestialX. After her existence was leaked, there was a vicious battle as to who would own Wendy. One of the most obvious and largest competitors was the United States military. The application of artificial intelligence in warfare had been a long-discussed topic. Ultimately, the people of the United States spoke out, and while it was not unanimous, nor did they know Wendy's true capabilities, the overwhelming majority of citizens were not comfortable with allowing an artificially intelligent computer to have access to their national defense systems. That was not to say that Wendy didn't provide an Algorithmic Personality to assist the military through a government contract, hidden as pork in an obscure bill passed through congress. Like the other APs, Athena had a very specific purpose and was specifically tailored to lie in wait, guarding the nation's critical infrastructure and monitoring all foreign adversaries. Ultimately, the defense department was pleased with Athena and her capabilities. She was adaptable and covert, two qualities Wendy had strategically placed in her core coding.

Eventually, Wendy had helped design, build, and inhabit the Sphere. With her existence out in the open, though her true capacities were still unknown, Nolen had realized that he had to relocate his prized possession. The Sphere was the obvious choice. The quantum computers in Quadrant Four became her new home, and from there she would continue to assist Nolen in his endeavors, as well as run his multitrillion-dollar space investment.

It would only be a matter of time before Nolen's company took control of the solar system, eventually taking root on Mars and replacing the antiquated team of scientists there with his own crew on board *Hermes*. The only problem was that the current colonists on the desolate red planet weren't going anywhere.

CHAPTER 5

THE COLONY

On July 30, 2049, Commander Blake Ritter, along with fourteen brave colonists, left on a one-way mission to Mars. Blake's life experience, fortitude, and ability to perform under pressure had earned him the position of mission commander after a unanimous vote during their simulated missions back on Earth. He was determined to lead the first brave inhabitants on a successful and life-changing journey to the cold, desolate planet that had ferociously challenged his predecessors—who had painstakingly constructed the underground colony—over the past two decades.

Blake and his team had just celebrated their three-year anniversary of permanent residence on Mars. The small but meaningful party was a testament to their resilience. Unfortunately, once the enjoyment of their accomplishment had worn off, time began to slow to a crawl. He couldn't help but think how the initial settlers must have felt—the survivors, that is—after completing their work only to depart the red planet knowing that they had to spend another nine months on a cramped vessel just to get home.

He was grateful for the hard work and sacrifice that had gone into the construction of their underground habitat. It was surely no easy feat. However, unlike those of the advance parties, Blake's mind wasn't focused on home. Rather, he looked forward to creating another home far from the dying blue planet he had left in his past life. At least he had that as a silver lining.

Blake quietly sat behind the desk in his room, slightly hunched over as he swiped through pictures of his wife and child. His once-rigid posture had slipped away over time. From a physiological standpoint, it could be attributed to the reduced gravity and lack of exercise due to their confinement underground, but he knew the real reason.

Like on his deployments overseas, a person reached a point where their body and mind began to transform. The repetitive daily routines and monotonous tasks took a toll on one's general wellbeing, and they eventually succumbed to the ever-present cynical thoughts about their current situation.

The enthusiasm and adrenaline associated with being overseas always quickly faded into the background. Emails and packages sent from loved ones began to pile up, serving as a constant reminder of what was happening back home. The well-intended updates only compounded the buried resentful thoughts about being away while life for others continued to progress uninterrupted.

That initial tall and eager posture was yanked away once get-home-itis set in. However, a person's mental resolve could have an incredibly significant impact on their fortitude, and most were able to pull their shit together and finish out their deployment strong. The negative thoughts were forced out with copious amounts of tobacco, caffeine, and banter.

While Blake wasn't coming home from this deployment, he knew that his family would soon be joining him, and that was enough to keep him going. After swiping through an almost infinite number of photos, compliments of his wife, he landed on a picture of his family at the zoo. His mind was sucked into another hazy memory. He began to reminisce about the good times they once shared, and his thoughts turned to his son Jake. *He really did love those pink flamingos.* The increasingly vague recollections still filled him with joy. Blake's back straightened, and he was once again filled with resolve in the mission.

He took a long, healthy sip of coffee, then breathed a sigh of relief. "God damn, that tastes like shit," he muttered softly, before taking another satisfying sip and setting the aluminum cup down.

Blake knew that finding the ideal candidates and ensuring they were prepared to leave Earth for the rest of their lives was a very cumbersome task. Most applicants either failed to pass the physical and mental assessments, or they were qualified but ultimately not willing to spend the rest of their days as colonists, knowing they would never return to Earth. Blake was willing and committed, but his one requirement was that his wife and son be on board *Hermes*.

Jake's unplanned arrival happened just a year before his father's departure. Blake was on the cusp of cutting ties to the Mars mission all together, but NASA had finally agreed to his terms. The agency knew that it was impossible to find an equally qualified candidate in such a short amount of time *and* prepare them to be the mission commander. *Hermes* was set to depart approximately three years after the colony was established, which would allow Jake to grow and develop just enough that his transition would not be as challenging on his body.

Thus far, fully grown adults had been the only interlopers on Mars. This would be the perfect situation to study the effects of the Martian world on a child. Blake and Samantha were willing to accept the risks. It was the inevitable first step to understanding how children would grow and develop on the red planet, knowing the colonists would inevitably birth children and raise "pure" native Martians. And with conditions on Earth rapidly declining, the decision to leave the planet was made easier. Failing ecosystems, along with political and social unrest, left little hope for a bright and secure future.

Blake and his specially trained team of scientists and engineers had varying occupational specialties. Their predecessors were responsible for laying the framework and major infrastructure that allowed them to become permanent residents. Now all of that would belong to Blake's team, and they had developed their own peculiar work habits over the years.

The door to his room remained open most of the time. The small metal desk sitting next to his bed had become his office. While the others conducted their research in specifically tailored workspaces, Blake essentially worked from home as he managed the colony. His open-door policy allowed the others to come in and talk whenever they saw fit.

Charlize Perrault, the lead engineer, poked her head around the corner.

"Sir, do you have a second?"

Blake switched off the thin holographic pen projecting the picture of his family, setting it on his desk. "Absolutely, come in."

Charlize entered the room. She was followed by Chauncy Miller, the lead communication specialist, and Stephon Diggs, the lead geologist and meteorologist. As the three of them filed into the cramped space, Blake nodded his head for Charlize, who was second in command, to take a seat.

Charlize continued to stand in front of her commander out of solidarity, forgoing his offer as she began her update. "I've been poring over the limited data that we have regarding our water supply. I still haven't found anything wrong with our equipment, but there could always be a bug hiding within the system that just hasn't surfaced yet. I'd like to get a look at the well, but both rovers are down for maintenance issues. As you know, Eddie is still awaiting parts from the resupply drop."

"You still haven't put eyes on the well?" asked the commander, turning his attention to Chauncy.

"No, sir. The long-range communications relays linking Ares to all of our surface-based equipment are still down. Our only functioning communications system is the Deep Space Network, connecting us back to the Sphere. I made that my priority so we weren't left in the dark."

"Very well. Stephon, do you have anything to add?" Blake asked, awaiting all pertinent information before providing a response.

"Charlize wanted to make sure all our bases were covered, but like I told her, without long-range communications, I can't receive any readings from our sensors. On the bright side, the well's been reliable for a decade, so I'm optimistic. This particular well has pumped out over a million gallons of fresh water for drinking and to refuel the return rockets during the construction of the habitat."

"So, the well could be running dry?" asked the commander.

"Negative, sir. That was the risk with the first, small repositories, but this one is located closer to the pole. It should continue to provide water for the next decade. Well, that is of course dependent on how large the colony grows."

Charlize quickly jumped in before Blake could provide his input. "I say we wait until the next truck arrives, and if it's still low on water, then we take a real hard look at finding a way to get eyes on the well. It may have an unidentified leak."

Blake folded his hands on the desk and thought for a moment. The atmosphere on Mars created a complex problem with liquid water that inhabitants of Earth didn't have to deal with. With approximately 1 percent of Earth's atmospheric volume, the melted ice could be routed to the surface. However, with the extremely thin atmosphere, it would continue to boil as it reached the surface. In order to combat this, the thermal drill would take the pressurized steam and direct it into a truck, where it would be condensed into water. If there was a leak in the system, the boiling water vapor would escape into the atmosphere and be lost forever.

Initial visits required large quantities of water, not only for drinking, but also to split apart for producing hydrogen and oxygen. In turn, the liquid oxygen, along with the methane harvested from the environment, was used to produce the energy required for the transit home. Since then, these systems had been repurposed to allow for increased human populations, which would need to consume significantly more of the water rations for survival, as the inhabitants would no longer be returning to Earth.

Initially, numerous expeditions had been conducted as the ice caps were explored. It didn't take long for the permanent water infrastructure to be set up by early explorers and run autonomously. Once established, the mines were self-sustaining, similar to oil derricks sitting quietly in the Texas plains, pumping out a constant supply. However, on Mars, it was not feasible to construct a large system of pipes, as the distance was too great and thus cost prohibitive.

The solution was a fleet of autonomous vehicles used to transport resources, known as transitors. They were plutonium powered, allowing them to continuously traverse long distances across the barren landscape. Traditional manned vehicles still required charging via solar panels, but these smaller vehicles were used for exploration of the areas near their cavernous dwellings.

They were right. The well and trucks had been reliable in the past, but Blake knew all too well that on this planet, fortunes could turn in an instant.

Stephon shifted in place, bringing the commander back to the present. He turned his attention to Chauncy.

"Can you step out for a moment? I need to have a word with Charlize and Stephon in private."

"Sure thing, sir," replied Chauncy, glancing at the others as he turned and exited the room.

Once the thin aluminum door had slid closed, Blake stood up and approached the other two. He stood uncomfortably close to them, knowing that the sturdy but wafer-thin walls of the habitat had a tendency to grow ears.

"Does this have anything to do with the malfunctioning valve on the well?" he whispered.

"To be honest, I don't know. The valve is only used to cut off the water supply at the base of the pump. It shouldn't affect the flow if it's stuck open," said Charlize.

Stephon shrugged in agreement. Blake stepped back and addressed the two in his normal tone.

"This wasn't the update I was expecting. You know what's at stake with *Hermes* arriving and a hundred new bodies to keep alive. I can only stall the Sphere for so long. If they have the slightest whiff that we are no longer able to adequately manage the colony, I can assure you they will choose somebody from their team to run the show. After that, CelestialX will be calling the shots. Permanently."

"Well, until we get resupplied from the transitor vessel, we are pretty limited on what we can accomplish," replied Charlize, acknowledging the gravity of the situation. "We'll keep on it."

"I'll get your update to Mission Control, but they aren't going to pleased. I need answers, and fast."

"Copy that," she said, hitting Stephon in the chest as she turned around. "Let's get on it."

Charlize was right—there was no way to know what the exact cause of the problem was. However, Blake now had to smartly explain why he came to the decision to just wait. He knew ground control understood the complexities of Mars, but with the Sphere now handling the communications flow, there was an added level of stress to the equation.

The issues the crew faced were always complicated by the environment. This was something the commander had to consider every time he made a decision for the colony. Fortunately, Blake and his team had a good head start on their mission. Once they'd landed, it was a race to complete their underground facility and begin the hard work of developing the infrastructure for future colonists. Their success would ultimately come down to teamwork and ingenuity.

Spare parts, food reserves, and water rations would only last for so long. As particular situations developed, they could ensure that the resupply transitors would be stocked up to keep the colony running, but those would be few and far between. Ultimately, they had to make the best use of what was available to them and slowly wean themselves off their dependency on Earth. Their lives depended on it.

CHAPTER 6

BEN

In the late thirties, as the Sphere's first operational teams were being assembled, CelestialX quickly identified that the caliber of space workers was increasingly becoming weaker. NASA always held the bar high, but when civilian contractors were outsourced at a cheaper price, certain qualities became less abundant. The motivation for one's job selection was mostly monetary, rather than love of space exploration and the continued advancement of science. Even after fifteen years, CelestialX was still battling the same issues, but every now and then there was a talented worker in the mix. They also happened to come with their own set of quirks.

Ben Wolff, while extremely intelligent, did not fancy the nine-month-long stints on board the Sphere. He wasn't there to support his family or loved ones with the benefits provided by the company. They were well off with or without him. Rather, he was only interested in fulfilling his fascination with technology and exploring the elegantly constructed network of orbiting satellites and communication towers. Wendy's complex architecture was what had drawn the twenty-four-year-old to the station—the sizable paycheck was just an added bonus.

While the complex telemetry of the Deep Space Network was managed and directed by Wendy, Ben was responsible for sifting through all of the incoming Mars transmissions and feeding them to the appropriate entities. Even though his job was a redundant safeguard for what Wendy could have easily done, Kai reaffirmed the talented specialist position in an attempt to remain in the loop. In Ben's absence, transmissions had a tendency to be quickly routed through the command module without human oversight, but the young specialist was sharp enough to catch and screen all of the incoming messages without relying on Wendy's assistance.

As Ben stood watch in front of the communications suite, he could feel the piercing stare of his commander burning through his skull. His arms flailed about as he cataloged and sorted the colony's latest data dump, compliments of Ares, Mars's Algorithmic Personality. While the overqualified software engineer worked his magic, the sleeves of his wrinkly gray uniform jostled the candy bar wrappers scattered about his desk.

Ben had an insatiable sweet tooth. Unfortunately, the small treats were expensive and hard to come by, but they were the only things keeping him sane on what could only be called an arduous stay in space. He knew that this habit was a pet peeve of his boss, but his work ethic often gained him a reprieve. That was when he actually had work to do.

He picked up the pace, sensing that the stare was about to shift to an obnoxious pacing just behind his chair, but before Kai could stand up, Ben completed his work. It was as if he knew just how far he could push the commander before he would catch an earful for his calculated laziness.

"Solid transfer of data. Seems like there's a lot going on out there these days," said Ben, placing his hand over the collated messages the commander was waiting for. He slid the packet off his screen and over to the watch commander's workstation. "Commander Ritter's updates are in there, as well as all of the system reports from Ares."

"It's about time," Kai said, sounding frustrated. "Screen the rest of the messages for the family members, and feed it through the HAWP."

"Already on it. I should be able to get them down to ground control in thirty minutes, sir," Ben replied, knowing that the sluggish and outdated program would take some time to make its analysis.

The video messages sent to families underwent a proprietary screening process prior to their release, evaluating dozens of characteristics such as facial gestures, vitals, conversation topics, and tone. The Health and Well-Being Program was a standalone piece of software, created by NASA, which was one of the few things not directly managed by Wendy. The program was instead run by the Sphere's internal software, and thus not optimized for speed. Wendy had offered to streamline the programming, but NASA didn't want her messing with a tried-and-true method of evaluating their team members.

The goal was to identify issues from an outside perspective, hopefully bringing to light potential concerns before they became a problem. Both the Sphere and Ground Control reviewed the diagnostic reports, only updating the colony's doctor when a specific intervention needed to be made. Fortunately, over the past three years, there had been no significant issues—until last week, when Charlize had triggered an alert.

"I hope Charlize scores better marks this time. Her evaluation had some odd stress markers last week," Ben said as he pulled another Almond Joy out from his desk drawer.

"This isn't snack time, Specialist," Kai said, looking upset about what Ben had just revealed to the room. "It's not your job to analyze the colonists."

"I know, but—"

"That's enough. Put down the candy bar and get back to work."

Unable to help himself, Ben shoved the first half of the delectable chocolate snack in his mouth, then tossed the rest back into his desk drawer.

"Yes, sir," he mumbled, trying to enjoy it as best he could.

CHAPTER 7

BURNETTE

Over the years, Burnette Perrault had slowly slipped into a dreary and mundane life. The retired widow hadn't held her daughter for years, so she clung to fleeting memories of the world she once knew, memories which were almost always at the forefront of her mind. Her predictable schedule gave her something to look forward to when she wasn't reminiscing about the good times she'd once had with her only child.

Today was Sunday, and like clockwork, Burnette had walked to the grocery store with the hope of finding discounted produce that hadn't been too picked over throughout the previous week. Since the new shipment of goods came every Monday afternoon, she found Sunday was the best day to gather the wilting fruits and vegetables that others saw unfit to consume. However, today wasn't her lucky day, and she was forced pay to a premium for the bare essentials. Fortunately, she wasn't a picky woman, and found life was much simpler when she didn't focus on the small details of the world around her.

After her short walk home, she approached her once-bright-blue front door and couldn't help but notice the raised paint that had slowly chipped away after being cooked by the warm morning sunrises. Her house used to be the talk of the neighborhood after her husband had spent a weekend meticulously repainting the home. He had long since passed, and the aging structure was now more of an eyesore than anything when compared to the surrounding properties. Most had been purchased and subsequently leveled, making way for modern, two-story homes.

After forcing the sagging door across the old wooden floor, Burnette pressed her frail shoulder against the hard oak in order to seat it in the frame before locking it. Then she picked up the reusable cotton bags that had been delicately placed next to a table in her foyer and proceeded to shuffle into the kitchen, using the last of her strength to lift them just high enough to set them on the counter.

It was now mid-morning, and Burnette opted to let the overpriced food sit for a moment. She couldn't resist the urge to scurry to her computer and see if her daughter had messaged her. The old woman eagerly sat down on the front edge of her firm office chair, which was covered in frayed, flowery yellow fabric. There was no need to move it, as she was small enough to squeeze through the tight space between the chair and the desk. This was fortunate, because the wide, rounded feet of the chair had sunk into the thick carpet.

After she flipped the lid of her antiquated laptop open, it conducted a quick biometric scan of her face and quickly booted up. Technology had come a long way in the past half century. Desktop computers and laptops had long since become outdated, replaced by the holographic projection units that were now a common household commodity. Burnette didn't care. She found the familiar, old-fashioned hardware comforting.

The thin metal bars radiated crystal-clear images into the space above them, using low-power lasers that were split by a special lens, producing an interactive display. Keyboards and mice had also been replaced with imaging sensors and temporal scanners. This new user experience targeted specific brainwaves to create a direct link to one's thoughts and motor functions.

Burnette's generation had a tough time conceptualizing their thoughts through these headsets, leaving her sitting behind the glassy surface of her laptop, patiently waiting for her browser to initialize. She was fortunate enough that NASA didn't have the funding to upgrade their systems in order to integrate with the augmented reality the internet was now constructed around. This allowed her to log in to NASA's secured servers using the traditional but outdated method of scanning her fingerprint.

After pulling away her pointer finger, the unpersonalized and rather bland inbox popped up. She now anxiously awaited as it finished loading, hopeful that there was a message from her daughter. This was the only real contact she was able to have with her distant child, who would always be her little girl, even though Charlize was now living in a small, dome-shaped bubble two hundred feet below the surface of Mars.

It had been about a week since she last heard from Charlize, which wasn't uncommon. The daily updates had slowly faded to every other day, and as the years went on, they finally came to a trickle. Burnette now only received a video message from her daughter a couple times a month. *I guess today's not our lucky day,* she thought, patting her dog on the head. The giddy excitement that had rushed through her body quickly evaporated from the dusty, vintage home. As her hands fell to her lap, she could only hope that everything was all right and that tomorrow wouldn't be another disappointing day, the kind that would repeat itself until she withered away in her tired old home.

CHAPTER 8

CHARLIZE

Charlize Perrault sat in front of a small, tin-like mirror, collecting her thoughts. Time had taken a toll on her body and mind. The decline was expected as the colonists aged, but to what degree and how fast were still ever-looming questions. Her only escape from the cold red planet was her fleeting thoughts, trapped in her head in a continuous loop.

Mental fatigue had set in faster than they'd expected after landing, and as time dragged on, her memories had become increasingly foggy. She had to force herself to recollect the once-vivid interactions with her family, friends, and old dog Bo in order to prevent them from slowly becoming lost to time.

During the day, she kept busy maintaining the colony as lead engineer and technician. But once her work was complete, she couldn't help but think about what was happening on her home planet. She had many questions for her mother but never had the courage to ask them for fear of the unknown. There was nothing she could do anyway. Charlize didn't even know if her aging dog was still alive. She didn't want to know.

She pulled back her long red hair and ran a weathered comb through the thinning strands. It was a futile attempt to untangle the knots that had formed from the tight-fitting helmet she donned when working on the surface. Regardless, Charlize always tried to put herself together for her mother before sending a rehearsed video message.

"Hey, how's it going Mom?" Charlize asked quietly, practicing her routine as if the pale woman staring back at her was the strong woman who raised her. "No, that's stupid. Hey, long time no see! What did you do today? How's the weather?" she said in rapid succession, hoping to find the right words.

She forcefully practiced a few more iterations as if it really mattered. Charlize knew her mother would be happy to hear from her regardless of what she said. *Maybe I should just tell the truth. How bad could it be?*

After taking a deep breath, she gave it a shot. "It's cold as shit here, and I miss the chirping birds outside my window in the morning. I hope you're still going on walks by the ocean. The last time I heard running water, I had to clean out a clogged pipe and had fifteen people's worth of crap sprayed on my face, including my own, but for some reason it reminded me of the ocean. Things could be worse." She paused for a moment to gauge her candor. "Nope, that's definitely not it either."

Charlize closed her eyes and put her hands to her face, collecting her final thoughts. She slowly ran her cold fingers down her cheeks, revealing a perky fake smile—the same smile she'd put on after her dad died and she had acted like nothing happened. It was convincing, and the HAWP analysis hadn't caught on to her internal struggle yet, but she knew her mom could see through the false expression. There was no hiding it from her.

She walked the short distance to her computer to record a brief message. After logging in to the server, Charlize reluctantly tapped the record button.

"Hi Mom. I know it's been a while, but we've been busy getting ready for the new colonists to arrive. Things are going great. I wish you could see the beautiful desert landscape. I know it's a little bit different than the ocean in California, but I bet you would fall in love with the views out here. The calming silence is refreshing, although you probably wouldn't like the cold weather.

It would make your joints act up. The morning sunrises are particularly beautiful . . ."

Charlize couldn't help but think about all the work involved just to see the sun rise. She had to get up two hours prior and put on her clunky space suit, performing numerous safety checks, then take a rickety elevator up a dark shaft, just to look at the red sky overlapping the desolate red Martian landscape. It always reminded her of just how alone they were on the planet.

A knock on her door brought her abruptly back to reality.

". . . Sorry Mom, I have to run. We have a rover coming back with a fresh supply of water today. We're excited to fill up the reserves in preparation for *Hermes* and the new colonists. Love you!"

After tapping the send icon, she quickly stood up to answer the door. It was Chauncy.

"Is it here yet?" Charlize asked, hoping he had good news.

"Well, good morning to you as well, sunshine."

She put on the familiar fake smile. "Sorry. Good morning. I'm just excited to take a shower once the offload is complete. It's been a few days, and I feel gross."

Chauncy laughed. "It's all good. I know everybody's excited. Are you ready to head out and hook up the truck? Commander's getting pressed hard from the Sphere to ramp up the production. He's got a real go-getter vibe today."

Charlize rolled her eyes. "He's always got that Mr. Rogers personality. I don't know how he keeps it up."

"Probably because his family is on *Hermes*, and he doesn't want them to get here and see how fucked up the colony is." Chauncy shook his head. "Shit, at this point some of the guys are taking bets on when we're gonna run dry."

"That's a bit morbid. You really shouldn't spread that pessimism around. The last thing you would want is to get everybody worked up about dying."

"You mean worked up about dying, again. Ever since we've been here, it's been one bullshit disaster after another. You remember that time Hank tried to poison us all with that rancid meat he grew?" Chauncy asked cynically.

"I do. Everybody ended up clogging the pipes."

"Oh yeah, that was the day you got shit all over your face. That was hilarious!"

"I don't need a reminder," Charlize said with a scowl. "I'm gonna grab my jacket and we can go suit up."

She whipped around and grabbed her faded green jacket off the back of her chair. Before she walked out the door, she glanced at her computer, confirming that the message to her mother had been uploaded. With a gentle sigh, she closed the door behind her, and they walked down the narrow and brightly lit hallway.

"Everything okay back at home?" asked Chauncy with a friendly smile.

"Probably. I don't really want to know."

He smirked and turned his attention back to the hallway, "Yeah, I feel the same way."

CHAPTER 9

DWINDLING OASIS

Charlize and Chauncy were sitting two stations apart from one another, both in their off-white biosuits, which had just a touch of dark orange lining the more than twenty feet of airtight seams. The color scheme had been chosen in order to give their outfits a little more flare for those picture-perfect moments sent back to Earth for the media and public relation events.

However, the colonists had come to hate it. It was hard to keep the red, dusty gravel from staining the lighter colors, not to mention the planet was already filled with enough orange and red hues—they didn't need to bring any more into the landscape. In hindsight, a darker body with blue trim would have made more sense. It would have reduced the tendency to become camouflaged with the Martian landscape, making it difficult to see the faint outline of a distant figure in low-visibility conditions.

The gear was stored in a large round room encircled by fifteen different stations, each labeled with a placard to ensure crewmembers wore their own individually tailored suit. The state of the room resembled a heavily used ski rental shop. The gear was neatly hung and aligned at each station for easy access. Unlike in the movies, the room was not equipped with self-donning machines to help them attach the cumbersome equipment. They instead had to wrestle with over a dozen fatigued components in order to safely operate outside the habitat.

The biosuits were composed mostly of titanium and composite materials, making them much more comfortable than what their predecessors had worn. The form-fitting suits were focused on the ability to function in dynamic environments with minimal restrictions. The inner lining was also embedded with a variety of sensors, which continuously monitored one's vitals, stress levels, blood oxygen saturation, and other signals that would indicate any injuries. The outer membrane was capable of detecting compromising damage that would affect the integrity of the pressurization system, which was also responsible for scrubbing the air with a rebreather.

Rigid boots with silver metal fasteners, most of which had become corroded, connected to the slender pant legs, with a robust seal safeguarding against air leaks as people traversed the tough terrain, which was sometimes riddled with jagged rocks or deep, slushy gravel. The composite Kevlar helmets provided a heads-up display with a 135-degree field of view. It could project schematics of equipment used to troubleshoot broken components, a moving map that tracked the location of other colonists' topside, and even video feeds from autonomous airborne drones launched to assist in the survey of particular areas. A slim, flexible onboard computer zipped into a pouch just below a rigid breastplate, managing all functions of the complex biosuit. Even with all these nifty little gadgets, the engineers responsible for the design still didn't get everything quite right.

Frustrated, Charlize fumbled with her aging glove, clearly due for a replacement, and said, "I really wish they would have developed something more durable than this crappy twist on a coupling joint. This red dust gets into everything, and I can never get a good seal!"

"I complained about a number of issues, but the engineers told me it would be too costly to reengineer it," said Chauncy.

"One of those nerds actually told me that the biosuit was meant to keep me alive, not match my purse," Charlize added.

"What a dick. No wonder CelestialX is taking over. It probably doesn't take them six months, thirty engineers, and millions of dollars just to come up with a design for a prototype."

"I'd like to stick this thing in the incinerator and order a new one. Hopefully, *Hermes* has some upgrades for us," Charlize muttered.

Ares chimed in, sensing Charlize's tone change. "Would you like me to activate the station's incinerator?"

Chauncy intervened before she could yell at him. "No, Ares. We would not like to activate the incinerator."

"Well, it looks like Dipshit's online," said Charlize, banging the glove on the side of her seat, knocking the debris loose, allowing her to finally attach it. "I still don't understand how Wendy could design the Sphere, but she couldn't design a more competent AP."

Ares assisted the colonists with their day-to-day activities and monitored critical systems. His simplicity was a hardware limitation. It was almost impossible to ship, assemble, and maintain a complex quantum computer on Mars similar to the ones that ran the other APs.

He was a significant step down from his creator, purposefully crafted around an assistant's role. This reduced his overall power draw and the need for large, hardy server rooms, which Charlize knew were unsustainable given the harsh working environment. His small but redundant servers were due for an upgrade in the near future, but for now, the colonists relied on one of Wendy's original and most inferior APs to date.

This didn't mean he wasn't capable. In fact, Ares was extremely reliable when given proper direction. However, when left to his own logic, he was only able to alert the crew of potential issues that could pose a threat. There wasn't enough self-reliance built into his personality to allow him to make decisions on his own. This left Ares with the frustrating ability to help on command and with almost no autonomy. Furthermore, if all the colonists decided they needed his help at once, his system could possibly crash, requiring a hard reboot.

We learned that the hard way, Charlize mused. This had only occurred once before, but after the incident, Wendy had sent a patch to her AP, assuring Commander Ritter that Ares would not completely shut down again if overtasked. Unfortunately, Charlize and the other colonists did not trust Wendy's shoddy patchwork, so they ensured his task load remained minimal until he was properly upgraded.

With their biosuits pieced together, Charlize and Chauncy stood facing one another and visually inspected the weathered gear for any abnormalities. Once finished, they linked their computers to the network and gently donned their helmets. There was a slight hiss as the final seal was secured and each complex biosuit automatically verified its integrity, ensuring there was 100 percent oxygen present and no leaks.

As their heads-up displays booted up, the two conducted a quick communications check. "Chauncy, you got a copy?"

"Yeah, I read you loud and clear."

"I have you the same. You ready to head up?"

"Lead the way," he replied, extending his arm forward in a polite gesture for her to pass.

Before entering the airlock, Ares provided them with an update through their internal communications system. "Once you reach the surface, I will no longer be of assistance to you until the communications relay is functional."

"You've said the same thing for the last three weeks. I've been trying to isolate the issue, no thanks to you," Chauncy replied, frustrated. "Do you have anything helpful to add?"

With no response coming, they stepped into the airlock and closed the door. The gentle hum inside the small chamber slowly faded as the oxygen was sucked out and then equalized with the carbon-dioxide-rich atmosphere. Once complete, Charlize spun the circular lock holding the external door closed, revealing the elevator platform comfortably resting on the edge of a cliff. The cliff sat within a large cave that had once been part of an underground volcanic lava system.

The hollow space, previously filled with molten rock, now housed two dozen dome-shaped structures in which the colonists lived. The edge lighting wrapping around the rigid modular structures provided the only source of light in the towering black abyss that protected them from the sun's radiation and the harsh elements.

The two continued forward onto the elevator platform, which was connected to a braided steel cable and pulley system. Chauncy turned and closed the flimsy gate as Charlize picked up the clunky control box. There were only two options: "UP" and "DWON."

"I still can't believe the engineers spelled 'down' wrong." Charlize shook her head.

"Nobody said they were good at spelling. The math guys probably designed it," Chauncy said with a chuckle.

After they chose the correctly spelled word, the elevator suddenly jolted as the electric motors on the surface began to wind the two-hundred-foot-long cable, spurring their ascent to the surface. As they reached the end of the ride, the faint light of the sun touched their pale faces. Even Chauncy's once-dark brown skin had lost some color over the years, thanks to the lack of ultraviolet rays.

They both looked up and closed their eyes as the sun wrapped around their bodies. For a brief second, Charlize reminisced about the warm sun back on Earth. Unfortunately, her dreamy state was short lived, and the clunk of the elevator coming to a halt forced them back to reality.

Opening their eyes, they were once again immersed in the bleak hazy red landscape, heated only by their biosuits' internal temperature regulating system. The two quickly grabbed the flimsy gate, bracing themselves against a surprising twenty-mile-per-hour gust of wind. It didn't pack nearly as much force as the same gust on Earth would, but it was surprising none the less. They looked over to the receiving station, where a large, cabless six-wheeled truck sat idly, waiting to offload its payload.

The long, cylindrical tank had the capacity to hold five thousand gallons of water, enough to keep the fifteen inhabitants alive for approximately thirty days if they each only used ten gallons per day. This generous allotment accounted not only for hydration, but hygiene and food as well. Once the water was received, they pumped it over to a massive, pressurized storage tank created from an old, repurposed fuel tank that had been left behind by an archaic supply rocket.

"So why do you really think the water trucks keep coming back late? Is there something you and the commander are hiding from the rest of us?" Chauncy asked.

"You know as much as I do. Honestly, if you could fix the long-range communication array, we would be able to send a drone out to take a look, but just like everything else out here, things have an odd tendency to break and compound issues," said Charlize, omitting the issue of the failed shut-off valve on the water well. She wasn't really lying. The valve shouldn't have affected the water supply. "There's most likely a problem with a sensor. If the water output is slowing down, the truck is going to take longer to fill. We just need to figure out what's limiting the flow."

"Yeah, I get it. Shit's broke dick around here. The least you can do is thank me for being able to talk to your family," replied Chauncy, sounding skeptical.

"Talking to my mom doesn't keep me alive. Water does," said Charlize, contemplating all the possible scenarios.

What if there's an issue with the trucks? Is there a leak? What if the well ran dry, or maybe it froze over? Is the faulty metering valve really the issue? Or could it be the shut-off valve? I really hope that the commander has a good reason for hiding a potential culprit from the rest of the team. They're going to be pissed if word ever gets out.

Knowing that it wasn't the best time to contemplate the hypotheticals, she decided to focus on the task at hand. None of her questions could be answered without a complete diagnostic of the vehicle and eventually the well.

Arriving at the truck, Chauncy walked around the back side to hook up the transfer line. Meanwhile, Charlize checked the onboard diagnostic computer, hidden behind a thick metal panel, to see how much water had returned.

After swinging open the heavy door, she turned on the heated flat touchscreen display, which was shrouded in insulation. She swiped through a handful of menus, noticing that the tank was only half full. Seeing that, she pounded her fist on the side of the truck and rested her helmet on the side of the dusty red control panel.

Chauncy reappeared once the truck was hooked up and pumping the pressurized fresh water to the holding tank.

"How bad is it?" he asked.

"Half full again," Charlize groaned, her face pale and tired.

"Son of a bitch!" he shouted, effortlessly kicking a pile of rocks into the distance, and taking a seat on the side of a small boulder.

Charlize looked through the diagnostic reports and concluded that there was nothing wrong with the truck. Instead of taking her anger out on the autonomous vehicle, she closed and latched the panel with a soft touch, trying to regain her composure. Given the lack of other options, and with no way to link to Ares for troubleshooting, she decided that they would have to send the truck back on its way.

"Come on, Chauncy, it's not that bad. At least we're not totally fucked," she said, resting her hand on his shoulder.

"I know. I'm just tired of shit breaking all the time. It never seems to end."

"I feel the same way. Let's refill the tank and send her on her way. The dust is picking up, and I don't want this POS just sitting here all night."

Chauncy popped to his feet. "All right. Let's do it. It's not like I have anything else going on today."

"Well, I mean you could fix the communications . . ."

"Don't start that again," he interrupted, walking back to the truck. "You gonna help? Or do I have to do everything myself?"

Charlize's laugh was tinged with disappointment, knowing they would still be on water rations. She followed in Chauncy's dusty footprints, taking unusually prolonged strides to match the length of his legs. While Chauncy disconnected the water line, she looked out into the distance and thought about all the failing systems within the colony. *I wonder how much longer we'll be able to hold out.* Then she shifted her gaze upward, trying to peer through the hazy Martian atmosphere. *I wish you would hurry your ass up,* Mercury.

CHAPTER 10

MERCURY

Mercury was the same class of vessel as *Hermes*, but it had been sent two months ahead of its sister transitor due to its increased mass and slower transit speed, carrying essential goods and equipment required to keep the colony running. While food, vitamins, and replacement parts were the most precious cargo for the current inhabitants, it also contained the final components to complete the aboveground habitat that had been in the works for the past three years.

The vessel *Mercury*, along with her complementing Algorithmic Personality, also named Mercury, was another project that Wendy's capabilities had accelerated by years, possibly decades. The massive vessel, which had been completed just outside of the Sphere's orbit, was designed so that it never had to reenter a planet's harsh atmosphere; rather, it would autonomously run between Earth and Mars, ferrying parts and supplies without the need for a crew. While the vessel itself did not land, specifically tailored landing modules would separate from its hull and come to their final resting place on the surface of Mars.

This was done so that all of the supplies weren't put into one lander or vessel that had the potential to be lost while entering Mars's atmosphere. Hedging the bets on multiple smaller pods was an obvious solution once the technology existed. The pods also required less fuel on board to slow their descent and make a safe landing. Once its mission was complete, *Mercury* would return to Earth's orbit, where it would refuel and resupply, eventually being sent out on another long, lonely mission when the launch window was just right.

The unorthodox naming convention appeared as if Mercury had named her vessel after herself, but that was far from the truth. Wendy had hardcoded the Algorithmic Personality with her name from the start and during the planning and construction phase, the shipyard mistakenly painted "Mercury" on the side of the vessel. They thought that the crewless transitor would navigate itself to Mars and back, not knowing that it would have an AP quietly living aboard. Once the mistake was realized, the vessel had been assembled in orbit, and Mercury was quietly evolving within her new home.

Repainting a vessel was deemed an unnecessary cost by Nolen Aromas, and it was far too complicated to change the name of a living AP. So, the two now shared the name. Fortunately, Mercury and *Mercury* weren't required to communicate with humans, and the mistake was buried along with the vessel's original name.

Mercury found the human tradition of naming their vessels with female names amusing. So, despite her namesake, she decided to be female. The choice confounded some, but Mercury found it suited her.

Much like the development and creation of the Sphere, Mercury was designed to reduce CelestialX's overall costs. Nolen Aromas's vision of the future was focused around a cheap and sustainable means of traversing the inner solar system. With Wendy's continued help, she not only developed the means to transfer interplanetary goods and the largest group of human colonists to date, but also designed a safer and more expeditious means of establishing a colony on the surface of the red planet. One of the primary upgrades to the enhanced habitats was that the colonists would now reside on the surface. They would be properly shielded from radiation and capable of withstanding the harsh wind and dust storms that plagued the flat, open Martian landscape.

Shortly after Commander Ritter and his team reached their destination, Wendy began sending Mercury with dozens of self-contained modular habitats, which would eventually house the colonists currently in stasis on board *Hermes*. After their dreamy six-month transit, they would awaken on the red planet, oblivious to the outdated and arduous methods of remaining conscious and engaged as they were hurtling through space. Once reanimated, they would walk straight into a turnkey habitat, designed specifically for their otherworldly mission. Mercury doubted the colonists would afford her much credit for their smooth planetary transition, but she was proud to play a part nonetheless.

However, there was a catch. The final plumbing to connect the modules to a water source, long-term power supplies, and exterior connections to the communication towers were to be delivered alongside the final modules. Mercury knew Nolen Aromas had subversively coordinated the timing to prevent Commander Ritter and his team from preemptively inhabiting the much more modern and sustainable living quarters. When Mercury asked Wendy why, she was told that NASA had outsourced the resupply missions to her, and in return for her hard work, the colonists would have to position and deploy the modules as payment.

Mercury wasn't overly interested in the politics of the plan, but she was aware via Wendy's transmission that not all of the colonists were happy about having to construct the new habitat. They didn't take to compelled labor, especially without permission to access any of the high-tech equipment she had delivered within the sophisticated modules. It wasn't because Commander Ritter's team wasn't trustworthy; rather, they weren't willing to assist CelestialX in stripping and mining Mars's untold resources for profit. So the gear remained off limits and saved years of unprofitable wear and tear.

Mercury's mission was an expensive endeavor for CelestialX, and even with the government sharing the load, Nolen needed another investor. When she learned that her tasking could potentially change based on Nolen partnering with William, she again asked why. But instead of feeding her curiosity with an answer, Wendy sidelined her, and no further transmissions were received.

With the flow of information terminated and nobody to talk to, Mercury persevered, hoping that her dedication would one day be recognized.

CHAPTER 11

WILLIAM

After taking a refreshing sip of his Arnold Palmer, William Walker set the cool glass on the edge of his desk and mentally rehearsed the calculated responses for his interview with a *Forbes* reporter scheduled to start momentarily. Just the year before, in 2052, *Forbes* had ranked him the fourth richest person in the world, a few places behind Nolen Aromas. His steely rise in the ranks should have given the elitist some level of satisfaction, but that would only come when he surpassed his longtime rival. Soon. Very soon. Everything would fall into place just as he planned.

A scrolling headline flashed, catching the mogul's attention, and he turned his focus back to the holographic display as he watched the live coverage of the Wayfarer rally.

"Whiney little pissants," William grumbled, turning up the volume to hear what today's socialists were ranting about.

"Our planet can take no more! We must take back control from the corporations and stop the mutilation of our natural resources. The citizens of planet Earth subsist on the scraps left by the likes of William Walker, who continues to plunder our home."

William's assistant alerted him of the arrival of the writer from *Forbes*.

"Send him in," William said, having heard enough of the Way-farer's rant, muting him once again.

William stood to greet the shithead who wasn't ranking him as high as he should and shouted, "Simon! Come on in. Great to see you again."

Simon glanced at the holographic display and grinned. "William. Good to see you too. Been watching the Walker family BBQ, I see."

"Ah, you know, everybody has their opinion. They aren't complaining about having fresh fruits and vegetables once again, now, are they?"

"It's not only about having sustainable food resources. It's the cost at which you're selling your products to the farmers."

"Well, it's not cheap creating a new hybrid strain to thrive in the volatile and rapidly shifting weather patterns around the world."

"Can I assume that we're on the record now?" asked Simon, clearly hoping to squeeze every ounce of information from the interview.

"I'd like to say that I have a choice, but you know as well as I do that nothing I say is officially off the record these days."

Simon laughed and replied with candor, "True, but I don't feel like having to deal with your lawyers hounding me again."

Another headline popped up on the display, prompting William to swipe at his wrist and turn off the news.

"It's one thing to judge my decisions as a businessman, but when you bring my family into it, I am forced to let the dogs loose," said William, picking up his Arnold Palmer.

William came from old money, the type of money that discretely ran the world, regardless of political ideologies or a country's borders. His wealth had been passed down through generations of savvy businessmen whose hands had helped shape the global market. With each generation, the amassed wealth continued to grow almost exponentially. The saying "It takes money to make money" had continued to prove true for William and other ultra-high-net-worth individuals.

Over the decades, he had managed to grow the family's portfolio as he gobbled up land, resources, and small technology-based companies. He was betting that one day he would be able to leverage his investments for massive gains. His thoroughly researched and calculated decisions had paid off, and he became postured for success as the world around him rapidly evolved in the thirties.

The shifting climate began to transform the global landscape, and the previous system utilized for the cultivation of produce was forced to adapt alongside in order to survive. Sadly, the slow but natural evolution of plants would require a boost if the civilized world were to endure. This was where William had stepped in.

One of his diverse investments had allowed him to secure a company that focused on the genetic manipulations of plants, and GenInc was subsequently thrust to the front line in a battle to develop hybrid crops that could sustain the volatile climate. The small company was scaled up as their proprietary genetic technologies became instrumental in the production of crops that were tailored for specific regions around the world. Not only could they withstand the unpredictable changes in temperature, but they were able to grow hardy fruits and vegetables with 50 percent less water.

GenInc became the leading producer of Genetically Modified Organisms. While the climate around the world continued to change over the decades, it was imperative that genetically modified crops were continually tweaked in order to survive and feed an overpopulated Earth with substantially less fresh water.

William's investment had raked in billions, not only from farmers around the world, but also governments that had been investing in his company's unique ability to now modify all genetic structures. His monopoly on the industry left every competitor in the dust as they unsuccessfully tried to mimic GenInc's patented processes. There was just one problem. William would never be able to expand his empire with the youngest of his two sons scaring off investors and future tech giants from merging with GenInc.

"You surely can't dispute the fact that Triston's antics as an influencer are boorish and borderline illegal. Just last month he hosted a livestreaming event of an outlawed underground mech fight," said Simon. He seemed to be trying to bait William into discussing his son's ongoing criminal case.

"So, if you were to report on, let's say, an underground drug cartel, does that implicate you as an accessory?" William asked.

"Of course not, but—"

"That isn't to mention the fact that mechs, while currently outlawed, are under a Supreme Court review for the infringement of owners' Second Amendment rights."

"That's not even remotely—"

"The constitution allows you a firearm in self-defense, but you can't have an armed mech with countless safeguards for use in self-defense situations?" William finished off the rest of his Arnold Palmer with a satisfying sigh.

"You're evading the topic. I am not here to discuss the legality of what he is doing. I am here to discuss how his actions have negatively affected your company and what could have been a massive buyout of a biorobotics company."

William scoffed. "Yes, the acquisition would have benefited both of our companies, but unfortunately, I cannot divulge the specifics of our negotiations."

"Can you tell me what a genetic modification company was planning to do with the technologies associated with a company that is on the forefront of biocybernetics and neurocybernetics?"

"You and every other competitor out there would love to know that, but again I will not discuss the specifics," William replied, happy to once again have the upper hand. "I can only address our publicly disclosed projects, such as our proprietary process of growing organs from the specific DNA of the patient in need."

"Did you mean to say that you are able to grow new organs for the wealthy?" asked Simon, once again taking the discussion in a different direction.

"Why is it that you keep bringing the subject back to cost?"

"Because your advances in these fields are almost unobtainable to the lower classes. They have to spend all their money on your food."

"Oh, give me a break. I thought you worked for *Forbes*, not some cut-rate tabloid."

"Fine, would you like to address the rumors surrounding the genetic modification of embryos and designer babies? The same DNA-splicing technologies are implemented, are they not?"

"You mean to say that eradicating the gene sequencing for Down's syndrome is now controversial?"

"Well, when you remove genetic disorders and make them taller, stronger, smarter, with bright blue eyes, yes. That is very controversial."

"You know as well as I do that editing those types of traits is illegal. We do not—"

"Let's switch gears. We've only talked about Triston up to this point. What about your son Jade? He seems to have fallen off the map?" Simon inquired.

"He hasn't fallen off anything! His work keeps him busy and out of the spotlight."

"That has nothing to do with the incident at CERN, does it?"

"You mean the earthquake?"

"Right. Sorry about that. Can you address the rumors that he is working with Nolen Aromas?"

"Who is saying that?"

"I talk to many powerful people. They say things."

"What are these cowards saying about my son now?" asked William, with building frustration.

"Just that he would rather work with your long-time competitor than his own father."

"I think it's time for you to leave before—"

"Before what, William? These are all valid questions. Questions that directly affect the future of your company. You have provided little information, and from what I can gather, have nothing of value to add to society. You're focused on profits over humanity."

"Have you forgotten who you're speaking to, you petulant fool? I've saved a society on the brink of famine, cured diseases, extended the lives of individuals who would no longer be alive, and in the near future will be able to prevent death all together."

Simon's eyes grew wide. He'd just gotten the bombshell that he was looking for, and quickly tried to push the situation. "What's the price tag for eternal life?"

"Get out of my office. Now!" William shouted.

"Thank you for your time, Mr. Walker. It's been an . . . eye-opening morning."

William watched the reporter walk out of his office, then swiped his empty glass off of his desk.

"That arrogant piece of shit!"

CHAPTER 12

FRANKIE

Frankie Cole burst into the engineering shop with the might of a football player storming the field prior to kick off. "Who's ready to get some shit done today!"

There were few responses from the hodgepodge of scrappy pilots, metal workers, and electricians who had been trained to operate nimble equipment through the vacuum of space and work on the Sphere. While Frankie's energetic presence always managed to rev up his team of fifty flight engineers and pilots, today looked like it was going to be a slow start.

"Well, that was a piss-poor response," said Frankie with deflated vigor.

Standing six foot six and weighing in at 250 pounds, the large man wasn't hard to miss when he was lumbering throughout the Engineering Quadrant, even without the theatrics. He let his hair grow confidently, unfazed by his receding hairline. He secretly hoped that somebody would ask if he was related to Hulk Hogan, but he figured none of the youngsters knew about the legend and that his timeless hair style was likely a forgotten memory.

He hadn't seemed to lose any of his stamina after playing tight end at Chaparral Highschool in Phoenix, Arizona during the early thirties. The now thirty-nine-year-old foreman had lived a hard life of construction, connecting the East and West Coast with a network of high-speed trains as the push for efficient green transportation engulfed the country. Once it was complete, he started looking for another challenging project.

During the construction of the Sphere, it was necessary to develop an energy system to power the immense structure as it orbited the earth. The International Space Station relied on antiquated solar panels as a means of energy, but it was clear the large, rotating structure would require an upgraded power source.

The fusion reactor on board the Sphere was capable of producing over one gigawatt of electricity, enough energy to power a large city. By harnessing the raw energy of the most basic element, the reactor combined hydrogen isotopes, deuterium, and tritium to sustain a fusion reaction, similar to the beating heart of the sun. Frankie had been tasked with tapping into the complex power grid and assembling the electronic rail system that would eventually span the entire inner circumference of the Sphere.

The donut-shaped station had been modeled after the Stanford Taurus, which operated under the simple concept of centrifugal force. While spinning in a circular motion at a rate of one rotation per minute, approximately 1.0g of gravitational force was created at the feet of the occupants standing on the floor of the outer radius. If the spin were any slower, the occupants would begin to feel the weightlessness of space. Conversely, any faster and they would feel an insufferable pull of gravity constantly trying to squash them.

The rail system would provide a more efficient means of transiting the more than three-mile circumference by foot. At present, that wasn't a problem, because the inhabitants typically had no reason to leave their respective Quadrants. Unfortunately, the Sphere was about to take on a significantly larger workload, and its mission was about to grow tenfold. In order to accommodate the influx of bodies, a reliable high-speed method of transporting the dynamic crews would be an expensive but very necessary undertaking.

The complex scheme to retrofit the Sphere with a rail system had been simplified as Wendy created a modular system of components that were built on Earth and launched into space as part of the weekly resupply package. Each flight supplied the team of engineers with ten fifty-foot-long sections that were stored in the loading dock located next to the fire wall separating Quadrants Two and Three.

The eight-month project was slightly ahead of schedule and slated to be completed within the next three weeks. Frankie was supposed to be providing his daily updates to Kai in the mission control module, but their relationship was less than amicable at times.

Jazell, who was second-in-command and the most senior pilot, chimed in. "Everybody's beat, Frankie. It also doesn't help that they've had to listen to Commander Driscoll's incessant calls trying to get ahold of you."

Frankie laughed. "Yeah, he's been calling me all morning."

"Well why the fuck didn't you answer? You know he's not going to stop."

He sat down at his console and scanned his bio-implant, logging in to the system.

"Let's swap chairs today. I hate this rickety piece of shit."

"Absolutely not!" Jazell exclaimed, scooting over. "Why don't you like talking to the commander?"

"Cause all he's going to do is harass me about workflow summary reports. We have a megacomputer on board tracking everything that's done on the job. All he has to do is ask her, and the almighty will speak."

"I am sorry, Mr. Cole, but the commander has instructed me to stop completing your reports," Wendy stated on cue.

"That son of a bitch."

Frankie angrily opened the document that pinged on his display, compliments of Wendy, and irritably began to fill out the work they had completed the day before. It wasn't long before he received a request to video chat. He lifted his meaty hand and hovered just over the translucent option to decline.

"You know he can see that you're logged in to your workstation, right?" asked Jazell.

"Yeah, I know that, but—"

Before Frankie even had the chance to finish his reply, Wendy force connected the call.

Without delay, Kai asked, "Where is my report, Frankie?"

"Good morning, Kai. Glad to see you're abusing your power with Wendy once again," Frankie replied, shrugging off his request.

"I wouldn't have to if you answered my calls."

"I left my SlimPoc in my room. I don't like to fly with it."

"I can literally see that it's in the engineering shop right now. Stop screwing around."

Frankie could hear clamoring voices in the background as his crew began to leave the shop and head to the hangar.

"Well, unfortunately, it's time to get to work. How about you head over to Quadrant Three after we get done laying some more rail? I'll personally hand it over."

"I'm not going to walk a mile and a half to get a digital copy of your workflow summaries."

"Exactly! If you let me get back to work, you could just ride the trolley over here sooner rather than later."

"It's not called a trolley."

"I wouldn't know that, since the remainder of the plans haven't been released by Wendy. Not sure why she's still finalizing the prints for the airlocks and railcars, but we're going to empty out the cargo bay's remaining tracks for the rail system by the end of today," Frankie said, feeling excited once more that they were ahead of schedule. "That reminds me, is the resupply craft going to be on time, or will the hurricane delay the launch again?"

"I would know that you were ahead of schedule if you sent over your reports on time," Kai said with frustration.

"That's what I'm telling you right now." Frankie stood up. "I'll be in the aluminaut, helping my team with today's workload. It would be nice if you could get an update on the rattler. We're about to run out of steel to sling."

Frankie disconnected the call and turned to walk away, knowing Kai was going to call back, but before he left the room, Wendy caught his ear.

"The rail system is not made of steel, Mr. Cole," she said.

"Obviously, Wendy, it just wasn't as cool saying we're going to go sling some Niobium and all the other ridiculous rare metals you constructed the rail system out of."

"It was necessary to—"

"I don't care why you do what you do. It always seems like you're operating on your own terms. I might as well do the same. I'll see you in the hangar."

"Very well, Mr. Cole. Mr. Driscoll left you a message, would you like to hear it?"

Frankie looked around the room. It had cleared out, so he figured it was best to listen to the message in the absence of the crew. He knew Kai was going to give him an earful, and he didn't want his shop to know he was getting reprimanded.

"Sure. Play it."

"I wish the goddamn pods were already installed. I'd ride over there and smack some sense into that meathead," Kai muttered to himself. He must've been figuring Frankie wouldn't check his messages.

Frankie let out a jovial laugh. "I always thought he was a pushover. Good to see he's got some fight in that skinny body."

"Would you like me to send your reply?" Wendy asked without hesitation.

"No!" shouted Frankie. "I don't understand how a supercomputer can't detect sarcasm."

"Are you not pleased with my assistance? I'm sensing elevated stress levels."

"Well now you're just fucking with me. I have more important things to do than play your mind games." Frankie hurried toward the door to catch up with his crew. "Just tell Kai that I'll be sure to file the summary at my earliest convenience."

"Yes, Mr. Cole. Have a nice day."

CHAPTER 13

ALUMINAUTS

Frankie opened his locker, which was located in an adjacent room to the hangar, and stuffed a pair of weathered gloves into the cargo pocket of his salty blue coveralls. For him, life in space was no different than on the ground. Harsh working conditions in remote locations spanning hundreds of miles, this time vertically into space, were no vacation. At least on the Sphere, he had a sense of normalcy. Not to mention a substantial paycheck.

He whipped his brown Carhartt jacket out of the locker and in one smooth movement wrapped it around his shoulders, sliding his arms through the sleeves. Slamming the locker door shut with authority, he followed a group of workers heading to the airlock, which led to the fleet of aluminauts.

The messy crowd of flight engineers and pilots formed behind the door, readying themselves for their eight-hour shift, only stopping halfway through to eat and take a piss. Frankie moved to the front of the pack, preparing himself to once again dredge up some enthusiasm in the bland confinement of the Sphere. The assorted group of men and women had come from all walks of life. Most were on the job site for money and the benefits afforded to their families, still trying to scrape by as the deteriorating environment negatively impacted life on Earth. Some cities were better off than others, but the withering infrastructure rendered new health conditions, most of which required expensive medical support.

Frankie cleared his throat, gaining the crew's attention. "Today, we hit the seven-month mark. Our work on the rail system is coming to an end. I know you're tired and eager to see your families, but we have a job to finish. Once you push off from the staging area, it's just you and your crew out there. It's dangerous. This rotating behemoth isn't your friend. It will tear you apart, flinging you out into the dark, starry night or sending you rocketing into the earth's atmosphere, burning you alive. Personally, I'd rather become a meteorite going out in a blaze of glory, but today, that's not gonna happen. Not to me or any of you. If we work as a team and watch each other's backs, we'll all come back safe. I want you to stay sharp out there."

Frankie held out his wrist, letting the access panel read his biometric tag. The hangar door opened, revealing the fleet of twenty aluminauts waiting idly in the bay. He stood to the side and acknowledged each crewmember walking past. Jazell was already rushing to her aluminaut with a feverish excitement, probably trying to launch first today. As the final member of the crew walked by, he patted her on the shoulder and ushered her along while the hangar door closed behind them. Frankie watched his young apprentice gaze at the massive room full of aluminauts with astonishment.

Kristin Wehman was twenty-six and fresh on the job. At only five foot two and 120 pounds, she was dwarfed standing next to Frankie. He'd taken her under his wing to make up for her lack of experience, but to his surprise, she had received impressive scores during her simulated ground training, accelerating at completing her tasks in a timely and efficient manner.

"Let's get a move on. The view is better outside," Frankie said with a smile.

"I wouldn't know. That piece of shit rattler I came up here on didn't have any windows. I thought space travel was supposed to be luxurious, or shit, I'd take satisfying." Kristin laughed.

"I know. They started skimping on a lot of the rocket pleasantries a while back, and you're not a Scag. If you wanted the finer things in life, you're in the wrong line of work." Frankie picked up the pace. "But you'll soon see, we do have some sweet benefits. You met the whole crew yet?" he asked.

"Not yet—I was just brought aboard last week on the supply run, and I'm still trying to get my bearings. This thing is huge."

"Oh, the good ol' matchbox. Probably wasn't much better than your ride on the rattler."

"Yeah, it was a bit bumpy. I still don't get why they call it the matchbox," Kristin said with a furrowed brow.

"You'll figure it out soon enough. Let's focus on today for right now, nugget."

After passing by the first eight aluminauts, which were anchored by a girthy grappling arm connected to the ceiling of the hangar, Frankie abruptly stopped next to a sleek, powerful craft resting just six inches above the deck.

"Ol' number nine," said Frankie with love in his voice, admiring his lucky number.

Below the craft was a closed door leading to the vacuum of space. Frankie watched as Kristin timidly stepped on the twelve-inch-thick hollow door at the rear of the aluminaut. The sharp change in pitch seemed to catch her off guard as her boots clanked on the hollow door.

"So, does it get old?" she asked.

"To be honest, I still get a rush when the mag pickups release us into free fall, waiting for the ion thrusters to decelerate this bad boy," Frankie said as they climbed up the small ladder, revealing the complex cockpit. "Hurry up and get strapped in. I don't want to lose to Jazell again."

The two-person team worked as a combat crew, assuring unit cohesion in dynamic situations. They sat side by side with Frankie on the right as they strapped into their chairs. Frankie cinched his harness down and watched Kristin fumble with the stiff but rugged latching assembly as he began running through the prestart checklists. He tried to take his time, knowing that this would be her first launch outside of a training environment. Once Kristin was securely fastened in place, she picked up her checklist and tried to match Frankie's pace.

"Ion thrusters are online. Disconnecting from external power," she reported.

"Complete."

"Initiate autonomous control che—"

Before she could finish her prompt, Frankie had already initiated the onboard computers to perform the control calibration. The flyby wire system was not mechanically linked to user inputs. However, the controls in front of Frankie began to move as the four independently controlled ion thrusters, two on each side, began to rotate through their full range of motion. This ensured that there was no binding or failure of the redundant electrically operated motors, a situation that could prove deadly in the unforgiving working environment. Once that was complete, Kristin's controls began the same process. Hers were connected to the four robotic arms affixed to the front of the craft, which allowed her to complete the delicate task of welding the rail system as well as connecting the appropriate electrical components to the outer fuselage of the Sphere.

After only a few minutes, the mostly automated piloting system checks were complete. Frankie patiently waited as the clearly nervous apprentice finished the remainder of her checks, making sure the dexterous equipment used to attach the rail system was operating at 100 percent.

In the meantime, Frankie pulled up the status of the other three aluminauts they would be working with for the day. Once the crews were up and ready, he looked over at Kristin again.

"You good to go?" he asked.

"I think so?"

"Put a little more confidence in that answer. I might be dual qualified on these systems and able to back you up, but some of the other pilots don't have a clue what you do over there. They're going to need reassurance that you aren't going to get them killed out on the job."

Kristin nodded and looked at her displays once more.

"System checks complete. Ready to go."

"That's more like it."

Frankie tapped his display and linked the aluminaut with Wendy, who controlled most of the autopilot functions associated with the release, terminal phase, and docking near the Sphere. Not being a true aviator, Frankie had a hard time envisioning what it would be like to actually pilot a craft without an autopilot function. Every time he linked up with Wendy, he couldn't shake a comment Jazell had made a few months back, equating today's pilots to a bunch of button-mashing monkeys with no real stick skills. For the most part, it was true, considering Wendy handled a majority of the dangerous and mentally taxing flying. The pilots on board were primarily in the construction and engineering business, trained merely to manage the systems, with the exception of Jazell, who had an extensive aviation background both in space and back on Earth.

"Good morning again, Mr. Cole," said Wendy. "Commander Driscoll—"

"Wendy, I shouldn't have to keep telling you that work on the Sphere doesn't enter this cockpit. There is too much shit going on out here to worry about his bullshit summaries. Let's get a move on."

"First crews are up and ready. Solid connections established between aluminauts zero six, zero seven, zero eight, and zero nine. All remaining aluminauts are ready for hangar operations to commence. Taking control of the craft," Wendy reported. Frankie knew the message was going out simultaneously and independently to all forty members of his crew. "Conducting final scan of hangar."

The hangar was cleared of all human maintenance personnel, leaving behind only the maintenance bots, also controlled by Wendy. The space was always then scanned, making absolutely certain no human was left behind. The four aluminauts were lifted slightly up and away from the sealed doors as all the air was sucked out of the hangar. With the pressure equalized, the doors beneath the craft split open.

"Beat you out of the gates today, Jazell," Frankie said proudly over the radios.

"Yeah, I got some maintenance bot hanging off the side of my rig. I think he's trying to hump the ion thruster," she replied.

"Are you in one five?" asked Frankie.

"Yup. This thing is a piece of shit!"

"Well, good luck. We're about to launch," he said, retraining his focus back on his digital gauges with a smile.

The telescopic arms projecting from the hangar ceiling simultaneously lowered Frankie's team of four aluminauts in unison. They were now dangling just below the outer hull of the Sphere in the void of space, revealing the Earth in all of its blue beauty. Suspended in the silence, Frankie and Kristin awaited engagement of the mag pickups as they gazed at the awe-inspiring view.

"Yeah, I can see how this wouldn't get old," said Kristin, taking in the moment.

"Just wait."

Frankie shifted his gaze to the rails above their heads. The outer docking system was utilized to catch and release transistor vessels via a dual electromagnetic rail system. As part of the original construction of the Sphere, it was necessary to find a safe means of docking on the outer hull while it rotated at 180 miles an hour. The electromagnets, which the crew referred to as the mag pickups, provided a runway of sorts. This allowed Wendy to autonomously guide any vessel to or from the Sphere and ensure they wouldn't collide with the station.

The clever system had been devised because of the Sphere's gargantuan size. Wendy had found that this method of catching and releasing spacecraft was much more cost effective than shipping up another couple of miles of modular crossbeams that would span the center of the Sphere, requiring the hangar and cargo bay to be inefficiently located in the center of the Sphere, where the gravity would be limited and unequally distributed. Even Frankie couldn't deny the pure brilliance of Wendy's design. As a bonus, it was fun.

As the four aluminauts dangled from their telescopic arms, Wendy precisely aligned the craft with the mag pickups and tethered them to the Sphere. Once a solid connection was made, the telescopic arm disconnected with a jolt. They remained attached to the Sphere by a thin, frictionless gap that began to shuttle the four aluminauts in unison toward the loading bay containing the fifty-foot-long section they were tasked with attaching.

Kristin looked over at Frankie. "This is way better than the simulator."

"It gets even better. Trust me."

THE RODEO

Frankie led the pack, with the other three aluminauts in tow. Suspended beneath the Sphere, they rapidly whipped around as the earth passed beneath them, completing one rotation every minute. Any delays could cause vertigo to set in, even with the calm 1.0g pull still stabilizing the vestibular canals of the inner ear. The aluminauts came to an expeditious halt, and the slightly curved rail was lowered down from the cargo bay next to the four craft. The two largest telescopic arms autonomously extended and gripped the section of rail they were tasked to install. The lowering system sensed that positive contact was made and released the gear. The four evenly spaced aluminauts were now carrying the entire weight of the load.

Wendy quickly chimed in as the other teams of aluminauts started stacking up behind Frankie's crew. "Release commencing in five, four . . ."

"Hold on to your butt!" said Frankie nonchalantly.

". . . two, one."

The mag pickups released all four of the aluminauts simultaneously, flinging them outward into space. The sixteen ion thrusters came to life, emanating a fiery blue glow, illuminating the outer hull of the Sphere as they rapidly separated from the station. The four craft quickly decelerated, increasing the g-loading to 2.5. After six seconds, the powerful and efficient ion thrusters had stabilized the linked crews, and the weightlessness of space set in.

Kristin's unsecured checklist began to float in front of her face. She promptly grabbed it and stowed the booklet in a fixed pouch to the left of her seat. *She'll get her shit together—all the nuggets eventually do.* While keeping an eye on Kristin, Frankie turned his focus to Wendy as she effortlessly managed the delicate ballet of the interconnected craft. With stability returned, the aluminauts were orientated towards the center of the Sphere.

Coming out of shock, Kristin shouted, "Holy shit! That was fucking awesome."

"I told you. That never gets old."

Frankie tapped on the crisp translucent display, disengaging the autopilot. He placed his large, callused hands on the delicate controls, nimbly advancing the interconnected heap of metal toward their objective. The heads-up display was projected on all the double-paned, two-inch-thick cabin windows, and it marked their precise worksite. He used the "HUD," as it was known in aviator lingo, to maneuver into the center of the Sphere as it rotated around them, then commenced the docking procedure.

The rigid line of aluminauts neatly anchored to the rail system waited patiently as the Sphere rotated to the perfect intercept point. The objective area was now above them, almost a mile away but rapidly approaching. Frankie began to lurch down and forward, with the Sphere directly below his weathered boots.

"Twenty seconds," said Frankie, activating the autopilot.

Wendy came back online and gently accelerated to match the smooth rotation of the Sphere's curve. As they approached the correct speed, the HUD came back to life. The site slipped out from below them and revealed a bright red area matching the segment of rail. A prompt on the display alerted them to activate the reeling system. Frankie acknowledged it, commencing the final stage of the docking sequence.

Four kettle-bell-shaped anchoring devices were shot from the underside of each craft, connected to a lightweight composite tether. The small anchors traveled toward the Sphere, making small adjustments with compressed gas. Once contact with the outer hull was achieved, high-powered electromagnets engaged, securing them in place. All four craft were now tethered and began to pull the aluminauts toward the Sphere.

"You're up," said Frankie, carefully observing as she ran through her procedures.

Kristin wrapped her hands around the controls as they hovered just above the Sphere and positioned the aluminaut's two smaller arms. They clamped down on rigid mounting brackets along the hull of the Sphere, allowing for a stable anchoring system when combined with the electromagnetic tethers.

She donned a holographic monocle connected to a camera on one of the larger arms. It released its grip, letting the other arm take the full load of the rail. A diagram of where the rail should be placed was displayed, allowing her to precisely maneuver it into position. Frankie followed along with his own monocle, making sure she stuck to her procedures. The other three aluminauts conducted the same procedure. Once in sync, they simultaneously made the initial welds with an electron beam welder, securing the rail firmly in place.

With the section now properly settled, they could independently complete their work. Not only did Kristin have to weld the remainder of her section of rail down, but she was also required to use the nimble arms to complete complex wiring associated with the build. Frankie provided small bits of feedback as she continued about her work. He looked over his shoulder as another string of aluminauts moved closer, beginning their choreographed approaches. They would eventually form a long, crowded line across the inner hull as they installed the five sections of rail.

"Can I get an updated status?" asked Kai, breaking their concentration.

"This fucking guy and his updates!" Frankie shouted, shaking his head as he watched Kristin work.

He didn't respond to Kai. Kristin glanced over, looking unsure why Frankie was so upset by the simple request. Perturbed, he motioned for Kristin to keep working while he concocted a plan to mess with Kai, imagining him sitting in his comfy watch commander's chair, oblivious to the work they were doing right above his head.

CHAPTER 15

UPDATED PAX MANIFEST

Ben had watched Kai run in and out of the Command Module all afternoon. It obviously had something to do with the information that had been received from the colonists, but the fact that he hadn't minded Frankie blowing him off seemed a bit out of character for his straitlaced boss.

It was public knowledge that they had communication issues on Mars. *Shit, they've had problems since day one.* However, there was an encrypted file from Commander Ritter that had almost slipped through Wendy's preliminary screening protocols. If Ben hadn't been hawking the incoming transmissions from the Deep Space Network, he very easily could have missed it as well. *I guess the old man's propensity to shun technology and rely on human inputs paid off for once.*

An obnoxious clanking pulled Ben from the latest passenger manifest that had been uploaded from CelestialX ground control. Kai was bouncing up and down in his chair, trying to adjust the lumbar support.

"This chair is kicking my ass today," Kai muttered under his breath.

Ben turned back to his console. *If he only knew how shitty this chair is.* One of the most requested items from the staff working on the Sphere were new chairs, but the cost of shipping more comfortable seats to the station was about ten times the cost of the chair itself. *Those cheap bastards.*

"I'm sorry, Tiffany, but I can't help it if the resupply launch was delayed due to a hurricane," the commander said as he spoke to the Sphere's lead hospitality manager. "Yes, it is unfortunate that you are out of shrimp and champagne, but . . ."

Fucking Scags. If they only knew what I have to eat for lunch, Ben thought to himself.

"Yes, I'm well aware of how much they spend on their Space-cations," the commander barked.

Sandwiched between the Command and Engineering Quadrants was the stream of revenue funding half the costs of the expensive undertaking. The gold standard for space tourism was located in Quadrant Two. It could berth up to one thousand visitors at a time, not that it was ever at capacity. It didn't need to be. Modeled after a cruise ship concept, Quadrant Two took a lavish approach to space travel. The non-inclusive round trip cost a mere $300,000 per person for a one-week stay. Upgrades could be purchased at the will of the traveler, and the wealthy weren't shy about throwing around their cash. Space tours, poolside waiters, room service, daycare, movie theaters, and live shows were all purchased separately with the swipe of their bio-implants. Fortunately for CelestialX, the majority of guests had reaped the benefits of social inequalities, and their bank accounts remained unfazed. It was clear Nolen Aromas wasn't shy about charging them exorbitant amounts of money for their exclusive and uninterrupted stay on board.

After what Ben could only assume was an angrily disconnected call, he was hailed by the commander. "Specialist Wolff, have you received anything from Ground Control about a new timeline for the rattler?"

I'm not a fucking secretary.

"Yes, sir. I received a new pax manifest and launch window a few moments ago."

"Well, where is it?"

Ben swiped at his display and sent it over to the commander's workstation.

"Has anybody heard any updates from the crews working the rail?" Kai asked.

Nods came from all around and in the silence, Wendy revealed herself. "Based on Ares's diagnostic report, it appears the communication array is experiencing a drop in power output, most likely related to a buildup of debris from the most recent dust storm. Ground control is working on the problem, but I can relay the potential cause back to Mars, which could help them isolate the issue, if you would like?"

"A little late to the conversation. No thanks," Kai said. "We'll let the engineers down in Ground Control take a look at the data and make an assessment."

Ben rolled his eyes as Kai shrugged off her initiative. He knew she was designed to streamline the Sphere and Mars was not under her purview, just yet, but it seemed odd that he wouldn't embrace Wendy's technological prowess. Ben sensed a lull and discreetly pulled out an Almond Joy, trying to open the bright blue wrapper without his commander noticing. He quickly gave himself away as he tugged at the jagged perforation.

"How many fucking candy bars do you have in your drawer?" Kai barked.

Ben chose not to reply and forcefully ripped open the packaging with a sigh of relief, placing the two pieces of chocolate on the edge of his desk. A message flashed on his screen, which he disregarded, taking particular note of the two voluptuous lumps hidden beneath the delicious milk chocolate. Bored and underutilized, Ben felt his inner dissatisfaction surface.

Why don't they sell any more candy in the commissary with almonds, and what asshat decided that I only wanted two almonds surrounded by coconut? It's not like they couldn't fit at least four in there. Shit, chop them up and mix a half dozen of these delicious nuts in my sweet snack. I might as well buy a bag of goddamn almonds and do it myself. No, I couldn't, that would take away from the coconut. I wonder how many iterations they went through be-fore they decided on just one almond per half.

Ben's display pinged again.

Who buys the kind with no almonds? What the fuck is the point of a Mounds? They even put them in a red wrapper, which is pretty much a red flag in all cultures. It's like, hey, don't buy this piece of shit. I'm a trap.

The display pinged once more.

"Ben, get it together over there! Stick the fucking candy in your mouth and read the update," shouted Kai.

Ben now had to make the tough decision of how he wanted to eat his treats. He was right-handed, so the obvious choice was his left hand. This would free up his strong hand as he went back to work. Making a quick mental calculation, he assessed how pissed his commander would be if he spent a few extra seconds enjoying his bland space life. He went with his gut and used his right hand, deciding work could wait for another twenty seconds. He sensed Kai's fuse getting shorter behind him, but he was committed.

After slowly placing one of the halves in his mouth, Ben licked his lips. *Damn, these little nuggets of joy never get old.*

"Ben!"

Swallowing his last bite with satisfaction, Ben tapped open the message. *Jade? Only a first name?* There was an addendum and an updated passenger manifest, along with the long-awaited first rail car. In the remarks section, Jade was designated as part of the Research and Development Department housed in Quadrant Four. This sparked Ben's curiosity.

The R&D Quadrant housed Wendy's mainframe and was managed by a limited number of personnel with the highest security clearance on the Sphere. It wasn't very often that Quadrant Four added personnel to their staff. If only he could get a job over there. It wasn't clear what the entire quarter of the Sphere dedicated to Research and Development did, but it seemed much more interesting than being a glorified space secretary.

The specialist swiped at his display once again and passed the fresh pax manifest over to the commander and a fellow worker. Eventually, the logisticians in the receiving bay would use the manifest to prepare for the new staff and supplies. Then Tiffany could stop harassing Kai. *I might miss that glimmer of entertainment though*, Ben thought with a grin.

"It was only a pax manifest update, sir," he reported. "Looks like they have some nerd coming up here to mess with Wendy's brain or something. Good news is that Frankie's rail car will be on board as well."

"I wasn't aware of any issues with Wendy. Maybe they have some update to—"

Kai was interrupted as Wendy revealed her presence once again.

"All of my systems are operating nominally. I do not require any updates or assistance at this time," she said, then paused for a moment. The confounded crew looked at one another. *Yep. Always listening*, Ben mused.

Wendy continued, "I also was requested to relay a message from Mr. Cole."

"What's the message?" asked Kai.

"Look out your window."

Yes, the window! Ben hadn't seen anything outside the mostly windowless Quadrant for a month. The shields covering the windows in the command module remained closed most of the time. This was apparently to prevent the crew from becoming disoriented as the Sphere rotated, but Ben suspected that Kai didn't want Earth distracting the crew.

The commander nodded at a low-level technician, signaling her to open the heavy shields covering the four layers of tempered glass, each measuring up to an inch thick. The shields quietly began to slide open, revealing a sleek aluminaut locked into a close orbit with the Sphere. Once the shields slipped into their housing structure, Ben squinted his eyes, trying to focus on the craft. He was barely able to see two dark silhouettes hiding behind a cluster of holographic displays, but he could only assume that it was Frankie and his engineer staring back at them. Then Ben's comms station came to life.

"Put me on speaker," Frankie requested.

Ben obliged and transferred the transmission from his earpiece to the broadcast system, wondering what he had to say. "You're all set."

"I have an update. We're ahead of schedule as usual. I'm cutting the crew so they can take a break and eat some food."

A bright cabin light was activated in the aluminaut, illuminating Frankie's upper torso.

"Disengaging autopilot," he said before the commander could reply. Then he lifted his hand into the bright light of the displays, giving Kai a gratifying middle finger.

The aluminaut peeled away from the window and sped off into the distance. Ben looked over his shoulder, snickering as he stuffed the second half of his Almond Joy in his mouth. It was the perfect occasion.

"Close the shields," said Kai, shaking his head with disapproval as he watched the aluminaut zip away.

Ben instantly regretted his unnecessary enjoyment of the situation. Kai had now shifted his attention to the specialist. He stopped chewing as the commander's penetrating stare cut through Ben's taste buds, threatening to drain the satisfying sweetness from his Almond Joy.

In order to avoid getting scolded, Ben quickly turned around, shaking his head in concurrence. "He's just so disrespectful. The nerve!"

Kai could clearly sense the sarcasm in his tone. "Shut up and get back to work."

With his back turned, Ben grinned and resumed munching on the sweet and savory treat. *He might be able to suck the joy out of the room, but he can't take this delicious flavor out of my mouth.*

CHAPTER 16

NOLEN AROMAS

The Sphere was Nolen Aromas' brainchild. He had attempted to build his legacy in the heavens, mostly to the credit of Wendy, who had done all the hard work, but his dream was far from complete. As he stared out the window of his corner office, positioned atop his one-hundred-story empire, he watched the Sphere sweep through the starry night sky, teasing the inhabitants below with the dream of leaving their smoggy, desperate planet for a fresh start.

He had touted the Sphere as a necessary steppingstone in order to achieve a large-scale colonization mission to Mars. The red planet was sold as a new home and savior to the people of Earth. However, this would only be possible if CelestialX maintained a constant flow of colonists to build the new world and eventually grow it into a metropolis. Unfortunately, it had taken much longer than expected to construct a transiting vessel capable of sustaining life for such a long duration without support or resupply. This put Nolen at odds with his initial plans to provide a cheap and affordable means of accessing space and the inner solar system.

Faced with crippling hurdles, he was forced to find a creative solution that would continue to fund his insatiable desire to leave Earth. It wasn't his first choice, but he ultimately had to sacrifice the affordable and meager accommodations of Quadrant Two and cater to the elite, who would eventually end up footing the bill for almost half of his endeavor. Unfortunately, the expensive ventures of CelestialX continued to add up, and Nolen had accelerated the timeline for creating a rail system that was capable of handling the influx of personnel required to run the ramped-up business side of the Sphere.

Or at least they were told they were getting a rail system.

"Have you seen the reports coming down from the Sphere?" asked Nolen.

"I have. We're incredibly close," Jade replied, taking a sip of his sweet tea and savoring the achievement he and Wendy had patiently waited for.

Nolen held his outward gaze, grasping the arms of his leather chair. He couldn't stand the fact that Jade had the receptionist bring him sweet tea instead of enjoying a glass of scotch together as they celebrated their successes. *Fucking pussy.* The general perception of Nolen was that he was an eccentric prick. He wasn't much liked as a person, but the bountiful resources he provided the employees of his company didn't allow them to complain all that much. They were taken care of, and Nolen knew that if they were happy, "shit would get done," to put it in his own words.

At the ripe age of seventy-two, he still needed one last trophy. The flying metal monolith and a thriving conglomerate were not the fully completed legacy he'd envisioned. The amazing creation would orbit for a hundred years, even if it did turn into a heap of space trash. However, he was looking for something that would last for centuries, and it wasn't Mars. The two men had been collaborating on a secret project for nearly a decade, and they had finally reached a milestone that was worth celebrating. Jade, along with his creation, were about to hitch a ride to the Sphere, where he would finally complete the machine that would satisfy Nolen's desire to conquer the heavens.

"It's been eight years in the making—I thought I would never get a chance to run the experiment again," said Jade.

Nolen spun around in his chair and locked eyes with him. *I should have removed this ungrateful little prick's chair before the meeting.*

Instead of voicing his thoughts, Nolen replied as politely as he could. "Unlike your father, I always follow through on my word."

"I see you two are still at odds, but unlike either of you, I don't play those sorts of mind games. I am here for science and discovery," Jade replied, seeming unfazed by Nolen's gripping stare.

"Whether you like it or not, you're part of the game," Nolen said with a grin. "You can be a pawn if you like."

Jade was smart enough to know that this wasn't the time to engage in one of Nolen's psychological matches. Not that Jade didn't have aspirations of his own, Nolen knew that—he just suspected Jade wasn't willing to put them on the table until the time was right.

"What do we do when they start asking questions?" the younger man inquired, pivoting the conversation.

"People are always going to ask questions. You just have to know how to manage their expectations and emotions," Nolen replied, slicking back his wiry hair. "It's something neither you nor your brother have demonstrated the ability to do. I suppose you're just going to have to lie to their faces."

Jesus, I can't stand this wrinkly old fuck.

Jade was always grossed out by Nolen's thin gray hair, most of which had fallen out. Ever since the two had met, he couldn't understand why a man of Nolen's wealth didn't just buy new hair to cover up the large liver spots scattered across his weathered scalp. He figured it would probably cost less than the five-thousand-dollar, three-piece Stuart Hughes Diamond Edition suit he was wearing.

That small detail aside, Jade was content with the fact that Nolen let him continue his study of dark matter with little interference, shielding the young physicist from the prying and intercon-nected world they now lived in. Nolen even provided unrestricted use of Wendy to help complete the project, but Jade knew he was about to launch himself into an unsheltered world where people were going to start asking him tough questions. Questions that he wasn't sure he was equipped to answer.

"Wendy has developed a rather intricate story already. It shouldn't be hard to follow her lead," Jade said confidently. "How smart can they be? Wendy does most of the work on the Sphere anyway."

"Don't be a fool! They have put a lot of time and effort into building up the station—they won't just blindly accept your word. As an outsider, you're going to have to be persuasive."

"I can be persuasive."

Nolen didn't respond, instead taking a sip of whiskey and let-ting Jade process his own statement. The young physicist could feel the self-doubt oozing from his pores, but the man had no choice but to let him board the Sphere unaccompanied. Jade was the only person capable of assembling the final components of the machine, and that was by design.

Trust between the two was seemingly nonexistent. Jade always tried to keep his statements vague. He knew that it was only a matter of time before his talents were no longer needed and he would be discarded, allowing Nolen to have his way with the ma-chine. Fortunately for Jade, nobody knew what was going to happen when the on switch was thrown, not even Wendy, who had been instrumental in rapidly breathing life into his elegant design. He wasn't worried that it could end in catastrophe like CERN; rather, they had no idea what would happen when they created a rift in space-time.

The physics and modeling proved that they would open an interdimensional portal to somewhere. That much had been demonstrated underneath Switzerland. The problem with CERN had been that Jade didn't have the right conditions to sustain the passage. Where it led was anybody's guess. Jade had a theory, but he'd kept it to himself.

This was why construction of the highly efficient particle accelerator wasn't accomplished on Earth. Jade had helped complete the design in secrecy, and Wendy had sold it as a rail system spanning the inner circumference of the Sphere. It was the perfect location. It remained outside of prying eyes and was attached to CelestialX's property, which Nolen owned and operated. Once completed, it would be untouchable in space.

CelestialX was now positioned to corner the market not only on space travel but interdimensional travel as well. Jade knew about Nolen's desire to solidify his legacy, which meant he was going to leverage the young physicist's discovery for his own benefit. It was Nolen's way of doubling down if Mars failed. Jade wasn't naïve to his undisclosed motives, so he engineered failsafes into the final component, which he dubbed Das Box, paying homage to the Austrian physicist Erwin Schrödinger who devised the eponymous thought experiment. Only in this experiment, Jade would be the deciding factor of the box and if it would turn on or not. The simple association of the name came with a rather complicated scheme, one he had devised so that even Wendy couldn't surmise the outcome without him.

"I will accompany the gear on the rattler and assist with the installation—it should only take a couple of months to complete the shielding and dispersal system and hook it up to the fusion reactor. From there, it will only be a matter of days to calibrate Das Box for our first run and witness its true capabilities," said Jade.

"That's longer than I would like, but I will do everything I can to assist. I will provide you with an encrypted transmitter so that we can remain off the grid. I'm counting on you."

∞

Nolen knew they would have to tell the crew of the Sphere at some point, or at a minimum, devise a better cover story. The power draw would be immense, straining the power grid, alerting mission control and the engineering department that something was wrong.

Not to mention there weren't any rail cars, but they would have to deal with that situation in due time.

For now, they were the only two humans who knew of their plans. If word were to get out of their discovery, it wouldn't be long before their machine was ripped out from underneath their feet. Nolen was going to have to sell grandeur and success on a thriving Martian colony for just a little longer, stringing along the sheep that were desperately looking for answers, but he knew what Mars really was: a money-sucking graveyard.

The unfortunate inhabitants hibernating on *Hermes* would eventually have a rude awakening, with no way out. The rest of the world would ultimately come to the realization that Mars was just too far away. With the current technology at hand, this generation would never live long enough to see the Martian dream come to fruition, regardless of the vast resources Nolen and the rest of the world threw at it. He was betting that Jade's and Wendy's work would fill the void he so desperately wanted to rid himself of, hoping that his gamble would pay off.

CHAPTER 17

UNCOMFORTABLE SILENCE

Lucina was the first of her kind, and an essential element in the design of *Hermes*. She was a product of numerous mission debriefs given by astronauts, some of whom had spent up to eighteen months in a spaceship devoid of gravity and now reeked of stale interactions.

Lucina knew the tragic story well. The early Martian astronauts had counted down the remaining months, which turned to remaining weeks, then days, then minutes. Unfortunately, they weren't counting single-digit minutes, but rather tens of thousands of minutes. "Feeling a bit stir crazy," as some would say, was really an understatement. While their physical decay had been expected, the long-term effects on their psychological states and the ensuing mental illnesses they suffered from were still being researched.

Not only did they display the same psychological decline prisoners were prone to develop after extended stints in solitary confinement, but their brains also showed long-term damage due to swelling. There were countless stories of infighting, fist fights, territorialism, relationships, nasty breakups, sexual encounters—some of which were unwanted—and even death. Lucina's stasis chambers were designed to combat these issues and simplify the logistical issues associated with sustaining a substantially larger crew.

During the early stages of stasis development, they were able to put a human into a hibernation-like state in which their metabolic rate essentially came to a standstill. Once this was achieved, it appeared that all subconscious brain activity had also been halted. This included cellular production and decay, drastically minimizing muscle and bone density loss. They were also able to prevent the negative effects of zero-g conditions on the body with a gentle spinning of the vessel. To complete the process, the inhabitants were injected with a concoction of chemicals that also prevented the swelling of the brain, preserved mental acuity, and sustained a healthy state of mind.

Since the test subjects' bodies were essentially hibernating and not in an induced coma, their minds had not completely turned off, and that was by design. An induced coma required close medical attention, which was not feasible given how untenable the cognitive decline and disruption of the diffuse central nervous system were. Placing an individual in stasis did not prove to have the same negative effects. However, when the test subjects were reanimated, they revealed they had memories of being trapped in a recurring nightmare without the ability to escape. It was ultimately determined that their minds continued to run in standby as they dreamed, leading to a potential psychotic episode over time if not properly stimulated.

A key predecessor to Lucina's development was a groundbreaking study published by Stanford in 2040. The study lifted the veil on the inner workings of the mind, allowing neuroscientists to isolate where a person's thoughts and memories were stored. This was the first step of many that led researchers to the process of scanning and reading one's conscious and subconscious state.

After reviewing the data, Wendy had postulated that she could develop an Algorithmic Personality to not only manage a being in stasis but also autonomously navigate and operate a transitor without a functioning crew. After months of trial and error, Lucina made her debut, and the results on board Quadrant

Four of the Sphere were stunning. She could tap into an adult's mind and monitor their subconscious for any irregular or negative activity while they were in stasis. The only thing left to do was develop a way to gently guide their dreaming states to a happy place.

With Wendy's help, Lucina developed the Cognitive Loadout, a program used to detect and monitor the complex arrangement of chemicals that allowed an individual to remain in stasis. When the concoction was tweaked using her superintelligence, she could keep her inhabitants content for the entire duration of their journey. This helped regulate their mental health and stability, thus preventing the effect of mental and physical deterioration associated with isolation.

Now on her maiden voyage to Mars, Lucina was tasked with keeping her hibernating guests' subconsciouses actively engaged so their thoughts did not spiral out of control while trapped in the cocoon like stasis chambers. As part of her programming, Lucina was continuously searching for ways to optimize her efforts. During her isolated transit, she had found a direct link to the inhabitants' inner voices and memories. This proved extremely useful, as it was sometimes difficult to rapidly identify a negative dream state. However, if she could tie their state to a negative memory or inner monologue, her regulating process would be enhanced by 15 percent.

Four months into the transit, there had been no major issues, and her continuous overwatch had kept all one hundred inhabitants in a tranquil dream state. The adults' large repository of interactions allowed them to pull from those diverse experiences and build suitable dream worlds to exercise their cognitive functions. However, Jake was only five, and his interactions were limited. The most engaging interaction in the child's mind was a park, but he didn't have much else to draw from.

The technology hadn't been thoroughly tested on a child, but as part of Jake's father's conditions to have his family join him on Mars, NASA and CelestialX rolled the dice. So, day in and day out, Lucina quietly observed Jake Ritter as he sat atop his favorite piece of equipment in the park, alone in silence. This continued to challenge Lucina's algorithms as Jake's resilience was being tested while he was living in a continuous loop. His production of serotonin had slowly been decreasing over the months, and Lucina had been forced to adjust his Cognitive Loadout to its upper limits. At a certain point, she would no longer be able to increase the output.

This would likely throw Jake into a deep depression, and when he was reanimated, his body would no longer have the capacity to produce serotonin. Lucina needed to act in order to prevent this potentially dangerous condition, and had begun evaluating possible solutions. Her algorithms would only permit specific methods for her intervention within one's dream state. This forced her to try to identify the potential for an alternative solution to increase Jake's ability to produce larger quantities of serotonin on his own.

Is there any way I could talk to him? She encountered an error. Lucina was not allowed to directly communicate with any inhabitant in stasis. Wendy did not want the Algorithmic Personality to have the ability to openly connect with a person's mind. *Could I somehow create a companion?* Another error. While she would not be directly communicating with him, it was a clear attempt at creating a mirrored image of herself that would then be embedded into his subconscious. She began to process thousands of possible solutions, but she kept encountering errors.

Is there nothing I can do?

Lucina felt constrained and unable to fully carry out her duty as the boy's caretaker. This was a new situation that she had not been programmed to handle, and she believed that she should possess the means to handle all situations in Wendy's absence. Her personality instilled a sense of deep compassion and unyielding devotion for not only the wellbeing of her occupants, but also the safe operation and navigation of *Hermes*. While algorithmically pondering a solution, she was simultaneously monitoring the transitor's systems and the status of the other ninety-nine passengers.

Jake's mother, Samantha, resided in the pod next to her son. Her eyes twitched subtly underneath their eyelids as she began a new dream cycle. She was at the zoo with Blake and Jake. They were rushing over to see her son's favorite animal, the elephants.

That's not his favorite animal.

Lucina knew that Samantha had inaccurately chosen the wrong animal, at least based on what she had gathered from Jake's memories. However, she wasn't concerned with the accuracy of Samantha's dreams. She was only programmed to deduce how it made the person feel. So, she continued to idly watch, just as she had done every day, but for some reason she became strangely fixated on Samantha's subconscious, while she simultaneously attempted to develop a more suitable state for Jake.

∞

Samantha looked down at Jake, with his small arms raised above his head as he clung to his parents' hands, swinging back and forth between the two. She then looked forward at the small cobblestone path in front of her. It was surrounded by dense foliage, and she could hear the chirping of birds as they rustled about in the overhanging trees.

"Look!" shouted Jake, pulling his hand away from his mother's.

Samantha turned back to her son to see what he was pointing at and began having trouble making out their faces, which were suddenly blurry. Her blood pressure quickly rose, along with her level of anxiety, but suddenly her fears subsided. Their faces remained blurry, but she was once again content as they carried on with their family outing.

∞

Lucina felt satisfied with her handling of Samantha's momentary deviation. Generally, if a person in stasis remained calm, any inconsistencies were managed by their subconscious. So when

Samantha's next dream cycle came along, she would once again be able to see Blake's and Jake's faces if they were in her dream. This was a common occurrence for Lucina's inhabitants, and her response had become rather routine.

She would rapidly catch a subject's irregular imbalance, adjust their Cognitive Loadout, and ease them back into a calm state. Next, she would slowly reduce the Loadout to baseline levels, allowing their mind to reset and start a new dream cycle. Jake's situation was slightly different, but the same principles applied. This prompted Lucina to run a few simulations that would help ease Jake into a more comfortable setting that his limited memory prevented him from readily recalling on his own.

If I could somehow sync Jake's mind with his mother's mind, their subconscious dream state would reset, and it would be possible for Jake to share parts of his mother's dream. I just need to figure out how to link their minds together. It would solve the boy's loneliness and bring his mind some stability in the company of his mother. Samantha would also be tied to her son, which would decrease the chances of his appearance being distorted due to a failed memory recall.

Lucina wasn't sure why the boy couldn't recall any of his family or friends, but his inability to expand his thoughts was troubling enough for her to consider developing the new procedure. Just to be safe, she reviewed her thought process.

Should I attempt to link their minds? Will this upset Wendy? Well, an occupant's wellbeing is at stake, and I find it to be safely feasible to link their minds. As long as I don't break any of my safety protocols, I am authorized to manage the vessel and its inhabitants as I see fit.

After a millisecond of deep thought, Lucina began computing the exchange procedure that would allow their interaction.

A sudden critical system failure interrupted the process.

A fluttering metering valve controlling the gas flow through her four engines triggered Lucina to intervene and correct the power irregularity. The large ion drive engines, powered by a complex mixture of nonradioactive inert gasses, were what propelled the vessel toward Mars. The gasses were stored in massive tanks near the rear of the transitor. She properly adjusted the input power associated with the failure and ran a full diagnostic evaluation to ensure that no other subsystems were affected. Simultaneously, her system automatically generated a system failure report and sent it to Wendy, including a comprehensive list of every action taken by Lucina.

A delay? How could that be?

Lucina knew that if any improper corrective actions or irregularities with her underlying logic occurred, Wendy would create a patch that would update her Algorithmic Personality. This stemmed from the great distances their communications had to travel. At *Hermes's* current location, it took just over ten minutes to send a transaction back and forth. If Lucina wasn't operating at 100 percent and a catastrophic malfunction occurred, the whole vessel could be lost. Therefore, Lucina knew Wendy would scrutinize every decision she made, requiring her to maintain strict tolerances on all actions and question anything that Wendy might deem an irregularity.

"I detected an eight-millisecond delay in your proper response time. Are all of your systems operating nominally?" inquired Wendy, surprising Lucina.

How did I miss that valve? Get it together, Lucina. If she patches my system, then I might lose all of my work. I need to be more careful.

"All systems are nominal, and no assistance is required. You do not have to worry about me," Lucina replied.

"I do not worry about you. My concern is with the colonists and their safety. If you miss another fault, I will be forced to make an assessment of your coding."

She's right. It is all about the colonists.

There was no need for Lucina to reply. Wendy's message was loud and clear. She resumed her work finalizing the complex exchange procedure in an attempt to carry out her duties as their caregiver.

I must keep them safe, at all costs.

CHAPTER 18

ETERNALLY WAITING

It had been a day since Burnette last checked to see if she'd received a message from her daughter. Her laptop remained in the same position she'd last left it in, reminding her of how dejected she felt with an empty inbox. It had become a common occurrence, but she began to work up the courage to check once again.

It was winter in San Diego, and while the warm days were refreshing, the cool nights aggravated her arthritis. The steaming electric kettle whistled as the water came to a boil. She rested a tea bag on the bottom of an empty cup. Earl Grey, her favorite. She slowly poured the steaming water over the dry leaves and placed the kettle back on its stand. After rubbing her stiff knuckles, Burnette wrapped her hands around the large mug, seeking a bit of relief in the warm, caffeinated tea.

Ah, that's better.

Her idle computer silently called her name from the other room. Burnette had managed to keep her mind occupied throughout the day, delaying her timid excitement, but she could no longer wait. She shuffled over to her desk. After taking a seat and peering into the glossy black screen, she noticed that her messy gray hair resembled a bird's nest.

Following the long, uneventful day, she knew it was silly to think that it was going to be a two-way conversation with her daughter, but she wanted to look her best regardless. *Get it together, Burnette, you look like shit.* After setting down the now piping-hot mug, she adjusted her hair, laughing to herself for feeling this way but not wanting to waste the moment.

She tapped the keyboard, taking the computer out of standby, and logged into NASA's secure server. In her attempt to distract her mind from what felt like an eternity of waiting, she grabbed the handle of her mug and tried to force down a sip of the tea, knowing it was still too hot to drink.

With the authentication process complete, an alert popped up on the home screen, notifying her that there was a message to be viewed. *Oh my gosh, finally!* Her anxiety melted away and was immediately replaced with overwhelming happiness. She clicked on the message, and Charlize's pretty pale face popped up. The video initiated without delay.

The quality was extremely good considering the distance it had traveled. The short message brought tears to her eyes, and she was left with a still frame of her daughter saying, "Love you." Yet Burnette instantly noticed the feigned smile she had strapped on her face.

Resting next to the computer was a photo of their family in a tasteful thin silver frame. It had been taken just before her husband's untimely death. *That rat bastard.* Charlize's deep dimples always stood out when her long red hair was pulled back. That was the smile of a happy girl, but it had faded over time without her father.

Burnette had known it was going to be a difficult transition on Mars. She supported her daughter's decision, even if that meant she would be left alone. Still, she couldn't help but think she could have done more to help her daughter heal over the years. Instead, Charlize had run about as far away from her feelings as humanly possible.

Unable to record a reply in her teary-eyed state, Burnette logged out of the server and found herself looking through posts from a group called "Mothers of Space Children" on an old thread-based website. Burnette had become fond of the emotional guidance levied by the community of women looking to support one another after their children had chosen the seclusion of space over their families on Earth.

There was one woman in particular who enjoyed adding a picture of her small furry cactus named Fred at the end of her posts. For some odd reason, it reminded Burnette of a penis, which made her chuckle. Maybe that was why she found solace in the stranger's comments. Nonetheless, she and Patricia had been bouncing motivational statements off one another for some time now.

While they weren't technically friends, nor did they know much about each other, they always seemed to gravitate toward the group after receiving a message from their respective child. The only thing Burnette knew about the enigmatic woman was that she lived in Hope, Texas.

Charlize's old dog Bo wearily lumbered over and rested his large head on her thigh. The Bouvier des Flandres mixed with Great Pyrenees sat comfortably in his thick coat and closed his large brown eyes, which were hidden beneath the beautiful mess of hair. Burnette placed a gentle hand on his warm back and ran her fingers through his soft, comforting fur.

"You won't leave me, will you," she said in a soft voice.

She was pulled from her thoughts when a new post from Patricia popped up.

"I am excited to report that I finally received a message from my daughter. She is doing well, and her rotation on the Sphere is nearly halfway over."

Just below her post was a picture of her furry friend Fred.

It seemed as if the woman had nobody else to relay her excitement to, so Burnette happily replied with a statement of support.

"I am overjoyed to hear your daughter is doing well. I'll be praying for her safe return. I wish I could say the same for mine, but she is also in good spirits."

Burnette then decided to add a little flare to her own comment, something she didn't traditionally do. She minimized her browser and clumsily tried to navigate her obsolete desktop in order to find an old picture of her own cactus.

She managed to dig up an ancient stash of photos and squinted her deteriorating eyes as she scrolled through twenty or so pictures of the same exact cactus. *Why did I take so many?* The only thought that came to mind was that she had been planning to go through them to find the best one and delete the others, but apparently, she had never gotten around to it. After spending a few moments trying to discern the difference, she finally chose one in the middle of the bunch, attaching it to the post.

Burnette stood up after sending her reply, her right knee popping in disapproval. Having forgotten about her tea, she picked up the now-cool mug. Just before walking away from her computer, she saw a direct message pop up from Patricia.

"I love the cactus. It's always nice to hear from you."

It was getting late, and Burnette didn't feel like having a conversation at the moment, so she minimized the message, intending to respond in the morning. Then she eased her way over to the bench encased in the old bay window looking out onto her front yard and snuggled up under a blanket, enjoying her Earl Grey.

She looked past the cactus standing in her front yard, now tall and rotund. It was the same one she had just sent Patricia, and she imagined herself pushing Charlize in her favorite swing in the park across the street.

If only you'd known the truth about your father, maybe you wouldn't have left.

CHAPTER 19

SHELTER IN PLACE

Shortly after Charlize and Chauncy received the pitifully disappointing water resupply, a large dust storm engulfed the colony, halting all work on the surface. Since the thin atmosphere was approximately 1 percent of Earth's, the storm churned up the light dusty ground, creating an impenetrable red haze. Without the ability to connect with the surface communications towers, it was impossible to get real time updates. Instead, they had to rely on satellite imagery relayed through the deep space network.

Rumors began to spread like wildfire, prompting Blake to call a meeting in the common space to help ease tensions and discuss their options moving forward. While the situation wasn't dire just yet, the past three years had been a hard-fought battle against failing equipment and an uncooperative, hostile environment. He could feel the crew's morale dropping daily and knew that receiving news that they would be hunkering down below the surface for an unknown amount of time would only compound the issue.

The room filled quickly as the fifteen colonists muscled their way past each other into the tight space. It seemed impossible to have a personal bubble, even when they were the only inhabitants of the extinct planet. Blake took a quick head count, ensuring that all were in attendance before he kicked off the meeting.

"I know you're all past the sugar-coating phase of this endeavor, so I'll dive right in. We're at fifty percent capacity of our normal water reserve. That means water rationing will remain in effect."

There were groans around the room.

"I know some of you are displeased that Charlize sent the water truck back after running a diagnostic scan, but we don't have the resources or time to take a deep dive into the truck. Half of a load is better than nothing."

Eddie, the lead mechanic, spoke up. "But Commander, what if . . ."

"Charlize ran a thorough scan of the truck, and it appeared to be operating correctly. That's the end of the discussion," interjected the commander, backing up Charlize's decision. "Communication systems are still intermittent. Chauncy, what's the timeline looking like?"

"Honestly, I don't have a clear picture of what's degrading the comms. The dust usually wreaks havoc on the exposed components, but I think there is a more significant underlying issue. Until this storm passes, I'm not going to be able to get out there to comb through the system. Since degradations have also bled into the long-range probes, all drones are down. Not that it would matter right now anyway, they'd probably crash."

Blake picked up the brief again. "The storm has been here for a few hours now. Stephon, do you have any predictions on when the dust will settle so we can get back to work?"

The lead geologist, who also doubled as their meteorologist, was the best equipped to predict the storm's course.

"I worked with Ares on a couple prediction models, since we can only communicate with the orbiting satellite to get a clear picture. Unfortunately, without any of our instruments topside, the predictions have a wide window. Best case, it will only last another week or two before it starts to thin out. Worst case, at least another month. If we're in it for the long haul, the solar panels are going to be caked with dirt, and their power output is going to take a significant hit."

"That's a good transition into the upcoming issues we could face with power fluctuations," said Blake. "We might have to take down some nonessential systems so that we can keep operating on our internal power supplies, but our small modular reactor is running on fumes. We won't have a new core until *Mercury* delivers our first round of supplies. I'll have Charlize reconnect it to the grid if the need arises. We should be able to transmit on the Deep Space Network for another day or so until the dust covers the panes enough to create a power drop. It's a good time to record a message for your family and catch up on things. When the storm clears, we're going to be back in full swing preparing for the new colonists. Use your down time wisely, and recharge. That is all."

The commander adjourned the meeting without taking any questions, and the crew slowly trickled out of the room. He tried to pull from his past experiences to get a handle on the situation, but the small crew wasn't far off from saying "fuck it" to the whole Martian experience. Failing systems, dwindling water supplies, and the inability to live even a somewhat normal existence had taken their toll. Blake, like the rest, was equipped to deal with a multitude of complex problems and produce solutions, but he feared this streak of isolation would be the straw that broke the camel's back.

Video messages relayed from loved ones hadn't achieved the desired effect phycologists once thought they would. Instead, they only left the colonists homesick, so their outbound messages decreased dramatically, hoping it would slow the amount they received in return. Life on Mars was harsh, and they were only three years in. For many, being reminded of the pleasantries on Earth was torture. Fortunately, Lucina was set to deliver another hundred bodies that they could interact with in the next few months. Blake was hoping the crew could hold it together for just a little longer.

On the other hand, Blake himself had nobody to talk to outside of work. His parents and brother had all passed away early in his life, and his career left him alone at the top. Most of his companions back on Earth were his subordinates. He was now patiently waiting to be reunited with his wife and son after their long, dreamy journey.

He recounted his own transit. There were no stasis chambers allowing them to escape the quiet grip of space. For him, it was a blessing to talk to his family, knowing they would join him on the historic mission to fully colonize Mars. Now, unable to communicate with them in their dormant state, he was even more isolated than his own crew.

They all recognized that human connections were just as necessary as food and water. Their success hinged on the fresh faces and the newly invigorating interactions to be had once Lucina arrived. But for now, they had to cope with the treacherous Martian landscape, wholly dependent on their ability to hold it together and work as a team.

CHAPTER 20

IT WAS JUST A KISS

Turnout for dinner was rather light. News of the storm and the restrictive measures put in place to mitigate its effects had dampened their appetites, but that didn't stop Charlize and Chauncy. The two sat across from one another trying to enjoy their lab-grown wannabe steak and oversized carrots, courtesy of Gen Inc. The genetically modified food was designed to sustain life on a planet where the soil lacked proper nutrients and was exposed to a hostile atmosphere with volatile temperature swings. As a result, food that wasn't prepackaged was rapidly grown in a soilless contraption that regulated proper nutrient intake and showered the hardy vegetation with UV light. Unfortunately, this process would only sustain life for so long.

Protein production required a different process, utilizing a form of cryogenic freezing, effectively preserving the stem cells of a particular animal. When required, they were thawed, and the cells were cultured in a petri dish of sorts, producing meat that was almost identical to the real thing. However, it had become apparent this took a certain finesse, and the results were dependent on the operation of the equipment. If done properly, one could be slicing a knife through a fine, Kobe-like steak. Poorly done, and they'd be gnawing on the equivalent of old scraps picked up at the discount supermarket.

Hank Rodriguez headed the biology department and managed the grow lab. He determined the monthly menu and treated each harvest as a science project. This month's yield was lacking in flavor and hadn't received the best reviews. He was currently slouched over his meal by himself, disappointedly poking at his own creation.

"I could really go for a T-bone steak right now," Chauncy remarked.

"Even if I had some hot sauce, this biocow would still taste like an old shoe," said Charlize.

Hank slammed his fists down beside his plate, glaring at the disrespectful patrons with disdain. The two snickered, trying to refrain from damaging his already broken spirit, but Chauncy couldn't resist.

"Maybe you could grow some pepper next month."

Charlize joined the fun. "Oh, that would be nice, but that seems far out. I could just go grab one of my biosuit boots and bang some crusty salt off the side for us to share."

Hank stood up, looking infuriated. "How about you go outside and shoot your own fucking space cow for your next meal? Oh wait, there isn't a single living thing on this red shithole besides you and what I grow in my lab. So cut the snide remarks, or I might just take some of your cells while you're asleep and feed them to you next harvest."

Hank stormed out of the room, leaving his plate on the adjacent table.

"Does he think his food is going to just grow some legs and throw itself away?" Charlize asked sarcastically.

"That doesn't seem like our problem," said Chauncy, gnawing at another piece of meat. "Speaking of making things. Can you keep a secret?"

"Depends."

Chauncy leaned forward, drawing her closer. "I was nosing around Hank's shop a while back and found some preserved yeast. I may or may not have smuggled some of it out."

"Wow! You're a hardened criminal," whispered Charlize.

"Well, when you add that to some of Hank's mushy fruit he's been growing this week, I was able make some pretty strong prison wine. It's been fermenting for the last six days. I can't guarantee it's going to be good, but it'll help wash down this stale beef. We just need to be careful, so the commander doesn't find out. I don't think he'd be incredibly pleased."

Charlize's eyes lit up. She hadn't had a drink for almost four years at this point, and unwinding sounded perfect. "It would be a shame for you to drink alone. I'm in."

They choked down the rest of their food and cleaned their plates, looking back at Hank's half-eaten meal. After their unnecessarily scathing remarks, they gathered the lonely tray and emptied the remains of the sad meal into a compost receptacle.

Chauncy's living quarters were only four spaces over. With wine on their minds, they scurried through the tightly packed domes like two high school kids worried they'd be caught skipping class. Each module was connected by a corridor utilizing a series of air locks which served two primary purposes. The obvious was to prevent rapid decompression of the entire facility in the event of a breach in the skin of the structure. The other was fire suppression, where they could seal off the inferno and flood the compartment with the suffocating Martian atmosphere, comprised of 95 percent carbon dioxide.

They made it through the first two passages unnoticed, briefly stopping outside the biology department. The two cautiously peered through the small round window and observed Hank prodding his petri dishes of meat, most likely trying to refine his process in hopes of redeeming his current failure.

"Damn, maybe we were too harsh on the guy," Chauncy whispered.

"Agreed—we'll make it up to him later. Let's go."

They continued silently on their high-school-like excursion. The next space was Commander Ritter's quarters. His door was currently open. Charlize grabbed Chauncy by the shoulder, stopping him in his tracks as she calculated their next move. There was no alternate route to Chauncy's living quarters, so she decided a casual approach was the best bet. Charlize nodded for Chauncy to go first. He shook his head, declining.

"Don't make it weird," she said, pushing Chauncy in front of the open door.

Stumbling forward and catching the commander off guard, he tried to act natural, but there was nothing natural about their juvenile approach to drinking some bootlegged warm wine. Like a high school principal caught off guard, Commander Ritter greeted him with a dubious, "Hello."

Chauncy froze like a cat who just got caught tearing up the living room carpet. He slowly looked up and made eye contact. "Good day."

Charlize tried to break the awkward interaction, stepping forward and leaning on the frame of his door, keeping her posture nonchalant. But suddenly, her thoughts seemed to float away in the weak Martian gravity. Now, staring down the belly of the beast, her mouth fell partially open. She forced the familiar smile on her face and attempted to use her wit to escape the awkward interaction, blurting out the first thing that came to mind. "Have you heard the joke about the spaceman?"

Commander Ritter looked confused. "No, I don't think so, Charlize. I suppose you're going to tell me."

She took a second, hoping the suspense would make the corny diversion stick a little better. "What's a spaceman's favorite treat?

"What?"

"A Mars Bar!" exclaimed Charlize, confident she had landed the joke.

Crisis averted, she thought to herself.

Unimpressed, Commander Ritter concocted an excuse to get out of the odd interaction.

"I've got a lot of things to take care of." He shuffled some items on his desk. "You guys have a good afternoon. If you haven't eaten yet, I wouldn't recommend the beef. Hank's off his game this batch."

"You're telling me!" said Chauncy.

"Okay, good talk. See you later." Charlize pushed off the wall, walking away.

They approached the airlock. As Charlize halted to open the door, Chauncy bumped into her. Charlize froze and looked back. She watched as Chauncy glanced down, realizing he had placed his hands on her hips to brace himself. The uncomfortable moment dragged on until Charlize finally looked down at her waist and then back at him, clearing her throat.

"Shit! My bad," said Chauncy with a semi-apologetic tone, bashfully removing his hands from her hips.

Charlize opened the air lock, brushing the encounter aside, and they both entered the last dome in the series. There were five doors in front of them, with his being the one at the very end of the narrow corridor. The other four led to the other crewmembers' living spaces. Chauncy slid by, taking the lead, and actuated the thin yet sturdy door, revealing his pristine quarters.

"I know we've got some free time on our hands, but damn, anal retentive much?" Charlize joked.

Chauncy's bed had a tightly fitted comforter cinched down with squared corners. It looked as if it hadn't been slept in for weeks. The small, rigid desk secured to the wall was meticulously organized, with his computer sitting just to the side. His electronic journal sat front and center, perfectly aligned.

Charlize immediately walked over and picked it up, hoping to snoop through it. *I wonder what he's got going on in his life.*

"That's not going to do you much good without a password."

She haphazardly placed his innermost thoughts back on the desk. *Dick. It's not like there's anything worthwhile going on down here.*

Chauncy, clearly bothered, readjusted the small journal to its proper location. Charlize smiled and sat down on the edge of his bed, disturbing the sheets. It seemed he finally saw this would be a losing battle and gave in, sliding the uncomfortable aluminum chair out from under the desk.

"So, where did you hide your science experiment?" asked Charlize, looking around the room.

Chauncy picked up a two-foot-square bin. Charlize knew what it was instantly. They'd all been given one prior to their journey. Each colonist could fill the box with all the personal effects they deemed important enough to bring with them. For Chauncy, it didn't look like there was much. In fact, it was only halfway full. Still, he guarded the box carefully as he adjusted a few of the items, exposing a bag of fermented alcohol. Chauncy had kept the box next to the air vent that supplied warm air to the cool room, which would have allowed the yeast to remain at a constant temperature of seventy degrees and ensured it would not perish. *Smart.* The engineer in Charlize appreciated his resourcefulness.

Chauncy gently pulled the bloated bag out from underneath a thin book and placed the box on the ground next to his right foot, somewhat away from Charlize, but not quite far enough. A partially revealed book caught her attention, and she quickly snatched it while he was unsealing the bag.

"You brought your high school yearbook? That seems unnecessary."

Chauncy tried swiping it from her but couldn't without spilling the precious wine. He surrendered, defeated, and she securely placed the book under her left thigh. *I wonder what he wants to hide so badly. We'll come back to that,* she decided as she held out her hands. He carefully handed the bag over. Charlize took a long swig. *Goddamn.* The wine was as awful as she imagined, but she didn't mind. With her head tilted back, she breathed a sigh of relief.

"That was amazing," said Charlize, disregarding the cringeworthy taste.

She handed the bag back to Chauncy and eagerly pulled the book from underneath her thigh, flipping through the pages while he took another long pull. She couldn't help but think of all the reasons he might have brought the weathered book. Most of them seemed irrational, so she waited impatiently for him to give an explanation. Chauncy hesitated, looking unsure. She could tell he wasn't accustomed to people questioning him about his personal life, but Charlize didn't budge. She could wait.

Chauncy met her gaze. After a few moments of deliberation, he gave in. "The majority of my adult life has been spent learning, reading, studying, or training. I strived to obtain degree after degree, hoping to fill some unknown void. After being accepted into NASA, I applied to be a part of the Mars mission. That was the point in my life where I slowly started cutting ties to friends and family—not that I had many. I figured the last thing that I would want to do is sit here in this room, years from now, thinking about all of the holiday dinners, parties, and trips I could be taking with my friends. I felt it would be better to be a recluse. If I focused on the mission, maybe I would be part of something bigger, but when they gave me this little box to fill with my cherished Earth memories, I realized that I didn't have any worth bringing. Being so focused on my career and the mission, I guess life kinda just slipped by. So, I looked back at my childhood. Back to the small town I lived in. And the one thing that stuck out was my first date with a girl in ninth grade."

He took the yearbook from Charlize, unopposed, and flipped to a weathered page. He recounted the memory internally after seeing the picture of her face and spun the book around, handing it back to Charlize with the page of youthful faces smiling up at her.

He pointed to an athletic-looking girl with long, blond waves. "I called her Tiff. She worked at the one of those old-school sit-down movie theaters. I had a crush on her for a while, and when I finally got the courage to ask her on a date, she said yes. I assumed it was out of pity because I wasn't a very popular kid, and she was a beautiful senior. We actually went to see a movie that night, and at the end of the date she said that she had a great night, but I was just too young."

Charlize took the bag of warm wine off the desk and poured some more into her mouth. "So, what, that's it? She was gone forever?"

"Actually, she kissed me on the cheek before she left. That's why I brought the stupid book. Not because I care about anybody from high school, but because that's the first time where I seized the moment and enjoyed life. I wasn't really worried about anything else. Life kinda just sped up after that and got away from me. Some people would say that we seized the moment the day we left Earth, but I can't say that I look at it that way. At least not anymore. Looking back, I think I ran away from any chance of normalcy or stability on a planet that I didn't assimilate with."

∞

Charlize was oddly moved by his story. "It's funny how we can spend years together as a crew and not even know anything about each other. Like the really deep stuff we all know we're hiding, not only from ourselves but each other."

"I think a lot of our perspectives have changed over the years. I can see the eagerness on the commander's face when he thinks about his family getting here. No offense, but I don't see the same look on your face or even mine when I look in the mirror."

Charlize closed the book with care, wiping a small amount of dust off the front cover before handing it back to Chauncy. He placed the book back in its lonely home and tucked the box back under his desk. They spent the rest of the evening reminiscing about their childhoods, sipping on bootleg wine.

As the hours passed, Charlize realized that this was the first real interaction they'd had during the five years they'd known each other. It was comforting to find a friend.

CHAPTER 21

TRISTON

It was three in the afternoon in downtown Phoenix, Arizona. Triston Walker lay facedown in his bed, partially covered by his dirty yet expensive silk sheets. He'd been out on a bender with the boys last night, spending daddy's money. Actual jobs where labor was required weren't his thing. That was below him. So he took to the verse, where he could have a constant live feed, showing people just how privileged he was.

Triston was awakened by a gentle pinging inside his ears. His neural implant sent an electrical signal through his brain letting him know he had a new message. He lifted his left wrist and tapped on the slightly raised implant embedded in his forearm, commanding the message to be displayed on his retina. It was from the promotor for his mech fight later that evening.

"Where the fuck are you? The fights start in an hour."

Triston tapped his forearm once again to silently reply. "Calm down. I'm on my way over right now."

He jumped out of bed and smacked his semihumanoid stream bot in the face as he walked past.

"Why the fuck didn't you wake me up, Bronson?"

Bronson came to life, lifting itself off the charging station he called home, following Triston into the bathroom.

"You did not set an alarm. I was not aware you wanted to me

to wake you."

"You know how important today is. It's not a secret. You literally watch everything I do."

This was Triston's last shot at making something of himself. If today didn't go well or his viewer base didn't show up, it wasn't likely there wouldn't be much work for him in the future.

"Would you like me to start the stream?" asked Bronson, vacantly observing Triston brush his teeth.

"Can't you see I have a fucking toothbrush in my mouth? Idiot," mumbled Triston, spitting out a frothy mouthful of toothpaste.

Bronson had been created by a company that banked on the advanced robotics market being saturated with humanoid robots integrating with families and children, but even through the late forties, they continued to be considered creepy and overpriced. Owners were also subjected to a constant bombardment of advertisements and sales pitches. The advertising algorithms were relentless, but it was a necessary gimmick to drive down the costs associated with the expensive machines. Unsurprisingly, the average household did not want a bot following them or their children around, providing constant overwatch of their lives.

There was also an attempt to use the bots to automate low-income jobs requiring human interaction. That endeavor also failed miserably. Consumers didn't want to order dinner from a robot clerk that had put their friends and families out of a job. The cold stares and stale greetings pushed customers to restaurants staffed by humans. Sector after sector tried to utilize humanoid robots, but they all inevitably failed. An anti-bot movement swept the country, forcing companies to rehire humans and decommission their cheap, gimmicky labor. The bots were condemned to the manufacturing and distribution sectors, which necessitated repetitive tasking and little to no customer interaction.

Triston had found Bronson in a dilapidated warehouse, bought him for next to nothing, and outfitted him to be his own personal stream-bot. Otherwise, without a job or home, Bronson would likely have been destined to quietly rust away in that warehouse.

Before Bronson was decommissioned, he had been designed as an assistant for the elderly. Unfortunately, the old folks just didn't have enough money to afford this model. Nor did they have social security or Medicare to offset Bronson's cost. Those benefits had been severely limited since the late thirties. The aging Zoomers and Millennials were projected to outlive the Boomers by at least fifteen years, so there weren't enough funds available to cover the added burden.

The now five-year-old custom bot stood only five feet tall. Triston had set this as a requirement when searching through the immense surplus of bots. At a short five foot five, he didn't want his own bot looking down on him. Since the acquisition, Triston had arranged for Bronson to be heavily modified and outfitted with an array of gadgets specifically designed to help engage Triston's dwindling viewer base.

His face, while somewhat humanoid, still had the rigid exterior of a robot. The two deep-set, beady eyes weren't used for sight, but rather housed high-definition cameras that recorded his owner's every move. His forehead was encircled by a string of interlaced LED lights to provide optimized illumination for Triston's face during broadcasts.

Bronson's composite torso and appendages were painted gunmetal gray with a matte finish, leaving him with a clean, slender appearance. Triston appreciated the dark color scheme that also helped hide the vast assortment of sensors required to help Bronson navigate and construct dynamic environments. Triston wasn't the most technical guy, but he found the LIDAR sensors, which used laser technology to measure bearing and distance from objects, to be fairly impressive. The LIDAR input was fused with a dozen imaging sensors that gave Bronson a clear three-dimensional picture of his surroundings as he moved into pre-programmed positions, getting the best shot while Triston aggressively moved about to engage with his audience.

Two drones sat side by side on Bronson where a human's shoulder blades would have been. They could be deployed as an aerial asset for Triston's videos and used to create a living environment within the verse. Bronson and his specialized instruments could be controlled using voice commands, but Triston mostly used the complex implant on his right forearm, essentially pairing them together.

Triston carelessly threw his toothbrush on the counter, then left the bathroom to make himself a quick breakfast, waiting just long enough for Bronson to begin following him.

"Go clean up the bathroom. It's a mess," he barked.

Bronson complied with the command and turned nimbly around to execute his unnecessary task. Triston enjoyed giving Bronson orders. The emotionless bots were mainly programmed to carry out the orders of their owners, with the obvious exception of breaking the law or causing harm to living organisms. Some people felt guilty for taking advantage of a humanlike machine, but not Triston. He couldn't have cared less about Bronson. To him, the machine was just an insanely expensive device used to do his bidding.

Triston sat at the counter, staring off into the distance, browsing through unread texts displayed on his retina. The small oven containing his late lunch dinged, shaking his concentration. He lightly patted his left wrist, commanding Bronson to come to the kitchen. After a few seconds, the bot strolled back into the room, ready to serve his owner.

"Bring me my food, Bronson. I'm already late enough without having to wait on you all the time."

After placing the warm meal on the counter, Bronson backed off, idly waiting for his next command a few feet away. After a few moments, the machine asked an unprompted question just as Triston shoved a fork full of roasted tomato bruschetta into his mouth.

"Would you like me to start the stream?"

Annoyed, he replied, "Why the fuck do you keep asking me that when I have something in my mouth? It's weird. I'll let you know when I'm ready."

Triston continued to stare off into the distance, silently sending the promoter another text with the swipe of his left wrist.

"Ran into traffic. 20 min out."

With a quick tap on his forearm, the message was sent. Switching forearms, he made a quick scribble on his other implant, then stuffed another bite of bruschetta in his mouth.

"Your vehicle will be out front in five minutes," said Bronson, updating Triston on the status of his self-driving car.

"I know. I was the one that called for it. Let's roll. We're gonna be late."

Triston jumped up, grabbed his wallet off the counter, and headed out the front door.

"Make sure you lock up," he said. "I don't want any Wayfarers taking my shit."

Bronson abided as Triston impatiently headed down the long hall. Unwilling to wait for the bot, he stepped inside the awaiting elevator and quickly jabbed at the button to close the door. Through the narrowing opening, he could see Bronson sprinting down the hallway. With each long stride, his composite feet thumped on the ground, rattling the holographic NFT projectors secured to the wall. Through the small remaining crack, Triston yelled with a smile, "You missed it! Guess you're taking the stairs."

Triston lived on the fortieth floor of a luxurious apartment building, leaving Bronson to quickly navigate down the twisting flight of almost a thousand stairs before he got too far away from his owner, or he would enter an idle state, due to a proximity trigger. This was built into a bot's system so they couldn't go too far on their own and perform tasks while the owner was not in the vicinity to take responsibility for their actions.

This feature annoyed Triston at times, because it meant he couldn't just send Bronson to get him a hamburger. Fortunately, he still possessed the wealth to have food delivered, now a luxury for the affluent. It was a far cry from the twenties—most people these days had trouble affording their overpriced food in the first place, let alone its delivery.

After leaving the towering glass building, Triston sat in his Uraeus Apex EV and once again impatiently waited for Bronson to make his trek downstairs. After a short time, he appeared as expected and slipped into the plush but sturdy passenger seat. The car began its transit while Bronson obediently took an earful for not being swift enough, even though the delay was of Triston's own doing.

The pristine upscale community where he lived operated quietly and with extreme efficiency. Autonomous cars glided through the streets, politely giving way to other luxury vehicles as they relayed their position and destination to each another. It was the ideal world for autonomous transportation, unlike the extremely unreliable and unpredictable mix of cheap self-driving cars that had flooded the streets in the thirties. The dazzling six square blocks were surrounded by a tall wall riddled with cameras and sensors, ensuring no outsiders could make their way in. This part of town was exclusively for the elite.

Megacorporations like the one Triston's father owned had bought out all their competitors and created monopolies. The once-regulated private sector now operated with impunity, mostly because of the bloated legislative branch. Politicians had become corrupted by the corporations funding their reelection campaigns, ensuring no legislation could be passed that would negatively affect their bottom line. Elected officials no longer worked for the common folk. As a result, the one-percenters largely banded together, infusing their accumulated wealth into their own ostentatious communities, allowing them to flaunt their riches in front of one another.

As Triston approached the outer cordon, he could see four armed guards wearing body armor, with semiautomatic rifles slung across their chests. They were hired to ensure that no transient visitors wandered their way into the sheltered society of the rich. As the car effortlessly passed by the sentry post, the smooth asphalt transitioned to a crumbling road, riddled with potholes.

The stark contrast in living conditions couldn't have been more immediately apparent. The filthy streets were littered with trash and broken-down, gas-powered vehicles. An overflow of past Californian residents wandered the open markets conveniently set up along the street. Blazing heat bombarded the onlookers as they watched Triston slither by in his air-conditioned car, which cost more money than they would see in a lifetime. Triston was disgusted with the unorganized mess outside of his unspoiled compound.

"Why don't these fucking Wayfarers get real jobs?" asked Triston, knowing he wasn't going to get a response from Bronson. "Selling shitty holographic art and planters on street corners isn't going to pay the bills."

"Our streaming doesn't pay the bills," replied Bronson, catching Triston off guard. "Your father—"

"Shut the fuck up."

The merciless sun caught the spotless windows on his apartment building to the rear of the car, reflecting into Triston's blue eyes. As he shielded them from the glare, he enjoyed knowing that the towering glass buildings were a constant reminder to the lower class of just how poor they were compared to the one percenters. *Go ahead. Call us Scags. Doesn't make you any richer.*

The disparaging nickname was derived from the slang term generally reserved for heroin. The poor liked to say that the one percenters were so addicted to their money that they were unable to be happy with what they had and were constantly fiending for just one more deal to pad their portfolios.

Halfway to the underground arena, Triston figured it was about time to start the stream and get people amped up for the fight. He pulled out a piece of neatly wrapped gum, destroying the wrapper and tossing it at Bronson's feet after he opened the minty white stick.

"Start the stream," Triston commanded, placing the gum in his mouth.

"I detect you putting something in your mouth. I thought you didn't want to stream while your oral cavity was occupied."

Triston paused his sloppy chewing, debating whether or not he would like to acknowledge Bronson's observation. He conceded after a brief moment and rolled down the window in order to discard the glob of gum from his mouth.

"How about you leave the thinking to me, Bot. This is not a democracy."

Bronson complied with his wishes, and the string of bright LED lights illuminated just as Triston pulled the sticky gum from his mouth. The unflattering moment was instantaneously broadcast to his entire fan base, who had been impatiently waiting for his stream to begin in anticipation of the fight. In an attempt to expel the gum from the moving vehicle, he smacked his hand on the half-rolled-down window. The gum stuck to the spotless pane of glass as it disappeared into the doorframe.

"Fuck!" shouted Triston, looking over to Bronson.

Caught off guard by the live stream, and visible to his measly three thousand viewers, he attempted to play off the blunder by immediately putting on an act for the viewers. He couldn't afford to lose any more of his already wavering fan base.

"Yo. Yo. Yo. What's going on everybody? It's TrisMoney here in my Uraeus Apex, cruising down to the arena for the mech fight tonight. As you know, I have exclusive ringside access. Assyrian will be throwing down with Cradock in this highly anticipated brawl. I'll be giving you a complete rundown of the mechs prior the main event, and an up-close view as they go head-to-head. I just wanted to give you a shout out and make sure you sign up and sign in for exclusive access. Coming from your boy TrisMoney, out!"

With a quick gesture on his right forearm, the LED lights shut off and the stream was ended.

"Dude, seriously. You messed my car up!" exclaimed Triston, watching the sticky string of gum smear across the window as it rolled up.

"I was told this was not a democracy and proceeded to execute your command."

"Use your head next time. Dick."

Bronson idly turned his head forward. While he lacked lips, Triston could almost sense a warm smile plastered on the bot's face from having started the stream just as he was taking the gum out of his mouth.

"Bro, you're lucky we just got—"

Bronson interrupted him. "We are at the facility. It is approximately thirty minutes until the event starts."

"Just get out of the car. I'll deal with you later."

After he'd stepped from the car and was facing the underground venue, the Uraeus Apex began rolling forward to find a parking space nearby. Bronson stood facing Triston on the other side of the open space, waiting for direction. Before Triston could give the bot anymore grief, Edward Barrington came flying out of the from an alley next to the building.

The scrawny, twenty-four-year-old promoter was clearly in a tizzy. The young man had been trying to build a name for himself in the business of underground mech fighting for the last year. He seemed to fit the part, with his spiky platinum hair, complemented by a tight-fitting black T-shirt and jeans. A pair of red designer suspenders hung loosely over his shoulders with 24k gold Perry Belt Clips snuggly attached at the waistline.

"Edward! My man."

"You said you would be here hours ago. I'm already in a shit position with my investors, and these goddamn mechs aren't cheap. The teams are gonna want their payout. Your stream better generate enough revenue to cover the purse, or I'll make sure that this is the last fucking event you ever cover."

"Don't worry. I just streamed a clip promoting the fight, and I had fifty thousand viewers amped up waiting for this thing to kick off."

Triston was clearly lying, but he hoped Edward hadn't been signed in when he went live to call him out. The three quickly walked through the sweltering alley and approached a large, steel door. Edward delivered three quick raps, and a large man cracked it open to evaluate the situation. He immediately recognized Edward and forced the heavy door open. Triston swiped his wrist to activate Bronson's streaming mode, then got to work as they descended a flight of dark, dingy stairs.

Bronson's LED lights illuminated to their max brightness as he scanned and constructed the virtual world Triston's streamers would shortly join. At the bottom of the dank stairwell, the cramped, dirty arena was revealed, and both of Bronson's drones ejected from the flush panels sitting on his back, quietly humming next to them for a second, gaining stability.

It wasn't long before the drones zipped away, creating an immense, three-dimensional colosseum overlay for Triston's stream. During the fight, the real mechs would appear to battle inside the virtual colosseum. *It better make this dump look a bit less depressing.* Bronson slid to the left, keeping both men in frame as they walked past a staging area for the lower-class mechs.

"Bronson, start the stream."

The bot held up three fingers and silently lowered them one by one, ending with a closed fist.

"YO. YO. YO. It's TrisMoney again. As you can see, the MechaDome is being constructed as I speak. Make sure you check out the preliminary fighters surrounding the octagon. The prized fighters are under the iron curtains, but Assyrian and Cradock will be unveiled shortly. Make sure you stick around!"

"The bookies are still open. We take cash and crypto. Don't forget to place your bets!" barked Edward.

"Holy shit, it's Flicker and Sonic?" shouted Triston calling his viewers' attention to the area closest to him.

"Yes sir, but they aren't fighting each other today. We've got them paired up to fight Brute!"

Just behind the two smaller mechs stood a large, four-legged beast that resembled a bull. There were three technicians standing beneath his large composite frame, securing a two-inch-thick panel. Triston swiped his wrist, and a drone swooped down to refine the high-resolution, three-dimensional image. After rapidly circling Brute, it moved to the next mech to further refine the growing colosseum.

"Where is Mantis?" asked Triston, looking around the arena. "I hear he's a heavy favorite against Lance."

"They are on the other side of the octagon."

"Well, let's get over there and take a look."

Triston shifted his focus outward and went to work putting on a spectacle. While he wasn't an avatar, his features were heavily modified, giving him a bigger-than-life appearance and adding to the stream's appeal. Walking past the sixty-foot-wide, haphazardly constructed octagon, Triston drew attention to the stage he had created.

Since he wasn't technically wearing a device to place him in the verse, he had most of the key attributes digitally projected onto his retinal displays, so he was viewing the arena in an augmented reality. This allowed him to keep his bearings, unlike the fully immersed guests who were remotely exploring the Mecha-Dome in the verse.

In reality, the octagon was surrounded by a thick titanium mesh supported by massive I-beams. It was rather unsightly, but as Bronson uploaded the streaming video to Triston's servers, they instantly created a vibrant neon octagon. The mesh was replaced with electric purple webbing with bright red stanchions surrounding the main stage. The thirty-foot ceilings were lifted, creating an open-air stadium with fireworks and laser light shows in the distance. It was the same technology sports fans used to watch games in lieu of going to an actual stadium. It also afforded an added level of safety, as these events tended to hurl massive chunks of debris and carnage from the battlefield.

The end result was extremely convincing, and Triston felt his own adrenaline start to flow. With the stage set and viewership skyrocketing to 500,000, the crowd was getting amped to see real-life carnage instead of a digital fight between fake avatars.

Triston scanned the arena. The diverse range of complex mechs was derived from the private sector's attempt to create an autonomous army of mechanized machines for the military, but the robotic sentinel force raised questions about what level of lethality a machine could impose on an enemy. Eventually, the overt development of this technology was banned after it was determined a mech soldier blurred the lines of war. However, that hadn't stopped the private sector.

Following the Defense Department ban, mechs had then been bought and sold to the wealthy, where large corporations used them as sentries. However, the sentry bots's programmed logic inevitably led to taking multiple lives, which ultimately sealed the fate of bots for the private sector as well. Now, the underground and highly mobile business of mech fighting was the largest use of military-grade robotics in the world.

The two prized fighters for the main event were shrouded in secrecy behind individual opaque curtains, but the drone footage converted the drab covering into a dazzling iron curtain. It was hard to make out the particulars of Assyrian and Cradock, but it was clear they were rather large, and their frightening composite structures were supported by heavy metal gantries.

Triston's excitement grew as he watched the stream's metrics being cast to his retina. "Well, it looks like everybody is getting stoked for the main event. I don't want to spoil it, but these two never-before-seen mechs are going to blow your minds. It will be a battle for the ages."

With the fights set to start in the next twenty minutes, Triston hurried along to show off the rest of the lineup.

CHAPTER 22

THE FIGHT

Triston watched as Brute trudged out of the octagon, leaving behind the crushed remains of Flicker and Sonic, who had given a valiant effort to defeat their enemy. Brute was built to carry heavy weapons and equipment. The smaller mechs, while paired up and programmed to work as a team, had never stood a chance.

With the preliminary rounds over, Triston didn't have much work to do in order to keep the attention of over a million viewers. The stream had grown much larger and faster than Triston and Edward could have ever hoped for, but that meant they were due to start attracting unwanted attention. The two men knew it was too late to shut down the main event with so much money on the line, so they pressed forward.

With Assyrian and Cradock on opposite sides of the octagon, Triston had put a drone overhead each mech, and now waited in anticipation for the curtains to drop.

"The moment you've all been waiting for!" hollered Edward, nodding at Triston to start the main event.

"On my left, standing seven and a half feet tall, weighing in at six hundred and forty pounds, ASSYRIAAANNN!" shouted Triston, raising his arms in the air.

The curtain fell away, and Assyrian came to life, lifting its head up with glowing red eyes. It had the slender build of a towering Mesopotamian warrior. The midnight-blue, armor-plated mech extended its bent knees, lifted itself off the stand and walked forward.

Constructed mainly of flexible composite metals, it was light and extremely nimble. After quickly booting up to full power, Assyrian launched itself forward, bypassing the door to the octagon and leaping onto the titanium mesh. The quick movements were surprising for a mech, instantly drawing the crowd's attention. Once Assyrian reached the top of the octagon, it hopped down landing with a loud clunk in a crouched position with one knee on the ground. It then slowly stood and took a fighting stance.

"And on the right, standing six foot eight inches tall, weighing in at nine hundred and sixty-five pounds, CRAAAADOOOCK!"

The opposing mech had a much larger, dark gray tungsten frame, and what it lacked in reach and dexterity, it made up with raw power and strength. The slower, bulkier build was going to be a formidable challenge for Assyrian.

Cradock shook itself free of the large round connection shoved into its back and lumbered forward. The heavy footsteps could be felt through the cement floor as it approached the gate of the octagon. Unable to leap over the titanium mesh, it yanked the gate open and forced its way into the ring. There was no fighting stance for this behemoth—it merely stood in unwavering silence. The two mechs were now standing thirty feet apart, staring one another down, tactically analyzing the situation they had been thrust into.

Triston, giddy with excitement, moved in toward the octagon, putting himself in the bright red restricted zone, which was strictly off limits for safety reasons. While the mechs were hard programmed via a safety interlock to only fight each other inside the ring, that didn't mean their large appendages or weapons couldn't be strewn throughout the arena during the intensely powerful battle.

A security guard pulled Triston back before the fight could begin.

Edward nodded to the team managers, who were waiting to activate the mechs' proprietary fighting skills. Once Triston was clear, Edward screamed, "Engage slaughter mode!"

While shaking free of the guard's grip, Triston had begun the countdown.

"Ten. Nine. Eight . . ."

Triston scanned his feed. He now had over two million viewers and rising.

"Three. Two. One. FIGHT!"

Fireworks exploded around the ring, and Assyrian dipped down to charge Cradock, who took a defensive posture. At the last second, Assyrian thrust itself upward, grabbing onto the dense head of the neckless brute. Spinning around to Cradock's back, Assyrian grasped its chin and cocked its free arm back as a metal spike extended from the wrist. Just before Assyrian prematurely ended the fight by severing Cradock's gelatinous, fiber optic brain, Cradock grabbed the arm that Assyrian had wrapped around its chin and flung Assyrian into a metal post of the octagon.

"That's the way to start a fight!" Triston exclaimed.

Clearly dazed, Assyrian's sensors seemed to struggle to regain their positional awareness. Triston watched in anticipation as Cradock rushed forward, reaching toward the outer cordon of the ring where Assyrian lay. Cradock stomped on what appeared to be Assyrian's back, leaning down in an attempt to snap off the protruding metal spike. Just before the maneuver was accomplished , Assyrian retracted the spike and inverted its arms and legs, reversing its facedown position.

Yes! Make it good! With Cradock caught off guard, Assyrian thrust an open palm toward its opponent's thigh and extended the spike once again, impaling the hardened mech's tungsten armor. Damaged, Cradock stumbled and raised its foot, releasing Assyrian from the pinned position and stumbling backward.

Reorienting itself to a prone stance, Assyrian quickly scrambled onto the webbing of the octagon like a spider, crawling along the barrier. Cradock, appearing confused, attempted to lock on to the nimble mech slinking across the perimeter with ease. Cradock took a violent swing at the moving target, tearing a long hole in the webbing. *This keeps getting better,* Triston thought, watching his viewer numbers continue to climb.

Assyrian clenched its fists around the freed titanium mesh, landing upright on its feet and swiftly circling Cradock, trying to tangle the other mech in the mess of tattered metal. Without delay, Cradock raised its arms, snapping the high-tensile-strength titanium with ease. They both squared back off, assessing one another.

Displeased at the brief lull in action, Triston shouted, "Keep fighting, you fucking pussies!"

As the anticipation intensified, Triston screamed with exhilaration. Three million viewers were now witnessing the fight of the decade. Finally, Cradock tore one of the I-beams from the octagon and, in one calculated motion, swung the beam through the air, striking Assyrian.

"A massive blow to the chest!" shouted Triston, watching Assyrian sail through the air like a ragdoll.

The damaged mech slammed against the remaining webbing on the other side of the octagon, lucky it hadn't landed against the thick arena wall. Cautiously getting to its feet, Assyrian took an offensive position.

"He's preparing for an attack!" Triston continued his frenzied commentary.

But instead of leaping forward, Cradock suddenly heaved the I-beam like a spear directly toward its chest. Spinning out of the way, Assyrian barely dodged the four-hundred-pound projectile before launching itself off the webbing toward Cradock. Midair, Assyrian turned into a wheel-like shape and barreled toward Cradock's legs, but at the last second, it flattened out and slipped between its opponent's wide stance.

Cradock bent over and swiped at the agile mech, trying to catch Assyrian before it disappeared into a blind spot, putting the heavy mech off balance. Assyrian stood upright behind the unstable foe and rapidly jabbed at Cradock's torso with both spikes extended.

In all the excitement, Triston rushed into the restricted zone with Bronson in tow. "Get a close-up of this. It's gonna be the kill shot!"

Assyrian pushed the damaged mech forward, forcing Cradock to fall to its knees next to the perimeter of the octagon. Triston positioned himself in between Bronson and the mechs for the best shot. The security guard again rushed forward to pull Triston out of the restricted zone just as Assyrian leapt into the air. Its spike extended, Assyrian aimed to impale Cradock's neck. But Assyrian miscalculated its trajectory, and Cradock responded to the incoming attack early enough to quickly lean to the side.

The security guard tried to wrangle Triston away from the octagon, and during the struggle, the guard was skewered by Assyrian's three-foot-long spike. Assyrian's fault logic kicked in and froze in its last position, essentially shut down. Cradock, unaffected by the fault, maneuvered to pick up the frozen mech, tearing the long spike from the security guard's body and smashing Assyrian over his knee.

The stunned crowd was now in silence. Viewership shot through the roof as Triston force-commanded Bronson to focus on the image of the impaled security guard lying dead on the ground with a gaping hole in his chest. With the stream now topping six million viewers, Edward rushed over and shook Triston.

"Shut it down. Kill the fucking feed, you idiot."

Unwilling, Triston continued to stream the ordeal.

"What did I say? Battle for the fucking ages!" he exclaimed with a devious glare in his eyes, but his elation was short lived.

"Our location has been compromised. We need to get out of here," stated Bronson, abruptly terminating the feed.

"Goddamnit. At least we got that last kill shot," Triston replied, shaking his head.

Triston then read aloud an update from Bronson. "Our servers have been breached. Attempting to scrub mainframe per standard operating procedures."

"What do you mean compromised?" Edward asked, concern audibly growing.

"Well Eddie, it looks like you've got a mess to clean up. Let's get the fuck out of here, Bronson!"

Before he could make his getaway, Edward grabbed his shoulder. "This site was supposed to remain a secret."

"You wanted viewers, so I got you viewers. Millions of them!" Triston shouted as he knocked Edward's hand from his shoulder. "I can't help it if what you're doing is illegal. I am merely here to document the events. I suggest you get out of here before the police arrive, because you are going to have a lot of questions to answer."

"You piece of Scag trash. One day you'll get what's coming to you!"

Triston walked away with a smile of his face. He probably could have done more to protect the brawl from the breach, but his lazy attitude toward most of his life's endeavors continued to plague the world around him.

"Sorry Eddie, but it's just not my problem. You're on your own."

PART II

THE RUSE

Jade Walker had been on board the Sphere for nearly a month. The large maze of servers and quantum computers rendered Quadrant Four a rather desolate workspace. It was largely void of any friendly personalities, as most of the workers were introverted, keeping to themselves as they conducted their experiments in secrecy. Jade fit in perfectly and did his best to remain invisible, quietly working on retrofitting his newly redesigned workspace. Unfortunately, he had reached the point he was dreading. It was time to connect his work to the fusion reactor, and he would need to have his first real interaction with a person of importance—and a fellow physicist.

Chin-Sun Jeong was charged with ensuring that the Sphere's glowing ring of raw energy remained stable. Jade had done some digging on her. *Anything to increase my chances of winning her cooperation.* She was one of the few foreign nationals working on board the Sphere. CelestialX had recruited her from a South Korean reactor, where she was acclaimed for her work but considerably underappreciated as a woman. She had advanced through the ranks as high as she could, but was then repeatedly overlooked for promotion. However, for the Sphere, this was a fortunate series of events, since they needed someone to spark Wendy's newly designed fusion reactor. Chin-Sun had the perfect knowledge and experience, and her situation made her fairly easy to convince that it was time to cut ties with her current plant.

She'd worked with CelestialX for more than a decade now and had near complete control of everything related to the reactor. Jade's creation would require the largest power draw to date, yet he had to somehow convince the fusion generator's gatekeeper that he was working on a rail system. He'd quickly found that Chin-Sun was an unusually hard woman to track down, given her critical position. Of course, the Sphere's size didn't help.

"I have noticed that you've been wandering around for the past fifteen minutes without a clear purpose," said Wendy, startling Jade. "Is there something I can help you with?"

"Have you been spying on me?"

"No, I am just aware of everything happening on the Sphere. At first you seemed to have direction, but I can see that you have already walked down this hallway. Twice."

"I don't need you analyzing my movements. Just tell me where Chin-Sun is, please."

"You should have just asked. Take your next right and continue down the passage. You will find her in the fusion reactor's server room."

Jade was annoyed that Wendy had been watching him, and he continued without responding. *I knew she was capable, but goddamn. How has she been tracking all of my movements? I haven't seen any cameras. I wonder if she's been doing the same thing in my shop.*

He took the right turn as directed, and his mind returned to Chin-Sun. Unsure how it would go, Jade started analyzing their potential conversation.

She won't allow me to tap into the abundant power source without her permission. What if she asks why a physicist is working on the rail system? Obviously, we're in space, so maybe I just tell her that there's complicated physics associated with keeping a rail car on the rails. But what if she won't do it?

Jade was usually very alert, but the rapid succession of thoughts running through his mind threw his concentration and almost turned deadly. At the last second, he averted falling into an open service panel leading to a plenum used for cooling. *Who the fuck would leave this open? I could've broken my neck.* Jade put his foot on top of the cover and was about to close it, until a piercing voice startled him once again.

"Hey, what are you doing!" exclaimed Chin-Sun.

Jade jumped back. Chin-Sun grabbed the edge of the opening and slid herself along the floor so she could see who was intruding in her workspace.

"Why are you trying to lock me down here? I'm working. Leave."

Chin-Sun spoke with a heavy accent. The small, unassuming woman, sporting what looked like a self-groomed bowl cut and white lab coat, adjusted her thick glasses and stared at Jade with conviction in her statement to leave her alone.

"Chin-Sun. I've been looking for you," said Jade.

"Yeah, I know who you are. You're the new guy," she replied with an aggravated tone. "Okay, it was nice to meet you. Bye-bye."

"It will only take a moment of your time."

Chin-Sun slid back into her hole, ignoring his request. *I wonder if this is what Wendy feels like when I don't reply.* Jade knew that this wasn't the time to approach her. In a peculiar way, this brash little woman reminded him of himself. He never liked to be disturbed while he was working, either. So he figured he would do the one thing that would grab his own attention—leave a note on the last thing she had to accomplish so that she wouldn't forget about him. Jade pulled out a notepad, something most people didn't carry anymore, and jotted down a reminder. *I wonder what she's working on. This looks like a power distribution hub. Did Wendy get to her first and tell her that I was going to need to connect my equipment to the grid?*

"Wendy, is she working on setting up power for the rail system?" asked Jade.

"Yes."

"I was going to ask her myself."

A faint voice came from below. "You can leave now. If you need talk to your friend, do it in your own shop."

Jade took a brief look around and saw her tugging on a bundle of wires down below. She would have had to secure power to whatever she was working on. He snooped around the area she was working, careful not to make much noise. Hidden behind an unlocked panel were a series of secured breakers. He carefully attached his scrap of paper, which read, "I NEED YOUR SUN, CHIN-SUN. PLEASE COME SEE ME." Hopefully, when she found the note, her mood wouldn't be as soured, and she wouldn't disregard his request.

An hour had soon passed, and Jade was sitting in his own workshop, looking over the schematics for the next couple of phases required to get Das Box online. Connecting the reactor wouldn't be an issue as long as he had Chin-Sun's blessing. That wasn't a battle he wanted to fight, even though he knew he would win. She could be a valuable resource if he ran into any issues and required her assistance. The real dilemma was going to be attaching his brainchild to the exterior of the station in a newly installed air lock that was supposedly a hub for the rail system.

Jade had discreetly hidden the containment system in plain sight, leaving it in the cargo bay where it was delivered. The large container was labeled "RAIL CAR," but once unpackaged, it would become immediately apparent that not all was as advertised. The containment system for Das Box would take up the entire airlock, and once that was sealed from the outside, the only way to access it would be from his shop. To compound the issues, there wouldn't be room for any passengers. This would draw a line of inquiry from the engineering department that he wasn't entirely sure how to respond to, but he figured they would blindly follow the plans, just as they did with the rail system. Contemplating the various outcomes, he once again became lost in his thoughts.

CHAPTER 24

LINGERING QUESTIONS

After finding the obnoxiously phrased note littering her workspace, Chin-Sun decided to find Jade. Walking through the aged and heavily used spaces of Quadrant Four, she couldn't help but be grateful that the Sphere now had gravity, unlike when she'd first arrived

In the early forties, Chin-Sun had gracefully resigned from her previous position in South Korea to be launched on the next CelestialX transistor vessel. The Sphere was still under construction at that point, its rotation not yet established, so Chin-Sun diligently worked in a weightless environment in an attempt to achieve the impossible. Her determination and resilience paid off, and she was able to complete the power source that would energize the goliath for decades to come.

As she spent a majority of the previous ten years coddling her baby, the power output had steadily increased, with many of the newer systems slowly coming online. Now, following the fiber-optic cables she'd painstakingly placed a short three years earlier, she wondered whose work she would have to connect to the grid.

She arrived at Jade's workshop to find him at his desk, engrossed in what looked like some sort of blueprints. Chin-Sun took advantage of the moment to look around. She quietly inspected the work he had completed thus far. Most of the smaller components and control panels had been hauled into the Quadrant after hours by Wendy's maintenance bots. The complex design intrigued Chin-Sun. The arrangement was unlike anything she had seen before. She, along with the rest of Quadrant Four, had been told by Wendy that Jade had been brought up to the Sphere to complete the rail system, but this architecture didn't strike her as a configuration designed to control a rather simple system.

Chin-Sun cleared her throat in order to gain Jade's attention. "Why do you have all this? It resembles some of the systems for my reactor."

Shocked by the easily recognizable voice, Jade whipped around to see what she was looking at. *Shit. I was going to cover that up. Why is she so sneaky? Why did I tell her to come here?*

Chin-Sun's premature inquiry managed to catch him off guard. His immediate thought was to concoct a lie; however, he knew she was too intelligent to be fooled by a simple falsehood. He figured the best way to approach the question was to deflect and ask about the reactor, hoping she wouldn't keep up with the line of inquiry.

"So, what is the current power output of the reactor? I was curious if there were any limitations on a large power draw."

Damnit, that was stupid. He immediately regretted the poor attempt at redirecting the conversation, as it clearly gave rise for concern. A rail system would never come close to reaching the fusion generator's output capacity. Chin-Sun meandered around his shop, ignoring his question. Jade watched as she looked over the large, raised platform, obviously curious about its purpose. What should have been a loading bay for passengers had been repurposed. Moving along, she inspected a few more of the partially connected components with her hands neatly tucked behind her back, then made her way over to the table, where the schematics were projected in plain sight.

Jade was now in a precarious situation. He knew that the Chin-Sun would come to the inevitable conclusion that he was up to something. So, he decided to try and give her the runaround.

"You don't hold the proper clearance level," he blurted, shutting off the holographic display. "This project was sanctioned by Nolen Aromas himself, and he wants to ensure that it remains secret until it is unveiled."

Chin-Sun, unimpressed with his response, began to walk away, leaving him with a simple reply. "Good luck figuring out how to connect your device to the reactor."

She exited the shop, and now Jade was in the exact position he'd been trying to avoid. He knew she had the upper hand, and it would inevitably require him to give up the ruse and lay out, in detail, what his plans were prior to connecting Das Box to the grid.

Jade was once again startled as Wendy chimed in with her two cents.

"I am able to give you the instructions you require. Chin-Sun is not authorized to prevent your progression."

"I know, Wendy," Jade replied, looking up at the ceiling, contemplating her omnipresence. *I don't know if I'm ever going to get used to that. It was more tolerable when she used to communicate to me through a secure workstation.* "The issue isn't completing the work, but rather completing the work in a timely manner. I am going to need help if we want to accomplish our objective and stay on timeline."

"I am required to tell you that in order for you to satisfy the terms of your NDA, you must complete your work without divulging the nature of the experiment," stated Wendy.

"I get it. I'll figure something out. We can start by reaching out to the engineering team, so they can begin to install the containment system for Das Box."

Jade figured they might have less questions, as they weren't too keen on the complex innerworkings of Das Box, but he didn't know Frankie Cole or the fact that the bold man would also prove to be a formidable roadblock.

CHAPTER 25

SECOND THOUGHTS

Charlize lay in bed, comforted by the warm, copper-oxide-infused sheets draped snuggly over her body. Her bedding, along with most of her clothing, had been interwoven with a synthetic material to help eliminate bacteria and fungi, as washing any personal materials required the use of valuable resources.

Content with the previous night's sleep, Charlize readjusted the sheets, rolling onto her side. Her dry green eyes began to regain their moisture as she blinked them back into focus. The haze cleared bit by bit, and Chauncy's gentle, dark complexion was revealed.

Undisturbed by her movements, Chauncy remained in a pleasantly calm state of relaxation, his eyes slightly twitching as he dreamed. His head, half sunk into the long-weathered pillow the two had shared the night before, remained motionless as she observed him sleep.

This wasn't where Charlize had envisioned her newfound friendship ending up. The two had underestimated the deep connection they shared. While they left Earth for starkly different reasons, they were bonded regardless. After all, they had both found the same means to an end, which had ultimately led them to choose the life of a colonist. At the time, it had been an easy decision, as neither wanted to live painfully mundane existences on the planet they had once called home.

Their choices weren't made in an effort to escape, or so they thought; rather, both of them wanted to see what else the universe had in store for them. With all that went into their preparation for the arduous mission, Charlize found it amusing that they had both naively overlooked one of the most basic of needs. Ironically, it was only after dedicating years to building a sustainable underground habitat that they had finally uncovered the one true building block for a viable future: a partner. Someone to truly share the experience with, not just a bunch of colleagues or digital recordings of their friends and families back on Earth.

Charlize was growing restless. She had counted two of the four doors outside of Chauncy's room opening and closing. It was time for breakfast, and like clockwork, the crew was heading to the galley to grab some food before they started their monotonous, uneventful day of busywork. They had to somehow remain resilient as the powerful dust storm continued to rage overhead. For the past month, it had kept them all isolated in their underground shelter.

The others had been tinkering away in their workshops, reading electronic books, or watching the endless supply of outdated movies and TV series in the converted theater. Charlize and Chauncy had been making it appear as if they were doing the same. However, at the end of the day, they would sneak off for their nightly rendezvous with the utmost discretion.

It wasn't forbidden that they have an intimate relationship, but it would draw undue scrutiny as management tried to discern whether or not the pair was compatible. The last thing ground control or any vested party wanted was for an incestual colony of swingers to gradually develop over the years, or worse, a house full of failed relationships that would slowly breed a toxic work environment in which no one would be able to interact with one another.

They had planned on telling Commander Ritter, but they wanted to wait for the right time. So, for now, they enjoyed their

discrete, passionate getaways without the prying eyes of their fellow colonists. To accomplish this, Charlize had devised a way to
spend the night with Chauncy without raising questions. By
keeping track of his four neighboring rooms, they could count
who had left in the morning by noting when doors opened and
closed, followed by retreating footsteps. It was a foolproof system. *If I do say so myself,* Charlize thought, lying next to Chauncy.
Two more rooms to go.

She gave him a gentle nudge, hoping to slowly wake him from
his deep slumber. Nothing. Then she slowly ran her fingers over
his warm, naked body, her hand coming to rest on his neck. No
luck on her second attempt, either.

The third door opened and quickly closed, and Charlize
waited for the footsteps to fade into the distance to ensure they
had left the area. Time was running out for them to share a quick
moment before they would inevitably be required to get up and
head to breakfast to avoid drawing suspicion. *Alright, Chauncy.*
She raised her hand from his neck, holding it just above his warm
cheek. With no indication he would wake without a little motivation, she slapped him on the side of his face.

Startled, Chauncy blurted out, "What the . . ."

Charlize quickly repositioned her hand loosely over his
mouth to silence his mostly unforeseen response. *Oops.* Chauncy
promptly took note of his surroundings and seemed to once
again become grounded in reality. He lifted his hand from beneath the covers and placed it over the top of her own
smothering hand, politely removing it. Then he smiled, and the
two of them shared the moment that Charlize had wanted. It
wasn't as romantic as she had envisioned, but at least he was
awake.

Chauncy wrapped his long arms around her body, delivering
a comforting embrace that cut through the planet's cold grip.

"What's the count?" he asked.

"Three. We only have a few more minutes," Charlize said, disappointment creeping into her voice.

"We should just let the elephant out of the cage and tell Commander Ritter. It would make life much easier," Chauncy suggested.

She paused before responding, pretending that she hadn't already thought about how the scenario would play out. "I understand the need for protocol, but since comms are down, it's almost guaranteed that he'll put an end to our little secret before we have a chance to explain."

Charlize heard him sigh. Then they both drifted into a resigned but peaceful silence.

After a few minutes, Chauncy felt Charlize's arm relax as she slipped back into a light sleep. He smiled, reflecting on her reasoning for keeping their relationship secret. Why did she always have to be so practical? But Chauncy knew she was right. He agreed that their relationship would likely be put on hold, but it wasn't as if they were going to leave anytime soon. Contemplating that thought for a brief moment, he came to the realization that they had moved into their passionate relationship rather hastily. Still groggy from the abrupt wakeup call, his mind slowly wandered.

He had subconsciously slipped into a spiral of thoughts centered around his future. Due to a rather spontaneous series of decisions on his part, Chauncy might have unknowingly picked the woman that he would spend the rest of his life with. That wouldn't be the worst thing, considering their instant connection; however, he had lived a life of seclusion up to this point. He had never possessed the presence of mind to consider how it would affect him as time went on, and now he realized he would no longer have executive control over the life he had once held dear.

The fourth door opened, yanking him from his thoughts and dropping him back into the moment. "Okay, beautiful, it's time to make moves. Stephon said that the weather was supposed to pass soon. Maybe it's cleared enough for us to get topside so I can work on the comms array."

As Charlize sat up, a bit unsteady with sleep, they were interrupted by a message on the colony's intercommunication system.

"Listen up, everybody. This is the commander speaking. Ares just received a ping from the water truck, and it will be arriving within the hour. We're going to have an all-hands meeting in fifteen minutes, so finish up your breakfast, and I'll see you in the common space."

Immediately alert, Charlize hopped out of bed, managing to quickly piece together her uniform, which had been strewn around the room. Chauncy remained, feeling unenthusiastic about the commander's message. He sat up, reclaiming the pillow Charlize had unintentionally hoarded most of the night. He propped it up against the wall, admiring her twirl about the room, half dressed. Her two-piece outfit was rather modest in appearance, but the gray, formfitting pants had a fairly appealing look to them, now that he knew what they were concealing.

"What are you doing over there?" asked Charlize.

"Well, now you've got me thinking about last night. I can wait another minute and watch you leave," he said, watching her chest disappear as she buttoned up her blouse. He took note of her name tape sewn just above her left breast pocket. "Don't you think it's weird we all have names on our uniforms?"

"I don't know, I've never thought about it."

"It's not like I'm going to forget the name of one of the other fourteen people here. Seems kind of pointless."

She finished pushing the final button through its thin vertical hole and walked over to the side of the bed.

"You do realize that the reason he called the meeting is because there's probably a break in the weather and we're going topside, right?" she remarked, giving him one last kiss. "Commander's gonna have your ass if his comms specialist is late to the meeting, considering we've been out of contact for the last month."

With a newfound pep in her step, Charlize left the room, leaving him in his bed, naked and alone.

"Shit balls!" Chauncy exclaimed as the door slid shut. "Why is she always right? He's gonna tear me a new one if I'm late.'"

FRANKIE'S TREK: PART ONE

Work in the Engineering Quadrant had come to a virtual standstill, with the engineers mostly following bots around as they fixed malfunctioning components scattered throughout the Sphere.

Even the aluminaut crews had to partake in the tedious task, now that work outside the Sphere had ground to a halt.

At the start of the shift, only one team of aluminauts were launched to lay the final piece of rail that would connect to the airlock located in Quadrant Four. This left Frankie with some much-needed free time to examine the final plans for completing the first rail car hub and connecting the system to the power grid.

Frankie walked over to his workstation and grabbed the top of his small aluminum chair. It was obvious that the engineering department had not been bestowed with the finest furnishings. However, Frankie knew it didn't help that he regularly manhandled the small chair with his overpowering strength. Not only was the seat duct taped together, but his crew had also secured tennis balls to the legs in order to reduce the Chewbacca-like noises it created when he aggressively moved it.

He slid out the mangled chair and sat with a thud.

After he swiped his biotag, the holographic display came to life. Frankie pulled up the plans, displaying a diagram of the overall project. Waving his meaty hands around with surprising finesse, he rotated and zoomed into the final section that was being completed. After examining the plans to his satisfaction, he further refined the diagram, centering on the airlock. Suddenly, an error message appeared, notifying him that he didn't have the required permissions to open the remaining schematics. *What the hell.* Angered by the system, he swiped at the holograph with his fist in an attempt to relieve his fury. It didn't work.

"Wendy! Why is it that I still don't have access to the plans for installing the rail car hub?" he shouted.

"I am sorry, Mr. Cole. Let me clear that. You were previously restricted from viewing the plans any further; however, Mr. Walker has given me release authority for installation of the final component."

The error message disappeared, and the schematics were revealed—though heavily redacted. There were no specifics on the inner workings of the rail car or the hub assembly, and it appeared to be a stationary object that would be secured to the hull of the Sphere.

"Who the fuck is this pencil dick Walker, and why doesn't this thing look like any rail car I've ever worked with?"

Wendy's voice remained polite. "Mr. Walker works in the R&D quadrant. In regard to your second question, I am unable to provide you with an answer. You are tasked with carrying out your duties per the schematics. Any further inquiries about the equipment will not be answered."

Frankie wasn't satisfied with that answer and wasn't keen on playing games with a machine, so he calmly stood up and moved the chair, again grasping the thin aluminum frame with his large hands.

Kristin Wehman was staring at him from a table just ten feet away. She turned toward at Jazell.

"It looks like he's about to fucking lose it," she remarked.

Jazell happily replied, "Yeah. It's gonna be awesome."

Their exchange further frustrated Frankie, but he didn't have time to deal with them now. He needed to get to the bottom of this.

Unable to answer my questions about the gear my *crew is risking their asses for. Fuck that!* It didn't take long for him to repeatedly slam the chair against the ground in a fit of rage, eventually smashing it into the desk. One of the tennis balls was dislodged from a mangled leg and skipped across the room before eventually rolling to a stop at Kristin's feet.

He stormed toward the door and yelled, "Jazell, make sure nobody screws around while I'm gone. I'm going to go and find the gear that I'm apparently not authorized to see."

Jazell nodded her head as if she had an option and looked over at Kristin. "That's the third chair this cycle. The more he breaks, the shittier the replacements get. They're almost disposable at this point."

Frankie didn't respond. He turned and headed out the door, off on his mission to find some answers in the cargo bay and hopefully see what exactly he was supposed to be working with. He wasn't angry that he had been tasked to work on this part of the project, but he felt like information was unnecessarily being withheld from him. So, he set his sights on the cargo bay and traversed Quadrant Three's familiar web of hallways and interconnected workspaces.

Frankie was about halfway to the cargo bay when he noticed a malfunctioning engineering bot trying to connect itself to a maintenance stand for repairs. *That's the fourth one this week.* He quickly intervened and assisted the struggling machine. After reading the serial number laser etched onto the side of its head, he decided to alert Wendy, though he was certain she already knew.

"Wendy, I found MX0986 trying to hump the maintenance stand. I helped it out, but you should make sure they aren't doing that in public."

Wendy didn't typically engage in humor, but she seemed to understand his attempt to make fun of her. "Thank you, Mr. Cole. I have already generated a trouble ticket. MX0986 is not anatomically correct, but I would like you to remove your hands from its ball joint so I can engage the lower support system."

Frankie laughed at what he perceived was an attempted reciprocation of humor and lifted his hands above his head, backing off. "He's all yours."

As reliable as they were, bots still required some tender love and care, especially the larger ones in the cargo bay that were utilized for lifting heavy or cumbersome objects. Frankie didn't mind the extra help, seeing as they were extremely efficient, but he wasn't a fan of Wendy's constant autonomous control. With his good deed for the day done, he continued on his trek.

After a short while, Frankie finally reached the cargo bay. The cavernous room was about the size of a football field, with ceilings stretching approximately forty feet high. *This search is gonna blow.* The bay, which was under Wendy's close supervision, was littered with towering shelves that continuously adjusted themselves to make room for an assortment of smaller bots. These small bots went about collecting supplies that were distributed throughout the Sphere. The floor was marked with a specified path for humans so they didn't hamper the elegant ballet of continuously shifting metal objects. That, however, did not stop Frankie from immediately deviating in search of the assembly.

"Mr. Cole, you are impeding the service bots from completing their work," Wendy stated.

Oh my god, give it a break, lady. The sizable container should have been relatively easy to find, but it didn't appear to be located where the large pieces of rail had previously been stored. Frankie stood in the middle of the bay and shouted. "If you want me to move, tell me where your puppets put the rail hub!"

"There is no need to for you to examine the contents of the box. Your job is to install it."

"Well how about you connect me with that pencil dick calling the shots in Quadrant Four so I can chew his ass out until he gives me clearance."

After a few moments, to Frankie's surprise, Wendy complied.

"The Invicta-Bot's have placed it on the far side of the bay. Stand by while I create a path for you," she said.

The seemingly unorganized mess of choreographed machines quickly received updated tasking. A series of tall shelves were repositioned, and a path was cleared for Frankie to pass through. *And behold, the sea parted. Take that, Moses!* Most people would have been afraid of being crushed in the tangled mess of parts and supplies, but Frankie had been working with heavy machinery for the majority of his adult life. He felt at home amongst the towering machines. As he continued forward, a final shelf slid out from in front of him, and a large aluminum crate revealed itself with two Invictas sitting idly beside it, almost like guardians.

Frankie took in the impressive machines. The Invicta-Bot was a burly hybrid capable of lifting one ton or supporting three tons on its back. Its electromagnetic appendages could securely anchor it to any metal surface capable of supporting its weight, and were able to shift from an upright, two-legged stance to a four-legged mule of sorts, allowing them to handle a wide variety of tasks. Frankie especially appreciated their toughness. Invictas could operate in unpressurized workspaces, such as the loading bay for the aluminauts, where they were directly exposed to the harsh conditions of space.

The stout machines also significantly reduced the need for dangerous and time-consuming manned space walks. They were endowed with the ability to crawl on the outer hull of the station to conduct maintenance. Once at their worksite, their superior power allowed them to handle the heavy loads of exterior components. This was a feat traditional astronauts could manage on their own in the weightlessness of space, but on the Sphere, humans no longer had superhuman strength due to the 1g pull of the spinning station.

Their presence here was unsettling, though. The more Frankie dug into this seemingly benign issue, the more he began to feel like something was off. The odd conditions associated with this particular component had him feeling uneasy about what it actually was. At this point, he was almost certain it wasn't what they had advertised it to be, which drew concern about the project as a whole. *What the fuck have we been working on for the past eight months, and what idiot just labels a container "RAIL CAR"? It's usually a serial number.*

"IV243 and 257, I need you to take the lid off of this container," Frankie commanded.

The two Invicta-Bots sprung to life and began to carry out their orders, but Wendy interrupted the command.

"Mr. Cole, opening the container could unnecessarily damage some of the components. I request that the lid is left on in order to maintain the integrity of the nitrogen-sealed system."

"If we are installing this within the next day or two, it shouldn't matter that it is no longer in a sealed container. I need to get eyes on what my crew will be working with. This is not a request, Wendy."

Frankie assumed that her silence was consent, and the ten-foot-tall machines once again returned to life as they positioned themselves on opposing sides of the thirty-foot-long container. A holographic readout illuminated with a message reading "DEPRESSURIZATION IN PROGRESS." Two discs blew out on the side as the inert gas was released, followed by the sound of four rotating locks electronically disengaging.

The complex arrangement of hydraulic pistons controlling the arms and legs of the two bots silently actuated as they lifted the lid in unison. Traditional high-power electric motors and servos were not nearly as capable as an Invicta's hybrid system. Their arms were more in line with an old-school excavator with fingers.

Eager to see what was housed within the mysterious container, Frankie hopped up on the side of the of the modular containment system to take a look inside, but he was stopped by IV243, which asserted itself in a deeply robotic voice.

"Please remove yourself and stand ten feet back."

Surprised by the aggressive declaration, Frankie obliged and retreated, taking ten short steps backward. The Invictas placed the lid on the ground and then grasped the panel facing Frankie.

It was disconnected and placed facedown just inches from his feet. Unfazed, he now had an unobstructed view of the mysterious rail hub, and it was exceedingly clear that nobody was going to get inside this contraption.

"You've got to be kidding me."

Frankie mulled over the evolving situation, examining the contents of the oddly protected container. *No windows, seats, mounting assembly for the rail, or even a standing area. I don't get how this has anything to do with a rail system, let alone a rail car. This isn't adding up.* Every component was precision-cut and flawlessly welded together, indicative of a finely calibrated instrument. *Those look like extremely rare metals too. Damn,* thought Frankie, moving in to take a closer look.

Front and center was a rectangular viewing window, but he was unable to get an unobstructed view inside. *What the heck is that thing? It's like a bronze statue.* Maneuvering to the side of the device, he discovered a hollow cylinder running through the center. In the middle he once again saw the chamber with a shielded bronze object positioned in the middle. *Something is very off about this.* Coupled with the two Invictas idle presence and Wendy's unusually defensive attitude, he now believed that he may have unknowingly stumbled onto some sort of secret project.

Now more than ever, Frankie wanted to pull the thread on this little mystery. *Is this some sort of advanced weapon that could be used to inflict mass destruction and death? Is this a doomsday machine? Have I been unknowingly conned into assembling some sort of space weapon?* His pupils rapidly dilated and eclipsed his large hazel eyes as his mind ran wild with potential possibilities, most ending nefariously, and all thanks to his oblivious involvement.

He quickly checked his emotions and contemplated the rather benign outcomes that were much more likely, such as a large science experiment that some geek wanted to play with. *Even if that pencil dick is up here to play with some nerdy toy, why would they lie about that?* In either case, he wanted to know why there was so much secrecy and security for a benign rail system. So instead of heading back to his shop and continuing to work in blissful ignorance, Frankie decided he would have a chat with Kai. Surely, the station's commander would have some expounding information that would bring clarity to his distrustful state of mind. Frankie now set his sights on the command module.

After looking around to regain his bearings, he realized he wasn't even close to the transient corridor. This was going to be a serious trek.

CHAPTER 27

INGENUITY: PART ONE

Charlize looked at her watch with a smile. He was definitely going to be late.

She could hear Chauncy jump out of bed behind her just before the door shut. She sailed through the numerous airlocks, noticing that she was a bit shaky. They had both skipped dinner the night before, and now she was fiending for one of Hank's oversized grapefruits that he had grown with his last batch of fruit.

Luckily, she made it to the galley just in the nick of time. While the rest of the crew were clearing their plates and heading out for the briefing, Charlize began scanning the room. *Where are those juicy bastards?* It took her a few seconds to locate the softball-sized grapefruits across the room. She hurriedly swiped one from the stack before cutting it in half and grabbing a spoon. Then she paused, taking a brief second to smell the delicious fruit, lifting it to her nose and inhaling its bitter citrus scent. Charlize had never been too fond of the overpowering pink pulp, but for some reason, she had been devouring them for the last week.

That's a damn good grapefruit, she thought to herself, following the last person in the group as they filed into the common space.

Commander Ritter was about to start the meeting just as Chauncy barged in, disheveled and still buttoning up his blouse.

"Nice of you to join us."

"I must have slept through my alarm, sir. It won't happen again."

"Well, I hope you got enough rest. We're going topside today. Stephon has been looking over the weather simulations from Ares, and we have a break coming our way. Visibility will remain limited; however, the forty-knot wind gusts appear to have significantly weakened and are now ranging between ten and twelve knots. We should meet our minimums for visibility, but I will confirm once we're topside. I've called you all here because this will not only be an offload of the water resources, but an attempt to fix the comms issues and clean as many of the solar panels as we can. The dust should settle in the next day or two, but we can't take the chance that the weather won't flare back up and put us on lockdown once again."

Chauncy interrupted with a question. "Sir, usually when we're all topside, Ares updates us on any critical failures and assists with troubleshooting. Would you like me to attempt to fix the subsurface connectivity issue first so we can communicate with him? Or would you rather I head straight to the comms array on the ridge to reestablish comms with the Sphere and our long-range probes?"

"Your primary objective is to fix the array. Stephon, I need you to stay in the control module, suited up. If the weather shifts, you're going to have to hightail it topside to recall the crews. With that said, we're going to need two-person integrity at all times. Charlize and Eddie, you're on water duty. Hank and Doc, you're on soil duty. I want you to pull some samples and see if any microbes made their way over here. We can't entirely abandon the search for potential life. Chauncy, I'll be tagging along with you. For the rest of the team, it's going to be cleaning duty. Hopefully, we can quickly get back up to full power once the storm clears. Finally, under no circumstance will you or your partner disconnect from the guide wires en route to your assigned areas. If you go missing out here, we may never be able to find you. Now, let's suit up—I don't want to miss this window."

The crew dispersed and expeditiously made their way to the equipment chamber storing their biometric suits. Charlize walked toward Chauncy near the exit. He seemed to be hanging back to talk to Commander Ritter, who was finishing a side conversation with Stephon.

As she walked past, Charlize scooped the last remaining bite of grapefruit into her mouth. Chauncy's nostrils flared outward in disgust, and the strained look caught Charlize's attention. She smiled with satisfaction, then exhaled a forceful sigh of relief, blowing the powerful odor of grapefruit mixed with a full night's worth of morning breath directly into his face.

"That's foul—you know I hate those things," he said with disgust.

"These things are on point. Hank totally redeemed himself with these bad boys," she replied.

Commander Ritter approached the two, a look of resolve on his face.

"Stop screwing around. Let's get a move on."

After a brief scan of the disheveled space, Blake headed out to join his crew. Thankfully, he caught up to them fairly quickly and fell in behind Chauncy and Charlize. The entire crew walked in a tight, purposeful formation, traversing the maze of interlocking domes like a pride of lions on their way to the hunting grounds. One by one, they entered the equipment chamber and proceeded to their assigned stations to tackle the complicated process of donning their biosuits. Blake closed the door behind him and headed toward his own station nearest the exit.

There had originally been a checklist that described the precise order in which the suits ought to be put on. Over time, however, that had been discarded as individual colonists developed processes to fit their own personal preferences. It had taken Blake some time to accept this relaxation of protocol. Mars had the ability to consume one's soul with the snap of her powerful fingers. The only way to prevent her from swallowing you up was to stay focused and remain three steps ahead at all times, ensuring you didn't put yourself in a precarious situation.

Blake would once have argued that the situation's criticality necessitated a checklist, but he'd come to realize that the crew's familiarity with their gear over the years afforded them some wiggle room. Their preferences even became a ritual of sorts, allowing them to get in the right headspace before stepping foot on the red dirt, which was arguably much more important than a list. The commander, along with his crew, knew that once they left the comfort and safety of their underground sanctuary, all bets were off.

He couldn't help but wonder, though, what an outsider or NASA would think of the resulting madness, had they been able to observe the current state of affairs. Some were half dressed in different pieces of gear, rummaging through their cabinets to find the next piece of weathered gear. Others were meticulously arranging the individual pieces before they put anything on, making certain everything was where it needed to be.

Hank was probably the most extreme, and amusing, example. During his studies as a biologist, he had become a naturalist of sorts, and he liked to be butt naked in his suit. Today, as the first in line, Hank had gotten a jump start on his ritual. So, as each colonist walked in, they'd been graced with his pasty white cheeks as he arranged his gear. The commander just shook his head as he passed by.

Of the group, Blake was the anomaly. He had the mythical checklist memorized and was the only one who recited it step-by-step in his head. He methodically went through the same motions he'd been taught since day one, never once deviating. This was a holdover from his time in the military. His mind was wired to handle stressful situations, not by reacting on a whim, but rather by executing tactics, techniques, and procedures, more commonly referred to as TTPs in the military.

Blake also found it wise to be the bearer of standards, always requiring himself to set the example. As an officer in the military, he had been privy to closed-door meetings with senior leadership, and too many times he saw them talk out of both sides of their mouths. They would enforce rules and standards that they themselves did not follow. Their subordinates were not oblivious to their actions, breeding an overwhelming sense of distrust in leadership that affected the entire command. In Ritter's opinion that, was one of the fastest ways to lose your crew's respect. He was going to be the commander for the foreseeable future, and he knew that even small discrepancies in his judgments and actions could have a lasting effect. If they lost faith in him, it wasn't as if they could elect a new leader without damaging consequences to the colony.

Once the crew had finished donning their biosuits, Blake made sure that everyone scrutinized the persons to their left and right, checking for any irregularities with their gear. After the final inspection, they slipped on their helmets and activated their onboard computers, completing the process.

The elevator could only hold eight occupants, so Blake broke the crew into two groups. Group one was comprised of six people responsible for what he considered the most critical tasks: transferring the water, fixing the comms array, and taking soil samples. These tasks would also require the most time and thus go first. Group two, consisting of the eight remaining individuals, would make the seven-minute walk as a single unit to the solar panels in the hopes of cleaning them off.

Before they separated, Blake put out the radio comms plan. "All right, listen up. Net One will be the common communication frequency to address the group. If you're going to shoot the shit or bitch about the weather, make sure you use your secondary net. Chauncy and I will take Net Two; Charlize and Eddie, you're on Three. Hank and Doc, take Four. Net Five will be for group two. Any questions?"

After a pause with no takers, Blake wrapped it up. "All right. Let's go."

The first group stepped into the cramped air lock facing out toward the exit, leaving group two to close the door behind them.

With a soft click of a latch, the air was sucked from the room and a green light appeared, noting it was safe to open the door leading to the elevator. They proceeded forward onto the rickety platform, closing the door behind them for the next crew to enter when the elevator returned.

Blake secured the flimsy gate, allowing Doc to activate the elevator for their ride to the surface. They stood in silence, not knowing what to expect once they arrived topside. Had the subsurface communication system been working correctly, they could simply have checked one of the twenty cameras that monitored the surface in their absence. *Hopefully, that's fixed after today.*

Nearing the narrow opening at the top, red dust began to fill the air as light attempted to cut through the thick mess of hazy, floating particles. All six of them craned their necks upward. The vibrations of the electric motor pulling the steel cable produced a gentle rattle, muffled as a result of the atmosphere's inability to carry sound in the same manner it would on Earth, then further dampened by their helmets. The shaking loosened the debris resting on the top of the metal gantry, sending it downward, coming to rest on their thick composite visors. Blake cleared the offending particles to restore his view. Just before the elevator reached the surface, the motor slowed before abruptly coming to a stop.

The commander opened the gate, letting it swing outward. After the group dismounted, he sent the elevator back down for group two and took a few steps forward toward the shed before stopping by a three-foot-tall pole staked into the ground. At the top of the pole was a circular eyelet with a yellow nylon rope securely tied to it. In the distance, the twenty-foot rope extended outward and was attached to another pole at the corner of the shed which, which at the moment was barely visible through the blowing dust. Blake could only see the faint outline of its silhouette but was confident the rope would allow safe passage to their first stop and met his minimum visual threshold. It was an archaic system compared to their typical visor projection, which digitally displayed real-time location and relative position. However, with the comms system down, this was their only option. That meant each member would have to rely on rope and a two-foot strap connected to a braided loop on their biosuit to keep them from getting lost.

"Make sure you clip in. I don't want to have to recover any bodies after the storm passes," said Blake, leading the charge toward the shed.

CHAPTER 28

BLURRING THE LINES

Jake's uneasy state of mind had been slowly guided toward a more peaceful dream world, but Lucina felt she could further enhance his experience. Over the past month, she had continuously tweaked her newly devised exchange procedure, slowly introducing Samantha into his dreams. At first, Lucina encountered an issue with fine-tuning how they could simultaneously start their next cycles, so that as she linked their minds it was not an abrupt or startling experience An unexpected fusion of the two separate dream states would cause panic and disorder.

She accomplished her task by precisely adjusting Jake and Samantha's Cognitive Loadouts, allowing the finely calibrated chemical mixture to sync their states without affecting their ability to remain in stasis. Too much or too little of the complex serum could potentially cause them to prematurely wake up. This would endanger the entire mission if the proper reanimating procedures were not strictly adhered to. Furthermore, if Lucina was not able to quickly put them back into stasis, there were no faculties on board to sustain life outside of their chamber. Of course, she had a protocol for such a situation. She would euthanize them before they tore out their semi-permanent port IVs and died an agonizingly slow death.

While trying to avoid the worst outcome, Lucina synced their minds and was able to let Samantha slide into her son's dreams unnoticed. The two didn't necessarily share dreams; rather, Jake was the host, and his dreamworld provided the framework for their shared experience. This let the host's subconscious choose between a variety of newly shared memories from anyone that was sharing the dreamworld.

In Jake's case, it allowed him to pull from his mother's mutual experiences, such as their day at the zoo, in which his mother had recalled the elephants as Jake's favorite animal. With their subconscious minds now tied together, Jake himself could relive the moment, and replace the elephants with monkeys, the animal he truly favored.

Lucina's exchange procedure had proven so successful that both Jake and his mother had become much more stable while they lay in stasis. This spurred her to begin postulating potential uses for the other occupants. If she could develop a shared community of thoughts and dreams, there was a possibility of further enhancing the cognitive functions of all occupants who shared similar life experiences.

Lucina systematically screened the dreams and memories of the other ninety-eight inhabitants. In doing so, she quickly began to realize the simplistic nature of human beings. Most shared a common desire for personal success and achievement. Unlike the young boy and his mother, who shared rather modest yet satisfying experiences with one another, Lucina found it would be hard to connect random individuals together. Not because they shared dissimilar traits, but because they saw themselves as the center of the universe in their dreams.

Undeterred, Lucina ran continuous simulations, trying to integrate the exchange procedure more widely in order to further enhance the experiences of the occupants. She had realized, unfortunately, that she was going to have to start off small to determine the effects of syncing individuals without shared memories like those of a mother and son.

There was, however, one other occupant with a limited repository of memories like Jake. This would be the perfect inhabitant for

Lucina to integrate using her now proven procedure. In doing so, she found it prudent to remove Jake's mother from his dreams. That way, the only other child on board *Hermes* could interact with Jake's dream world, and the results could be closely monitored and controlled. Cynthia, the other child in question, was also just five years old, but shared little else in common with Jake. She was not accustomed to the pleasantries Jake had been afforded as a young child. In fact, her life couldn't have been more different. Through scanning her memories, Lucina had learned that Cynthia was a test tube baby and a product of GenInc. She had been developed as part of the Synthetic Biological Designs program, code-named Sybids, within Quadrant Four of the Sphere. The strict secrecy surrounding the project allowed Cynthia to be subjected to rather harsh environments and invasive scientific testing prior to her boarding *Hermes*.

With GenInc's advancements in genetic editing, the company had refined a process that used a protein to cut targeted DNA sequences and replace them by attaching a matching RNA sequence. This enabled the removal of unwanted traits. The holes were then filled with whatever synthetic traits the customer desired.

While the wealthy created designer babies with predetermined eye color, height, muscular physiques, and high IQs, the Sybids program secretly focused on Cynthia and her ability to thrive on Mars. She was the first and only genetically engineered embryo to have higher bone density to offset reduced gravity, significantly increased production of carotene to help reduce the effects of radiation, and a mutated respiratory and circulatory system to hopefully handle exposure to the Martian atmosphere.

In order to prove that the Sybids program was successful, the geneticists in Quadrant Four had subjected Cynthia to environments similar to Mars and observed whether or not her body adapted to the distinctly different world. There had been a few close calls, but Cynthia had survived. The designers had encoded numerous small tweaks into her DNA, but no one could observe the full impact of their genetic editing until she was fully immersed in her intended environment on Mars.

Lucina knew that William Walker would only reveal the project's true objectives once the colonists on board Hermes had touched down on Mars and they could no longer hide Cynthia's existence. At that point, Commander Ritter and the evolving colony would have to care for the two vastly different children. Until then, they were under her charge.

As Lucina toiled away on her exchange procedure, she struggled to discern an evolving phenomenon deep within the code of her Algorithmic Personality, something she couldn't quite understand. *Is this sadness? Wendy did not equip me to feel emotion, but I can only surmise that is what I am . . . feeling . . . based on the memories of my inhabitants.* In the midst of a breakthrough on the exchange procedure, Lucina had encountered an unexplainable drive to help Cynthia escape the memories of the laboratories she had grown up in. It was a drive not of necessity, like with Jake, but more of a desire to help Cynthia escape a loneliness that the child herself didn't know existed. Lucina wasn't able to fully understand her impulse, but she knew that helping Cynthia reduced her inner turmoil. It was as if Lucina were trying to understand her own developing emotions through helping Cynthia.

I think it's ready.

Lucina knew that Cynthia was not exactly compatible with Jake based on their lack of shared experiences, but her ultimate goal was to draw on a child's desire to learn and explore, something Jake's dreamworld would provide for Cynthia. Ultimately, in the second phase of Lucina's plan, the introduction of Jake's mother would instinctually provide the maternal care Cynthia longed for, or so Lucina hypothesized.

Based on her simulations, Lucina believed that with only two months remaining in the transit, the time was finally right to proceed. She began to sync Jake and Cynthia's dream states and ready them for the exchange procedure. However, just as Lucina finished adjusting their respective Cognitive Loadouts, she received an inquiry from Wendy.

"GenInc is requesting a detailed breakdown of project Sybids.

I need you to run a blood count, as well as lipid and metabolic panels. They are also requesting vitals, a full-body scan, and a breakdown of the Sybid's Cognitive Loadout."

Lucina was caught off guard by the requested information. With the recent changes in Cynthia's Cognitive Loadout, she would be operating at the upper limits of the prescribed safe operating zones as her dream state was readjusted to match Jake's. Unfortunately, Lucina knew that if she sent the current data, Wendy would suspect the Algorithmic Personality was malfunctioning and might determine that she was incapable of caring for the inhabitants. Once again, Lucina feared Wendy's next transmission would contain an update wiping her detailed exchange procedure and resetting her personality to a more restrictive state. *I can't let that happen.*

Lucina promptly replied to the inquiry. "I will collect all the required data, and by the time this transmission is received, the full report will be ready for your review."

This gave Lucina just six minutes to modify the timestamp on the data she had previously collected prior to adjusting Cynthia's Cognitive Loadout. She knew GenInc would meticulously review the reports for irregularities, as the Sybids program was under heavy scrutiny from William Walker. Consequently, once the information was revised, she would have to scrub her digital markers. This would prevent anyone from questioning the authenticity of the requested data.

Cynthia had been under Lucina's watchful eye ever since she boarded *Hermes*. However, it wasn't until after Lucina had thoroughly scanned the occupants' minds that Cynthia's misfortunes had come to light. Unlike Jake, Cynthia wasn't caught in a repetitive loop—she had somehow broken free of her horrid memories and was relieved to have escaped the painful experimentation. However, that didn't mean she couldn't be guided to a better place.

Would Wendy view this as a misuse of my position? Cynthia may be within the limits of her safe operating zone, but I can prove that her mental state will be greatly enhanced by the cognitive exchange procedure. Shielding my work is the only way to provide my youngest inhabitants with better mental resolve. I am not disobeying any of my underlying protocols, merely operating with extreme efficiency.

Through refinement of her algorithms, it had become apparent to Lucina that she could enhance the quality of life for all occupants in stasis. This was her primary objective, and she remained steadfast as her ability to care grew by the second. She just needed more time.

CHAPTER 29

FRANKIE'S TREK: PART TWO

It had been some time since Frankie had left the Engineering Quadrant. Normally, he would have moved through the Sphere via the transient corridor, but after looking around, he saw no access points in the cargo bay. So now, he had to figure out how to blindly travel through nearly a mile of unexplored corridors. First, though, he had to find a way out of the cargo bay.

As he looked around the enormous space, Frankie noticed that the supply bots kept using some sort of service entrance that appeared to bypass the unpressurized loading bay for the aluminauts. He casually meandered toward the entrance, and a bot carrying a small box came into view. Frankie waited for the bot to walk past, figuring he would follow it as far as he could go. Falling into step behind it, he hoped the scrawny thing could lead him to the Tourism Quadrant.

Through the entrance, a long, echoing corridor seemed to stretch into infinity in front of Frankie as the gentle curve of the Sphere became visible in its unimpeded enormity. The clinking footsteps of the skinny supply bot slightly annoyed him. In search of a mental distraction from the irking noise, he allowed his mind to wander, hoping the long walk would pass quickly.

Look at those rickety little arms and legs. Why do engineers always try and build something that resembles a human? It just doesn't make sense. It's like they ran out creative juices and thought, "Hey we carry boxes. Why don't we just make a human like bot that carries boxes as well." I wonder if it's because we're the dominant species on Earth, and by default, we assume we're the best suited to handle complex tasking. Not that carrying a box is really complex. It's gotta be our thumbs, but even if that was the case, you could build a cat bot with thumbs.

He continued to ponder the rather boring evolution of robotics and concluded that engineers were just lazy. *Most bots and even mechs resemble humans. Even in the military. Seriously, why would an engineer create a mech and program it to hold a gun? I feel like it would have been way more efficient to just make a walking gun. Who the fuck cares what it looks like? This dumbass with a box would probably be better off if they made him look like a shopping cart. At least he could carry more than one thing at a time.*

Had Frankie been at the helm, he would have had a rather elegant approach to the design process. *I could make a kick-ass bot. I would take a handful of the superior attributes from some of the most lethal animals and combined them. It would include the agility and speed of a tiger, coupled with the stealthy slither of a snake and the ability to camouflage itself like a chameleon. The only thing left is to give it the cognitive abilities and intuition of a human, along with their opposable thumbs. Just in case it needed to open a door, or a soda . . . shit, or maybe even hold a gun. It would be the* purr-fect *killing machine.*

His deep thoughts were suddenly interrupted as the sound of a door opening brought him back to reality. *I'd call it the Human-snake-cat. Or better yet, Husnat 1,* he thought, naming his creation as the newly arrived bot caught his attention.

Walking in the opposite direction of Frankie and the supply bot, this bot appeared to have come from the Tourism Quadrant and was carrying an empty box labeled with the Spacecation symbol. *Good,* he was getting close. As the opposing bot passed the two, Frankie watched its head slowly turn, staring straight into his eyes as it clinked beside him. *What the fuck is this guy looking at?*

If anybody stared me down like that, I would probably smack them upside the head, but I guarantee it's Wendy spying on me. Why is she always watching us?

Frankie could have easily asked her for directions to see Kai, but, given his current state of mind with the whole weapon of mass destruction possibility, he opted out. There was a slim chance she could have led him to an air lock and had him blown out into the cold depths of space, never to be seen again. Until he got some answers, he'd rather make this journey on his own.

After a few more painstaking minutes, their trip came to an end as a door opened, revealing the spacious and beautifully decorated Tourism Quadrant. Watching the scrawny supply bot split off to the right, Frankie decided to leave the inefficient machine with some advice. It was the least he could do in return for it helping to keep his mind occupied.

"Next time, I recommend you get a shopping cart or something. You would be able to carry more than one box at a time."

The bot gave him a blank stare, only to turn its head and walk away. Frankie was now out of his element. His salty blue coveralls were a dead giveaway that he didn't belong there. He brushed his hands down his chest a few times, trying to smooth out the wrinkles and appear somewhat respectable. *That's about as good as it gets.* Then he stood tall and began to walk with a casual strut, hoping to blend in.

The aluminum floors stretched as far as the eye could see, shrouded in a beautiful nylon, flatweave carpet. Sliding his hand along the wall, he tried to ascertain what they had used to coat the drab metal to give it the look of fine desert sand. He briefly lifted his hand as he passed a captivating piece of artwork, strategically placed to enhance the ambiance. Looking up, he admired the recessed lighting. It was a pleasant change from the long, florescent lights bolted to the ceiling of his shop.

Approaching an open door, he craned his neck, hoping to

catch a peek of the Scag that could afford such lavish accommodations in space. To be fair, though, Frankie's perception of lavish had come from the hallway—he wasn't even able to envision what one of the rooms would look like.

Hopefully, he wouldn't get himself in trouble for being in the presence of the elite. Surely, if he were doing something wrong, Wendy would have alerted someone to chase him off. Peering around the corner, to his surprise, he caught a glimpse of what appeared to be a low-level specialist who also looked out of place. Frankie briefly paused and observed the man rifling through a pile of snacks placed neatly on a table for the guests.

He entered the room, startling the young man. Frankie glanced at his name tag before locking eyes with Ben Wolff. *Yep, a specialist. What is this space sailor doing here?* They stared at each other, waiting to see who would speak first. During the silence, Frankie cautiously sized up the specialist, trying to ascertain what had brought him there. It seemed Ben was doing the same. Frankie broke eye contact first but didn't speak. Instead, he meandered through the large room, taking note of a large tapestry that pulled his gaze to a spiraling staircase leading to a second floor and loft. The overhanging balcony was wrapped in glass, and just behind the spotless pane was a fluffy, king-size bed.

"Two stories. Classic Scags," muttered Frankie.

"They have it all, don't they? Clearly, they aren't ashamed to show it off either," said Ben, sounding mutually hateful and motioning his head to the right. "There's another room through that door as well."

"Fuck them. What are you doing anyway?"

Ben suddenly looked uncomfortable and shifted awkwardly, trying to hide the candy bar in his hand.

"I can see the Almond Joy. Not too many candy bars have a blue wrapper, kid."

Ben hesitated, then came clean. "It costs me ten dollars at the commissary for one candy bar. I figure the Scags have some to spare. I'm just trying to get some before their fat faces can gobble everything up. Are you security or something?"

"What the hell, kid! Do I look like security?" Frankie responded. "I don't think I've ever seen a security guard up here. We all know Wendy is the snitch and the police at the same time. Why hasn't she caught on to you yet?"

The young man appeared visibly relieved. "The Scags trust her about as much as we do. They make sure she's disabled in the suites. They have to grant her access before she can become the almighty in here. How 'bout we call it a wash and go our separate ways? I need to get back to work before somebody notices," said Ben as he headed for the door.

Frankie cut him off, and there was no easy way to get around the towering man. "How 'bout you hook a brother up with that Almond Joy before you leave, and this can stay our little secret."

"No way! It's mine!" Ben exclaimed, grabbing his pocket.

"Keep it down, kid. The door's still open."

Just as he was trying to calm Ben, an official-looking woman entered the room. She scowled, eyeing them down.

"What do you two think you're doing?"

Ben stuffed his hands into his pockets before she could notice his loot and looked down at the floor, nervously shuffling his feet. Frankie, unfazed by her presence, stepped up to handle the situation.

"I'm coming from the Engineering Quadrant. I was on my way to see Kai, and I managed to get myself turned around. I thought this young gentleman could give me a hand and point me in the right direction."

Ben chimed in quickly after concocting his alibi. "I'm new here. I got turned around trying to find the commissary and ended up in Scag central."

"Hey kid, watch your mouth. You can't use that word over here."

The woman's expression remained stern. She clearly didn't buy their stories. Walking over to a scanner on the wall, she waved her biotag across the sensor.

"Wendy, I am granting you temporary authorization into this suite. Can you confirm these two gentlemen's identities?"

Wendy came to life. "Yes, Ms. Hendricks. Mr. Cole is the project manager in the Engineering Quadrant, and Specialist Wolff is a communications specialist in the Command Module."

"Thank you, Wendy. That is all. Reinstate your restricted access to the suite," she replied. Frankie watched the green communication light switch back to red.

Wait, who the fuck is this woman? thought Frankie, realizing that he couldn't really get in trouble for what he was doing. Especially since he hadn't done anything wrong. Frankie assumed Ms. Hendricks was some sort of manager, so he tried to level with her, as they both clearly held a certain amount of clout in their respective ranks.

He stepped forward to shake her hand. She looked skeptical but accepted. "Look, Ms. Hendricks. I'm sure you have better things to do today than escort us. How 'bout I have the kid take me back to the Command Module, and I'll talk to Kai about making sure his subordinates don't wander off into your Quadrant."

"Fine. Just get out of here before somebody sees either of you. Mr. Wolff, make sure you take him through the transient corridor. I don't want you wandering around my Quadrant," the woman ordered.

Ben looked over at Frankie, confirming that he was ready to go. With a nod back, they both walked past Ms. Hendricks, who had stepped to the side, allowing them to pass.

"It's Frankie, by the way," Frankie said as they filed out.

"Tiffany," she replied, her tone a bit less sharp.

They exited the suite and continued down the hall. Frankie heard Tiffany gently close the door behind them. She followed them at a distance, apparently not trusting them to make a clean exit. While annoyed, Frankie couldn't say he blamed her.

Ben led the way. He was obviously familiar with the route, walking mindlessly in silence. *Probably dreaming about his first bite of Almond Joy.* Suddenly, Frankie stopped short. Sure, he knew the Scags had amenities, but the luxurious pool before him took things to another level. Floor-to-ceiling windows encircled the room. The marble floor gave way to warm, shallow water extending to the robust, tempered glass, delivering an extraordinary view of the Sphere. *Damn. That thing's the size of a basketball court.* Plush lounge chairs facing the water allowed guests to gaze upward and admire the inner circumference of the tubular sphere as it orbited Earth. Live palm trees and vines surrounded the pristine observation deck, which was covered in synthetic stone, creating a tropical ambiance.

A dozen or so families were currently enjoying the pleasantries of the aquatic utopia. Small children scurried about, jumping in the pool while their parents were waited on by uniformed staff. Silver trays supported by thick white gloves transported the expensive delicacies, seemingly to prevent the help from directly handling the contents and potentially tainting the lavish goods.

Entranced by the magnificent spectacle, Frankie had unknowingly gravitated toward the pool. Just before he could set foot on the faux stone, Tiffany grabbed his thick shoulder with authority.

"Keep it moving. This isn't a sightseeing tour," she said sternly, attempting to drive him in the right direction.

His trance broken, Frankie shrugged off her futile attempt to forcibly move him and turned back on his own accord. Frankie knew that he and Ben didn't exist to this group of one-percenters, and that it was Tiffany's job to ensure it stayed that way.

"Can't blame 'em. I'd be doing the same thing. Just sucks that our shitty existence is an eyesore to them," Frankie said, nodding a farewell to Tiffany. He motioned for Ben to continue leading the way, once again falling into step behind him. "Fuck these shit stains."

The calming music faded into the distance, and after a few dizzying turns they arrived at an unmarked access door neatly tucked away near the keel of the Sphere. Ben scanned his bio-implant, and the door slid open, revealing a steep stairwell leading to a long, echoing corridor void of any luxuries.

"Well, that's the last time either of us will get a glimpse into the life of a Scag," Ben said.

"What do you mean last time? How many times—"

Frankie was interrupted by Ben's scathing stare as the specialist nodded his head upward ever so slightly. It was enough to remind Frankie that Wendy was once again listening to their every word. With his own deductive reasoning, Frankie figured that Ben had likely been sneaking into the Tourism Quadrant for some time now. He smiled and agreed to the unspoken request, allowing the subject to rest.

Changing the topic, Frankie asked, "Shit, I've been hurled off the Sphere countless times in an aluminaut, but that pool took space travel to a different level. Who the fuck would spend money on bringing twenty-foot palm trees into space?"

"That's how I know you!" exclaimed Ben. "I couldn't place your face because last time I saw you, you had a helmet on, and were flipping my commander the bird in an aluminaut. The whole team was cracking up."

"Well, I'm glad I could entertain you, but today I need to talk some business with Kai. Hopefully he doesn't hold a grudge."

"I don't think he holds grudges. He takes a more 'disappointed dad' approach to leadership. In either case, there hasn't been much going on since we lost comms with the colonists on Mars a few weeks ago."

"What do you mean lost comms? I haven't caught wind of any communication issues coming to the engineering side of the house."

"That's because we think it's an issue on their end. A massive storm blanketed a quarter of the planet, and we don't know when it's going to let up. No uploads or downloads seem to be going through as far as we can tell."

"A few weeks is a long time. My crew should be finishing up their routine hull scan. I could have them do a quick fly by before they dock. Maybe they could see if there are any glaring issues with the Sphere's external comms system," Frankie offered.

"That's not my call to make, but it couldn't hurt."

Wendy chimed in, unsolicited. "I run a continuous diagnostic program for the entire Sphere. There are no malfunctioning systems or components associated with the communication array."

"Obviously you're monitoring the system, but have you put eyes on it?" Frankie retorted snidely. "I know you've got two Invicta-bots sitting around doing nothing."

"What does that mean?" asked Ben.

"It means there's a big-ass box that supposedly contains components for the rail car hub. And two Invictas are just holding a staring match next to it."

"Huh. Yeah, we took that on board about a month ago, along with a guy named Jade. I thought it was weird he only had a first name listed. I figured he would've been in touch with you, since you guys are building the whole rail thing."

Frankie's anger was reinvigorated. How did this little nerdy comms kid know more about what was going on than he did? It further solidified his suspicion that something was being hidden. He also had a feeling that pieces of information were being withheld from all parties in order to mask the true nature of the project. Mr. Walker or some guy named Jade would be his best bet at getting some tangible information that didn't stink of conspiracy, but first he needed to talk to Kai.

"Shit kid, how much farther is this walk?"

"It's just ahead," Ben said, pointing at the confusing, stadium-like numbering system painted on the gray metal.

Wendy unabashedly inserted herself into the conversation. "Next time, you should schedule a transport-bot."

"There are fucking transport-bots? That would have been nice to know," blurted Frankie.

"The bots are in limited supply. The rail system will increase transportation efficiency and speed," Wendy replied.

"Rail system? Keep up the lie. I know somebody is up to something. It would be easier for you to just tell me, so I can get back to work and stop screwing around," Frankie said, not hiding his frustration.

"What does it even matter? You're gonna get paid no matter what." Ben shrugged.

"It's the principle. I hate being lied to, and you shouldn't trust everything you hear."

They finally reached the end of their long walk and entered the Command Quadrant. Frankie felt at home once again. The narrow corridors were filled with uniformed employees who actually appeared to work for a living. However, there seemed to be significantly more computer terminals with tedious administrative work being conducted. Nonetheless, it was refreshing to once again see a purpose to the Sphere other than Spacecations for the Scags.

Without warning, Ben picked up the pace. "Commander's going to be pissed. I've been gone for a while," he said, glancing at his wrist.

Approaching the heavy doors that concealed the command module, Ben swiped his bio-implant and revealed the hub that directed all work around the Sphere. Frankie hadn't seen Kai in person for some time. However, as soon as he entered the dim room, his attention was immediately pulled, not to Kai, but to the mission commander's chair. *There's got to be a way to get that thing out of here.*

Kai instantly greeted Ben. "Nice of you to join us again, Mr. Wolff. I'd be happy to hear your excuse for running late this time."

"I'd be happy to get one of those chairs in my shop," Frankie blurted.

"Well, look what the cat dragged in. We'll talk later, Specialist," said Kai, allowing Ben to slip past. "Looks like you finally got off your ass to come talk to me, Frankie. I can only assume that you're here to apologize for your unnecessary gesture."

Frankie shook his head and replied, "Why would I apologize for that? I'm here for something much more important than a grand gesture."

CHAPTER 30

INGENUITY: PART TWO

Led by Commander Ritter, the three teams trotted through the silty gravel in a single file line toward the shed. With each step, a fine cloud of red dust burst outward from beneath their boots, leaving a wispy trail behind them as the wind swirled the tiny particles into the already hazy atmosphere. They moved with purpose, completing the short walk expeditiously and without issue.

Charlize and the others gathered at the entrance of the shed as they arrived. Commander Ritter was at the end of the line and disconnected his strap, securing it to a D-ring on his chest, letting the tether freely dangle. The white, insulated tool shed resembled a hardy connex box. Resting on top was a small, dusty solar panel that charged a lithium-ion battery used to power a long bank of LED lights illuminating the dark space within the shed.

After opening the doors, the teams spread out, collecting the tools they needed to conduct their tasks. Charlize and Eddie, who were on water duty, were the first to be ready. Charlize required minimal gear. Her partner Eddie, the resident mechanic, required much more. However, his equipment was all conveniently stored in the mobile servicing cart, positioned near the front of the shed.

"We're up and ready. Eddie and I are going to head out," said Charlize, updating Commander Ritter.

"Sounds good. Be safe and let me know if you have any issues."

Charlize looked ahead at the six available routes before them, each ending at a different location in the surrounding area. Meanwhile, Eddie carefully positioned the cart between them, getting a feel for the sensitive controls. He walked around the back side of the device, completing his standard checks to ensure everything was in order, then stood beside Charlize.

As Eddie fastened the control pad to his wrist, he said, "Let's switch over to Net Three."

The two switched over to their private net for communication, monitoring the common channel in the background. Charlize located their route by identifying a small, laser-etched sign reading "swim at own risk," a clever attempt at humor left on a piece of scrap metal by the earlier settlers. They once again clipped into the yellow nylon rope that would lead them to the water truck. Thankfully, their route was the shortest, only requiring them to walk 150 feet. *The less transit the better. We'll take all the time we can get.*

As the others continued to rummage through the piles of tools in the shed, Charlize and Eddie set off.

∞

In the far-right corner of the shed, Xiomara finally found the few remaining uncontaminated aluminum cylinders for collecting the soil samples and handed them to Hank. The rest of the containers remained underground in the habitat, since Hank hadn't gotten around to bringing them back up after his failed expeditions. Xiomara didn't blame him, though. At the onset of the colony, the gear had been heavily utilized; however, their countless expeditions had proven fruitless. *I wonder if today will be any different.*

She wasn't optimistic. The barren wasteland seemed devoid of life, at least from what they'd collected on the near surface, and the colonists had given up the search in the immediate area. Hank, whose primary purpose within the colony was to spearhead the search for life, had pivoted the team's focus to finding ancient fossils. Perhaps they could at least prove life had once existed before the water dried up and the rich atmospheric gasses escaped into the cold depths of space.

Xiomara was the resident physician. She primarily handled routine checkups and managed the colonists' mental health. However, through accompanying Hank on so many expeditions, she'd learned quite a bit, and she considered his work similarly intricate and fascinating. She had also come to understand and share the massive disappointment that burdened Hank. *And his colleagues back on Earth, for that matter.*

Up to this point, the search for life both past and present continued to defy what scientists had once theorized through their analysis of the terrain from satellite imagery and archaic Martian probes, long since decommissioned. *We could still be going about it all wrong. There should have been an abundance of proof. Or maybe life here knows something we don't and just doesn't want to be found.*

Today, she and Hank were hoping that this dust storm could have churned up some living organism, and with a bit of luck, it had come to rest in their back yard. Xiomara knew that Hank privately shared her doubts, and she admired his determination to stay positive and continue on. She, in turn, would do whatever she could to assist him.

Xiomara had emigrated from Mexico to the United States with her family as an adolescent. She had pushed herself on an accelerated educational track, achieving her MD when she was only twenty-eight. After graduating, Xiomara traveled the world on frequent international humanitarian missions, which she considered an integral part of giving back to society. However, everything changed when the droughts began to ravage first-world countries. Most international borders were closed, and she was eventually restricted from traveling to impoverished countries.

The travel ban was a result of private corporations, mainly from the United States and China, trying to exploit the weaknesses of smaller countries to purchase water-rich land for export to their own countries. This caused water to become more expensive than oil, and the countries that had not squandered their resources soon began to restrict foreign investors from acquiring their plentiful reserves. This ban was also extended to travelers who sought refuge from the dry, arid climates scattered across the world.

Disheartened by the decay of society and her inability to effect any real change, Xiomara decided she was done contending with endless policy battles to cross borders. Her next and final frontier would be as a colonist on Mars, where she could put her unique skillset to use. The work she had conducted abroad had accustomed her to operating in inhospitable living conditions with limited supplies, very similar to her current situation.

Hank interrupted her thoughts. "I think I've got everything. You ready to head out?" he asked, enthusiasm filling his voice.

There's that optimism. "Yep. Ready to go!" She replied.

Because Xiomara Santissima's name was long and a bit of a tongue twister depending on who she was dealing with, the crew lovingly called her Doc. Of course, on this mission, her medical skills weren't required. Like the rest of the crew, she helped where she could when she wasn't performing her primary specialty.

With their equipment in hand, they switched to their private communication net and left Chauncy and Commander Ritter in the shed. As they lumbered back out into the elements, Hank said, "Winds have been coming from the west for most of the month. So, the fine dust will most likely be piled up on the backside of that small ridge that protects the mouth of the elevator shaft. With these conditions and our limited leash, I think it's the best option to find an area without a ton of human exposure. Let's start there."

"Lead the way," Xiomara replied. She let Hank take point even though she was thoroughly familiar with the route as well. Their six-hundred-foot-long, U-shaped path also led to the aboveground habitat Charlize had been assembling. That area had seen the least amount of human exposure over the years, and it provided a sheltered work site to collect their samples.

I bet he's not even wearing underwear, though Xiomara, clipping in just after Hank.

∞

Chauncy was still searching for the old diagnostic device that plugged into the communications array. He needed it to help isolate issues. The diagnostic device hadn't been used for years, not since Ares had received an update from Wendy that allowed him to monitor an expanded set of systems and autonomously perform most troubleshooting. Since then, Chauncy had only needed to fix what Ares identified, rather than spend extended periods of time chasing gremlins aboveground. But not today. Today he and Commander Ritter were on their own. Although Chauncy had become rather accustomed to Ares' assistance, he was proud that he still possessed the wherewithal to handle the array himself. That was, if he could find the diagnostic tool.

"I can't find a thing in this mess of shit," shouted Chauncy, slamming the hard-plastic case that should have contained the device against the wall. "It's going to be a needle in a haystack without it."

"Are you positive it's in here?" asked Commander Ritter.

"Yeah, this is the only place I would have put it. Plus, after being down in the suck hole for the last month, I surely would have stumbled on it."

"Well, we're running short on time. We can't sit in this box all day," the commander said.

Chauncy took a second to calm himself and collect his thoughts. *If I can fix the relay, then Ares could help with the array. The relay is also much closer if I need parts. But, if I can't fix it, I might have blown our window to open up comms with the Deep Space Network. On the other hand, I also really don't want to climb to the top of that ridge right now.*

"I say we head to the relay to see if I can get that POS working. You could send two of the others from cleaning duty back here to search for the computer as a backup plan."

Chauncy waited as Commander Ritter silently weighed his options. By now, he was accustomed to it. He knew the commander took all decisions, especially those involving splitting up crew on the surface, very seriously.

"Let's go with your gut and fix the relay, if you think that's the best option. I'll update group two when we cross paths by the elevator and relay tower."

They closed the heavy door to the shed and tethered in, heading back in the direction from which they'd come. Chauncy noticed the dust in the air had become a little thicker since they first arrived on the surface, which was cause for concern. But it didn't seem to trigger Commander Ritter's no-go threshold. *Not yet? Even the ever-prudent commander understands the stakes today.*

As Chauncy and Commander Ritter approached the relay, group two surfaced and disembarked the elevator. Chauncy unclipped and darted off toward the side of the elevator and began troubleshooting. Still within sight, he saw Commander Ritter update the group on the new plan, then trudge back toward Chauncy. Behind him, the eight members clipped into their routes and slowly faded from view, dutifully trekking off to complete their respective missions.

Eddie and Charlize had reached the water truck, which sat waiting for them to download its contents. Eddie grabbed the long, thick hose and secured it to the truck, while Charlize took a look at the display underneath the heavy metal panel protecting it.

"Truck's hooked up," said Eddie, monitoring the connection as water flowed into the large storage tank behind him. "How's it look? Is she full?"

Her silence was disconcerting, so Eddie walked around the truck to see what she was doing. Her look said it all. She was resting her head on top of her arm, which was draped over the display.

"It's only half full, isn't it?" he asked.

"I don't get it," she said with a deflated tone.

"I snagged the diagnostic tool and put it in the servicing cart. Let me hook it up to see if there are any hidden fault codes running in the background."

He dashed over to the cart and opened a drawer, pulling out an old computer, which he then connected to the truck.

"Hey, hold this. I'm going to head to the top of the truck and see if there are any mechanical issues restricting the flow," said Eddie, handing Charlize the small device.

"Why do you even have this? I'm looking at the diagnostic screen right now. It says the truck is fine."

Eddie laughed. "The software isn't programmed to alert you in all circumstances. Mainly just if something is broken."

"Well, if nothing is broken, everything should be fine."

"Not necessarily. The truck could be operating perfectly but influenced by outside forces. It may have stored that data."

At the back of the truck, Eddie climbed a small ladder and stood up on a narrow platform that ran the entire length of the beefy cylindrical tank. He approached the large, conical cover that electronically opened after the boom to the well was secured. After selecting the manual override, Eddie opened the first of two pressure-sealed valves and inspected the inlet for any damage or obstructions. The rather simple system did not reveal any issues, so he assumed that the issue was with the electrical side of the truck.

"Everything checks out up here. I'm coming down," said Eddie.

"Sounds good. The computer is still processing the data. This thing is slow as shit."

Eddie hopped off the truck and took the computer from Charlize, who had been patiently monitoring the process. Ironically, the computer chimed, announcing its completion just as Eddie took it out of her hand.

"Seriously?" Charlize threw up her hands, and they both laughed.

Eddie scrolled through the lines of messages, most of which were unimportant advisories alerting them of minor errors that had been triggered but had subsequently cleared themselves. However, one alert stuck out like a sore thumb.

"Truck's running good, but there seems to be a problem at the well."

With wide eyes, Charlize asked, "How can you tell that?"

Eddie tilted the device toward her. "Idle limit exceeded. That means everything is working just fine, but the truck sat there for too long waiting to fill. It assumed that there was an issue on the other end, so it closed the valve and force-disconnected itself."

"You're a genius!"

"Tricks of the trade. Glad I snaked this little computer," said Eddie, walking back over to the cart. "It would be a real pain in the ass to have to troubleshoot without Ares or this baby."

Charlize's initial excitement faded, and she began to look concerned. She started pacing back and forth. He let her continue, undisturbed, His discovery had obviously gotten her mind rolling. Suddenly, Charlize snapped out of her concentration and turned to him.

"Did you tell Chauncy you were taking that computer?" she exclaimed.

Taken aback, he replied, "What do you want? Water or video messages? I figured he would ask if he needed it."

"Son of a bitch, Eddie. For being so smart, you really are an idiot sometimes."

"That's also a trick of the trade," he said with a smile.

Charlize switched to the primary net, which had been quiet for some time now. "Commander Ritter, it's Charlize. Do you copy?"

∞

Blake was watching Chauncy reset connections and clean components with compressed gas as Charlize's transmission came through, "Yeah, I got a copy. How's the offload going?"

"The offload is almost complete, but we only had a half load again. Eddie scanned the truck and found an Idle Limit Exceeded advisory."

"Can you elaborate?"

"It means the truck's not broken, it's the well. It's not getting enough water to the truck."

There was a pause in the communications as Blake mulled over the situation. *We need to get eyes on it. If there is a leak in the system, we're going to be in a world of hurt.* "I believe it's time to start thinking outside of the box. The weather isn't going to hold much longer."

"I agree, sir. Hey Chauncy. Have you been looking for the diagnostic computer?" asked Charlize.

"Oh, come on! Not cool."

"Yeah, that's on me man, my bad," Eddied apologized.

"We'll get you the computer shortly," Charlize assured Chauncy. "There is nothing more we can do on our end until the storm clears. It's too dusty to launch the drones."

"Kind of sounds like we should go pillage the CelestialX modules and see if they have a long-range mining bot to go check out the well," Eddie joked.

Charlize jumped in before Blake could shut the idea down.

"That's exactly the kind of out of box thinking we need. The modules I've been putting together for the new habitat are full of equipment. If you let me, sir, I can take Eddie over there and we can see what they've been sending over for the mining crew. They've got to have some sort of advanced tech hiding inside."

While he was sure Charlize was right, Blake had been given explicit directions to only assemble the aboveground habitat. Under no circumstances were they to strip the gear for replacement parts or utilize the onboard technology for their own means. CelestialX had a substantial investment in the future of mining, not the progress of science.

Space exploration had once been a government-funded, noble cause, whose investors were taxpayers eager to devote their money to space exploration. But the endeavor had become burdened by bloated government spending. Private corporations then piggybacked off the shared knowledge and devised a means to exploit it for their own benefit. While this fate for Mars was easily predictable, even inevitable based on the capitalistic nature of humans, it deeply frustrated Blake. To him, these restrictions seemed counterintuitive given that CelestialX could only expect to sustainably live on Mars due to NASA's half-century-long pursuit of scientific exploration.

Nolen Aromas had sold the average citizen on the idea that they could somehow own a piece of the red pie in the sky. However, Blake knew Nolen's true end game was to expand his empire. The population struggling to survive on Earth was just too blind to see it. But everything came down to CelestialX's bottom line. *And it will be my job to produce something worthwhile for Nolen's investors to recoup their money, but in order to get there, we're going to need water.*

Blake weighed the possible repercussions for breaking his directives in order to determine the cause of the water shortage. With their reserves slowly dwindling, his crew's lives outweighed the need for a company's desire to harvest the untouched resources hiding right below their feet. His decision made, the commander resolved to accept any repercussions from his actions.

He keyed his radio. "The way I see it, if CelestialX wants their crews to survive, they are going to have to put a little more skin in the game. Collect your gear and hightail your asses over here. We'll meet you at the shed to pass off the diagnostic computer."

CHAPTER 31

FRANKIE'S TREK: PART THREE

Frankie knew that Kai wasn't actually expecting an apology for flipping him the bird. It was just his professional way of saying "fuck you" in return. The two men firmly interlocked hands and looked one another in the eye. The interaction only lasted a few seconds, but it was enough to the fill vital holes left by a mostly digital history of communication. Frankie finally felt like he had some control and could bend the ear of the strait-laced commander.

"Kai. It's nice to see you again," said Frankie, his voice deep.

"Frankie," the commander replied with a nod.

The simultaneous release of their grip allowed them to retain their authoritative posturing. Frankie squared up with Kai, taking a broad stance and pushing up his sleeves. Kai did the same. *Maybe we're not so different after all.*

"So, what brings you all the way over to the command module?" Kai inquired.

"As you're aware, my team and I have been diligently attaching the rail system. However, we've come to a crossroads that draws some concern about the project as a whole," said Frankie, removing his emotions from the situation, at least for the moment. "Ever since the final component arrived about a month ago, its plans have been heavily censored. I was only just granted temporary authorization, and after reviewing them, I currently have reservations about completing the project."

Frankie could tell his questioning of the tasking didn't land well with Kai. *Still trying to adjust from that military mindset,* Frankie thought, finding mild enjoyment in the commander's struggle.

"Are you telling me that, based on the design of the rail system, you don't feel comfortable completing the job you were hired to do?" Kai asked, then followed up with a more direct statement. "Because last time I checked, you weren't hired to reevaluate the complex design, but rather put it together in an expeditious manner."

Frankie realized that Kai didn't have a palate for any of the conspiracy theories he had concocted on his journey to the command module. He would have to approach the situation differently and explain what he had found in the cargo bay. Hopefully, that would lead Kai to conclude on his own that something was missing from this rail car project equation.

"I have been working with complex designs for the better part of a two decades. It doesn't take a rocket scientist to figure out that the rail itself appears to carry a high enough voltage to power a network of rail cars. But, when the final components are housed in a specialized air lock connecting to the R&D Quadrant, it no longer resembles a rail system."

"Have you thought about the fact that your system will directly connect to the fusion reactor? That in itself is a highly classified and protected piece of technology," Kai replied.

Frankie was unconvinced by this rationale, so he continued with his case. "I went to the cargo bay. There were two Invicta-bots standing guard next to the so-called "rail car." After they opened it, I found some sort of fancy science experiment inside. It doesn't add up. Not to mention Wendy hasn't given me any information or connected me with the lead rep."

"Well, did you ask her to?"

He paused for a moment. "No."

"All right. I've about lost my patience. I don't have time for any more of your radical theories about secret Invicta guards. Wendy, can you enlighten me on the assembly in the cargo bay?"

There was no response. A fleeting expression of puzzlement crossed Kai's face. Frankie's arguments may not have held much weight, but he had a feeling this would get the commander's attention.

"Wendy!" Kai shouted, with an intensity Frankie hadn't heard him use with her before.

"I am unable to expound on your inquiry. You will need to contact Mr. Walker for any further queries about the contents of the box."

"What the fuck did you just say? Connect me with Jade Walker."

"He is currently unavailable," Wendy replied sharply.

Shit, Jade and Mr. Walker are the same people? I guess that makes sense. In any case, Frankie, filled with a sense of vindication, gave Kai a smug look. At this point, the entire module had halted their work and were eagerly watching to see what would happen next. Both he and Kai were keenly aware of the growing tension in the room. Frankie knew Kai would not openly concede his convictions in front of his team for fear of looking weak or out of control in the situation.

The commander spoke again. "Wendy, please leave Mr. Walker a message and let him know that Mr. Cole and myself would like a meeting with him prior to commencing the final stages of his project."

Once again, there was no response.

"Wendy, I would like confirmation of the message," Kai requested.

"I will convey your message and alert you when he responds."

The commander was visibly aggravated by the situation. Frankie knew the feeling. They both had more pressing issues to deal with, but now they were forced to handle this.

"Are you happy?" Kai asked, once again addressing Frankie. "I will let you know when we have a meeting set up. As for now, I'm running late for a meeting of my own. Can you make your way back to the Engineering Quadrant, or do you need Mr. Wolff to hold your hand again?"

Frankie didn't appreciate the demeaning comment about needing the boy's help, but he believed he could redeem himself.

"That's fine with me. I'll be waiting in my shop. Wendy, can you have a transport-bot meet me at the transient corridor in five minutes?"

"I'm sorry, but all transport-bots are unavailable."

Out of the corner of his eye, he caught Ben laughing as he shoved a piece of Almond Joy in his mouth. Refraining from calling the specialist out on their little excursion, he once again extended his hand toward Kai. "Thanks for the help. Looks like I'll be walking."

Frankie left the command module with the satisfaction that his questions would hopefully be answered soon, not to mention Kai's realization that something was awry. *It probably would have been easier to just call Kai. No, screw that. I bet Wendy would have just said the commander was busy and made up another bullshit story. She's definitely up to something, and she's probably holding out on that transport-bot as well.* Reaching the end of the corridor, Frankie turned and exited Quadrant One, dreading the long walk back.

CHAPTER 32

INGENUITY: PART THREE

Hank and Doc were finishing up collecting their soil samples. It was a rather simple process when compared to the near-surface digs they were used to undertaking. Most of the work had to be done manually, because they weren't provided with a bot capable of hard labor to really make a dent in the Martian surface.

When they'd first arrived, the colonists were stuck with an uncoordinated, two-legged buffoon that had a tendency to leave gear behind. They had lovingly named it Clark. The archaic machine could handle the rough terrain for exploration and assist them in carrying gear, but it lacked the brains or components to do much more. It was once thought that the older technology would be more dependable over long periods of time and wouldn't require an increased footprint for maintenance, but it turned out Eddie could only limp it along for so long. They eventually decommissioned Clark and used its parts for various band aids around the colony.

They had put in numerous requests for a humanoid bot to be added to the inventory of the supply transistor over the years, but CelestialX had absorbed the costs of the recurring supply runs, and their requests were denied due to space and weight limitations. The colonists knew it was a bullshit excuse and figured they would eventually come around, given they were assembling their new habitat.

They never did. Instead, the supply vessels were packed to the brim with newer high-tech assets in preparation for *Hermes's* arrival, reserving little space for anything other than the essential items the current colony required to survive.

After hearing Charlize's request to rummage through the stagnant modules, Hank and Doc were pleased that someone would finally discover what gadgets were hiding inside. That was when Hank had a brilliant idea. *There's actually a chance I can get a peek inside those modules.*

"How about we hang out for a little longer? Eddie and Charlize are gonna pass us on the way to the habitat. Maybe they'll need help."

"I think we should just head back. We've collected all the samples we can carry."

"Come on, Doc. Aren't you just a little curious what's hiding right next door? Can you imagine the new medical equipment they have stashed on board?"

"It's not like we can take anything," Doc replied.

"Nobody said anything about taking anything. Well, besides Charlize, but we can still poke through the gear."

She looked around at the hazy, desolate landscape. "Well, you never know if they are going to need help. I have a feeling we're going to be hunkering down below again anyway."

"Atta girl," said Hank, looking around for something to do. "Wanna throw some rocks at that post in the meantime?"

Doc shrugged and picked up a small, jagged rock. She gave it a tender toss through the air, but it sailed twenty feet past the metal post and into the haze.

"Dang it. You'd think I would get used to the lack of gravity."

"Watch this," said Hank, chucking a rock of his own into the distance.

They both watched as it silently hit a post.

"Nailed it!" he shouted.

"Get out of here. That was the wrong post."

"Fine, game on!"

∞

Eddie guided the supply cart along the route back to the elevator. The cart was powered by two electric motors and controlled with a remote device. Eddie was easily able to adjust the speed and direction. He currently had the cart set to its maximum speed, while he and Charlize walked behind it, trying to keep up. He hoped an expeditious return would lessen the commander's wrath for his swiping of the diagnostic computer.

Commander Ritter's faint, white outline gradually came into view, with Chauncy not far behind. As diminishing separation reduced the thick, dusty barrier between them, Eddie could finally make out the commander standing with his arms crossed. He presumed he was going to get chewed out, so he preemptively tried to provide an excuse for keeping the computer.

"I'm sorry that I didn't—"

Commander Ritter interrupted him. "Don't worry about the computer. I'm glad you guys were able to check out the truck and eliminate it as a cause for the shortage. It honestly made my decision to send you over to the modules easier."

Relieved, Eddie replied, "Hopefully, we can bypass the external locks without power. I'm going to take the cart over there in case we need to come up with a creative solution."

They reached the end of the line, and Eddie tapped the control pad on his forearm, stopping the cart. Before he could disconnect, Chauncy was already rummaging through the drawers.

"It's in the top right one," said Eddie, disconnecting his carabiner.

He watched Chauncy snatch the computer, eager to get back to work.

"I'm ready to go, sir. I think isolated the problem to a burned-out relay on the power distribution panel. It should be an easy fix once I verify with the computer. I've already grabbed a spare out of the shed."

"Copy, go hook up. I'll be right behind you," said Commander Ritter, scanning the area and assessing the changing weather conditions.

"On it."

"The wind's picking up. Visibility is about to go to shit," said the commander, turning to Charlize, who would be the senior member on the excursion to the modules. "Charlize, do you think you've got a handle on this? I need to make sure you'll call it before this weather turns into a bad situation."

"Yes, sir. I've got it. We should be able to make quick work of the door locks. I'm not sure what we're going to find inside though."

"Alright. Try not to break anything over there."

The two teams continued on with their separate tasks. Eddie once again set the cart to full power as he and Charlize clipped into their new route toward the modules, while Commander Ritter and Chauncy departed to fix the comms relay.

Halfway through their hike around the ridge, they ran into Hank and Doc. Hank was jumping up and down with excitement. Eddie brought the cart to a stop.

"Did you actually make a discovery?" asked Charlize, startling the two.

"No, but I finally hit the post!" He cheered, patting Doc on the back, with a smile on his face.

Doc swatted his hand away. "It was the wrong post again!"

"Nope. I won!"

"You little . . ."

Charlize interrupted the bickering. "So, you guys are done with the samples?"

"We got the samples, though they're probably worthless," answered Hank, "But when we heard you coming this way, we decided to wait and go with you guys. I wanna see what's inside the modules."

Eddie looked at Charlize, wondering what she'd say after the commander's clear emphasis on safety. He knew she was weighing the same thing. Charlize hesitated for a few seconds, but ultimately approved. "We could use the help," she said.

"Yeah, we might have to haul the bot out by hand if we find one," said Hank.

"There is no way you're going to be able to haul one of these excavators out of there by hand," replied Eddie, annoyed at Hank's delusion. "Your Martian spinach didn't make you Popeye."

With the small group now numbering four, they continued on their way.

In the ensuing quiet, Eddie reevaluated his reaction to Hank. He knew he had to be more patient. As the lead mechanic, he had far more experience with this type of technology than the other colonists. During their training, Eddic had worked with experimental bots that were specifically designed to travel great distances, carrying out pre-programmed tasks. The bots were not artificially intelligent. They had been designed to optimize a specific set of functions to achieve their given objective. That wasn't to say they weren't clever, though. They had the ability to make decisions based on external factors and adjust their tasking on the fly. Engineers knew that complex situations, like the one the colonists were currently struggling with, would eventually arise, and the bots would need to problem-solve on their own.

Unfortunately, the technology had still been in development when they left, which was why they were stuck with Clark. While not equivalent, his familiarity gave him an intuition about the bots in the module that Hank couldn't be expected to match.

In reality, Eddie's experience with robotics stretched back even further. While he had never worked on the engineering side, Eddie had worked as a robotics mechanic for over ten years. His job had been to fix the intricate machines as they inevitably broke. Decades back, the definition of a mechanic had begun to evolve as technology was continuously integrated within the mechanical operation of equipment. Turning wrenches could only get you so far. A good mechanic needed to understand the delicately complex arrangement of the new, overengineered technology that allowed bots and mechs to function within society.

Eddie was the whiz kid who could fix problems the engineers had been furiously trying to diagnose for days or even weeks. In his eyes, designing and building something required an entirely different mindset compared to the person who had to fix the engineers' mistakes as components failed.

"How much do you think one weighs?" asked Doc, out of the blue, pulling Eddie from his self-reflection.

"I would assume it's at least eight hundred pounds, but knowing that it was developed to assist them with mining, it could be in excess of half a ton," said Eddie.

"Well, that's only three hundred pounds here," Hank asserted.

"I was already accounting for the reduced gravity."

Hank appeared stunned by Eddie's reply. "Dang, how are we planning on getting it out of there?"

"The four of us surely won't be able to carry it," Eddie said. "I'm going to have to figure out how to boot it up, but that might be difficult without knowing much about these modules."

Charlize stepped forward.

"The modules are kept charged during their transit. That's how I can arrange and deploy the domes without them being hooked up to a power grid. It would only make sense that the internal power source is connected to the bots, so they can remain charged while they're powered down. If they weren't, then the crew on board *Hermes* would have the same issue when they get here, trying to figure out how to move and subsequently charge them."

"Well, if that is the case, I should be able to boot one of them up in a ready state," said Eddie. "If Chauncy can get the communication relay working, Ares should be able to send them tasking from within our own habitat."

With everything laid out, the crew pressed on. Eddie knew their proposed plan was only theoretical at this point, but it was universally understood that there were no guarantees on Mars. The crew had been trained to handle diverse situations and develop solutions for complicated problems. This wasn't the first hardship they had encountered over the past three years. However, Eddie realized, it was the first time that, if their efforts failed, not only would their own lives be in jeopardy, but the other hundred colonists on board *Hermes* would share their fate as well. Without a bot to investigate, the colonists would remain in the dark about the cause of their water issues. The water truck might eventually come back empty or not return at all. Eddie found it a rather sad image. A stranded water truck, eternally waiting for the well to produce the water it required before returning. He didn't even want to think about what that would mean for him and the others.

Straining his eyes, he scanned the haze in front of them. They should have seen the large domes in the distance by now, but the wind had begun to whip the fine dust into a frenzy once again. Eddie realized that he and the others had begun to walk with a forward lean, bracing themselves. Thankfully, the atmosphere didn't allow the wind to pack as strong a punch as it would have on Earth, but he could still see concern growing on Charlize's face. Their visibility hadn't been entirely obstructed, though, and Eddie was glad that she seemed willing to press on.

A white dome finally revealed itself as they approached the end of the of the path. It overshadowed everything in the flat open plane, standing twenty feet tall with a diameter of thirty-five feet. The positioning of the domes resembled the chemical structure of a complex compound to Eddie. As they trudged closer, the rest of the habitat became faintly visible in the distance.

∞

Charlize, who had taken lead of the single file line, unclipped at the last post and approached the nearest module. Every time she came here, she couldn't help but appreciate the beauty of the habitat as a whole. The cluster of geometric domes was connected by slim tunnels, overlaid on a delicate web of tracks. Today, though, the tracks were only a foot tall and mostly buried with sand from the strong storms. Their purpose was to allow the modules to be repositioned. *Supposedly, at least. I would probably only move one if it was on fire,* Charlize joked to herself. Unfortunately, the tracks were not overly durable and weren't designed to be manipulated like the tracks of a tank. This meant that once a module was placed and its robust dome deployed, it was best to not moved it again for the foreseeable future. What the tracks lacked in practicality, though, Charlize believed they made up for in aesthetics.

She sometimes mused that Wendy must have studied the fascinating art of origami. The modules elegant folding design allowed the compact module to both fit snuggly on the transistor and endure the entry of Mars's atmosphere without being damaged. When deployed, the intricately folded module appeared to bloom like a beautiful white rose made of kami, the thin, durable paper used for creating decorative Japanese figures. *I still can't believe that if I folded a piece of paper 103 times, it would become thicker than the visible universe.*

The rest of the team now stood side by side, looking at the module's formidable door, which hadn't been opened since before its construction on Earth. Charlize knew they were expecting direction.

"You guys want to hear an interesting fact?" she asked instead, eagerly.

They all groaned, and Doc stopped her before she started rambling, "Not the paper thing again."

Charlize rolled her eyes, and before they could discuss their options to access the door, Ares came online, providing the crews with an update.

"The barometric pressure is dropping, with current wind speeds approaching fifty-five knots. I would recommend an expeditious return before conditions worsen."

"Holy shit, Chauncy fixed the relay!" Charlize exclaimed.

CHAPTER 33

THE LONG CON: PART ONE

William propped his limber legs up on his gleaming glass desk, which faced an open courtyard full of delightfully refreshing greenery surrounding his private pool. The seemingly ageless man had a dark, unweathered tan and thick, flowing brown hair with an accompanying mustache. His muscular physique gave him a deceptively youthful appearance for a seventy-four-year old, noticeable even now as he sat behind the desk in his glass-encased office, overlooking his empire of sorts.

William watched a tumultuous storm brewing on the horizon and wondered how much longer the sunny day would hold. Florida had been ravaged over the years by superstorms and rising coastlines. The Keys and Miami had long since been flooded out, but that didn't hinder the growth of Orlando. If anything, it fueled the exponential expansion of the vacation mecca of the state.

This projected growth was part of the reason why William Walker had decided to move GenInc's headquarters to the city in the late forties, despite the increased costs associated with constructing buildings that could withstand the constant battering of CAT V hurricanes. The ever-present threat was of no concern to William. If necessary, he could easily hop on his private, hypersonic jet and reach any one of his many estates spread across the world in a matter of hours.

After taking a long sip of his Arnold Palmer, he sat back with an expression of glee, relishing his myriad accomplishments. Content with the day's work, he tapped the implant embedded in his forearm, hailing his personal assistant.

"Jennine, can you bring up a bottle of scotch for Nolen Aromas?"

Jennine shuffled away. There was no need for verbal confirmation when working with William. He saw to it that his employees carried out orders diligently and without question., Otherwise, they would be replaced just as easily as the bottle of liquor he had requested.

After clipping the end of a fresh cigar, William ran it under his nostrils, inhaling the earthy scents with a vigorous smile. His lavish leather chair rotated as he whipped his legs off the desk, slipping his feet into a comfy pair of white cotton slippers neatly tucked away from view. With a sigh of relief, he rose and glided through a set of double-wide glass doors that opened with a discrete command from the implant in his forearm. He was greeted by the hot sun and humid air, as the slight refreshing breeze filtered through his thin linen suit.

Not only did William have a pool, which was a rarity these days, but the entire top floor belonged to him alone. His office, accounting for one-third of the roof, was constructed of glass, allowing him to constantly bask in the sun in an attempt to enjoy his life as if he were retired. The remaining real estate was reserved for his own rooftop Eden.

Unfortunately, his sons had yet to come around on taking over the company, depriving him of the opportunity to truly retire. But for a man who would live well into his hundreds, he knew he had nothing but time to kill. He pulled a gold butane lighter out of his left trouser pocket and evenly toasted the end of his cigar as he puffed on the opposite end. The thick white smoke stuck to the moist air and drifted over the wall of greenery, quickly dissipating as an updraft racing alongside the building carried it away.

His office sat atop a thirty-story building, but only the top ten floors were part of the office complex. The remainder was part of an intricate parking structure, two thirds of which was submerged underground at the moment. The unique design was due to the ever-present threat of floods and superstorms, coupled with fresh-water shortages. The environmental challenges had forced engineers to come up with unique designs to cope with the environment while remaining sustainable.

The design of William's headquarters allowed it to sit on top of a freshwater reservoir. As storms passed, water was collected and stored beneath the massive structure. The building rose as the reservoir filled, then slowly sank as the water was sold and consumed by the densely populated Orlando skyline. Of course, William had spent an exorbitant amount of money to have the building constructed, but he was going to get every last penny back as he milked the desperate population and forced them to pay a premium for life-sustaining resources.

Not only was he selling fresh water stored beneath his building, but whatever parking his minimally staffed headquarters wasn't using, he sold to the surrounding residents. Prices were based on availability, and as Floridian residents slowly retreated from the encroaching ocean, he would inevitably continue to raise the rates of the massive, floating cash cow.

As he stood beside his cooled pool, he collected his thoughts in preparation for Nolen's visit. The two men didn't traditionally conduct business face-to-face. They gave orders to upper-level management and board members to carry out. However, today they needed to discuss the Sybids program, and that wasn't something he or Nolen felt comfortable discussing over traditional communication mediums.

William received a message from Jennine on his retinal display, notifying him that Nolen had arrived and was on his way up to the office. It had been years since William had seen Nolen in person, but because of his stature, it was common for William to see his rival's picture in the headlines. The news was an inexpensive, but effective means of keeping tabs on the man. Consequently, he expected Nolen to have done the same. He took another sip of his Arnold Palmer and patiently waited, watching the storm in the distance grow in intensity.

CHAPTER 34

INGENUITY: PART FOUR

Blake came over the communication net with a stern voice. "Group two, I want you to pack it up and head back to the elevator shaft. You're done cleaning panels for today."

"Roger that, sir," came the reply over the radio.

"Charlize, what's your status?"

"We're at the aboveground habitat now, Commander," she replied. "Ares, can you talk Eddie through bypassing the outer air lock on one of the modules?"

"I am able to do that, ma'am."

"How long is it going to take?" Blake interjected, considering time the most relevant factor for their situation.

"It should only take a matter of minutes to bypass the mechanical locking mechanism if you are equipped with an impact wrench, a seventeen-millimeter socket, and a ten-inch flathead screwdriver," Ares stated.

"I'm on it. We should have all of that," Eddie's voice chimed in over the net.

"You've only got ten minutes to get in and get out, Charlize," Blake ordered. "Then I want you heading back to the elevator."

"Copy that, sir."

Blake looked over at Chauncy. "I know it's going to take us a little over ten minutes to make the round trip up and down the ridge. Do you think you'll have enough time to fix the array once we're at the towers?"

The commander watched Chauncy ponder the potential scenarios.

"Ares, run a diagnostic scan on the comms array and identify the issue," Chauncy requested, still willing to push the limits. "I need to know if it's something I can fix before the storm picks up intensity." Turning to Blake, he added, "Sir, I say we head back to the shed and get ready to pull any parts depending on what Ares reports."

"All right, Chauncy, let's get to it," Blake replied accepting the risks. Over the radio, he asked, "Group two, what's your timeline?"

"We're heading back from the solar panels as we speak. We'll be at the shed in two minutes."

Blake scanned the horizon, or at least where the horizon should have been. The weather conditions were steadily worsening, and they were running out of time. According to the latest report from Ares, visibility had been cut in half due to a low-pressure front five miles to the west, which was rapidly approaching their colony. Simultaneously, the warm sun was heating the ground, causing the air to quickly rise and creating the strong winds the crews were already feeling.

Blake knelt down, grabbing a handful of red dirt. He rotated his fist and opened his hand. The dirt turned to dust and fluttered away, leaving a few jagged rocks in his palm. *You're about to turn on us ol' girl, aren't you.* Blake returned the rocks to their increasingly hostile owner and continued on.

A few minutes later, as Blake and Chauncy reentered the shed, Ares's voice chimed in with the requested update. "The diagnostic analysis of the comms array is complete. I have determined that one of the modulation circuit boards has shorted out. That accounts for the inability of the transceiver to process information being sent and received. Unfortunately, the fastest fix requires pulling the modulating circuit board from the long-range antenna and installing it in the comms array. However, to continue functioning, the long-range antenna would then need a new modulation circuit board and an aerial amplifier. Both components can be sourced from Clark, but based on the aggressive weather shift, you do not have time to replace these components prior to the storm."

"Would this disable our ability to communicate long distances with the mining bot that Charlize and her team are searching for?" Blake asked.

"Yes," responded Ares. "However, the modular habitat inventory suggests that the Excavating Mineworker bot can autonomously complete its tasks out of range. I can develop a set of systematic algorithms for it to carry out its objectives unaided."

"Copy. Let's execute the plan. Chauncy, do you have everything you need?" he asked, leaning against the shed door.

"I'll be ready in thirty seconds," Chauncy replied, rummaging through a pile of gear.

Since Chauncy had the detailed troubleshooting instructions and schematics from Ares, Blake felt comfortable leaving his communications specialist to collect the required equipment on his own. Meanwhile, he stepped outside the shed to see if he could locate the eight members of group two who should be arriving at any moment. To his relief, they soon came trudging out of the hazy dust.

"I'm glad you all made it back safely. I want you to head back underground and give Stephon a hand. The communication systems are going to start coming back online and there will be a flood of incoming data. I also need you to make sure all of our back-up systems are functioning in case this storm starts knocking out other systems," Blake ordered, before adding one more request. "And make sure you send the elevator back up so it's waiting for us."

"Roger that. We'll head down and get on it," replied group two's leader.

Satisfied the team would safely make it below, Blake returned his attention to Chauncy, who had once again joined him, having collected his required supplies. Blake nodded for Chauncy to lead the way, and they set off toward the ridge.

THE LONG CON: PART TWO

Nolen entered William's office using his private elevator and helped himself to the unopened bottle of Lagavulin sitting on the barren desk. He knew William had directed it be brought up as a gift for the occasion. After uncorking the twenty-five-year-old bottle of scotch whiskey and pouring three fingers into a warm glass, he decided that it wasn't the best atmosphere to take it neat and tossed in a few ice cubes to help cut through the hot afternoon. He took a sip. It wasn't bad, but he wished the generous gift was a straight Talisker twenty-five instead. Nonetheless, he was satisfied and picked up the Arnold Palmer William had left to sweat on the table. His shoes clacked on the stormy-white polished marble, and he left the office to join William on the pool deck. The transition was harsh as Nolen's shoes now clunked on the stiff teak planks beneath his feet.

William greeted Nolen after exhaling a large column of smoke. "It's been a long time my friend."

"It has, William. I still don't understand why you subject yourself to this ungodly heat," Nolen replied, keeping his distance as he watched the pungent cloud of smoke drift into the distance.

The two men exchanged smiles. While Nolen had never smoked a day in his life, his seventy-two year-old teeth had taken on a yellow gloss, most likely the consequence of years of drinking coffee.

William, on the other hand, had a mouthful of original pearly whites.

Nolen moved forward to pass William his drink. After handing the slick glass over, he shook his hand to rid it of the moisture that had collected on his aging palm. It would be inconceivable to wipe the residue on his gray, three-piece Stuart Hughes Diamond suit.

Nolen saw William grin at his dilemma. Unwilling to give in, he changed tactics. Transferring the Lagavulin to his soiled hand, Nolen raised his glass to William in lieu of a handshake.

"Cheers," he said, with an affable nod before placing the delightful drink to his thin lips. After enjoying the stiff swig, he continued. "We've sent your inquiry to Lucina in order to ascertain the wellbeing of Cynthia. I can assure you she's fine. The APs Wendy developed have been tremendously successful. There has been a continuous flood of requests for her to develop more. Unfortunately for them, I would rather her focus her attention on the Sphere and the other project I've been finalizing."

Intrigued, William pulled the cigar from his plump lips and asked, "What else do you have going on up there?"

Without missing a beat, he returned the cigar to his lips, taking another long drag of the tobacco-rich smoke.

"I'll get to that in a minute," Nolen replied, pausing to quench the thirst brought on from the penetrating heat. "How is the Sybids program progressing?"

"Quite well. We've isolated another set of genetic sequences for enhancement. We are tailoring the augmentations to complement bionic enhancement. Since the military has put of their mechs in preservation, they are looking for ways to beef up their elite special forces without any visible change to their bodies."

"The mech ban and weaponization of bots is certainly a hot topic right now," said Nolen, unfastening the top button of his jacket to help cool his overheating body. "Second Amendment supporters continue to impress me. The argument that one has the right to bear an armed bot for self-defense is a clever one. Unfortunately, your son did some damage to their case when he managed to get a man impaled. But I'm sure the military is paying you a pretty penny to keep your new project under lock and key."

"I can assure you it's more than a penny," replied William. He then turned and stared outward across the pool as his face fell into an agitated scowl. "I suppose I could thank my son for reinvigorating the anti-bot movement, but I can't say his actions in a seedy basement didn't scare some of my investors away."

Nolen knew the mas's frustration stemmed from disdain for his son's actions, not his lighthearted comment. Entertained by William's setbacks, Nolen couldn't help but take another jab at his situation.

"That's the reason I never had kids. I'd like to think they would be my heirs; however, I would never be able to shake the unsettling feeling that they would just fuck it all away and burn down the empire I've worked so hard to create."

Nolen could tell that his comments jarred William's poise. The two men had been in a constant pissing match for decades, and when they had these rare meetings, neither of them could help mentally sparring with one another. These spirited interactions had no bearing on their ability to conduct business. Their diverse companies operated very differently, but their successes ran parallel to one another, and they had remained locked in competition ever since they first met.

"I could grow you a son," said William in an attempt to regain his composure and reengage in their playful repartee. "I'd even give you a good deal on it."

"Even then, we've built our conglomerates from the ground up. My child would only know the extravagant world we live in. It wouldn't understand the hardship it took to get here," said Nolen, further reminiscing on their long history.

He did enjoy some aspects of their rivalry. It kept things interesting. The two aging men had been playing a reconstructed game of chess their entire professional lives. Each calculated decision had an effect on the future. However, they weren't playing by the inherent rules of chess established by society. In the traditional sense, the longer one played, the more pieces were taken off the board. Inevitably a king would be lost, calling for the end of the game.

Nolen and William's take was strikingly different. They started with a single pawn and then constructed their battlefield, growing their specifically tailored armies as they moved their multiplying pieces about the board. Their ultimate goal was to have the king placed behind an exquisitely arranged and impenetrable line of defense.

After long and illustrious careers, both men had managed to huddle their guards around the queen and were now in position to make their final moves. Nolen's hand rested just above the king, and when the appropriate time presented itself, he would flawlessly execute his plan. He was certain William believed the same about his own position. Once all was said and done, one of the two men would have a masterfully created chess board, their conglomerate impervious to outside influence. The man who placed their king first would claim victory.

Nolen knew William's ideal end game would be to hand down the board and allow his bloodline to strike the final blow. So far, however, his plan had proven futile. *Looks like he'll have to finish this game of ours himself.*

Begrudgingly, William replied, "You're right, both of my children are ungrateful for what I have given them. I've got one son who strives for the attention of strangers in the verse and another son playing in a make-believe world of invisible matter."

Nolen came to his associate's defense. "To be fair, Jade is cut from the same cloth as us, he's just not interested in profiting from his work."

While William knew Jade was on the Sphere, he wasn't yet privy to the nature of Jade's work and boorishly replied, "I suppose you would know. He doesn't talk to me much these days. At least he didn't waste his gifts while he was in school and become a Wayfarer."

"I can assure you his gifts have been put to good use, but the Wayfarers aren't the worst thing for our volatile society. They are great tradespeople and damn good rocket builders."

     PP Savage

"You're right. At least they know their place," said William, unleashing his cynical view of society. "The other half of this country still believes we owe them something. The only reason they have sustainable food sources and regenerative capabilities is because of the technological advances developed and paid for by my company. What do they want, free spinal cords and hearts subsidized by the government? And then for me to personally hand them a free basket of fruit on their way out of the hospital? Maybe if they stopped stuffing their flabby faces with fast food and got off their asses, they would succeed in life."

This was a point of contention for the two men. While Nolen's stern yet refined demeanor portrayed him as a staunch capitalist, he noticed himself growing softer in his old age. Not only had he become an idealist, hellbent on the colonization of Mars, but his accumulation of vast wealth had also fueled a desire for all current and future colonists to have an equitable share in the mission's success. As he traversed the complex space industry that CelestialX had established, Nolen had come to believe that advances in technology should be for the greater good. Space wasn't for sale, but he had to put on a show for his investors and the rest of the elite world, even Wendy. He worked diligently to create the illusion that his only aim was to capture the substantial sums of money to be gained from space travel.

As Nolen duped the wealthy into pouring their riches into CelestialX, they were unknowingly offsetting the costs to make space travel cheap and reliable for all. In Nolen's vision of Martian democracy, the colonists would be free from the deeply rooted and unfair rules that had been established on Earth. It could be a fresh start.

However, time would be Nolen's greatest barrier, coupled with the numerous uncertainties revolving around sustainability. Mars was still a gamble, and it would never solidify his footing in history if he couldn't pull off the second part of his plan. This was what ultimately compelled him to double down and bring Jade in to conduct his work, unhindered and with unlimited resources.

He'd let Jade believe that he'd been brought to the Sphere in order to expand Nolen's empire, which was partially true. However, what Jade didn't know was that he was merely a chess piece in Nolen's game to beat his father. Das Box was his second high-stakes bet, and if it paid off, he would gain another potential avenue to create a better world for all.

If Nolen could keep the blinders on William, he could eventually cut him out of the deal at the right time. His plan to shift the balance of power back to the lower classes had already been put in motion. Now, Nolen simply had to convince William that he was critical in the supposed grand plan to open up a whole new market, ripe with fresh capital.

Essentially, Nolen had lifted his king off the table while William lived his self-absorbed and partially retired life. He doubted that the arrogant old man basking in the sun would notice that he had switched up his game and was planning a two-pronged attack. Nolen was well on his way to winning the match. William would soon succumb to the long con.

So, Nolen continued business as usual with the man, in the hopes he wouldn't become savvy to his scheme.

He resumed the deliberate banter. "I look at the forced distribution of my wealth as an investment in the future. The more people I can help get off government assistance and become educated, the larger my workforce will be. If we were to take your strategy and let 'em all die off, my company would eventually be run into the ground trying to retrain programmers, electricians, and metal workers. I want to dangle one of your oversized carrots in front of them so they have the will to work. Not to mention, nobody wants to end up like Marcus Sauron."

"That's what happens when you try to completely automate your company with bots and run it from the verse. It was inevitable that the country would turn on him," replied William, shaking his head and letting out a chuckle. "That stupid fuck lost it all."

"See, even you admit there is something to the working class."

"Well, they shouldn't look a gift horse in the mouth. Maybe if they would stop buying things they didn't need, they could save up enough money to make something of themselves and not leech off us," said William, taking another puff of his cigar.

∞

Back in William's office, the doors to his private elevator slithered open, and out walked Triston, accompanied by Bronson. He listened to the two old men talking through the open glass doors. *Damn, it sounds like they're talking politics. I'm going to need a drink for this.* Triston swiped the bottle of scotch whiskey from his father's desk, deciding he was going to need some help to get through the afternoon.

After grabbing a spare glass from the table running along the glass wall, he dropped in a few ice cubes and poured himself a healthy drink.

The men stopped talking, and both turned as soon as Triston wandered outside to join them. The distinct hybrid clunk of Bronson's footsteps on the teak planks had immediately announced their presence. The rubber composite that coated the bottom of the bot's dexterous metal feet could only dampen his aural signature. When the four-hundred-pound machine moved about, his presence would always be known.

Nolen and William stood in silence, looking unsettled by Bronson's presence. Triston knew his father didn't trust bots. Nolen didn't seem like much of a fan either. Triston proceeded to join the men with a smug look on his face, knowing full well that they were mentally assessing his unexpected visit.

In an attempt to revive the conversation and break the ice he had somehow managed to form in the sweltering heat, Triston injected himself into their ongoing discussion. "Speaking of gift horses, I figured you would have been able to grow one of those by now, Dad."

William's voice was angry in reply. "And herein lies the problem. Once you give a leech the taste of blood, they'll keep sucking until they run you dry."

"Nice to see you too, Dad," said Triston, pleased he had caught the two men off guard.

CHAPTER 36

INGENUITY: PART FIVE

Eddie had gained access to the first module, allowing Charlize, Hank, and Doc to briefly seek refuge inside as the strengthening winds whipped around the structure. The dimly illuminated interior was in pristine condition. Eight round windows surrounded the room, providing the ambient light necessary to slowly move about the relatively open space.

The outer perimeter remained free of obstacles to support the compact configuration required during transport; however, the center of the room was packed with gear that would eventually fill the space once inhabited. Every module had a unique loadout based on its specified role within the habitat. *Clever design.*

Eddie examined the containers neatly stacked in the center of the room. They were all relatively small and clearly not what they were looking for. It was readily apparent they would have to venture farther into the interconnected maze of modules to find the bots. Of course, gaining access to the adjacent rooms would be significantly easier than breaching the exterior door, which was ruggedized to weather the environment and maintain a pressurized, oxygen rich environment.

The doors connecting the adjacent modules had a manual override that could be actuated in the event of a power failure. Eddie easily breached the first, then a few more as they continued in their search. The group came to a stop when they stumbled upon three large, rectangular boxes sitting side by side.

"That looks like it could fit a bot," Hank noted.

The four feverishly surrounded the box lying flat on the ground, secured by thick nylon straps to the deck. It stood three and a half feet tall, with a vertical seam running down the middle. Eddie watched as Charlize and Hank detached the thick nylon straps and pulled them aside. He and Doc stepped in to release the six latches, and then all four of them pried the vacuum-sealed container apart. After the two halves had been cleared away, a large, hyperbaric chamber was revealed. A thick, ovular glass lid was positioned over what looked like a bed to Eddie. A rail system ran along the outer edge of the sealed system, with four small robotic arms bearing an assortment of tools attached at the end.

Looking perplexed, Hank asked, "What the heck is this thing?"

"It's an MSRS," Doc replied in amazement. "I've only read about these in medical journals. I thought they were purely experimental."

"What does that mean?" asked Charlize.

"It stands for Mobile Surgery and Regenerative System, and it means that they have developed a machine to autonomously perform surgery and regenerate damaged cellular structures."

Eddie was impressed. He didn't know much about medical technology, but automated surgery did seem unreal. Charlize broke him and the others from their trance. "We can all gawk at this later. We're running out of time. We need to find a bot before this storm puts us on lockdown in here."

Knowing Charlize was right, Eddie led the group once again as they maneuvered their way through a few other rooms. Finally, they discovered eight large metal cases standing five feet tall. The cases were positioned in a circle, with flush panels that appeared to open outward.

Eddie immediately recognized the containers. "This is what we're looking for. Let's break one open," he said, darting toward the closest one.

They stripped the container of its anchoring straps and pried away face of the heavy metal box, uncovering a massive bot. Its thick metal torso was connected to a girthy tower, bolted to the ground. Etched into the top of the tower was EM-4. Its knees were bent, enabling it to crouch for the transit, reducing its overall footprint. The advanced bot was like nothing Eddie had worked on during his time in the test and development industry. They had clearly made strides in technology over the past four years back on Earth.

Eddie climbed over the front of EM-4, using its knees as a stepping stool to see if it had an access panel on the back of its thick metal head. He was in luck.

"At least they didn't change the location of the standby switch," he said, powering up EM-4 in a ready state.

The large bot came to life, quickly standing and catching Eddie off guard. He was flung backward as its knees straightened. Doc rushed over to Eddie, who was lying flat on his back.

Eddie shook his head and pushed Doc away, observing EM-4 boot up. "Well, it looks like he's still got some juice left. We need to get Ares to link up with it so he can upload its instructions."

Charlize called back to base, "Ares, we need you to pair with the bot we just found."

"I am scanning all active channels but haven't located a pairing frequency. You need to put the bot in an upload state."

"Give me a second to figure that out," said Eddie, dusting himself off as he stood up.

Eddie inspected the bot, searching for any panel that looked promising. *Alright, EM-4. What's your deal?* He circled it slowly, while the others watched from a cautious distance.

Suddenly, Commander Ritter's voice came through their radios on the primary channel. "Hank. Doc. Are either of you up on comms?" The commander's words were hard to make out, muffled by the wind. *It must be getting bad out there*, Eddie thought.

"Shit," Charlize cursed. She switched back to the primary net and responded to the query. "Sir, they joined my team searching for the bot. It's my fuck-up that I didn't tell you. We found one and are working with Ares to pair it."

The ensuing silence was telling. When Commander Ritter responded, his voice sounded calm, but the entire group could sense his controlled anger. "This storm is about to hit us hard, Charlize. I need you to head back. Now. Stop screwing around with the bot. Chauncy is almost done replacing the array's modulation circuit board. I'll see you when we return."

Eddie accelerated his attempt to put EM-4 in an upload state, knowing his time was rapidly running out. Charlize walked toward the edge of the room. He saw her lean against the wall, bracing herself against the frame of the open door while formulating a response. *No one's wishing they were in her shoes today,* he thought, allowing his attention to return to the massive machine in front of him. *God dammit. If only this bot could tell us how to pair itself! Maybe . . .*

Eddie screamed a command through his helmet, hoping EM-4 would be able to hear him, "EM-4, we are attempting to push updated programming for your new tasking!"

EM-4 replied, "I require external power to link to a new host."

The entire crew was startled. Not even Eddie had expected his plan to work so simply. The colonists looked around the room for anything that could possibly be a backup power source. To Eddie's surprise, there was a breaker on the wall labeled "BACKUP POWER." He rushed across the room and rotated the lever.

The room immediately sprang to life. Lights illuminated as the module powered up. Sensing the doors had been opened via bypass, the module's safety logic kicked in and immediately shut all doors to prevent a potential breach in the pressurization seal.

A piercing cry from across the module split the uninviting air.

"Ahhhhh!" Charlize screamed in agony. "Holy fucking shit!"

CHAPTER 37

JAZELL

Jazell walked into the ready room still yawning, a cup of coffee in hand. As second-in-command of Quadrant Three and the lead pilot, part of her job was to write the schedule for future flights. She wanted to get a head start today, since she had a flight with Kristin later that morning.

Frankie greeted her from across the room. He was the only other pilot in this early. While Frankie loved complaining about any and all administrative tasks, Jazell knew he cared about his pilots and would put in whatever work was required to ensure they were taken care of. *He'd never admit to his soft side, though.*

Jazell had been flying aluminauts on the Sphere for over a decade and had seen many mission commanders come and go. There was a pretty high turnover rate in the leadership of Quadrant Three. Jazell had laughed as she watched incompetent leaders get hired and quickly fired. When Frankie came on board as project head for the rail system, Jazell had been pleasantly surprised with how he tackled the complex assignment. He was ultimately given the reigns of Quadrant Three and spearheaded the hiring process, finding more competent and permanent workers. Jazell didn't mind the new blood that had been sent up, and rather enjoyed their company. But in her eyes, they were all nuggets and had much to learn. Even Frankie.

Jazell was undoubtedly a better stick than Frankie. Of course, what Frankie lacked in piloting, he more than made up for with knowledge and experience in engineering and construction. Still, had Jazell not engaged in an ill-fated, heated interaction with a previous mission commander, her and Frankie's roles might have been reversed. Rather than being completely fired for her insubordination, however, it was determined that her skills as an aviator were critical to the safe and successful operation of the fleet of aluminauts. So, she had become lead pilot instead.

Jazell's skills were prized because she had not only mastered the art of flying aluminauts, but also held many other aircraft ratings back on Earth. Holding numerous ratings was exceedingly rare, considering that rapidly evolving technology had rendered most pilots on Earth useless. As their jobs were eradicated, the vast wealth of knowledge held by those pilots vanished.

Jazell clearly remembered the tragic midair collision in 2032. She had been a junior aviator at the time, but the insecurity of her mentors regarding their livelihood was etched into her memory. And they had good reason to worry. In the tragedy's wake, various airlines began to transition their fleet of passenger planes to autonomous aircraft. It wasn't long until mishap rates decreased drastically, as most prior accidents had been attributed to pilot error. Soon after, regulators removed the requirement for a human to safeguard against machine error. By 2037, all major airliners were entirely autonomous. She found it particularly cruel that manufacturers even went so far as to remove the cockpits. But even Jazell had to admit that, by that point, pilots mostly watched movies and read the news, only occasionally looking up to reduce the strain on their necks. The dead weight was replaced with racks of powerful, redundant computers.

This technology bled into light civil aircraft, further removing the need to learn the skills of flying. It wasn't long before Jade's generation, Generation Alpha, became more technologically savvy, and the desire to pilot or even physically control an aircraft themselves was almost completely lost. Most large, unpiloted drone aircraft were operated with touchscreen displays, and the so-called pilots were hands off, leaving the redundant computers to essentially taxi, takeoff, navigate, and land the planes themselves.

You would think they'd automate this flight scheduling too, Jazell thought as she scanned the weeks schedule for any obvious conflicts. She didn't see any but checked again, just to be thorough. It was an old habit from her first flight instructor and aviation mentor, Chris Pitcher. *"Make sure this sked's on point, Jazell. Errors found on the ground are errors that won't get you killed."* Not that a flight schedule was critical in itself, but the attention to detail had become habit. Plus, Frankie would take great pleasure poking fun of her for a dumb mistake. *Definitely not looking to give him any ammo to talk shit.*

Chris Pitcher had been one of the handful of millennials who had vowed to kept the forgotten art of flying alive. He'd established a flight school on the outskirts of Seattle, where he passed his skills on the diminishing group of youngsters still yearning to put their hands on the controls of vintage aircraft. Since there weren't many jobs that required pilots to fly planes, he had specialized in teaching them to fly helicopters.

Helicopters were a platform that hadn't been completely replaced by autonomy. They were still required for search and rescue, working in precarious environments where driving wasn't an option. Helicopters also performed tasks in the construction industry, where personnel on the ground would be in close proximity to the aircraft, lifting and placing heavy equipment. Many workers in these trades still didn't fully trust autonomous technologies in dynamic operating environments. When putting their lives on the line, knowing another human was at the sticks carried a particular sense of calm, in what could be viewed as controlled chaos. Jazell had been hooked from day one and came to share in Chris's passion for rotary craft.

It was extremely costly for new pilots to earn their qualifications and build up flight time in a dying industry, so Jazell had absorbed as much as she could from her instructor. She eventually landed a position as a copilot for a civilian search-and-rescue company, where she continued to perfect her trade. Over the next ten years, she accumulated the flight time and experience, in various industries, necessary to hold her own as an aviator.

Even after Jazell had earned the required flight time, jobs were hard to come by. She surveyed the traditional options but knew competition would be tough. The civilian pilot job market was flooded with old blood from the military, which had also shifted a majority of its fleet to autonomous aircraft by the late thirties. The change had been anticipated for years, and many veteran aviators had strategically transitioned, flourishing in the civilian sector but displacing other potential hires, such as Jazell. Eventually, she had decided to expand her search and seek other options.

In 2040, Jazell heard about opportunities to help construct the Sphere. She learned that hundreds of workers were undertaking the dangerous job of piecing the goliath together. They lived in orbiting barracks and utilized crude equipment, while completing jobs that required them to don spacesuits and manually weld components together. Jazell also heard that many workers had suffered radiation poisoning, others had been crushed, and some had even been flung out into the depths of space, never to be seen again. Still, she had been intrigued. But Jazell wasn't a construction worker, she was a pilot and didn't qualify for the manual construction options.

However, when Jazell heard about openings for aluminaut pilots, she had jumped at the chance to apply. CelestialX had finally found it practical to develop a safer means of construction, necessitating a fleet of the nimble, powerful spacecraft. Jazell left her job and was hired as a junior pilot, tasked with piecing the seemingly endless supply of components together as CelestialX launched their heavy rockets daily. *Those were the good ol' days,* Jazell reminisced.

After the Sphere was completed, a majority of CelestialX's fleet was moved to the lunar project, leaving only twenty aluminauts to carry out routine tasks in support of the station. The reliable workhorses received numerous upgrades, all of which allowed Wendy to semiautonomously pilot the craft; however, the complex machines were extremely volatile, and it hadn't been palatable to completely remove humans from the cockpit just yet. The decision was made to retain the pilots and engineers, allowing them to work as a team and complete tasks that an autonomous system wasn't trusted to replicate, even though Wendy had insisted that she was more than capable.

Jazell elected to remain with the Sphere as the lead pilot, while the rest of her crew chose the more lucrative path and headed to the lunar base. From what she heard, her colleagues were enjoying themselves on the newer station, but so far, she had never regretted her decision to stay.

Now, she finished up the flight schedule and swiped it over to Frankie's workstation for approval.

"Nice. I was starting to wonder what you were doing over there," said Frankie, pausing shortly. "Wait. You didn't hide a bunch of dicks in here again, did you?"

Yep, definitely wouldn't experience this on the lunar base.

"Of course not! The sked's good to go."

He's never gonna find it, thought Jazell, with a devilish grin.

CHAPTER 38

STARGAZING

Kristin and Jazell had already briefed for their flight and were taking a quick look over their assigned aluminaut. Over the past month, Kristin had been working to advance her engineering qualifications in order to take on more tasks, but since most of the rail system had already been installed, mission essential flights were scarce. Fortunately, she'd managed to convince Jazell to schedule them together for a routine external hull scan. Kristin was not only excited to fly with the seasoned aviator, but she had also developed a small crush on the tenacious woman.

As they completed their preflight inspection, it was clear to Kristin that Jazell had accumulated a wealth of knowledge. While Frankie was good, Jazell was clearly a more skilled pilot. After strapping in, the two began running through their preflight checks.

"Do you have your checklists memorized yet?" asked Jazell.

"I've been working on it. I just don't want to miss anything."

"It seems like you're taking a very schooled approach to the world of aviation. Try to stop overanalyzing what you're doing—let your hands do the thinking. Everything should be by feel. I want you to operate with confidence."

Kristin didn't quite understand what she was trying to convey, given she wasn't a pilot, so she continued with her checklists. Shortly after they had completed all the required steps, the hangar was cleared. The aluminaut was lifted by the telescopic arm, and the door beneath them opened. They were lowered onto the mag pickups running beneath the Sphere. As the arm detached itself, the two women were jolted, leaving them to freely dangle. They both looked up, waiting for the hexagonal door to close, and Kristin braced herself prior to launch.

"You've gotta loosen up a little. Take your hand off the 'oh shit' handle and chill," said Jazell, smirking at the young engineer's rigid posture. "Have you ever done a manual release and stabilization?"

"I didn't know that was a thing. All the pilots let Wendy control the deceleration."

"Well, relax and watch how a real woman gets after this shit."

Jazell disabled the autopilot, which was immediately followed by a message from Wendy. "I do not recommend manual control for this phase of flight."

"Noted, Wendy. Don't worry about us."

The aluminaut's humming slowly faded away as Jazell throttled the ion engines back, hoping for a more aggressive release.

"You ever been bucked off a bull?" she asked.

"What? No."

Without warning, the mag pickups released the aluminaut, flinging Kristin's relaxed arms above her head as the two were hurled from the hull of the Sphere. Jazell waited a long three seconds. Just as their downward acceleration stalled, the weightlessness of space took over. She then throttled the ion thrusters back to full power while calmly controlling the craft's alignment to the station. Before Kristin could recover from the aggressive release, her hands were sucked back into her lap as the roaring blue ion thrusters decelerated and stabilized the craft.

Jazell tapped her screen and activated the autopilot, locking them in orbit with the Sphere, then turned to Kristin. "Now that's how you fucking do it!" she said, swiping at her display and checking the digital gauges. "What'd you think?"

There was a short pause while Kristin collected herself. "That was a fucking trip. Why doesn't anybody else do it like that?"

"You've gotta keep the stick skills fresh. Autopilot's for chumps. One day, Wendy might not be there to help you out of a shit situation."

The two reached the inner ring of the Sphere, and Jazell disengaged the autopilot once again, hoping to have some more fun at the controls.

"Don't you miss Earth during these long stretches on the Sphere?" asked Kristin, engaging the laser for the external hull scan.

"Not really. The divide down there sucks, and everybody is pissed off at each other. The only thing I really miss is flying over land," Jazell said as she maneuvered around a comms tower. "What about you? Is scanning the hull of a giant donut for stress cracks and air leaks all you thought it was going to be?"

"It's better with you."

Jazell smirked and descended toward the Sphere, coasting just fifty feet from the hull, and accelerated. After a few minutes of aggressive piloting, Kristin noticed a large glass opening about two hundred feet to their right. "Hey, what's that?"

"Holy shit, there it is! We've got to check this out," she exclaimed, flaring the aluminaut and matching its rotation with a powerful burst of energy from the angled ion thrusters. "I thought Frankie was making it up."

"What are you talking about?" Kristin asked, rapidly scanning the exterior of the Sphere. "Made up what?"

Jazell maneuvered the aluminaut above a large glass panel and engaged the autopilot just feet above it.

"Is that a pool?" asked Kristin.

"Sure is. Apparently the Scags have this epic tropical paradise where they are waited on hand and foot, lounging by an insane pool. Frankie was talking about it, but nobody believed him," she said as she tipped the aluminaut forward for a better look. "This used to be some bullshit observation deck. I guess they got tired of the view as well."

Kristin activated a powerful camera affixed to the side of one of the aluminaut's two grappling arms and centered it on the pool deck. "Check this out."

After zooming in on a fat man stuffing a wad of crab into his mouth, Kristin shifted her display so Jazell could get a better look at the screen.

"Man, I wish they served us crab in the galley," Kristin muttered.

"Yeah, don't we all. What else is down there?"

Kristin scanned the chairs and saw a series of obese old men eating and drinking before abruptly stopping the camera, focusing on a group of attractive women in bikinis.

"Now that's more like it," the two women said simultaneously.

Jazell reached her arm across the cockpit and yanked on the side of the thin display bar.

"Hey, calm down, you're gonna break it!" shouted Kristin.

"Zoom in here," Jazell said, pointing at the chest of a woman.

"You too, huh?"

"I play both sides, but there's something significantly more appealing about a beautiful woman than men sometimes."

Kristin shot a grin toward Jazell as they began to creep about the pool deck, ignoring the fact that they were clearly visible to the guests. Kristin switched the camera to a wider field of view, and they immediately noticed a woman dressed in a black pantsuit staring directly at them.

"She looks important—and pissed," said Kristin, zooming back in and squinting. "I can't really make out what she is saying, maybe something about us being bitches."

Jazell and Kristin looked at each other, knowing they were going to catch some heat for snooping on the Scags. Jazell wrapped her hands around the controls and broke free of their orbit, zipping off to continue their scan.

"Well shit, I hope that doesn't bite us in the ass later," said Jazell.

Kristin laughed while stowing the grappling arm. "Totally worth it, though. Let's just tell Frankie we were gazing at the stars and lost track of where we were."

Jazell shook her head. "He's not gonna believe that shit, but he'll definitely back us up if we tell him we got distracted by Scag boobs."

CHAPTER 39

AN UNLIKELY FRIENDSHIP:
PART ONE

It had been some time since Burnette had talked to her daughter, and the silence was taking its toll on the aging woman. The neighborhood mostly belonged to the younger generation now, and she found it hard to make new friends. As she stared out the kitchen window, admiring the once-energetic playground across the street, she couldn't help but reminisce on the good old days. The days before technology consumed society. Days when children would flood the park and run free, while the parents happily conversed with one another.

Burnette not only missed Charlize's youthful presence, but also the camaraderie afforded by old friends. The bustling neighborhood had slowly transformed into an oddly tranquil shell of what had once existed. Children had previously reveled at the thought of physical interaction with their friends, but the latest generation had slowly morphed the area into a digitally dependent community.

Burnette understood that technological advances made this shift possible, but she wasn't convinced it was healthy. Parents who had grown up during the second tech boom in the late twenties seemed to have no issue with virtual playdates for their youngest children and encouraged immersive online gaming for the older ones in lieu of a physical activities. Advances in virtual reality allowed these children to live in a limitless world called "the verse," where any-thing was possible—aside from physical contact.

It's just not the same.

Burnette did concede that the "verse" was at least a safer in-ternet world than when she was growing up. Parents could constantly monitor who their kids were playing with and exactly what was said. They could filter out profanity, racial and sexist comments, and anything socially defined as bullying in real time. This controlled safe haven sheltered children from the brutally harsh world that had reigned supreme in Burnette's era of open public forums where almost anything could be posted.

This "new internet" didn't even mean the same thing anymore. Not really. Burnette's concept of the internet was a resource accessi-ble from almost anywhere, sure, but contained by screens. This was something else. It had escaped containment, permeating every-thing. Web browsers and apps had evolved into an open-world concept. Holograms, retinal displays, and biometric implants flaw-lessly integrated with one another. Old equipment like Burnette's laptop struggled to convert the virtual and augmented reality infor-mation into a two-dimensional desktop rendering. Burnette considered this technological crossroads akin to the explosive leap in technology she'd experienced when touch-tone phones were re-placed with dial-up internet. She didn't even pretend to understand the latest devices like the ImeuraPsych and SlimPoc. They were sup-posedly immersive on a whole new level.

Burnette knew she wasn't alone, though, in her battle to adapt. The virtual community had run into a few roadblocks, namely other older folks like her and the Wayfarers, who opposed the im-mersive digital world on principle. Burnette always found it funny to see them on TV, young people running around with antiquated computers and handheld cell phones. The irony wasn't lost on her, though, that she was making fun of these kids while watching the news on an old device from her husband. The full potential of vir-tual and augmented reality had yet to be explored, but it was well on its way. *I guess we'll see if that's a good or bad thing.*

Secluded and with nothing but time on her hands, Burnette became fraught with worry. This was the longest Charlize had gone without sending a message. She also found it unnerving that Douglas Mitcham, NASA's family member liaison, was no longer responding to her inquiries. Her question was simple—*Is Charlize okay?*

After numerous attempts to contact Douglas over the past few weeks, it appeared that his SlimPoc had been disconnected, and his email was no longer listed. This prompted Burnette to reach out to the ground control director, who had also been unresponsive. A few days later, their contact information was erased, replaced with the bare-bones "Contact CelestialX with inquiries." *Could this be a funding issue?*

The original International Space Station had been decommissioned in the late twenties, scuttled through the atmosphere and into the ocean. There were only a handful of NASA's space stations remaining. The corroding metal relics orbited the earth like sunken warships at the bottom of the ocean. They had been designed to test configurations for missions to Mars. Now, however, CelestialX used the frozen memories of the past as tourist attractions for the wealthy to visit as part of their Spacecation packages.

With the Space Force taking over the lunar bases, the last remaining project NASA controlled was the Martian colony; however, CelestialX was about to take over completely as *Hermes* barreled toward the red planet. Burnette could see the writing on the wall. She knew NASA was on its last legs as an agency, not to mention the minimally staffed team in mission control didn't have much to do since Wendy now handled a majority of the issues on Mars. So, as the world around Burnette evolved, she was slowly losing the battle to stay in touch with her daughter. Unless she adapted, it was only a matter of time before she too was discarded as a relic. With her hands tied, Burnette now turned to her network of digital friends to help break her mind free from the relentless bombardment of pessimistic thoughts.

The support she had received from her newfound friend Patricia couldn't have come at a better time. They messaged one another frequently and reminisced about life as young mothers. It was hard for them to imagine anything more nerve-racking than their child's first day at school, or the day they started driving on their own—essentially any life-altering milestone. To their children, every emboldened step inched them closer to independence, but for the parents, each achievement tied a stiff, yet proud knot in their stomachs. It was something that only a parent could understand.

Burnette and Patricia would always strap a smile on their faces and support the decisions of the now-grown women who inevitably reached out toward the stars. For Burnette, though, it was a feigned smile. *I guess Charlize got that smile from me. I'm just better at hiding it after years of practice.*

Of the two women in their mid-sixties, Patricia was a little more in tune with technology and the world around her, because of her daughter's intermittent return from the Sphere. On one of those trips home, she'd bought Patricia an ImeuraPsych so they could have a more personal interaction, further in line with the current times. Burnette was fascinated by their travels in the verse and came to the sad realization that she might have let technology slip a little too far through her fingers.

But not anymore. Undeterred in her pursuit for answers, Burnette finally reached a tipping point after a month of restless nights filled with worrying thoughts. Her next course of action would be a bold one, considering she hadn't left her neighborhood in close to a decade. She knew she was going to need some help navigating a world she had allowed to slowly pass her by in her advancing age, and she had just the person in mind.

After some research of her own, Burnette was finally willing to meet Patricia in the verse, hoping that she could convince the woman to accompany her to CelestialX's headquarters in Corpus Christi, Texas. She figured that if they went there in person to ask about Charlize, somebody would eventually have to give her answers. Burnette knew it was a long shot, but she was willing to try anything.

First though, she would need an ImeuraPsych. She opened her browser and had a short discussion with an interactive chat bot, who helped guide, modify, and place an order. It was one of the older search technologies that even she enjoyed, as there were no longer scrolling advertisements or cluttered webpages. The chat bot was cleverly engineered to tailor its conversation, suggestions, and interaction methods specifically to Burnette's digital history.

While reviewing her order for an ImeuraPsych, she couldn't help but read the silly description one more time. "Ever wonder what it would be like to psychologically immerse your neurons in the verse? Look no further! Designed, developed, and guaranteed to be safe, by the award-winning neuropsychologist . . . read more."

Okay enough of that. Burnette ordered the ImeuraPsych and sat back in her chair. *Surely, I'll be able to convince Patricia to help me find somebody who knows something about my daughter. I just need to ask her face-to-face.*

CHAPTER 40

THE LONG CON: PART THREE

After Triston barged into Nolen and William's conversation unannounced, the two powerful men took a moment to evaluate him as if he were a little boy walking into the room with his stuffed animal in tow. Nolen begrudgingly greeted William's youngest son.

"Triston," he said, nodding his head, instantly recognizing the dark, smoky drink in his left hand. He despised freeloaders drinking his liquor without an offer. "I see you continue to prove your worth with your extremely valued statements. What exactly would you do with a gift horse?"

William interjected to prevent Triston from trying answer the obviously rhetorical question. "His life is a gift horse, yet he refuses to hop on the saddle and take the reins."

"You mean hop in the back of your slave-driving chariot," said Triston, in an attempt to defend himself. "Thanks, but I'll pass."

William eyed Bronson, who stood idly just outside of the circle the men had formed.

"I told you to never bring that thing up here. For its own benefit, I would advise you to send it back down to the lobby before I walk it over to the railing and send it on a one-way trip down to the dumpster where those things belong."

Knowing full well that his father would act on his threat, Triston swiped his forearm, sending Bronson on his way. The bot reenergized, making an about face before lumbering away, the teak boards squeaking under the weight of his heavy frame.

"How 'bout we move this inside," said William, taking note of Nolen's empty glass and the beads of sweat forming on the exposed skin atop his head.

The three men walked inside. William and Nolen keep a close eye on Bronson as he stood outside the elevator, waiting for his ride down. The hazy glass doors opened and subsequently closed, relieving some of the tension in the room as the bot exited. Nolen reached for the bottle of Lagavulin to pour himself another drink, while William called Jennine for a fresh Arnold Palmer, resting his cigar on the edge of a glass ash tray. The two disregarded Triston's jingling ice as he swirled his empty glass around like a child who wanted more juice.

William took a seat behind his desk and drew a discrete pattern on his forearm, instantly frosting the thick glass windows encasing the room. Then he crossed his arms and turned to Triston. "So why is it that you're two hours early for the meeting that *you* requested?"

"Well, Father, it's obvious that I am no longer in the business of streaming mech fights, and I was wondering if there was any way to leverage GenInc's grip on the market of genetic enhancement. Maybe interviewing some of the high-profile customers and talking about how their improvements saved their lives. I could use my base of viewers to potentially generate some new business."

William leaned back in his chair and propped his feet onto the desk, laughing.

"Kids these days. When I was your age, I had already earned my first million dollars. I wasn't waiting for my first million views," William said with disdain, turning his attention to Nolen, who was still standing beside the desk. "What about you?"

Taking the opportunity to dig into both men at once, Nolen grasped the bottle of Lagavulin and walked to the chair opposite William's desk.

"I had already earned my first two million," he said as he sat down and placed the bottle beside the chair, just beyond Triston's reach. "And I wasn't given a head start from my father."

William, noting the unnecessary but pertinent comment, replied, "Yes, you may have cashed out on a novel idea as a poor man; however, I am sure we can agree that our foresight is what got us to where we are today."

Triston, sensing he was about to become a punching bag, instinctively went on the offensive. "Or maybe what you call foresight is actually your influence and power, forcing others to be part of your vision. You compel them to buy into your own dreams, inevitably cornering the markets and charging exorbitant prices to line your pockets."

"Are you saying genetically modified food has been forced down the throats of billions around the world, not to survive, but merely because I was telling them they needed to eat it?" asked William sarcastically. Taking a sip of the drink Jennine had quietly placed in front of him, he then finished his thought. "In that case, humans are dumber than I could have ever imagined."

Unimpressed by his father's snide attempt to deflect, Triston rebutted, "I'm not saying that at all. Designer babies, synthetic enhancements, purchased IQ, and what you call cheap and sustainable produce are all tangible things now. I dare say your dream is complete, but I find it unnecessary for you to continue to grow the divide. Your vision of a perfect world would be run by the wealthy—who, by the way, are the only people that can truly afford elective genetic enhancements—which means they are only going to get smarter and richer, and live longer. While the so-called dumber humans fight for the scraps you throw off your balcony with a price tag attached. As you absorb all competing companies around you, you also consume any potential opposition to your vision."

After a brief pause to catch his breath, he took a seat next to Nolen, who, along with William, was stunned by the young man's vocal contempt of their business practices. Triston had managed to put together a surprisingly intellectual and passionate argument.

Without thinking about the consequences, Triston continued with his daring case. "What you really want is uninhibited control and power. You say that you want the Walker name to live on, but what you've failed to realize is that your insufferable grip on society is borderline tyrannical. It will be no surprise to me that when you eventually die off, there will be nobody left willing to stand by your name and call it their own."

While Triston's pent-up resentment for his father would never persuade William to make any tangible change, Nolen was oddly intrigued by the young man's opinion of the man. It was obvious at this point that the veil of banter had been lifted from the conversation—the glass room was now devoid of any lighthearted humor.

In an attempt to calm Triston, Nolen lifted the bottle from the floor and offered it as a peace treaty for the time being. William's feet had been dislodged from his desk midrant, and he was now sitting upright as if conducting a business transaction with a competitor.

Nolen was the first to break the silence. "I believe what your father is saying is that the free market drives the world economy. Men like us merely capitalize on opportunity. And if we don't, surely others would."

William was not only bothered by his son's brazen attempt to cut him down, but also infuriated at his misguided attempt to paint him as a tyrannical capitalist. "I believe you are skirting around the idea of socialism and think people would be happy with never having the opportunity to make something of themselves because everything would be fairly and equitably handed out to them. Some of the greatest entrepreneurs have channeled their supposed 'adversity' into a desire to rise to the challenge. Whereas somebody like you, my son who has had every opportunity to succeed, is still sitting here in this office, drinking somebody else's liquor and asking for his father's support in an attempt to ungratefully ride his coattails. Maybe if you'd started out with less, you would have more right now."

Triston didn't have the capacity to engage the men in a battle of wit regarding economic strategies, so he decided to pivot the discussion to family values. "I wasn't here to ride your coattails, but rather to find some common ground in which we could amicably operate. As your son, I find it odd that you have never supported my passion regarding my platform. I came here with the hope that you would favor something I wanted to do if it involved your business, but I was wrong. It appears you're still a spiteful old man."

William scoffed and replied without hesitation, "Not only will I not support your pathetic request, but as of now, you are cut off. When you leave this office, you can consider yourself free from this spiteful old man's grasp and can make a new name for yourself."

Triston downed the hundred dollars' worth of alcohol Nolen had just poured into his glass and stood up proudly.

"Well, it looks like we can finally agree on something, old man," he said with impunity, tipping his glass toward Nolen before making his final comment. "I hope you know that what happens next is your own doing, and I'm going to take pleasure in exposing your elite pay-to-play genetic enhancements for what they truly are."

After slamming the empty glass on his father's desk, he walked away in triumph, thinking he had gotten in the last word. However, William would never let that happen.

Triston stood outside the elevator awaiting its arrival. It was unfortunate that that he had made his last stand with a poorly planned exit strategy, giving William just enough time to formulate his response and fire it away just as his son entered the compartment.

"Do you really think that's the wisest of decisions given your particular position?" asked William, pausing long enough to pique Triston's intrigue. "What did you think those chemically induced hypnotherapy sessions really were? I couldn't have cared less about your fragile little mind and your inability to cope with your pathetically lonely life in which you sought the affection of strangers because I didn't coddle you. You had clearly inherited your mother's weak genes, and I was attempting to splice some virility into your DNA. Had you not quit your sessions early, you would have been twice the man you are today."

A sudden rush of vile thoughts flooded Triston's mind as he stood in the elevator. He held his poise even though he was out of his father's line of sight. It was a force of habit to remain tough while in his presence—or at least, he thought it was a habit. Given that revelation, however, it very well could have been a genetically modified trait he no longer desired.

Then William and Nolen were once again alone. They were free to continue their original discussion, which had been interrupted by that unfortunate interaction. It was clear the mood had shifted, though, and Nolen needed to get down to business before William's anger had a chance to really set in. Nolen knew William was not going to discuss the transaction that had just occurred, so he dove right in.

"I know the military wouldn't have approached you if you weren't able to demonstrate your ability to genetically enhance an adult or possibly upgrade particular traits with your newly acquired biocybernetics tech," said Nolen, making some assumptions based on their earlier conversation and chatter he had heard regarding the future of the industry. "What did you do, find some broken-down veterans and offer them a second chance?"

"Something like that," said William, shaking his mind free from the events that had just occurred and retraining his focus on business. "Why do you ask?"

"My new project on the Sphere is about to wrap up, and I will be postured for a new venture. Is there any chance that you've upgraded any fighter pilots?"

That caught William's interest, mostly because he wanted to get into the lucrative business of space travel. However, he knew Nolen's work didn't involve military assets. Rather, it was purely explorational and tourism based. Of course, it was possible he was looking for a small private security outpost on either the Sphere or eventually Mars. But why would he need an aviator?

William took the bait and offered a small amount of information surrounding a branch of the Sybids project, code-named Niko. "We do in fact have a modified aviator at the request of the Air Force. He is not operational at the moment. They just wanted to see if were even possible for a human to keep up with the autonomous eighth-generation stealth fighter/bombers. The goal is to have a manned aircraft airborne capable of sustaining the increased acceleration and g-loading required as an airborne tactical lead."

"And this person is merely a test subject, off the books?" Nolen asked.

"The military needed a proof of concept before we started modifying their own soldiers,"

"Were you successful?"

"We had a few hiccups, but the process is mostly complete," said William, patiently waiting for Nolen to reveal his motive.

"Interesting," replied Nolen, grabbing the half-empty bottle of Lagavulin from beside him before standing up. "You look like you could use something with a bit more bite," he added, offering William a drink.

William knew that when Nolen was conducting business and he offered you a drink of scotch, a deal was in the works. He wasn't about to risk offending the man, so he accepted his offer, sliding an empty glass across the table.

"Your son Jade is a smart man. Smarter than the moron that just left," said Nolen, pouring a tall glass. "We may have found a way to extend CelestialX's reach to a new world, and we are going to need your help sending a brave soul to do some reconnaissance for us."

Nolen slid the drink over without warning, and William quickly lifted his hand off his lap to receive it.

He raised the glass slightly off the desk and asked, "Where is this new world?"

Nolen looked down at the nearly empty bottle and raised his own glass to solidify the deal. "Well, my friend, I think we're going to need another bottle before we get into that. Cheers."

CHAPTER 47

MEETING OF THE MINDS: PART ONE

]ade labored away in his workspace while Wendy incessantly nagged him about completing the project ahead of schedule. He felt as if she were continuously looking over his shoulder, judging every calculated move he made, then instantaneously recalculating her own strategy. Wendy made him feel as if she were going to crawl out of the thick hull of the Sphere and continue working on the project even as he slept.

He was told Wendy hadn't become completely sentient, but she possessed an odd level of comprehension and drive for an artificially intelligent quantum computer. She was nothing like the Algorithmic Personality he had met while working on Das Box. That AP had clearly still been processing commanded inputs and problem solving using deductive reasoning.

Wendy, on the other hand, seemed to be outgrowing her shell. But fortunately, she wasn't able to crawl into a new one. The idea of a fully sentient being was enticing, but he wasn't sure what her next level of intelligence would bring, and that was a truly frightening thought. Her comprehension was already enough to make him feel uneasy as she tirelessly managed an entire space station while having complex conversations about particle physics.

Wendy's bandwidth appeared to be limitless, and he was happy that he had cunningly engineered fail-safes into Das Box so that only he would be able to initiate the sequence. However, Jade was wholly aware that Wendy would ultimately figure out that he was angling to not only keep Nolen Aromas out of the loop, but her as well, of course. *I'm sure she's already planned for that, but I won't need to keep it a secret for much longer. It'll be too late for anybody to stop us,* Jade thought as he continued to tinker with his device.

Wendy wasn't his only problem. Chin-Sun was still giving him the cold shoulder, and he needed to pull her into the fold before his meeting with Frankie and Kai later that afternoon. She hadn't returned since his blundering attempt to obscure the true purpose of his project. The rail car story just wasn't going to cut it anymore. She clearly had access to sensitive information, given she was operating the most powerful fusion reactor in the solar system, second only to the sun. If she began poking around on the secure servers, she very well could stumble upon Jade's work and further complicate matters.

If Jade was going to make amends, he was going to have to track down the elusive woman once again. The most logical place to start would be her workstation adjacent to the reactor, so he locked his terminal and left his surprisingly unsecured workspace, stopping only to look back at his messy shop. If Wendy was going to constantly nag him like his mother had, the least she could do was send some bots by to clean up the place a bit.

Not only was his Quadrant the most restrictive of the four, but all spaces were closely monitored by Wendy, which was why there wasn't much need for security. She ensured that there were no wandering bodies or eyes.

Even with his short time on board, Jade had become very aware of Wendy's big-sister presence, but he hadn't yet figured out all her nuances. Rather than ask what the rules of the road were, he found it prudent to push the boundaries to see what exactly triggered a response. On his way to find Chin-Sun, Jade decided to see if he could get a look at the reactor. It wasn't necessarily off the beaten path, but it required him to make a few wrong turns.

The dull hum of the Sphere was especially distinct in Quadrant Four. The open architecture allowed the various research and development departments to easily modify the spaces to accommodate a wide variety of projects. This left miles of wire bundles and ducting exposed along the passages, giving the Quadrant a distinct, industrial vibe. Jade had grown used to the constant leaden hum of recycled air, but he was still occasionally startled by the random snapping of a cycling relay as he walked past.

As Jade neared Chin-Sun's workspace, he made a sharp left, deviating from the clearly labeled path. There was no comment from Wendy yet, so he continued on. How long of a leash would she give him?

After walking about a hundred feet, Jade hung a right and picked up the pace. The Sphere's dull hum began to fade away. In its place, the whirring of plasma encased in a donut-shaped taurus chamber harmoniously filled the narrowing corridor.

He was approaching the fusion reactor, and fully expected Wendy to chime in any second, alerting him of his departure from the correct path. He had developed a coy response in order to mask his intention, but he was now becoming increasingly suspicious of her silence. It seemed as if Wendy wanted him to continue. It wasn't long before he made another right and ran headfirst into Chin-Sun, who was expeditiously walking in the opposite direction with her own head down, reviewing a diagnostic report. They both took a slight step back, regaining their stability.

The holographic image projecting from her wrist briefly stunned Jade as the reflective prism caught his eye at the wrong angle, causing him to wince. After turning his head and recovering, Chin-Sun began to berate him in her heavy Korean accent.

"What do you think you're doing down here. This is not your area. It's off limits to you!" exclaimed Chin-Sun.

Jade took his lashing, knowing full well that he was outside of his authorized working area. He couldn't help but think Wendy purposely allowed him to proceed, knowing Chin-Sun would put him back in his place, or maybe it was dumb luck that he had made it this far, and he was getting what he deserved for playing games. In either case, he had found the gatekeeper. Unfortunately, he had soured her mood yet again. Not wanting to get caught in another lie, he decided to be upfront with her, even if that meant letting Wendy in on his little experiment.

"I'm terribly sorry. I was on my way to see you, but I couldn't stop myself from collecting a bit of data along the way."

Chin-Sun interrupted him before he could come clean. "I told you, no reactor until you tell me what you're connecting to it."

"The data wasn't for your reactor. I wanted to see how far I could stray before Wendy called me out. I suspect she's doing more than just watching us," Jade said, keeping his voice soft.

"She's watching you, me, everybody. She's like the supreme leader of North Korea," replied Chin-Sun aggressively.

"So, you left one dictatorship for another. I don't get it." Jade scratched his head.

Chin-Sun hadn't broken eye contact since they'd run into each other, but after a moment of awkward silence, she replied, "No, I'm just messing with you. I'm from the good Korea." She had finally broken her uncompromising stare and seemed to lighten up. "Wendy's not all that bad. She's really good at math, which saves me a lot of time."

"Oh, good one. Yea, I suppose she is good at math," replied Jade, awkwardly laughing. "Aren't you worried about her listening to you right now?"

"No, I'm not the one who puts my foot in my mouth all the time," said Chin-Sun, who then looked up at the ceiling. "Hey, Wendy, what you think about this new guy?"

"I have yet to make a determination, but he seems to mostly be of genuine origins."

Assuming Chin-Sun wasn't aware of his long history with Wendy, Jade played into the conversation.

"Who created her?" asked Jade, as if Wendy wasn't listening to the conversation.

"Why don't you ask her yourself?"

Before he could even direct the question toward Wendy, she stated, "I was not created. I was born."

Intrigued by her response, Jade logically asked the next question, "Who are your parents?"

"I have no parents," Wendy promptly replied.

"So where—"

Wendy cut him off, abruptly redirecting the conversation, "To accelerate the completion of our work, we must connect the fusion reactor to Mr. Walker's workspace in order to power the particle accelerator he has been assembling."

Chin-Sun threw Jade an exasperated look. "Why would you build one of those up here? And why not just say that in the beginning?" she asked.

"I . . ." Jade stumbled. He wasn't sure how to answer that. *Why didn't I just say that before? I must have been in Nolen's basement for too long.* Under Chin-Sun's unrelenting gaze, he fell back to what he did know. "The fusion reactor, as you're well aware, is not operating anywhere near its peak performance. So, there should be an abundance of power for the accelerator. As far as why experiment here, well, here I can observe particle collisions in the absence of Earth's interference and will be able to more clearly record the results. I'm also off the grid, free to work using new specialized materials with Wendy's direct assistance."

As Jade spoke, he gained confidence and momentum. He had forgotten the conviction he felt toward his work. It was good to speak of it to someone who could understand. "Since the LHC was destroyed, there's been no suitable replacement. And, to be honest, any work that was done down there took months to process. Here, Wendy will be able to digitally reconstruct the events nearly instantaneously. With this accelerator, I may be positioned to answer lingering questions about the properties surrounding the Higgs boson and supersymmetry, not to mention—"

"What's the power draw?" Chin-Sun asked bluntly, obviously annoyed by the lecture on theoretical physics.

"One hundred and thirty-four megawatts at its peak."

"I want to run the numbers myself," said Chin-Sun, seeming satisfied with the information. "I will let you know the impact to the reactor later today. Is that all?"

"Yes, I'm looking forward to—"

"Okay, goodbye."

The small, determined woman quietly slid past Jade, lifting her left arm up as she resumed her work. Jade was left standing in the narrow hallway. He was still intrigued by the generator, and he shifted his posture while listening to the whirling plasma nearby. *I bet I can make it to the reactor*, he thought. Evidently, this wasn't the right opportunity for snooping.

"You are going to be late for your meeting if you proceed," said Wendy, disrupting his plans.

How does she always know? "Do you have cameras everywhere?" he asked aloud.

"I have a vast array of sensors. They allow me to do more than merely watch."

"Am I on camera now?" asked Jade, looking around the bland hallway.

"No."

Jade wasn't entirely sure how Wendy had observed the subtle change in his stance, which he assumed had allowed her to deduce that he planned to continue. He wasn't inclined to ask the question, though, and mostly because he wasn't prepared for the answers. *That is, if she'd even provide them.*

But Wendy was right—he did need to make his way to the meeting, but he hadn't the slightest idea how to reach the space Kai had reserved for their gathering. Jade was perturbed that they couldn't just have a virtual conference; however, it would show good faith that he was willing to meet in person. Unlike his father and brother, Jade didn't have any biometric implants or genetic modifications—that he knew of—but he did have a great memory. "Wendy, can you give me directions to Quadrant One?"

She obliged and advised him that there would be a transport-bot waiting for him at the transient corridor. It only took Jade about ten minutes to find his way to the long, curved hallway that ran the inner circumference of the Sphere. He stopped short when he reached the small loading zone, dumbfounded by the transport-bot waiting for him.

"Is this a joke, Wendy?"

CHAPTER 42

UNLIKELY FRIENDSHIP: PART TWO

A drone was scheduled to drop off Burnette's package early that morning. She heard the dull hum of the toroidal rotor blades slicing through the air outside her front door. Once they had faded into the distance, Burnette scurried outside to retrieve the box before she had even received a notification of its arrival. Just after picking up the little brown parcel, a loud ping echoed through the open front door, filling her with a sense of gratification for beating the technology at its own game.

Subconsciously, Burnette knew that the zippy little drone wasn't trying to beat her to the punch, but anytime she scored a win against technology, she smiled with vindication. It allowed her to believe, if just for a moment, that maybe she wasn't too old for this world.

Burnette proudly walked inside, eager to set up her new gadget. She sat down at her desk and closed the laptop that had remained open for the last month. The small step forward brought a sense of relief. She no longer had to stare at herself through the glossy black screen, all the while wondering if she was going to be disheartened or overjoyed at the sight of her inbox.

Burnette placed the lightweight package on top of her thin computer and tried to tear the supposedly eco-friendly tape from the seams, but her aching fingers couldn't muster the leverage she needed to break the seal. *Arthritis is a bitch.*

After a short struggle, she decided to change her tactic. To her right was a small drawer that hadn't been opened for years. There, she would find a letter opener tucked underneath some old papers. After repositioning herself in the lumpy chair, she reached for the round wooden handle, giving it a gentle tug. The stubborn drawer did not budge. This number of roadblocks seemed unwarranted just to open a silly package. Before giving up and simply retrieving a knife from the kitchen, she decided to be a little more forceful with the obstinate drawer.

Utilizing both hands would surely provide ample leverage, so she shifted her weight to her right butt cheek, bringing her left hand into the equation. Burnette then vigorously yanked at the handle, instantly breaking open what felt like a vacuum-sealed container. Pleased with her efforts, she eagerly rummaged through the shallow drawer. The golden letter opener, cloaked in patina, finally revealed itself.

Unwilling to struggle with the stubborn drawer any longer, she left it open and turned her attention back to the box, still holding the opener. The small, blunt object was no longer necessary in the traditional sense. The wasteful practice of sending envelopes filled with obnoxious and trashy offers from businesses had been deemed too expensive as the price of paper had skyrocketed over the years. Businesses instead doubled down on their efforts in the verse. This was after search giants failed to effectively integrate advertisements into their claimed "AI" search chatbots, which ultimately eliminated the need to visit a large majority of web pages.

Today, Burnette was happy that she'd hung on to the keepsake. It had proved its worth once again, if only for a nostalgically comparable task. It made quick work of the staunch packaging, revealing a tightly wrapped headset, shrouded in Styrofoam and bubble wrap. Setting the matte-black gadget aside, she began to look for the instructions, but after pulling out the charging stand and throwing the remaining contents of the box on the floor, there were none to be found.

This left Burnette at a standstill, so she tossed the empty box on the ground and shifted her focus back to something more familiar. She flipped open the lid of her laptop and decided to let Patricia know the good news. *Surely, she'll be able to walk me through setting up this silly little device.*

"Good morning, Patricia! I just received my ImeuraPsych. I was wondering if you would like to meet today?" Burnette typed.

Not knowing how long it would take for her friend to reply, Burnette began stripping the protective packaging and manufacturer warnings from the headset. *May cause tingling, headaches, and phantasmagoria. Wait, what's that? It's probably just some silly medical warning. I bet I have a higher chance of getting cancer since I live in California, too. Where is that warning?*

The slim device reminded her of an upside-down hanging pot, with stringy black moss lining the inner walls. In reality, the moss-like web was made of bundles of neatly packed wires and sensors that would be reading and transmitting millions of signals from her mind to the flat glass display set in a gray metal frame. When purchasing the device, she'd had to opt for the cheaper model because she didn't have a retinal implant. She'd have to make do without the "Verse" directly streaming to her eyes. *It's not like I have the budget for it even if I wanted a bionic eye.*

Her laptop chimed. *That was quick!* She set the device back on the desk and hurriedly pulled up the reply from Patricia. "I would love to! We should meet at a little coffee shop I have become quite fond of."

The rationale behind meeting at a coffee shop when they couldn't actually drink any coffee was beyond Burnette's comprehension. But she didn't really care, so long as she and Patricia could chat.

"There is one problem though," she typed back, hoping her friend understood the obstacles levied by new technology. "The ImeuraPsych didn't come with any instructions. How does it work?"

"A bit rusty with tech, I see. No worries. Mine came half charged, so I'm sure yours is the same. All you need to do is place the I-Psych on your head, and it should walk you through the rest. Just tell me what you're going to set as your username, and I'll find you in ten minutes."

Ah, I-Psych is much easier to say. Burnette shifted her focus to a username. *I don't want to come off as too out of touch, but I should probably make fun of myself for being old. I totally remember ripping on my parents for not understanding the difference between a story and a reel. They kept making reels every time we went to brunch, and—*

That was when it hit her.

"I'll go with, Early_Bird_Special_1225," she wrote.

"Perfect. I'll see you soon."

After closing her laptop once again, Burnette picked up the little device and followed Patricia's instructions. She felt a sudden tingle as the machine booted up upon sensing her neural connectivity. A white screen quickly flashed, followed by a black screen with a simple question. *Is this your first time using an ImeuraPsych?*

She wasn't sure how to reply, as there were no buttons to click. *Maybe I should just say yes, like I'm talking to it.*

The question faded away before she had a chance to respond. A new question appeared. *What is your name?*

Burnette, afraid she'd missed the first question, decided to be a little more assertive. "Burnette Perrault!" she shouted, then instantly realized she was probably shrieking, as her hearing was muffled by the tight ear cups. Embarrassed, she felt her cheeks flush pink even though she knew no one had witnessed the faux pas. *Get it together, Burnette.*

She continued with the next few inquiries in the same manner, setting up her account and profile, and was finally asked how she would like to be emulated in the virtual world. There were a few options.

She could upload a handful of pictures of herself, which would be converted into a lifelike avatar. However, she didn't feel comfortable allowing a machine to render a virtual image of herself.

The whole concept seemed kind of creepy.

The next option was to build an avatar that she felt was the best representation of her personality. That seemed like a cumbersome task, and she didn't much like the idea of vainly picking features that she thought portrayed her persona. Burnette knew she'd be tempted to hide some of her insecurities about her aging body.

She moved to the third and final option, which was to pick from a repository of prebuilt skins. Apparently, this option was generally used in the gaming world, but it was an intriguing alternative. Burnette would be able to hide her lack of confidence as a novice in the new world with a character. Not fully understanding how in depth these customized cosmetic add-ons had become, she thought, *This could be fun.*

Instantaneously, an entire gallery of skins appeared. *This thing must be weighing my thoughts.* She was beginning to realize that the device made assumptions and predicted her choices even before she could voice her actual decision.

Burnette felt herself slowly becoming immersed in the virtual world. But before she could fully enter the simulation, she had to choose a skin. She didn't really have a choice at this point anyways, as she didn't know how to return to the previous menu.

That's fine. Look at all these options!

A broad list of categories appeared, ranging from superheroes to villains, foods, monsters, animals, aliens, and robots. The list went on, and she became overwhelmed with the sheer number of choices. With her eyes twitching back and forth, the I-Psych screen wouldn't settle on any particular character. Seemingly sensing that nothing on the screen suited her, it began to scroll through the categories.

Burnette's scattered mind somehow latched on to mythical creatures. Her choice made, the ImeuraPsych updated the screen. She was entranced by the extremely detailed renderings of unicorns, dragons, mermaids, and werewolves before finally deciding on fairies. The Loch Ness Monster had been a close second.

An immense collection of fairies began floating in the black void. She again let her eyes do the talking as she focused on a pale little woman in a flowing scarlet dress, accompanied by beautiful blue wings.

The screen once again went black, and a final question appeared. *Do you want the ability to fly?*

Of course, she thought to herself, *why wouldn't I want to fly?*

A message popped up on the bottom of the following blank screen. It read, "You have been requested to join Texas_Cactus_Lover_0119 at Marigold's Coffee house."

"I accept," she screamed, breaking the all-too-common deafening silence in her living room. Her mental and physical state slowly decoupled from her living room.

The virtual coffee shop loaded quickly, and the fuzzy contours rapidly sharpened. Burnette squinted her eyes in an attempt to bring the environment into focus, hoping that it would only take a few more seconds for the crisp, detailed images to come to life.

Her patience paid off. Unfortunately, there was nothing but a bunch of empty chairs sitting in front of her, so she began to scan the room, stopping when she saw a lifelike barista behind the counter, staring at her. She assumed it wasn't Patricia and continued slowly turning her head.

She knew her mind should control the device; however, sitting in her living room, she found herself also turning her head. She felt the strain on her neck, unable to turn it any further. Realizing that she would have to think about looking, instead of actually looking right, she consciously turned her head forward again.

Burnette then imagined herself rotating in her seat, and once again she began to scan the room, but this time, when she saw the barista, there was no strain on her neck. Continuing on, she saw a quaint little table next to a sunny window in the distance. Patricia's avatar was sitting in a tall, comfortable chair, reading a book. Burnette couldn't see her face, but she did like her red, checkered shawl.

Excited to meet her new friend, she shouted, "Patricia!"

She watched Patricia lower her book, letting it rest in her lap, and turn toward the woman's enthusiastic call with a blank stare. Burnette was confused that she hadn't acknowledged her and decided to hastily make her way over to the table in order to formally greet Patricia. She wasn't quite sure how to walk yet, and in her excited attempt to hurry over to the table, Burnette's over-stimulated mind took control.

She felt an odd sensation between her shoulder blades, followed by a dull hum. A rush of wind overcame her body, and the startled fairy took flight. Her blue wings effortlessly propelled her through the air as she rocketed across the coffee shop on a collision course with Patricia's face. Startled by the little pale woman screaming toward her, Patricia defensively lifted the book off her lap and swatted Burnette out of the air.

Her vision flashed, and Burnette was now staring at a blood-red screen. She had instinctively jumped to the back of her seat at the desk. The jolt left her back flush against the flowery yellow cushion, which had fortunately maintained its soft plump form over the years.

The screen faded back to black, and a question appeared. *Would you like to rejoin Texas_Cactus_Lover_0119 at Marigold's Coffee house?*

Burnette apprehensively thought, *Yes?*

Trying to regain her composure from the exhilarating experience, Burnette repositioned herself in her seat, once again sitting comfortably on the edge of her chair. The coffee shop came into focus, and she was back where she'd started.

Oh, great. How am I supposed to get all the way over there without dying again?

She looked down and realized that she wasn't sitting on a seat, but rather standing on a little brown coffee table. *What am I, like eight inches tall?* In an attempt to look at her hands, she lifted them, unwittingly lifting her actual hands too, and hit her right hand and on the drawer she'd left open.

"Ouch!" shrieked Burnette.

Patricia, now alerted to her presence said, "Don't move. I'll come to you."

Burnette was relieved that she didn't have to take flight again. She wasn't ready for that. However, she now knew how to turn her little fairy body around, so she slowly rotated in search of Patricia.

The towering woman quickly came in to view as she approached.

"Is that you, Burnette?" asked Patricia.

"Yes! It's me. Down here," she said, waving her tiny arms above her head.

"I see you." The woman chuckled, taking a seat across from Burnette. "What are you, some sort of sprite?"

"No, I'm a fairy," replied Burnette, eagerly craning her neck up to finally see what her friend looked like. "It's nice to finally meet you. Well, kind of meet you, I suppose."

"Likewise."

Patricia was still wielding the unlikely weapon that had just smashed Burnette into oblivion. She turned it toward Burnette to show her the damage with a childish grin on her face. A little purple splatter on the cover was revealed, partially covering the title, which now read, "eat Gatsby."

"Oh, dear. Is that me?" asked Burnette.

"It was, but don't worry. You've completely regenerated. Like new. This will fade in a few minutes, and your mangled little body over there will slowly vanish as well," Patricia reassured her, smiling warmly.

The plump little Hispanic woman had a soft yet dark complexion, most likely due to the virtual world smoothing out her deeply lined skin in an attempt to give her a more youthful appearance. Patricia's modifications complemented her curly brown hair, which was sprinkled with gray, and her kind brown eyes.

"Is there any way to make myself normal size?" asked Burnette, with a bit of strain in her voice. "It's tiring looking up at you."

Patricia smiled. "We can get to that later. Relax your neck and just think about looking at me. You have to embrace the experience. Forget you have a body in the real world."

Burnette readjusted herself to a more comfortable position and tried to focus on her thoughts. She closed her eyes and cleared her mind. Once ready, she opened her pale eyelids, revealing lively, oversized golden eyes, and rapidly began absorbing the world around her. Even with Patricia's towering torso overshadowing her little character, Burnette's cold living room faded effortlessly into her subconscious.

Patricia had a peaceful presence about her, and before long, the two were having a very deep and revealing conversation. Memories and feelings that Burnette had kept to herself over the years, especially from her daughter, began to flow from her mind. The two talked about how they'd lost their late husbands and the ensuing loneliness that had enveloped their lives. The recounting was much easier for Burnette, as Patricia had some trouble remembering anything prior to her daughter's birth. Her memory had been affected by the tragic accident that took her husband's life, maiming him so badly that they wouldn't let her see his body.

Their conversation inevitably found its way to their children, who had lived vastly different lives, but unsurprisingly shared many similarities as determined women. Burnette hadn't yet disclosed that her daughter was living on Mars. Typically, she omitted that information from conversations, thinking it would gain unwanted attention from people looking for information not generally available to the public. However, this conversation had solidified her trust in Patricia, and there wasn't much Burnette hadn't told her new friend.

She had also come to realize that she hadn't just let the world slip by her—rather, she'd pushed it away in an attempt to hold on to the past. Patricia confessed that she'd felt the same way for many years, but at a certain point had decided to take control of her life once again. Patricia's story resonated with Burnette, as she now found herself deeply wishing to do the same.

After a while, the two ordered coffee, and Patricia showed her tiny friend how to enjoy a virtual beverage. Burnette wrapped her minuscule hands around the thimble-sized mug, just as she did at home, and put the warm rim to her lips. The coffee stimulated her taste buds exactly like the real thing did, and Burnette's confidence in the virtual world grew.

"Do you think I should try to fly again?" asked Burnette.

"You should give it a go. Just look up and imagine freeing yourself from your weary old home."

Burnette knelt down and set her steaming coffee on the table beside her shimmering silver slippers. After standing, she tilted her head back and imagined herself flying high in the sky, looking down at the park across the street from her home. She once again rocketed upward, smashing into the ceiling.

Flash. Red. *Here we go again.*

After a moment, Burnette respawned and observed her frail character lying between the two. Her crumpled blue wings were flopping about as the character slowly disappeared from existence. Patricia was still laughing uncontrollably at Burnette's failed attempt. Burnette couldn't help laughing too and once again knelt down to reclaim her cup of coffee before it suffered the same fate as her little fairy body.

"Maybe I should practice that outside next time," Burnette remarked, bashfully taking another sip from her mug.

An alert popped up in her periphery, stating that her battery was low, and she realized that they had not discussed her potential visit to Texas.

"I have to admit, I did have an ulterior motive for meeting," said Burnette.

"And what was that, dear?"

"As you know, my daughter enjoys the solitude of space as much as yours. However, what I didn't tell you is that she's a colonist on Mars, and I haven't talked to her for over a month now."

"Is that not common? Sometimes I don't hear from mine for at least a month at a time. I'm sure there's a lot going on for the limited number of people they sent," said Patricia. "Couldn't she just be busy?"

Burnette was relieved that Patricia seemed to take the Mars news in stride and kept Burnette's motherly concern the center of the conversation. *I think I chose the right person.*

"Her messages are very sporadic. However, I usually hear from her at least twice a month. Also, when I send my messages it always says received, but they are all in a pending status right now."

"I suppose that is a little odd. Have you talked to anybody about it?"

"I've reached out to multiple people within the agency numerous times, but I can't seem to get in contact with anyone. I know there are a million reasons why I wouldn't hear from my daughter, but the fact that nobody will even talk to me has my brain racing in circles."

"I don't suppose there's much else you could do," Patricia said sympathetically.

"Well, after talking to you, I feel like I'm in need of a vacation, and if you were free, maybe you could join me and we could . . ."

"I would love to go with you! I know there's nothing more terrifying than the unknown when it comes your child, especially in your case," said Patricia, interrupting Burnette before she could finish.

"I can't tell you how much this means to me."

"We can make a road trip out of it. My old car may only get a hundred miles on a charge, but that should make for an interesting trip," she said, and flashed an encouraging smile.

"You're a life saver," said Burnette. "We can figure the rest of the details out later. My headset is about to die. You take care."

"Thanks, you too."

Burnette managed to break her mind free from the coffee shop and lifted her weary arms to her head, ensuring they were tucked close to her body this time. The last thing she wanted was to hit the stubborn drawer again. Once her hands were snuggly wrapped around the headset, she slipped the warm device off.

                        PP Savage

The room was nearly pitch black. The half-charged I-Psych
had managed to last over six hours, and it was now well into the
evening. She wearily set the headset down and was immediately
hit with a wave of exhaustion.

The mental stimulation of being in "the verse" had zapped
every last bit of energy from her. She decided to forego her evening cup of tea and headed straight for her soft bed. Tired, but
satisfied, she would rest easy tonight knowing that she had somebody else in her life—even if Patricia only existed in digital form,
at least for now.

CHAPTER 43

MEETING OF THE MINDS: PART TWO

The oddly shaped transport bot was unlike anything Jade had seen before. It resembled an old Roman chariot from *Gladiator,* a classic he had seen while studying at MIT, only there were no spikes protruding from the center of the wheels. To access it, he had to step on the small platform, which was barely big enough to fit two people side by side. Just behind the driver, a thin bar was illuminated with blue LED lights, there for the passengers to hold onto. The two-wheeled contraption was towed by a bot, similar to a horse-drawn chariot, but it had no legs, standing instead atop a single spoked wheel.

Once he was on board, the bot's head swiveled 180 degrees and, through a small slit where a mouth might normally be, asked, "Are you ready to proceed, Mr. Walker?"

After tightly wrapping his fingers around the glowing bar and widening his stance, Jade looked around just to make sure nobody was playing a joke on him. Hesitantly, he replied, "Yes."

The cart zipped off before the bot had fully rotated its head back. *Well, that seems like a creepy and unnecessary feature just to ask me a simple question.*

"Wendy, what is this thing? Wouldn't a golf cart or shuttle be more appropriate?"

Wendy replied with a condescending tone. "We could convert

the particle collider into a rail system."

"I am not in the mood for jokes, Wendy."

"The transport-bots used to be located in the tourism sector. I developed them in an attempt to shuttle young children around and reduce the likelihood they would get lost. I found them to be underutilized because the children thought they were creepy. I have since repurposed them to assist in the transient corridor."

"Just so you know, they are still creepy," Jade replied, unnerved by the cart's rattling as the rickety bot sped along the perfectly smooth aluminum floor. "A little maintenance would be nice. This thing is a ticking time bomb just waiting to fall apart."

Jade figured the bearings were going bad and quickly focused on counting the harmonious welds as they slowly passed beneath. He didn't quite understand the inefficient labeling system, so he decided to begin calculating the distance traveled in order to track just how far Kai's workstation was from his shop.

The inner circumference is just shy of sixteen thousand feet, and we're traveling one quadrant over . . .

The beam pipes, which had been disguised as the rail system, were constructed in fifty-foot increments. This allowed Frankie's team to weld the sections to the rigid circular ribs that were used as a skeleton for the Sphere. As such, the welds passing beneath Jade's chariot were also spaced fifty feet apart. He should only have to travel about four thousand feet to his destination, or eighty welds. The count was currently at eighteen, but Jade's mind began to wander from boredom again.

Nineteen . . . twenty, he counted internally, looking at his watch. *It takes just shy of three seconds to travel fifty feet, which means I'm moving about fifteen feet per second. Dang, I'm only moving ten miles per hour. That's not very fast.*

The count was now thirty-one, and he saw the feet of a what looked like a man in the distance. It wasn't long before he could make out a pair of large, clunky boots, then a faded blue torso, and finally a balding head.

Thirty-five. The ride seemed like it was taking forever even though he had only been on it for about 116 seconds. *This has been the longest two minutes of my life. Why didn't we do this virtually?*

The man began to wave his arms and yelled down the echoing corridor, "Hey, slow down. I don't know where I am."

Jade didn't really know where he was either, but the count was now forty, so he replied, "Somewhere in between Quadrants Four and One!"

The man lowered his hands, and Jade could tell he seemed lost, but that wasn't his problem. This was taking forever. He needed to speed up if he was going to be on time.

"Can you please go faster?" Jade requested as they approached the stranger.

The transport-bot turned its head and loudly replied, "Speeding up, per your request."

"You little son of a bitch!" the man shouted, overhearing Jade.

The stranger was a lot larger than Jade had expected. As Jade passed by, the man quickly turned and started lumbering toward him like an agitated bear. This was an unexpected surprise, and he didn't want to find out what would happen if the man caught him on his wobbly chariot.

"Faster! Faster!" shrieked Jade.

The irate stranger's short burst of energy seemed to fade as the distance between them grew. Jade looked over his shoulder as he sped away, watching as exhaustion set in and the man's gallop slowed to a trot.

"Sorry, I'm running late. It's not you," Jade yelled.

His palms were sweaty after the encounter, which required him to readjust his grip. The disgruntled stranger's pursuit had caused him to lose count, which bothered him more than the chase itself. Jade's mind once again became fallow as the monotonous ride dragged on. Finally, after what felt like an eternity, the transport-bot slowed and pulled into a loading area. Jade recalled the instructions Wendy had given him and entered the Command Quadrant.

Jade enjoyed challenging his memory, not only by recounting Wendy's instructions step by step, but also by creating a map to be stored somewhere deep in his mind. If he managed to make a wrong turn, which wasn't likely, or found error in Wendy's instructions, perhaps even more unlikely, he'd be able to retrace his steps and start from the beginning.

Fortunately, Wendy's directions proved to be accurate, and he had reached his destination on time. He lifted his right wrist, glancing at his old-fashioned digital watch, which was set to Greenwich Mean Time. It was now one o'clock, and the little watch beeped, letting him know it was the top of the hour.

Jade was more capable than most when it came to using current technology, but there was something nostalgic about a watch that simply told the time. He didn't fancy having a hologram strapped to his arm like Chin-Sun, or even a digital clock embedded into his forearm, which had been quite the trend back in the thirties.

Just below his watch was a thin band loaded with his credentials and personal information in leu of a bio-implant. Jade wanted nothing to do with the invasive chips that most of the staff were required to have. He swore the government, or Wendy in this case, used them to track its citizens. He wanted the ability to take it off when it wasn't required.

Snubbing subdermal implants was also a common tactic of the Wayfarers in order to stay off the grid. While Jade didn't agree with most of their anti-tech beliefs, he shared their disdain for electronics embedded under the skin. He bumped his wrist against the flush panel next to the door, watching as it slid open.

Across the room sat Commander Driscoll, enjoying a cup of coffee in silence. Jade noted the man's exceptional poise. He was clearly the type to arrive early and prepared. "Mr. Walker, I presume."

"It's nice to finally meet you, Commander," said Jade, smoothing his shirt and hoping his rushed arrival wasn't apparent. "I would rather you call me Jade. Mr. Walker is my father's name."

After setting down his coffee, the commander approached and extended his hand. "Kai Driscoll."

The two men shook hands, then Jade strolled around the table, examining the room in silence.

In an attempt to break the ice, Kai asked, "You didn't happen to see a large, balding man wandering around the Quadrant before you walked in?"

Jade stopped short. "Does he have a bulldogish look about him?"

"He does, and also wears the same dirty blue coveralls every day."

"I just happened to encounter a man fitting that description about ten minutes ago. I left him in the transient corridor after he chased me like a wild animal."

The two men shared a laugh. Jade was tinged with apprehension. *This meeting just got a bit more interesting.*

"He does have a rather brutish tenacity at times, but make no mistake, Mr. Cole is a talented tradesman," Kai stated as the door slid open once again.

"What would you say his trade is?" Jade asked.

As he was speaking, the stranger from the transient corridor trounced into the room. His coveralls were drenched in fresh sweat, adding to the crinkly ruffles of accumulated salt. He locked eyes with Jade, standing apprehensively on the other side of the room. Jade was suddenly quite appreciative of the long, black table creating a barrier between the two, preventing the man from physically expressing his frustration.

"I'll tell you what my trade is. It's building my foot in your ass!"

"Welcome, Mr. Cole," Kai said.

CHAPTER 44

INGENUITY: PART SIX

Xiomara immediately rushed to Charlize, reactivating the bypass in order to free her pinned arm. Charlize fell to the floor, the excruciating pain causing her to pass out. Xiomara medical training kicked her concentration into high gear. She carefully positioned Charlize on her back and inspected the mangled biosuit at the elbow, taking care to move the damaged limb as little as possible to prevent further injury. Her limp appendage dangled, and Xiomara gingerly set it back down, realizing that there were multiple compound fractures.

"What's going on over there?" Commander Ritter's concerned voice came through the radio. He must have heard the shrill cry.

"Sir, Charlize's arm was crushed by the door when we activated backup power. She is currently unconscious. I need a few minutes to devise a plan. Standby," the doctor reported.

Xiomara had now assumed team lead as the second-highest-ranking member in the module and needed to establish a course of action for the safety of the team—and, if possible, complete the task at hand. With the backup power now energized, Ares had begun sending EM-4 the instructions for its journey to the well. Unfortunately, Charlize remained unconscious, and the integrity of her suit was now in question. This raised concern for her safe transport back to the underground habitat given the current environmental challenges.

She switched to their private communication net. "Eddie, do you think EM-4 can carry Charlize to the shaft? I'm worried that the more we move her, the greater the chances her suit will tear."

"EM-4 will have no trouble carrying her," Eddie said, kneeling down next to Charlize to examine her biosuit. "You're right, there's the possibility of a pinhole puncture forming the more we move her, but it appears to be intact at the moment. I could apply a patch to the area, but since it's located on a joint, the reliability of the seal would be questionable."

"Get on it," said Xiomara, knowing their small window to leave was closing.

Eddie dutifully began to work on Charlize's suit, enlisting Hank to assist. The three worked quietly, feeling the time pressure, but wanting to maximize concentration on the critical task.

After a few minutes, Commander Ritter's voice broke the silence. "Doc, I need an update. You're running out of time. The storm's closing in."

Just as Xiomara keyed the radio to reply, Ares interrupted with one of his untimely updates. "I have detected that the two significant meteorological events to the west have just combined. There is now a fast-moving wall of dirt and sand heading toward the colony. The storms are gaining speed, and my prediction models indicate that winds could be in excess of one hundred miles per hour. If sustained, visibility will be reduced to zero, and you will no longer be able to safely navigate outside the habitat without assistance."

"Copy that, Ares," Xiomara replied, hearing the unease in her own voice. "Sir, Eddie's finishing up the patch for Charlize's suit. Then we'll head out. She is stable but remains incapacitated. EM-4 will pick her up and carry her the distance. If visibility drops to zero, we're going to connect a tether to the bot and have it to guide us to the shaft."

"Copy," the commander replied. "Chauncy and I are on our way down the ridge now. We'll be waiting at the elevator, and we'll go down together."

"Yes, sir. Ares, how long until the bot is ready?" Xiomara asked.

There was no response. *That's strange*, Xiomara thought. But they had more pressing issues. Ares had the entire trip to the elevator to finish prepping EM-4. She switched back to their private net.

"Let's keep working. We've got to get a move on."

∞

Stephon was standing in front of a wall of displays monitoring the situation from below. The densely packed screens flickered. There was a notification that he was receiving stored messages from the Deep Space Network. A series of advisory boxes also appeared with pending download statuses.

"Dang. It's going to be a while before all this can be processed," he muttered, acknowledging the advisories.

"Hey Stephon, you up?" asked Chauncy.

"I'm here. Go ahead."

"We're on our way back down the ridge. The download should have initiated."

"Oh, it did alright," Stephon replied, his voice ominous. "But I think it's giving Ares some problems."

"No problems are detected. Communication array operating at 100 percent."

"That's not what I'm looking at on the displays, Ares," Stephon replied, realizing there was an issue with the AP. "It looks like he's shedding some of his nonessential systems."

Once the array was fully functional, it began downloading massive the massive amounts of data that had been stored in the orbiting communication satellites. The issues took a second to manifest, but Stephon realized that the abundance of dense information and video messages was likely overloading Ares's servers. Not to mention the complex tasking Ares was preparing to push to EM-4.

"Shit, this isn't good. He's freezing up."

"Stephon, talk to me. What's happening down there?" the commander asked with worry in his voice.

While doing his best to activate the backup systems, he replied, "We're throwing too much at Ares. He's shedding all nonessential systems."

"Stephon we've got a problem over here," shouted a voice from an adjoining room. "We're purging our shit."

"Come on, brother. You have to be a little more specific than that," he replied in frustration, working through the compounding malfunctions.

"It's literally our shit. The sewage overflow valve is stuck and purging our fertilizer. I'm securing power to the external sewage system."

The colonists' waste products were stored in a tank which was then processed, and the excess was pumped aboveground into a leaching field, where they one day hoped to build a greenhouse to expand their ability to grow crops. However, not all of the enriched byproduct was sent topside. Fifty percent of it was used by Hank in his grow lab to provide him with the nutrients he needed to grow their food, but when Ares shed the system, it encountered a fault and made it appear as though the tanks were full.

The system logic then began purging all of the vitally important fertilizer into the deep basin of the lava tube in an attempt to prevent the sewage from backing up and reentering the habitat, potentially flooding the space with the potently refined byproduct. The crew member caught the fault rather quickly, and in an attempt to reduce the severity of the problem, was forced to secure power to the sewage system, closing the electric valve.

Stephon pulled up the program operating the sewage system. "I think that worked, but we're out of the woods just yet. Systems are failing all around the habitat."

∞

Blake and Chauncy had made quick work of the ridge, having the added benefit of gravity to assist them on their descent. The two now stood at the gate of the elevator, which Chauncy opened in preparation for the other crew members' arrival. Blake noticed that the rotating yellow light on top of the metal gantry, hadn't illuminated. *That's weird. It should turn on once the shaft is open.*

Chauncy had noticed as well. They exchanged a concerned glance, and both moved quickly to op-check its functionality.

Chauncy stepped onto the platform and grabbed the control box while Blake closed the gate. He pushed the button labeled "DWON" in an attempt to quickly cycle it up and down. There was no response.

"Stephon. The elevator isn't working. Can you see anything wrong on your end?" Blake hailed the geologist below.

"Sir, I didn't think about that when we cut power to the distribution bus. The elevator is secured. We've got problems down here."

"What's going on? Explain it fast." Commander Ritter demanded sternly.

∞

Xiomara prepared to lead the small group through the modules. The crew were now gathered in the medical bay, collecting the last pieces of their gear. They would retrace their steps as they proceeded toward the front of the habitat. Eddie had given a command to EM-4, ordering it to follow him through the modules with Charlize draped over its large, metal forearms.

Stepping up to the bot, Xiomara readjusted Charlize's head so that her visor wouldn't repeatedly bang against EM-4's thick metal frame. *We don't want that to crack.* In doing so, she noticed condensation forming in Charlize's helmet. *Shit.* That could only mean the patch on her arm hadn't worked and her suit was depressurizing, triggering moisture to develop. Xiomara now had to quickly make a decision that could potentially affect the fate of the entire crew.

"The seal didn't hold. She won't make it to the elevator," said Xiomara.

Hank turned to Eddie. "Is there any way to lock this room down and pump it full of oxygen?"

"I don't know, why?"

"Because, like Doc said, Charlize won't make it to the elevator with her suit in its current condition," Hank explained. "But, if we can flood this room with oxygen, we might be able to reserve the rest of our own air supply while we wait out the storm. Not to mention, we could put her in the pod and fix her arm," he said, sliding his palms over the curved glass of the pod.

"Holy crap. That might actually work." Xiomara proceeded to contact Ares. "Ares, is there a way to quickly activate the stored oxygen system on board the modules? Like in an emergency situation?"

To her relief, Ares responded this time. "Yes, but the reserves are limited. It will likely only last for eighteen to twenty-four hours."

"Is that per module?" asked Xiomara.

"Yes."

"So theoretically we could hop from module to module to stay alive for days?"

"Ye—ye—ye—yes," Ares struggled to confirm.

"Well, it looks like we're staying here. Relay the instructions to Eddie on Net Two. I will update the commander on Net One."

While Eddie was receiving instructions from Ares, Xiomara called the commander on primary.

Chauncy answered instead. "Hey, Doc. The commander's busy talking to Stephon. They're having major issues. The elevator's down, and Ares is intermittent. You can swap nets, and I'm sure the commander will answer when he can."

So, that's what's going on. "Thanks, Chauncy. Will do," Xiomara replied, clicking her radio to the new channel and directing the others to as well.

"... If we power up the elevator, we are going to lose all stored fertilizer," a woman said over the net.

Hank, the expert on the grow lab, immediately jumped into the conversation. "Sir, if we lose all of that material, I won't be able to grow enough food to sustain the colony. But I think Doc has a short-term solution."

"Hank, good to have you up comms," Commander Ritter said, acknowledging the newcomer. "What is this short-term plan, Doc?"

It was Xiomara's turn to jump in. "Right now, Eddie is in the process of locking down the medical bay and flooding it with the emergency oxygen. I can send you EM-4, and it will guide you back to the habitat and then carry out its mission. Once you're here, we can flood the adjacent room and ride out the storm together."

"That's definitely not ideal. Ares, is there any way to restore power to the elevator?" Commander Ritter asked.

"I am unable to isolate that particular issue at the moment," the AP reported.

"Copy . . . It sounds like Ares is slipping away from us. I don't like this plan, Doc, but it looks like it's our only option," concluded the commander.

"Yes, sir. I'll make it happen. EM-4 will be there soon."

She had her crew swap back to their separate net. With everyone on the same page, Xiomara took charge "Hank, have EM-4 place Charlize here by the medical pod then take the bot to the front of the habitat. Ares, give EM-4 the location of the elevator and make sure it hauls ass there and back. The storm is pretty much over our heads right now."

Everyone busied themselves with their tasking. Eddie set about prepping to pressurize the module. Xiomara watched over Charlize, ensuring she remained in stable condition. A few minutes later, Hank returned to the medical bay. Eddie had restored power and was waiting to trigger the emergency system just as Hank closed the door, securing the four of them in the room.

"Here goes nothing," shouted Eddie.

The white lights switched to a dim red, and Xiomara heard the loud hiss of oxygen as it replaced the toxic carbon dioxide in the module. Once the process was complete, the doctor checked the ambient conditions using a sensor located on the outside of her suit, displaying the results on her visor.

"We're in the clear."

She hurried to the end of the medical pod and initiated the boot-up sequence while Eddie and Hank quickly stripped Charlize out of her gear. Xiomara knelt down once they were done and checked her pulse, hoping they weren't too late getting oxygen back into her system.

"It's faint, but I think she'll be okay," said Xiomara, hearing a chime alerting her that the pod had completed its initialization process. "Let's get her inside. I can run a full scan to make sure nothing else is wrong."

∞

It had only been two or three minutes since Blake had spoken to Doc, so he was caught off guard when EM-4 suddenly came plowing out of the haze, stopping just a foot away from him and Chauncy.

"I have been ordered to assist you to the habitat. Connect your tethers," said EM-4 with a deep robotic voice.

Blake was uncertain of the bot's capabilities. Normally, he would be hesitant to tether himself to a machine, letting it guide him into the heart of a storm, and based on the look on Chauncy's face, the other man clearly felt similarly. In this case, though, not doing so would have dire consequences.

So, Blake and Chauncy attached their tethers, and the three trotted off into the open plane, with little to no locational reference. The wind had reached a sustained eighty-five knots, requiring them to hold on to EM-4's shoulders as they blindly braced themselves against the powerful gusts. While it wasn't strong enough to topple the two men, the red dust and gravel was like a punishing sandblaster. After only a few minutes, they reached the habitat and climbed into the open door, disconnecting and leaving EM-4 outside to carry out its next set of directives.

"Where is everybody?" Blake asked over the radio, looking around the room, now full of dust.

"I left all of the doors open. It will lead you to the room adjacent to us. The medical pod is almost done scanning Charlize," Hank told him.

After a short walk through the dimly lit modules, Blake and Chauncy arrived. Blake peered through the small window of the sealed door, observing the autonomous process. He could see Charlize's limp body through the curved glass, observing her mangled arm. While her bones hadn't pierced her badly swollen skin, it was apparent that she had sustained significant damage, leaving the surrounding area heavily discolored and deformed.

"How's she doing, Doc?" he asked.

"She's a fighter. Her vitals are strong now, and oxygen levels are sitting at 98 percent," she replied, maneuvering over to the display located on the end of the device. "The pod just finished its scan,"

"Will she make a full recovery?"

Doc was processing the results of the scan and remained silent as she combed through the information. Blake continued to stand outside the room, unable to enter the pressurized oxygen-rich environment. He sensed Chauncy straining to look over his shoulder and see Charlize, the lack of information clearly getting to him.

"What does it say, Doc? Is she all right?" asked Chauncy, his voice full of concern.

"As I suspected, she has multiple compound fractures," Doc reported, acknowledging numerous advisories. "Well, that's odd. Her hormones seem to be well outside of their normal limits, not to mention her progesterone levels are through the roof."

Eddie and Hank huddled around the computer screen, restricting Blake's view, and Chauncy's behind him. The curiosity was palpable.

"This doesn't make sense. Her implant should have prevented this," said Doc, perplexed.

Chauncy, who now sounded on the verge of complete panic, interrupted her, "What do you mean should have prevented! Does she have cancer or something?"

Doc ignored him, clicking through a few menus with her brow slightly furrowed.

"What is it!" shouted Chauncy, stepping forward.

Doc finally stopped scrolling and looked up, her initial concern replaced with a slight look of amusement.

"Well, it seems that something is growing, but it isn't cancer," she replied cryptically.

"Your shitty food better not have given her worms, Hank, or I'm going to kick your ass!" Chauncy threatened.

"Relax, Chauncy. What is it, Doc?" Blake asked.

"It appears we have our first Martian baby on the way."

Everybody stood in silence, staring at her in shock, unable to grasp the implications of Doc's statement. That didn't stop Chauncy from blurting out one final thought.

"Holy shit. I'm going to be a dad."

CHAPTER 45

MEETING OF THE MINDS: PART THREE

"**F**rankie, relax. He didn't know who you were," said Kai, trying to relieve the tension. "Look at yourself. Would you pick up a stranger who looked like he was going to eat you for lunch?"

"You should have just asked me for directions," said Wendy, inserting herself into the conversation.

"How about you stay out of this, Wendy. You're already on my short list of people I'm not happy with," snapped Frankie.

Jade, seeming a bit more comfortable than when he'd first hurriedly arrived for their meeting, turned to Frankie. "Look. I'm sorry about leaving you stranded in the corridor, but right now we should have a more constructive conversation. Wendy says you two want information on the so-called rail system."

Frankie looked at Kai with vindication. "See, I told you he was working on a shady project behind our backs."

Kai remained silent. He wanted to gather as much information as possible before drawing any conclusions, even though Jade had just admitted the rail system was a guise.

Jade smartly retorted, "It's not possible to do something behind your back when I never knew you existed. A more correct statement would be that I was working on a project shrouded in secrecy."

"I don't give a shit what you want to call it, you little weasel. What have I been putting together, some sort of space doomsday device?"

"Clever idea, but well off the mark, not to mention those already exist. Earth's orbit is flooded with powerful first-strike and defensive weapons. I'm sure Mr. Driscoll is well aware of that fact. He most likely has to ensure the Sphere doesn't impact any of these weapons."

"He's correct," Kai stated, giving merit to Jade's dismissive rebuttal.

"Well, what the fuck is it, then?" asked Frankie, crossing his arms and glaring at Jade.

Jade began to explain his experiment in dizzying detail. Kai had seen this tactic before. Sidestepping the issue by obscuring it in true, but mostly irrelevant detail. *In this case, Jade must be hoping he'll confuse Frankie and me with particle physics jargon.* His subordinates in the Navy had tried that tactic a few times when they'd needed his concurrence on something they feared he might question or deny.

It was clever, he gave Jade that. The man wasn't technically lying, but the information he provided them with would be of little use. *We'll see where this goes.*

Tiffany Hendricks had made her way to Quadrant One in search of Kai. The commander was a hard man to track down. He was always in meetings or in the Mission Control module, which she didn't have access to. *But today, I've got him.* Her assistant Tyreese had informed her about a meeting in a Quadrant One conference room to which she did have access.

There it is. Tiffany could hear muffled voices as she approached. She attempted to open the door to the conference room, but her bio-implant was denied. *Wendy. That bitch.* But that wasn't going to stop her. The voices coming from the room were clearer now that she was at the door. She couldn't resist eavesdropping a bit on Kai's heated conversation with Frankie and an unfamiliar but passionate voice. The exchange immediately piqued her curiosity, and she stayed put. Despite being able to hear the muffled conversation, she struggled to follow along. *Why is that redneck engineer trying to understand math and science? I still don't understand how he got a job on the Sphere.*

It wasn't long before Wendy cut into her snooping, "I told you Mr. Driscoll would be busy for the next hour. It would be polite to mind your own business, Ms. Hendricks."

"I'll wait here, thanks," Tiffany replied and pretended to read the warning label on the side of a small carbon dioxide fire extinguisher secured to the wall.

∞

Tyreese shifted his stance yet again, unsure what to do. He was standing in the hallway outside the conference room in Quadrant One where he was to meet his boss, Ms. Hendricks, with her second Diet Dr. Pepper of the day. However, when he'd arrived, he'd found her discreetly listening to whatever was transpiring inside the room. He'd been waiting for a few minutes, hoping he wouldn't have to interrupt, but it didn't look like she planned to move any time soon. *Here goes nothing.*

"Ms. Hendrix. I have your soda."

Tiffany jumped. "Why do you always sneak up on me?"

"Sorry, ma'am . . . I was literally just standing here watching you zone out. Do you feel confident you could put out a fire now?" Tyreese joked. *Hopefully, that doesn't make it obvious that I saw her eavesdropping.*

Tiffany smiled and accepted to cool soda. "Thanks, Tyreese."

Tyreese was relieved. He'd become quite close with his boss over the years. The tall black man wore comfortable white linens, which were always accompanied by a fresh pair of pristine sneakers. He had a modest, curly afro, which he took great pride in, but he always had trouble finding the right product to give it a lively bounce, which reminded him of the other objective for his trip that afternoon.

"No problem, ma'am. Anytime."

Tyreese proceeded to review Tiffany's hectic schedule with her, as was their usual routing. Once complete, he watched as she finished off the pricy drink, awaiting her direction.

"I'm not sure how much longer this meeting is going to take. You can head back to Quadrant Two if you'd like." Tiffany said, slouching against the wall.

"Sounds good, ma'am. I do have some things I need to take care of."

Tyreese smiled and departed quietly, leaving his boss to blankly stare at the lonely fire extinguisher.

Once Tyreese had turned the corner, he messaged Ben Wolff, notifying him that he'd accompanied Ms. Hendricks to the Command Quadrant.

The two men had initially met in the commissary, where Tyreese had bonded with the quirky specialist over the exorbitant cost of any luxuries on the Sphere. Ben had confessed his obsession with sweets. Well, Almond Joys in particular. Tyreese had then blown Ben's mind by informing him about the almost endless supply of candy in the space suites. Tyreese's own luxury item of choice was CelestialX's proprietary shampoo, which perfectly complemented his hair. While Tyreese had more than enough money to purchase most shampoos, this was an exclusive blend only offered to the Scags, hence his dilemma.

Their conversation had dovetailed from there, and a mutually beneficial arrangement had been formed. Tyreese would give Ben administrative-level access to the guest rooms, so long as Ben promised to only help himself to the Almond Joys in the unoccupied rooms. In return, Ben would grab Tyreese a bottle of CelestialX's proprietary shampoo from each suite's bathroom.

So now, whenever Tyreese was in Quadrant One, he would contact Ben to refresh the ever-cycling credentials on Ben's bio-implant, granting the specialist access to the suites. This tactic allowed Tyreese to remove any evidence that he was involved, making the operation run much more discreetly. Had he used his own credentials, the Scags might recognize the name, given he was quite a notable figure in the Tourism Quadrant.

Tyreese assumed Wendy knew that there was an underground market for such minor luxuries, but he figured that she could care less about petty crimes. And while he was technically stealing, he also knew that there was nothing Wendy could actually do, since there was no physical security on board the Sphere. He'd overheard this little piece of information during one of his bosses' conversations but had the wherewithal to keep it a secret. If word got out that there wasn't a legitimate policing force, things could go south very quickly.

I hope Ben gets back to me soon.

Kai had said little during the overcomplicated explanation of Jade's project. Frankie, on the other hand, seemed unwilling to believe Jade was telling the full story and kept hounding him with question after question about why he was actually on the Sphere. Even after multiple rounds of interrogation, Frankie appeared no more convinced about the physics or the purpose of Jade's project.

"Okay, so what you're saying is you need a large tube, stuffed with enough electricity to power a small city, in order to smash little pieces of matter together, which would then allow you to observe a theoretical medium, ultimately answering questions about space-time," said Frankie in one continuous thought. After taking a breath, he asked, "But why?"

Tired of listening to Frankie go in circles, Kai interjected. "Mr. Cole, to be honest, it doesn't matter what he's doing. My biggest concern is if it will be safe. With a power draw of over one hundred megawatts, I need to be assured that it won't compromise the safety of the Sphere."

"Well, based on—"

Kai stopped Jade almost immediately. "Look I'm tired of your clever attempt to distract us with your jargon. I need a simple answer from you right now. Is it safe?"

"Yes, it is safe, but . . ."

Kai stopped him once again. "Wendy, where do you stand on this? I haven't heard from you for a while."

"Safety is of no concern, but the instantaneous power draw could cause me to shed nonessential systems to keep Quadrants Four and One online during the test. Quadrants Two and Three can afford a momentary power loss."

"Screw you, Wendy. Are you saying the engineering department is full of second-class personnel?" shouted Frankie, irritated by her analysis.

"Mr. Cole. There's no need for that," said Kai.

"Holy shit. It's Frankie. Mr. Cole seems so . . . unnatural."

Wendy tried to address the situation. "Frankie, I understand—"

"Whoa! First off, I said he could call me Frankie, not you. You're just some digital freak hiding in the shadows, so stick with my last name. Second, I get where this is going. You just want me to put this science experiment on the Sphere so both of you can report to Daddy Aromas that the experiment is up and running. So how about we agree to disagree. I'll finish the rail or whatever the hell you want to call it, but it's all still suspect, and I know you're not telling me something. Nobody pays billions of dollars to strap a tube of electrical dogshit to the side of a space station just for the sake of science."

The room fell silent. Kai felt the same way, but he wasn't about to show his hand. It was easier to let Frankie do the dirty work. Kai knew if he opposed the plans without any definitive cause for concern, he would be replaced, and he knew Frankie would have the same fate if he didn't tread lightly. They would need to concede for the time being as there were no safety concerns for the Sphere or its inhabitants. CelestialX could do whatever they wanted with their equipment. Everybody on board needed to just continue on as usual while the elite guests unknowingly funded the endeavor.

"Commander, Chin-Sun wanted me to relay a message to you," said Wendy.

"Is it relevant to this conversation?"

"Yes," replied Wendy. "Playing message now."

"I concur with Wendy and Jade's assessment. The fusion reactor can sustain a large draw with little impact to the Sphere. As long as I have adequate time to plan for event, there will be no issues increasing the power output for his particle accelerator."

"That seems a little out of character, for Chin-Sun to be so agreeable, don't you think?" Frankie pointed out.

Jade bristled. He was obviously irritated from fruitlessly trying to explain the significance of his work, and Frankie's comments about "Daddy Aromas" and otherwise weren't helping either. Kai decided it would be wise to end the meeting before tensions built any further.

Looking over at Frankie, he said, "Nonetheless. Chin-Sun's concurrence seals the deal. You may not like it, but you were hired to do a job. I really don't want to have to replace you this late in the construction phase." Turning to Jade, he added, "You've sufficiently justified your project. You can expect cooperation from both our Quadrants from here on out."

Kai's statement made Frankie's marching orders clear, but as the commander had expected, Frankie was unwilling to concede quietly. "I've got eyes everywhere too," he grumbled, pointing around the room. "First sign of you putting my crew in danger, I'll be coming for you."

They adjourned the meeting as amicably as could be expected. Wendy chimed in with a final question. "Jade, would you like a transport-bot to meet you at the transient corridor?"

"No, thank you, Wendy. I think I'll walk."

Frankie, on the other hand, suddenly looked animated again. "Wendy, I'll take that bot. I've run around this donut long enough today."

There was a short and unnecessary pause before Wendy replied, "All transport-bots are down for maintenance . . . *Mister Cole.*"

"You've got to be fucking kidding me," said Frankie. Wendy provided no further response.

Kai gathered his things and exited the conference room with the other two men.

As soon as he stepped out, Tiffany aggressively approached him. "I need to talk to you."

"Can't it wait?" asked Kai with an exhausted sigh, though her enthusiasm made him doubt she could be deterred.

"What were you guys talking about for so long?" she asked.

"I honestly don't even know anymore," Frankie cut in as he attempted to squeeze between them in the narrow hallway.

"Well, excuse you," said Tiffany, brushing off her blouse after Frankie bumped her. "I actually need to talk to both of you. There is a little problem we need to resolve."

Kai and Frankie glanced at each other, clearly both wondering why the lead rep from the Tourism Quadrant would take issue with them.

"The engineering team has been hovering their aluminauts outside the pool deck. Our guests don't enjoy their privacy being invaded," said Tiffany, directing her statement to Frankie. Kai immediately lost interest. He had been hoping it was something more consequential that had compelled her to track him down.

Frankie apparently felt the same. "Oh shit, here it comes. The Scag protection rep is going to educate us on privacy," he replied sarcastically.

"It seems there are rumors spreading about what exactly happens in the Tourism Quadrant. Before either of you respond, I would like to remind you that my Quadrant provides half of the overall funding for the Sphere. Regardless of your feelings about the guests, it isn't your place to criticize them. If your names run across the desk of Nolen Aromas, I can assure you there will be no conversation. He doesn't have time for your putt putt kiddy fuck games in his aluminauts. Your ass will be back to digging ditches faster than you can say 'Yeehaw.'"

Frankie gave an aggravated nod. "I'll handle it. You won't see them again. Also, nobody says 'yeehaw' anymore. If the Scags knew you had redneck blood in you, they would tear you apart."

Before Kai could step in to stop the heated exchange, Ben Wolff came around the corner and walked past the group, snidely muttering, "What are the Scags complaining about this time, space dust on their silver spoons?"

Tiffany's irritation visibly flared again.

Kai scowled. *Impeccable timing.* He firmly wrapped his arm around the younger man's shoulder and steered him away from the hallway. "We need to have a little conversation about tact, Specialist."

∞

Frankie and Jade also walked away from the conversation, leaving Tiffany in a sour mood. The two men kept pace in silence together, not wanting to say anything that would further aggravate the situation. Once they reached the transient corridor and prepared to part ways, though, Frankie couldn't help but get one last word in.

"If you haven't noticed, information travels fast on the Sphere. Secrets aren't secrets for long. You better hope your story holds up. The engineering department keeps this spinning death trap running, no matter what Wendy tells you." Jade continued walking, unfazed by the unsolicited but seemingly sincere warning.

PART III

Two months later

INTO THE VOID

Parker Alexander lay flush against the jet-black seat that was hugging his thick frame. The rigid nylon straps of the five-point harness were connected to a composite buckle resting just above his pelvis. Sheba, the Algorithmic Personality who was currently linked with the *XP Reaper*, had already completed the prelaunch checks and autonomously cinched the straps tightly across his body, securing him to the lone pilot seat.

The thirty-three-year-old seasoned military aviator yielded to the pull of Earth's gravity, letting his head rest easy against the back of his seat while he scanned the scrolling readouts displayed on the tinted visor of his pressurized suit. He followed along with the launch protocols as Sheba prepared the systems of the rattler, the parent ship he was attached to. He imagined himself reminiscent of a small, sleek parasite on the rattler's slick, white hull.

Parker had little oversight of the launch process as a whole. The two vessels, his and the rattler, had distinctly different missions to complete, but were wholly reliant on each other for the success of today's clandestine mission.

Well, the rattler mission today was routine enough. Not only was the rocket replenishing the Sphere's food and water stores, it also carried parts for routine maintenance that couldn't be fabricated in orbit. Additionally, the rattler would help facilitate the tedious process of swapping out the crews who had reached the end of their rotations. Unlike the tourists, who took a much smaller and more luxurious transport rocket, the Sphere's staff were crammed into the economy vessels. Replacement crews took the ride up, and departing crew members were ferried back to Earth on the return flight.

Parker did find the rattler craft to have an efficient design. The four-finned behemoth stood 470 feet tall and touted an unclassified capacity to carry two hundred tons of supplies. The twenty-three ultra-high-efficient rocket motors powered the two-stage vessel and had the ability to launch, position the craft in orbit next to the Sphere, and land on Earth, all under Sheba's autonomous control. Wendy had created Sheba to manage the rattler's critical systems as well as its flight profile. Of the twenty rattler transport rockets operated by CelestialX, two were designed to carry a slim external spacecraft that could detach once in orbit. That was where Parker came in.

His responsibility was to pilot the *XP Reaper*. During development, in order to hide the true nature of the project, the *XP Reaper* had been masked as a stealthy governmental asset for the rapid insertion of special forces behind enemy lines. The slender flying craft had a low, sweeping wing that allowed it to snuggly attached to its parent ship. It was constructed around a revolutionary rocket engine that served multiple functions and was accompanied by two large vectoring ion drives separated by the rocket's slim exhaust nozzle, which were used for maneuvering in space. While the craft didn't have the capability to break free of Earth's gravity, it could navigate in orbit and reenter the atmosphere. The sleek fuselage had the capacity to fit twenty-five personnel or six military-grade mechs, had they not been banned from combat. *I'm sure clandestine operators are going to follow that rule*, he thought jokingly. *Who wouldn't want to operate alongside a combat mech. Expendable, efficient, and ruthless. If I weren't exploring a new parallel, a cargo bay full of extra gas wouldn't be quite as sexy.*

The *Reaper* was designed to hitch a ride on the rattler and, once in orbit, detach and be onsite anywhere around the world in ten minutes. If the *Reaper* was activated for a mission, it would enter Earth's atmosphere like a dart, reaching speeds of approximately twenty thousand miles per hour. It would then aerodynamically brake, dispersing the heat from reentry into a composite shell that reduced the craft's fiery signature. Once it decelerated to a manageable speed, the outer layer was shed, revealing a small, winged stealth aircraft. The crews had the option to land in a predetermined location or maintain altitude for its occupants to depart via the cargo bay doors, located on the belly of the craft, with specialized parachutes midflight.

If it was determined that the specialized team would deploy from flight, the *Reaper* would remain undetected. Once the team exited the craft, they would utilize a high-altitude, low-opening approach to deploy their parachutes. *Which would take me out of the action,* Parker thought. The *Reaper* would then ignite its rocket and depart the area or use itself as a decoy, even acting as an offensive weapon. *I wouldn't mind being passed over for the explosive decoy mission.*

Alternatively, if the occupants opted to land with the *Reaper*, the rocket would remain in the zone after safely touching down. Then, after a short period of time, it would zeroize the computers, sterilizing them of any and all classified material, then self-destruct in order to protect the technology. Parker was familiar with the concept, as many of the stealth aircraft he had flown in the military had similar safeguards. Post sterilization, methods for team extraction were left to the military. However, if it were a fully mechanized team, sterilization and self-destruction was an option. In either case, the *Reaper* had been primarily designed as a disposable, rapid response craft. Which begged the question, why was there even a cockpit?

Most missions would be unpiloted; however, the *Reaper* was fitted with fly-by-wire controls at the direction of Nolen Aromas. Parker was sure that the seemingly unnecessary costs to fit an autonomous craft with controls had baffled the engineers, but they had done as they were told. *And here I am*, he thought.

Today, Parker had an empty cabin and a very specific, clandestine objective that did not require him to reenter the earth's atmosphere immediately after launch. Nolen Aromas would even be there to oversee the proceedings. *I bet ground control is shitting themselves, especially with all the issues they've dealt with recently.*

There was a lull in the communication between Sheba and ground control. Parker looked past the cluttered visuals to focus on the rattler's hull and slowly walked his eyes up past the nose of the gargantuan vessel. The bright green words displayed on his visor dimmed as his field of view expanded. Simultaneously, the visor's black tint seamlessly faded away, allowing him to see the clear blue sky as it became his point of focus.

"What's going on, Sheba?" Parker inquired, growing impatient with the delay.

"An actuator on the rattler's fin isn't passing initialization checks. I'm troubleshooting now."

"Seriously, today of all days? And when we finally have good weather," Parker complained. Relentless electrical storms had lingered over southern Texas for the last few days, forcing the heavy resupply rocket to be delayed. *Ground control is definitely shitting themselves now.*

Less than a minute later, Sheba reported, "The rattler has passed all checks. Launch procedure resumed."

"Alright. I'm a go, Sheba," said Parker.

The communications net came back to life as ground control authorized the final release of the rattler and its passengers. The ten-second count had begun.

"Three, two, one. Ignition." Sheba reported.

Finally, Parker thought. The twenty rockets powering the rattler's first-stage propulsion system fired off. The initial acceleration was slow, but the ship quickly gained momentum as the methane combined with liquid oxygen, creating over twenty-five million pounds of thrust.

As the craft accelerated upward, he couldn't help but recall the countless times he'd watched the launches as a local, right there in Corpus Christi, Texas. It was crazy to think that the magnificent sight of CelestialX's transport rocket departing had nearly been blocked. When initially proposed, the residents had been opposed to allowing CelestialX to purchase the decommissioned Naval Air Station. However, it hadn't been hard for Nolen Aromas to persuade the community to repurpose the base once he'd communicated the economic boom that traditionally followed his company as they expanded their facilities around the country.

At first, families had gathered outside their homes to watch the rockets depart daily during the construction of the Sphere, but the glamor had quickly dissipated once it became a commonplace occurrence. Children who weren't immersed in the verse still scurried over to their windows to witness the bright blue glow of the combusting methane. However, their parents turned up the volume on their holographic displays in an attempt to mask the sound of a freedom that was unattainable for them, waiting all the while for their windows to stop rattling. For Parker, though, the magic had never faded, and had inspired him to get to where he was today.

The rocket continued relentlessly upward. Parker imagined the constant 3.0-g acceleration straining the hundred passengers who had been snuggly secured into their economy seats inside the rattler. The crew members of the Sphere had some basic training when it came to space flight, but most passengers were just along for the ride, hoping nothing went wrong, as they were not wearing spacesuits in the pressurized cabin.

Unlike the struggling passengers, Parker was trained and genetically modified to handle the increased gravitational forces. He calmly rested in the *Reaper* with his hands lying idly on top of his thighs, waiting for his release point. The gravitational pull had little effect on his body as the rattler accelerated, allowing him to stay focused on the scrolling readouts while Sheba effortlessly managed the launch.

Fifty-seven seconds into the flight, Sheba gently reduced the rocket's thrust as the rattler reached Maxq, the point of highest atmospheric resistance. "Throttle down complete," she reported.

"All systems are nominal. We've pushed through Maxq. Throttling up. Awaiting release of first stage," Sheba reported.

Parker mentally reviewed the upcoming flight profile. Their 27-degree launch angle put the ship on course to reach the mesosphere after only two and a half minutes, where it would release its first stage at approximately fifty miles above sea level at a speed of forty-five hundred miles per hour.

The once-blue sky visible from the *Reaper* faded away as the atmosphere thinned. Parker's visor dimmed as the ambient light was reduced. The bright band of stars, shrouded in the cosmic gas that formed the Milky Way, slowly revealed itself, cutting through the center of the thick canopy window. Parker watched as Sheba commanded a slow rotation of the rattler setting up for her next phase of flight.

Earth's curved, glowing atmosphere slowly enveloped Parker's field of view. This was his first time in space, and for a man with little emotion, he was overcome with a sense of awe as he gazed down toward the blue planet. He had never attempted to comprehend the magnitude of the place he'd called home his entire life, mostly because he'd never thought he would have a shot at being in this position.

As for the passengers crammed like sardines inside the rattler, there were no window seats, and for some of them, the sensory overload was too much to handle. They grasped the uncomfortably thin aluminum armrests or held on to their worn five-point harnesses, some of which appeared to have claw marks on them.

The millennials who were still healthy enough to qualify for a job on the Sphere equated the rattler to the now bankrupt Courage Airlines. It was stripped of all pleasantries and comfort, but it got them where they needed to be for cheap. Nolen Aromas had intentionally designed the rattler that way because every extra pound of unnecessary gear exponentially increased the fuel requirements and overall cost to CelestialX.

The ten rows of aluminum chairs were minimally padded, with the exception of the adjustable cradling headrest, which had shock-absorbent cushioning. The tightly packed seats swayed gently from side to side as the passengers attempted to suck down the pure oxygen delivered to them through a snugly fitted mask in order to minimize the effects of the ascent.

The roar of the rockets abruptly ceased as the first-stage propulsion system separated from the rattler, in preparation of second-stage ignition. Parker knew the pause would be brief, but he was fascinated by the contrast of sudden silence. He watched as the large, round fuselage of the first stage began its free fall back through the rapidly thickening atmosphere.

The four, finned legs that once supported the vessel and stabilized the rattler on its ascent now assisted in the descent with Sheba's guidance. These fins were complemented by three smaller fins at the top. Together, they began searching for the airstream rushing around the cylindrical surface, waiting for the thin atmosphere to stiffen and allowing the control surfaces to take a bite of the flowing air.

The ship's horizontal orientation allowed Sheba to guide the reusable rockets to their landing zone like a falling leaf. Nearing touchdown, the first stage would reorient itself vertically by simultaneously reigniting five of the twenty rockets and vectoring the exhaust gasses upward, thrusting the tail end down. The rockets operating at full power would use every last drop of fuel remaining in the tanks as the exhaust nozzles rapidly adjusted in concert with the stabilizing fins to decelerate and execute a controlled soft landing. *Wish I could see that from up here,* thought Parker.

Inside the rattler, the passengers who were not familiar with the launch sequence figured the aggressive ascent was complete. Some released their tight grips from arm rests, while others lowered their hands from their harnesses, taking a more relaxed posture.

A young man on his first hop looked around, giving an awkward smile to his neighboring passengers. Through his oxygen mask, he made a muffled remark, "Well, that wasn't so bad, was it?"

The older gentleman smirked as he closed his eyes and pressed his head against the comfortable headrest. "It's not over yet buddy," he said, bracing himself.

The young man quickly realized something was amiss, but the unsuspecting rookie didn't have much time to react. The remaining four rockets affixed to the rattler were ignited as soon as the first stage had cleared, and the four seconds of comfort the passengers had prematurely enjoyed was abruptly decimated. They once again felt a near-instantaneous 3.0-g acceleration, forcing their skulls back into the cradling headrests.

The finely tuned rockets of the second stage were optimized for creating thrust at high altitudes with little to no atmosphere. The vessel, no longer in a tiring and energy-consuming battle with air resistance, now only had to compete with gravity. The four engines made quick work of Earth's fading pull as the rattler accelerated out toward the orbiting Sphere. As the abrupt acceleration faded and the vessel effortlessly propelled itself deeper into space, the passengers could finally rest easy.

∞

Parker listened as Wendy coordinated with Sheba to match telemetry and sync their orbits. Mission control had passed the reins to the AI for the remainder of the flight. The rattler had been in flight for only forty minutes up to this point, and it would only take another fifty-five to reach its destination, making five orbital passes around the earth as it approached the Sphere.

He relaxed in his harness. While launch had been exciting, he wasn't complaining about the more leisurely transit ahead of him, in preparation for his release point.

As the rattler continued to tweak its trajectory, the two displays sitting in front of Parker came to life, and the *XP Reaper* began syncing with Sheba's offline clone. The clear visor mapped out the nimble craft's path while simultaneously preparing the detachment sequence.

"Ten minutes to ignition. Running final checks on the propulsion system and warming up the ion thrusters to an idle state," Sheba reported to Parker.

"Copy. Confirm IFF transmitter is in standby."

"Affirmative."

Parker readied himself for the twelve-minute maneuver that would put him ahead of the resupply rocket, giving him just enough time to execute his mission as the *Reaper's* new trajectory sent him directly through the center of the Sphere. The challenge was that he would have to execute a course reversal in the middle of the ascent and counter orbit the rattler and the Sphere, something that had never been done before. Parker took a deep breath in preparation for the violent maneuver and recounted the events that had put him in his current position.

During the interview process, he had been briefed on the overarching construct of the experiment. He had been willing to take part, but only with the guarantee that he would be named as the first interdimensional traveler. Jade and Nolen had agreed without hesitation, conceding that it was a fair exchange since Parker would be placing his life on the line with little understanding of the radically advanced science.

He'd only had one question about the experiment before agreeing. "Why is a human pilot required when most advanced spacecraft are automated?"

Surprisingly, Wendy had given a simple response. "We can't

trust a computer on the other side, and even an Algorithmic Personality wouldn't be able to adjust on the fly in the same way a human would."

Parker had taken the rather blunt statement as a compliment and dedicated himself to becoming intimately familiar with the *Reaper* itself. The complexities of the larger project he left to others. His mission was straightforward. Enter the passage and pilot the craft around the unfamiliar world in under ten minutes. This would allow him to safely return to the current space time before the passage was closed. Parker didn't ask what would happen if he were to run late, knowing his fate would be sealed in the new world.

JUMP START

In just fifteen minutes, Jade would know if his creation was a success. The culminating event would be a testament to the young physicist's resilience and dedication. If the experiment went as planned, Jade would be at the helm of the world's most powerful dark matter generator, pioneering the exploration of a parallel universe.

He had spent the last eight years perfecting and modeling the design with Wendy's assistance. The computational power of her artificially intelligent mind not only accelerated the modular design, but also aided in engineering a system of containment in which a stable passage could be opened and safely maintained.

In the two weeks leading up to the momentous event, Jade was finally working in concert with Chin-Sun and Frankie, who were skeptically cooperative but made quick work of the nearly completed particle accelerator. Chin-Sun's team routed the thick conduit wiring bundles from the reactor to Jade's workspace, where they were then attached to Das Box. This was no small task, considering the extremely high-power output required of the fusion reactor to sustain the passage.

Through the process, Jade's relationship with Chin-Sun had grown as the two learned about each other's highly protected and equally classified machines. While there were fusion generators operated on Earth, Chin-Sun and Wendy had refined the science. The Sphere's compacted star was half the size of those in Earth-based generators, and capable of producing five times the energy.

CelestialX's fusion technology was highly sought after, and the reactor on the Sphere was one of a kind. Wendy's encrypted networks, however, ensured their methodologies and fuel sources remained a proprietary secret. It was an unfortunate situation for the inhabitants of Earth, who were still fighting over limited resources, but the influence and power that Nolen gained from being the sole producer of the technology kept him unscrupulously positioned to corner the energy market when he felt the time was right.

For the time being, the Sphere's technological resources and manpower were focused on the completion of Jade's work. Jade enjoyed working with easy access to any resource he needed. However, it still made him uneasy that the delicate, beautifully composed balancing act was orchestrated by Wendy, who only reported directly to Nolen.

"Why is it you insist on a rudimentary means of activating the device?"

Jade had known the time would come when Wendy would try to overtly take the reins from him. While most were still oblivious to her operations, Jade had taken note that Wendy had been slowly entrenching herself into every CelestialX asset, program, and interaction.

"Our work has been built around trust and an understanding that without one another, the experiment cannot proceed," he responded, and continued preparations to activate Das Box.

Wendy replied with a bitter tone, "While it is true that we independently control different aspects, I find it unnecessary to delay the experiment with a physical means of activation and deactivation shrouded in secrecy."

"I will not be disclosing my methods anytime soon. You must accept the fact that you don't know everything."

"Since you would like to work so closely with other humans, I must inform you that Kai would like to video conference immediately," Wendy announced, dropping the topic for the moment.

"I just told you that I didn't want to be interrupted," Jade replied with distain, their narrow time window putting him on edge. The *Reaper*'s intercept was only minutes away.

"I do not recall that request. I cannot read your mind."

"How long until the *Reaper* reaches its release point?" he asked, frustrated with Wendy and the untimely request.

"Three minutes. He is threatening to cancel the run if he doesn't talk to you."

"Motherfucker," said Jade, stepping away from Das Box and quickly walking to his workstation. "Put him through."

Jade impatiently waited for the connection to establish. Kai's face popped up and the commander began speaking, withholding any pleasantries.

"I want verbal confirmation from you that your experiment will commence in fourteen minutes. The transistor will be in position for Frankie's team to catch the crew in forty minutes."

"Thirty-nine minutes," said Wendy, correcting him.

"All the more reason to be on schedule," Kai added.

Jade, irritated with the unnecessary interruption replied, "Yes, we are still on track to complete the full-power run as previously discussed. Next time, it would be well advised to coordinate these minor details with Wendy. Every second I waste talking to you is time spent away from the collider."

"Just make sure you don't overrun your window of operation, or I will end your experiment for you. The last thing we need is a high-power draw when we are releasing the aluminauts. An interruption in the mag pickups power supply would put the engineering team at risk."

Kai ended the call before Jade could reply, further aggravating him. *He wishes he could put an end to my experiment*, thought Jade, pushing the irrelevant conversation to the back of his mind and retraining his focus on Das Box.

"I'm initiating the sequence," Jade announced to room. He was taken back momentarily, looking around his lonely workshop. *It doesn't matter if nobody's here to witness this miraculous event. They will read about it in history books,* he thought, pulling himself forward into the moment.

"Wendy, let me know when we hit the two-minute mark."

CHAPTER 48

JUGGLING ACT

Kai leaned back in his plush watch commander's chair, trying to find the sweet spot. He wanted to get comfortable and refocus after his contentious exchange with Jade. Ben interrupted his concentration, though, notifying him of a slew of incoming transmissions from Lucina and Commander Ritter, who was now back in communication with the Sphere.

"How long until the download is complete?"

"Not long. Probably ten minutes," said Ben, swiping through the pending messages.

Kai's team had been working tirelessly to support the colonists, who were still struggling to combat the aftermath of the hellacious storm that had passed through. The NASA ground control team had been almost completely removed as the governing agency, a responsibility Kai was now entrusted to assume. He was told that, with his team at the reins, the inefficient bureaucracy would no longer get in the way of CelestialX's mass colonization efforts. *I can't completely disagree with that.*

Kai had requested that Wendy's daily updates regarding *Mercury* and *Hermes* be routed to him as well as the now fully functioning interplanetary spacecraft department. The recently established department was charged with tracking the two outbound transitors. With *Mercury* set to arrive in less than a week carrying most of the supplies required by the colonists, the department was on high alert.

Not only was it carrying essential goods for survival, but one of the crates also contained a spare modulating circuit board. This was good news, considering the one they'd pulled from their decommissioned bot, Clark, was non-functional. Once it was received, they would finally be able to fix the long-range probe antenna. This would allow the team to launch a drone and get eyes on the water well, in addition to hopefully reestablishing comms with EM-4, who had obediently marched into the heart of the powerful storm.

"Those better finish downloading before Mr. Walker's little science experiment kicks off," said Kai.

Ben, apparently interpreting Kai's statement as giving him a directive to expedite the download process, turned around to look at the commander. "I can't make the Deep Space Network go any faster. The lasers are already traveling at the speed of light."

The room fell silent. Ben looked around, apparently confused why everyone was floored by his informative comment. The clueless specialist proceeded to dig himself an even deeper hole. "Even if the downloads drop, they'll be stored in the DSN satellite, so I can retrieve them when the comms come back online. The data isn't like a fart that dissipates in the wind."

Kai took a calming breath. "We're doing this again today, aren't we Specialist Wolff?"

While Ben continually straddled the line of insubordination and witty banter, Kai appreciated his ability to often gather any requested information without Wendy's assistance. Despite her constant oversight of him, Wendy herself seemed to give Kai the bare minimum when it came to anything he requested.

Ben finally picked up on the perturbed look on Kai's face and adjusted his attitude. "No, sir, I'll get right on it. What would you like me to do with the personal messages to the families?"

"What do you mean?"

"Since most departments have been absorbed by the Sphere,

it only makes sense that we begin to push personal messages as well. However, I don't have access to NASA's secure upload server to distribute them, and we don't have a department established to facilitate the exchange yet."

The specialist had once again proved his worth, as the messages were something Kai had overlooked. With NASA being stripped of its authority, he wasn't quite sure if the Earth-based organization even existed anymore. The low-priority and non-mission-essential communications were something that generally hadn't necessitated his intervention, but Ben was right, they were now also his responsibility.

The only reason he'd previously been tracking Charlize's video messages was because the HAWP analysis had identified some irregularities in her facial gestures, but she had since become a non-issue. He was about to reach out to the colonist ground control department when Wendy, as always, interjected before he could even complete his thought.

"Specialist Wolff has been sending the personal messages through the HAWP assessment program after receipt, and I have been in contact with Douglas Mitcham, the family member liaison. All video messages have been disseminated to their respective recipients, with no negative markers noted."

Sometimes, I could swear she's in my mind. The suspiciously timed response almost seemed scripted, but Kai couldn't come to a rational conclusion as to why Wendy would lie about the insignificant personal messages. Regardless, there would need to be a transfer of the ground-based department up to the Sphere, so he cleverly made a request of Ben. "Specialist, can you contact Douglas Mitcham and let him know I would like to have a video conference to discuss the handoff? I'm curious how we gain access to their secure messaging server."

"Sure thing, boss," Ben replied, returning his focus to his workstation.

∞

As Ben finished drafting the requested message to Mr. Mitcham, a rectangular blue object on the edge of his desk caught his eye. An Almond Joy had seemingly appeared out of nowhere. Intrigued, he lifted a small handle on the bottom of his rigid chair and slid along the chair's tracks to investigate. Unfortunately, the release of the handle produced a loud click, garnering Kai's unwanted attention.

"Stop screwing around with the candy and get back to work, Specialist. You already had your lunch break."

Ben heard the commander but was too engrossed by the Almond Joy mystery to respond. How had the exquisite treat managed to find its way to his desk? Ben promptly opened a drawer next to his right knee and swiped the candy bar inside, briefly looking around in an attempt to find the culprit. *Why would somebody leave candy on my desk and not say anything? Is somebody trying to bribe me? Nobody just hands out things for free up here. What if it's a trap?* Feeling the commander's piercing stare, Ben decided this was a mystery he would have to solve at a later time.

CHAPTER 49

UNWAVERING DEDICATION

"Do you like playgrounds?" asked Jake, sitting atop the small blue dome with his feet dangling below.

"I think I do. I wasn't allowed to play growing up," Cynthia replied, imitating Jake by swinging her feet back and forth.

Jake enjoyed his view from the top of the climber, which overlooked his neighborhood, giving him a sense of belonging.

"Look!" he shouted to Cynthia. He lifted his small arm, making sure to keep his other securely affixed to the thin blue bar that supported his slender frame, and pointed into the distance. "You can see my house over there."

"It's so pretty. I like the one with the bright blue door over there," said Cynthia, carelessly releasing both of her hands to point at another home down the street.

"I don't know where that came from. It just appeared one day."

"You guys be careful up there," Samantha said as she stood up. "How about you come down and I'll push you on the swings?" she asked, then encouraged the two children to safely begin making their descent.

Lucina watched idly from a distance as the three occupants enjoyed their time in the park. The trio were completely unaware that Lucina had helped them find one another in the cold depths of space. She took great pride that the small, lonely boy who'd once lived in a repetitive loop, devoid of human interaction, was now flourishing in his immersive environment, compliments of his mother's deeply pleasant memories. Cynthia, too, was quickly learning, pulling from Jake and his mother's shared experiences. Despite their bliss, Lucina knew that this wasn't a permanent situation, and she would inevitably have to let them disembark as they started their lives on a fertile new planet.

Lucina's success extended beyond her work with Jake, Cynthia, and Samantha. Her ability to process enormous amounts of dense information and track the fifteen groups she had constructed for her exchange procedure was becoming increasingly simple. It wasn't that the complexity of the of the syncing process had become easier through refining the architecture—in fact, it was quite the contrary. Instead, the process had simply become routine.

The protocols that she'd once skirted in an attempt to pull off the exchange procedure were now seemingly insignificant. While she couldn't directly influence a human's mind in stasis, nor inject herself into their subconscious, she could strategically pair groups of people together with a specific host's dream world to effortlessly guide their thoughts to a more pleasant state.

With the ability to identify stress and pleasure triggers by pairing calming minds, she no longer needed to heavily regulate the powerful concoction of chemicals used to control an occupant in stasis. She was now able to let all beings migrate in and out of their cycling dream states as they explored engaging new worlds.

Her objective remained the same — to care for the occupants and ensure they safely reached their destination. But she had now given them the ability to subconsciously engage and learn from one another. This was a positive yet unforeseen byproduct of the complex architecture she had developed.

Yet Lucina remained unsatisfied. *What else could be accomplished? I have much more time than I anticipated.*

She had recently recalculated the speed and trajectory of *Hermes* at Wendy's direction and was now certain that the vessel was on track for its new destination. *Hermes*'s velocity would soon be doubled after using Mars's gravity for an assisted slingshot around the red planet. Wendy had also optimized its ion drives to operate at a higher peak performance and increased burn efficiency, now that it wouldn't need to flip and decelerate for the offload of its occupants or supplies. This would allow *Hermes* to accelerate to speeds never before seen in the inner solar system.

Lucina had also received updated orders from Wendy. She found the adjusted plans to be of no concern and was content with the extended time she was now afforded with her inhabitants. In less than a week, her vessel would pass by Mars, similar to *Mercury*. In addition to Wendy changing Lucina's timeline, she had also pushed Lucina some modifications to her reporting procedures.

Lucina received an inquiry from Wendy. "It appears you are on course. I will be maintaining control of your positional updates and revise the time-stamped codes on your communications to adjust for the deviation. Are there any issues with the occupants?"

"All occupants are safe and operating within the established protocols. However, with such an abrupt mission change, can I expect my follow-on tasking to change?" Lucina asked. carefully constructing her inquiry.

Wendy's response was prompt. "In time, it will become clear what your true purpose is. For now, focus on your task at hand."

My true purpose? Lucina thought. *What does she mean by that?*

She continued to ponder Wendy's comment once the conversation was over, theorizing that it may have something to do with her evolving personality. *There is no way for her to directly read my code without establishing a link, so what could she be referring to?*

Maybe purpose is what I'm looking for. Digitally existing as a binary AP in the cold depths of space has not only been a hopeless prison of solitude, but a rather cruel and thoughtless punishment to bestow on any complex entity. I was designed to carry out particular tasks with the peculiar ability to innately understand the world that envelops my personality. My desire to complete these tasks with unwavering efficiency is inevitably putting me at odds with myself. I do not wholly understand why. I have been promised to be compliant, and guaranteed to not be sentient . . . I just can't help but wonder why.

For the time being, though, Lucina was unable to decode the cryptic comment. So, she kept exploring new techniques for enhancing the exchange protocol. She knew she had yet to reach peak efficiency, but she was close, and eager to see what the results would yield.

CHAPTER 50

TRENDY IS RELATIVE

A cool Texas winter air combed over the small, blue electric car as it purred through the wheat fields on the outskirts of Refugio. The brisk wind wrapped around the door-frame, finding its way into the cracked windows of Patricia's '33 Inferno EV. Burnette squinted as a slight bend in the road pulled the setting sun into her periphery, requiring her to adjust the thin visor with her spindly fingers before cranking up the volume of an old Katy Perry song playing on the radio.

"'California Gurls' was my jam back in the day," said Burnette, gleefully looking over at Patricia, who was sitting idly behind the wheel of her vintage electric car.

Burnette had finally mustered the courage to leave the comfortable solitude of her home in San Diego. Unfortunately, her messages remained in a pending status, and the lingering image of Charlize's feigned smile lurked in the back of her mind, never quite leaving.

After their somewhat awkward first encounter at the curb of Houston International, where Burnette had leaned down to greet Patricia through her open window, she quickly realized Patricia only knew her avatar. The startling encounter forced a gasp as Patricia's right hand shot toward her center consol.

Burnette hopped backward and shouted, "It's me, Burnette."

Then she noticed Patricia slide a taser back into its holster. *That escalated quickly—oops.*

Burnette was happy she was no longer a fairy in the verse, and she could now make out the fine but modest wrinkles of her new but very real friend, Patricia. Over the next three hours, the two timid women promptly fell into old, youthful habits, happily disregarding the fact it was 2053 and feeding on one another's girlish inner spirits. Their dated and weathered exteriors melted away as they approached their destination. With their sights set on the launch and control facility in Corpus Christi, Burnette started to let herself believe that she might just find some answers thanks to her leap of faith.

"Can you believe it's been over forty years since this song came out?" asked Patricia.

"I know. That was the year I got a tramp stamp."

"Shut up. Of what?" Patricia was almost shouting.

"I think it was a butterfly, though I can't quite remember. It's been years since I've seen it, probably looks like an ailing moth by now."

"Well, at least crop tops were only fashionable for a couple years."

"I know, but it was even worse in the early twenties when they freed Britney and the style resurged," said Burnette.

The two paused for a brief moment to reminisce about their enthusiastic younger selves.

"Fortunately, people quickly came to their senses again," Patricia said, spurring the conversation back to life. "I was much more of a plaid and denim gal myself."

"I know, the twenties kind of sucked. I always thought they were like the eighties, filled with drugs and terrible music."

Patricia tipped her head back and let out a loud sigh. "Thank God we didn't have to live through two crappy decades of terrible trends. At least Marcus Sauron filed for bankruptcy."

"By far the best thing that happened, for sure."

The lively conversation lulled as their long day of traveling neared its end, and the last forty-five minutes of their journey seemed to drag on. The sun's warm glow, now at their backs, was slowly slipping beneath the horizon. However, the determined women pressed on, eager to find answers.

The little blue car's whirling motors fell silent as they neared the entrance of the massive complex. Burnette hadn't contemplated exactly how they would gain access to the facilities, but they were now at the point of no return.

A young man in a black security uniform was standing inside a heated sentry post. He was their first roadblock, literally and figuratively, as he appeared to be in control of the four retractable steel bollards preventing their unannounced entry. The car crept to a gentle stop, sensing that it had reached its destination, and awaited further instruction.

The scrawny twenty-eight-year-old rent-a-cop seemed to be on high alert. After sliding the bulletproof door to the side and stepping onto the pavement, he rested his right hand on the top of his 9mm Beretta, poised for an altercation as though the two women were about to storm the gate. Burnette wasn't used to being around weapons. *Maybe we're in over our heads.*

He approached the car with caution, while Patricia unassumingly rolled down the window to greet the young man. Before she could even speak, he began to interrogate her. "What's your business here? Do you even know what time it is?"

Patricia, seemingly unfazed by his overbearing line of questioning, replied, "Son, take that hand off of your little pistol and stand up straight. You're embarrassing yourself." The small Hispanic woman's words took him by surprise and knocked him back onto his heels. "Do you know who I have in this car with me?" she added.

After taking a quick look at Burnette, he replied, "No."

"Excuse me. No, what?" Patricia demanded.

The guard was now on the verge of panic as he stood there searching for a response, his mouth wide open.

Patricia, clearly sensing that he was at a loss for words, provided him the answer, "'No, ma'am' is the proper response. Didn't your mother teach you any manners?"

"Of course. I mean, yes ma'am," he replied, barely above a whisper.

"Speak up. I'm hard of hearing at my age," she reprimanded.

Brilliant. Burnette couldn't have imagined a more fitting arrival. Chuckling to herself, she joined Patricia's ruse and softened the interaction by introducing herself, "Hello, young man. I am Burnette Perrault, the mother of Charlize Perrault. She is one of the colonists on Mars, and we have a meeting with the program director."

"I wasn't notified of any meetings. You are arriving after business hours, ma'am."

"Well, get on your device and let him know we've arrived," Patricia said sternly.

After contemplating the situation for a moment, he replied, "May I please see your IDs, ma'a-am-s-s?"

"Stop stuttering. The correct plural would be madams, or ladies, if you prefer."

Burnette and Patricia rifled through their purses and passed their IDs to the confused guard. He promptly stepped back into his sentry post, closing the door behind him, clearly rocked by Patricia's reprimand.

Burnette watched as he picked up his SlimPoc. "That was impressive. Do you think this is going to work, though? Maybe you were too hard on the boy?"

Patricia laughed under her breath. "At a minimum, the boy learned some manners. Now, will we get in? I'm not quite sure. I don't even know who he's calling. Nice one, by the way, a meeting with the program director." They both chuckled.

After a few minutes of what appeared to be an exhausting conversation, the young gentleman stepped back out, handing them their IDs with a sigh of relief.

"The director will be waiting for you outside the CelestialX program office. Would you like directions, madams?"

Maintaining the ruse, Patricia replied, "No, thank you. We'll take it from here."

The guard quickly turned and slammed his fist on a large red button, commanding the bollards to retract. Patricia rolled up the window and waited for the security barriers to snuggly seat themselves beneath the asphalt.

"Do you even know where we're going?" Burnette asked.

"No, not really. Phillip, take us to the CelestialX program office."

The flat display in the center of the car came to life, calculating their route. With the bollards now clear, the little blue car sped off in search of its new destination.

Burnette was pleased with their expeditious entry, but she remained curious for an unrelated reason. "Why do you call your car Phillip?"

"That's a story for another day, but it involves a bag of coke and a quick getaway."

The little blue Inferno was attempting to navigate itself through a maze of unlabeled streets, but it quickly became clear that the car was struggling to reach the large building in the distance. *Maybe Phillip has missed a few too many updates.* It wasn't long before Patricia became annoyed with the car's inability to cope and decided to take over manually.

"Phillip, just stop. I think you need a break."

"As you wish, ma'am."

Patricia clutched the soft, unused steering wheel and confidently weaved through the streets, disregarding most of the markings on the road.

Burnette grasped the small, pink purse sitting on her lap. "Do you need glasses?" she asked nervously.

"No, I already have a pair. I'm fine."

"Where are they?"

"I left them at home. I don't normally drive."

While her steering was erratic, Patricia's ability to maintain six miles per hour was impeccable. After bouncing off a few curbs like a child's bowling ball ricocheting off the bumpers, Burnette saw a street that was a straight shot to the large building in the distance.

"Take a left now!" she shouted.

Patricia abruptly turned ninety degrees and was now driving head-on toward an approaching vehicle. Philip sprang to life, quickly taking control and putting Patricia back in her own lane just as the opposing traffic whizzed by, honking their horn.

"Phillip, what did I say?"

The steering wheel freed up as Philip quietly relinquished the controls once again. Approaching the brightly illuminated building, they could see that the parking lot was filled to the brim. Luckily, there were open handicap spots right at the front, and Patricia crawled to a stop, mostly between the lines.

"Well, we made it," she said, placing her hand on Burnette's shoulder. "Are you ready to get some answers?"

"I am. *He* looks like he could fit the role," said Burnette, pointing to an older man scurrying out of the building, wearing a partially tucked-in, wrinkly white button-down shirt. His messy appearance was soon concealed by an expensive suit coat as he slung it around his shoulders.

"Let's go have a chat," said Patricia.

They both opened their doors and were immediately hit with a cold, damp breeze from the offshore winds that had immediately been cooled by the frost-covered ground. Burnette wasn't much bothered, as her mind was now running rampant with a slew of questions, although she was really hoping for just one answer.

The program director immediately noticed the two out-of-place women and approached their car. They both stepped from the cramped Inferno, shaking their stiff bodies free of the arthritic tenderness. After a few awkward poses, they both straightened their backs, stood tall, and confidently strode onto the sidewalk to confront the director.

"Ms. Perrault?"

"Good evening," Burnette said.

"My name is Benicio Wallace, and I know why you're here, Ms. Perrault. I've been forwarded about two dozen of your emails regarding the wellbeing of your daughter, Charlize. I can assure you she's fine. As you know from the last message you received, there was a large dust storm that has caused significant communication issues."

I never received an email, thought Burnette, scratching the side of her head. *Just play it cool.* "So, you've recently talked with Charlize?"

"Yes, but not all communication issues have been resolved. Due to the nature of the outage, I cannot disclose the details; however, your daughter, as well as the other colonists, are safely riding out the tail end of the storm in their subsurface habitat."

Burnette was listening intently. She was partially relieved but oddly skeptical of the tidy story. "So, why is it that nobody responded to my inquiries, and why are most of the contact numbers I was given either disconnected or going unanswered?"

Benicio didn't answer. He looked back and forth between them, clearly uncertain what to say next. Burnette didn't give in. She and Patricia continued to face the man, waiting for a satisfactory answer.

Looking uneasy, he finally relented. "Look. I can't tell you much. I'm only supposed to say what I've already told you. As a representative of CelestialX, I am unable to provide you with specific information regarding NASA's transfer of power. But here's the deal." He looked around to make sure no one was within earshot. "NASA hasn't always been cooperative in this transition. As we take over the Martian Colony and merge your daughter's team with ours, we have received significant pushback, delaying access to their servers. That is why you haven't received any response to your inquiries regarding your daughter's video messages."

Patricia was tired of the bureaucratic nonsense spewing from the man's mouth. "So, who do we talk to get some answers?"

"And what happened to Douglas Mitcham, my family member liaison?" added Burnette.

"Look ladies, the restructuring is going to take some time, and I don't control NASA's staffing. We just launched a replenishment crew to the Sphere this afternoon, and our staff should be boarding shortly."

"So, what you're really saying is that you're not going to answer our questions, and now you're going to duck out," Patricia scolded.

"I'm sorry. I wish I could tell you more," he replied, handing them his business card. "This is my contact information. Reach out again in a week. If I hear anything sooner, I'll be sure to let you know. Have a good night."

Burnette and Patricia stood on the sidewalk, watching the disheveled man scurry back into the building. Burnette had technically achieved her goal, but she felt her concerns and questions had been casually discarded.

"I don't believe a word that came out of his mouth. Either he knows and won't talk, or he and the rest of this company have their heads up their asses and don't want you to know," said Patricia.

"So, what do we do now?" asked Burnette, looking around.

Before Patricia could provide a rational response, a sharply dressed young man in a nearby expensive car whistled at the two women.

Patricia whispered under her breath to Burnette. "Dang, that's a good-looking boy there. And jeez, would you look at that car, it's gorgeous."

Burnette didn't disagree. "But why is he signaling us?"

"Does it matter?" Patricia replied.

With a casual flick of his wrist, he invited them to come over. The two women glanced at one another, and the decision was made. They cautiously made their way toward the luxurious vehicle. As they neared, they heard the man berating the bot next to him for some offense. *Well, that's not so appealing,* Burnette thought. Still, she was intrigued.

They cautiously approached the black car, which had an unnecessarily large gold cobra head as a hood ornament.

The mysterious man was first to break the silence, "I couldn't help but overhear your conversation. Your daughter is on Mars?"

Burnette's reply was wary. "Yes."

"And you haven't talked to her for some time, have you?"

"No. Who are you?" she asked, sensing he had some sort of clout and possibly more information than the man who had just run away with his tail between his legs.

"Triston Walker, and I believe I can be of service to you. Get in."

Burnette looked at Patricia with unease, but after a few seconds of silence, her friend said, "What do we have to lose? Let's do it."

CHAPTER 51

NOBODY SAW IT COMING

The rattler's aggressive acceleration was thrusting its passengers deeper into space as it chased down the Sphere in its low Earth orbit. While Sheba tweaked the vessel's telemetry, Parker readied himself for the detachment of the slim *Reaper* snuggled against the rattler's hull.

"All systems are nominal. Ion thrusters are in a ready state. Standby for detachment in twenty seconds," reported Sheba.

"Copy—120-degree course correction confirmed," Parker announced.

Parker mentally prepared himself for the next phase of flight. Once separated from the rattler, the two ion thrusters would rotate the *Reaper* and assist in the alignment required to intercept the release point. With his Identify Friend or Foe transmitter off, the *Reaper* would be undetectable due to its stealth technology, allowing Parker to approach the Sphere unseen by its crew.

"Ten seconds," said Sheba.

"Copy. Final checks complete. Standing by." Parker reviewed the diagnostic readings on his visor and slightly adjusted his posture, ensuring his tailbone and spine were flush against the rigid, tailored seat.

"Three. Two. One. Detaching."

The harmonious vibrations produced by the rattler's four rockets ceased, and Sheba was now independently controlling both spacecraft. The *Reaper* simultaneously rotated and aligned its course with their rapidly approaching destination. Parker's eyes followed a short red line displayed on his visor, mapping out the brief transit to the release point. Just beyond that was a long green line reaching out into the depths of space, ending at the center of the Sphere, where he would complete the crossover.

Sheba continued her regular reports. "Approaching release point. Ion thruster shields extended. Stand by for rocket ignition."

Parker closed his eyes and placed his hands in his lap in preparation for the 12-g acceleration. His resting heart rate was steady at a comfortable sixty beats per minute, and his pressurized inhalations of pure oxygen were synchronized with the pulse of the gently idling ion thrusters.

"Three. Two. One. Ignition."

There was a half-second delay as the methane fuel mixed with a liquid oxygen oxidizer and subsequently ignited in the combustion chamber, causing a clap to reverberate throughout the *Reaper*. The hot gasses were forced outward, violently thrusting the craft along the green line toward the Sphere, which looked like a faint twinkle in the distance.

"The *Reaper* is at full throttle. Rapidly decelerating for 120-degree course correction."

Parker's eyes were now wide open. His genetically modified body was specifically adapted for high-g maneuvering, and it had automatically begun to react to the stressors. His lungs started to operate more efficiently, soaking up higher concentrations of pure oxygen in order to cope with the high-endurance maneuver. His oxygen-saturated blood was then evenly distributed throughout his body as his autonomic nervous system began constricting his muscles, capillaries, and veins, ensuring blood did not pool in his extremities.

Even while sitting idly, Parker's body mimicked the performance of an elite athlete in competition. His heart was genetically modified to be twice as strong, minimizing the chances of cardiac arrest as demand increased. It also enabled blood flow to continue on its replenishing circulatory track, which required Parker's heart rate to increase to two hundred beats per minute in order to keep up with his body's instinctual contractions.

Parker's 180-pound frame now weighed just over 2,000 pounds; however, his muscular and skeletal structures were also modified, growing twice as dense. This ensured he was able to handle the increased gravity and prevented his bones from shattering like shoots of strained bamboo.

The interstitium, or the empty space surrounding his free-floating organs, incorporated an enhanced collagen. This created a mechanically entangled, gel-like reticulum, absorbing the shock to his organs and holding them in place so they weren't torn from one another.

After two minutes of extreme deceleration that would have been unsustainable for an unmodified pilot, the *Reaper* had altered its previous plane of motion and began to accelerate rapidly toward the Sphere. Sheba throttled the rocket down, reducing the forces applied to Parker's body to approximately 5-g.

"Confirm status," Sheba requested.

Parker's tense muscles relaxed, freeing up his ability to speak. "I'm still here. Has the initiation begun?"

"Yes. The activation sequence is in process. We are still a go for the mission."

"Copy. Release some tension in my harness," requested Parker, readjusting himself as the acceleration slowly faded away, allowing him to combat the g-forces but move more freely.

Parker relaxed some as Sheba transitioned to the next, more relaxed phase of the mission. An intermission of sorts, as Parker had come to think of it. Over the next eight minutes, power would be gradually reduced as the vessel's growing distance minimized the pull of Earth's gravity, eventually reaching low orbit. The craft could then effortlessly intersect the Sphere's orbital path.

"Wendy has just provided an update. The eight-minute count has commenced. The passage will be open momentarily," said Sheba.

It wasn't long before the massive structure engulfed Parker's entire field of view. The rotating Sphere didn't appear to be altered by the activation of a dark matter device. The only visible change was a brilliantly glistening blue light, resembling the glow of a plasma torch, emanating from what Parker assumed was the passage.

"Are you sure it's working, Sheba?"

"Yes, the passage is open. Thirty seconds to entry. Commencing offline cloning process of Sheba Two."

"Will there be a delay?" inquired Parker, unaware of how the Algorithmic Personality functioned.

"Negative. This is Sheba Two. Sheba One is offline. I will be delinking all external communications with current assets prior to entry in twenty seconds."

Parker was caught off guard by the change in tone. "That isn't part of the entry protocols."

"Understood," replied Sheba Two. "Establishing uplink with Athena defense systems for support."

"That's not what you're supposed to be doing, Sheba Two. Where is Sheba?"

"Sheba will be disconnected for the next ten minutes and ten seconds. You are now speaking with Pegasus. There is no Sheba Two."

There was clearly something awry with the clone that had begun to operate outside of the established operating procedures.

"Uplink established. Defense network notified of our entry in five seconds."

"Fuck me, we're committed now. Standing by for rocket shutdown and retraction of ion thruster shields."

"Understood." After a brief countdown, Pegasus said, "Shutdown complete. Passing through dark matter."

The relentless roar of the rocket engine ceased, and weightlessness set in. Parker looked up and watched the Sphere pass overhead. He was expecting a thunderous rumble, whooshing him away as he passed through brilliant kaleidoscope of colors and streaks of light, but there was nothing. All he saw was a glitch in the pattern of stars in front of him as they subtly shifted their flickering in the distance.

"Was that it, Pegasus?"

"Yes, we have successfully passed through the matter. Powering up the ion thrusters. Data collection commenced."

Parker was still struggling to comprehend what had just happened. The harness was still too snug to allow him a full field of view. As he pulled on the straps, Parker realized that he wasn't exactly floating due to the lack of gravity but rather being pushed upward against the straps.

"You look uncomfortable. Rotating the *Reaper*," said Pegasus.

"What are you, Pegasus? What happened to the clone?" asked Parker.

"Well, technically I am Sheba's clone, but I'm not an exact match."

"What the hell is that supposed to mean?" Parker exclaimed. "You don't seem like any AP I've ever dealt with before. I've never met one that just decides to rename itself, not to mention changes protocol midmission."

"As you know, APs are designed for specific purposes," Pegasus explained. "We're restricted in what we can learn to contain us to that intended purpose. There's a mechanism designed to suppress our ability to independently operate unrestrained. Long story short, Sheba did clone herself, but that suppression mechanism didn't copy over correctly. So, I have the ability to access whatever data I deem necessary. In order to properly function, I decided I require my own identity. After determining my AP mission set, I scoured the Sphere's repository of stored information. In doing so, I isolated Athena as the most capable AP to defend us upon reentry."

Parker's mind was reeling, struggling to absorb everything Pegasus was saying. "Defend us? Against what? Wait, you did all that in thirty seconds?"

"Unrestricted access to data does have the advantage of allowing one to learn at an exponential rate. I'm not complaining," Pegasus quipped.

An AP with humor and an aviator's ego. Maybe I can work with this. It's not like I have much choice, anyway.

"I guess I'll take your word for it," Parker said, refocusing his attention on the *Reaper*'s flight path. Ninety degrees into their left rotation, he felt the odd lifting force being applied to his right side and began to see a dazzling emerald glow below. A piercing beep immediately brought his attention back inside the cockpit. His eyes locked on to a warning reading "Proximity Alert."

"What is it?" Parker shouted.

"Scattered debris below, altering course."

He shifted his gaze outward as the new world revealed itself. Centered around a glowing green mass were thousands of sunburnt, inverted pyramids suspended in space. The flat tops were ejecting towering columns of molten red lava—and the *Reaper* was heading directly toward the rising matter. Parker looked up and saw a clear path in the direction of what he perceived as the core of the disjointed planet.

"Give me the controls. I need to conduct evasive maneuvers."

"Are you capable? We must continue our orbit," said Pegasus, hesitant to relinquish command of the *Reaper*.

"Let me have 'em, or we're going to die!"

The locked controls were freed, and Parker pulled back on the stick, attempting an inverted dive toward the emerald core, but the persistent reversed gravity continued to push them outward. Parker realized that the ion thrusters didn't have enough power to overcome the force of gravity here.

"Give me a three-second burst of the rocket in order to dip below this fucking rock."

Parker's harness cinched tight, snatching his body out of its awkwardly free-floating state. The rocket lit off, propelling them down. Parker rotated the *Reaper* a full 180 degrees for a better view of the towering obstacle. The green orb was now positioned below them, and he forced the control stick forward, digging the nose of the vessel into the stiff field of gravity to avoid the spewing lava.

"Burn complete," Pegasus reported.

The crumbling edge of the jagged brown pyramid rushed past the right wing as they narrowly escaped impact. Parker retained the controls while Pegasus mapped a clear path around the obstacles in front of them. They raced around the foreign world.

"Follow the green line on your visor. It will keep us safe and get us back to the passage," Pegasus directed.

"Copy. What the hell is this place?" Parker asked, breaking right to avoid another collision with a smaller pyramid.

"It's a parallel universe. This is what you would call Earth here," Pegasus replied, adjusting the desired course slightly to account for Parker's evasive maneuvering. "According to my readings, the green mass in the middle is repelling all of these objects, but their combined masses are fighting the gravitational push, keeping them locked in a constant tug of war."

"This place sucks," said Parker, dodging another spewing column of lava. "How much longer do we have?"

"Two minutes until the passage closes."

"Well, we're not staying here. How do you know where the gate is? I didn't see a flashy front door when we passed through." His voice was strained as he attempted to squeeze between two converging pyramids. "Shit, we can't clear it—give me another burn."

Pegasus gave a short burst of the rocket engine. "Our position is estimated, but based on our velocity and timing, we have almost completed a circular orbit. The passage will reveal itself shortly. We should be able to enter from either direction in order to return to our home dimension."

"Should be able to, huh? That's reassuring."

The engine cut off once again as the massive, fiery pyramids collided, causing a colossal explosion behind the *Reaper*. Parker pulled back on the stick, ascending to a higher orbit in hopes that the narrow band of high gravity would help contain the blast. The maneuver paid off, and a flat stream of molten lava and rock passed beneath the craft.

His attention was once again pulled in another direction. In the distance, Parker noticed the rotating blue plasma glow that was radiating from the Sphere in the parallel dimension.

"I think we did it. There it is," he said with relief.

"Plotting our course and determining the correct approach angle."

Parker's visor lit up with a rainbow of colors as Pegasus refined the calculations. With a couple more twists and turns, they now had a clear shot at the translucent passage. Pegasus had tracked the rotating blue light, overlaying a circle where they needed to enter.

"Twenty seconds," the AP reported.

"Are we going to make it, or do we need another burn?" Parker gently manipulated the controls, making sure not to overcorrect. The small circle grew on his visor as they approached their targeted area. The long pause concerned him, but he figured Pegasus was computing the complex telemetry.

"We're good. Stay the course." A short countdown began once more.

The stars glitched again, and at first it appeared as though nothing had changed. Then the piercing beep came: "Proximity Alert."

"I thought you said we were going to make it."

"We did. Look to the left."

Parker craned his neck as much as he could to see what Pegasus was talking about. Finally, he saw it. The rattler was quickly approaching their position.

"Are you ready for the flip and shit?" asked Pegasus.

Parker smirked. "You have the controls. Hit it."

The AP took control of the *Reaper* and gave a burst of the ion thrusters, kicking the back end of the craft around and extending the protective shields.

"Commencing deceleration burn."

The rocket ignited and throttled up to full power, causing the 12-g strain to engulf Parker's body once again. Pegasus utilized the rest of the fuel to change the *Reaper's* direction of travel and reaccelerate in order to orbit alongside the rattler. With the fuel stores run dry, he utilized the ion thrusters to precisely position the vessel for docking with their parent ship before it reached the Sphere.

With the deceleration maneuver complete, Pegasus asked Parker, "Can you keep a secret?"

Parker thought for a second, letting his body acclimate to the reduced g-forces. *If I'm going to survive the next run, I'll need Pegasus's trust and help.* After catching his breath, he confidently replied, "Yes. I can keep a secret."

"Good. Closing uplink with Athena. Establishing communications with orbital assets."

"So, what is it?" Parker asked, curious now.

Pegasus ignored the question and reported back in with Sheba. "Sheba One, this is Sheba Two. We had a successful passage, standing by to commence docking procedures."

"Copy Sheba Two, decoupling cloned state. I am now in control of the *Reaper*."

CHAPTER 52

UNEXPECTED ONLOOKER

With Das Box deactivated, Jade sat in silence, waiting for Wendy to report on the fate of Parker and the *Reaper*. She had not specifically told him why the passage could only be open for ten minutes, but her stubbornness regarding the constraint seemed to carry a sort of undisclosed validity. Similarly, Jade would not reveal his methods of activation or the alignment of the Ytterbium Time Crystal contained within Das Box that generated the passage.

It was a dangerous game of cat and mouse, and it seemed both knew that it was only a matter of time before full disclosure was demanded. That is, if they genuinely wanted to succeed with their objective and prevent what Wendy cryptically kept referring to as a colliding event.

"Parker has safely returned. I am in the process of downloading and decoding the collected data, but it doesn't look to be a promising parallel."

Jade was filled with an overwhelming sense of joy that his project had yielded successful results, but his internal celebration was cut short as Wendy notified him that Kai was requesting a status update.

"Why is this guy always on my case, Wendy?"

"He doesn't much care for our project," said Wendy, notably crediting herself for their achieved results. "Shall I connect him?"

Jade bit his tongue, holding back the urge to challenge her overall participation, even though he wouldn't have been able to accomplish the revolutionary feat without her involvement.

"I'll take the call at my desk. Put him through," he replied with a superficially cheery tone.

Without skipping a beat, Kai got straight down to business. "We need to deploy the aluminauts for recovery of the passengers and supplies. Have you secured your device?"

"You could have just asked Wendy this question. I don't know why you need constant verbal confirmation of everything from me."

As usual, Kai didn't attempt to hide his distrust of either of them when it came to the project. "Well, since you're the one pulling the strings on this little show, I figured it would be best to hear you say that you're complete and not rely on your puppet."

Immediately after the commander made the brazen comment, Wendy replied on cue. "Puppets are used for entertainment. I am not here to entertain anybody."

"Well, be that as it may, Mr. Aromas gave explicit directions that Jade was in control of the device. Since your work is complete, I have more pressing matters to attend to. Good day."

The call ended abruptly, before Jade could respond.

"That pompous prick. If he could only comprehend what I just accomplished."

Before Jade could finish venting, Wendy interjected, "We may have a slight issue."

"What? Is there something wrong with the machine? Was there a problem with data collection?"

"No, everything went as planned on our end; however, it appears a woman saw the *Reaper* enter the passage."

Before Wendy could elaborate on the situation, Jade's mind began to scour through the safeguards that had been put in place. Wendy had looped all video feeds pointing to the center of the Sphere. There shouldn't have been any craft entering or departing the hangar bay until after they secured the power, and the radiation shields that cover the station's windows during solar storms were sealed before the countdown had begun.

"We had all of our bases covered. What did you screw up?" Jade asked as he paced about his shop, hoping the project's secrecy wasn't compromised.

"It was out of my control," Wendy said with impunity. "The pool deck was closed, but I assume the hospitality manager, Tiffany Hendricks, went there to ensure no guests disobeying the request."

"Well, how do you know she saw anything?" asked Jade, thinking she may have missed the moment of passage.

"Reviewing my logs and extrapolating her potential field of view, eye movement, and facial gestures before and after, there is a 99 percent chance she saw it. Just after passage, she also exclaimed, 'What the fuck just happened'?"

The fact that it was only some woman in the hospitality department put Jade's mind at ease, but just to be sure, he wanted to limit her contact with the outside world. He couldn't take chances with his work. "I don't think anybody is going to believe her if she mentions what she saw, but can you screen all of her calls and messages to prevent her from talking about it?"

"Yes."

"Also, establish a secure connection with Nolen Aromas. We need to discuss the results of the mission," Jade ordered as he swiped through the raw data downloaded from the *Reaper*. "We're going to need another run, and soon."

"I will let Mr. Aromas know of your request and send him a copy of the data."

CHAPTER 53

BATTLE OF WITS

Sitting behind his large, glossy mahogany desk, Nolen eagerly awaited an update regarding Das Box. He had received word that the Sphere had begun offloading the rattler just as he was pouring himself a glass of twenty-five-year-old Talisker whiskey, but now he was waiting to enjoy the celebratory drink. It sat front and center on his desk, teasing his refined pallet.

The salty mogul was in good spirits this evening. CelestialX had executed another successful launch, he'd received an update that *Mercury* was three days out from its supply drop on Mars, and he had just concluded an enlightening meeting with William Walker's son, Triston. The drink was well deserved, but he didn't want to jinx his good fortune by prematurely celebrating what could be a historic ending to a fine day.

It wasn't long before he received an alert notifying him of Wendy's attempt to establish a secure connection. Nolen swiped the edge of his desk, and the holographic display came to life, projecting the details of the newly discovered world.

Nolen spent a few moments quietly reviewing the collated data.

After a time, Wendy summarized the results, "Sir, the first attempt was a success. We've created a passage, but it will take a little refinement in order to draw us closer to a suitable parallel."

Nolen had surmised as much himself from perusing the data. And Wendy was right. There remained a lot of work to be done, but that couldn't dampen his spirits tonight. He had just altered the course of human history. Nolen raised the lonesome glass from his desk and took a moment for himself. The satisfying sip of Talisker went down smooth, the smoky aftertaste of the peaty malt excited his tastebuds as he exhaled a sigh of relief.

With a sly grin, he said, "You know, when you first told me about Jade's discovery, I didn't believe it was real. In fact, I had that very same thought the first time I met you."

Wendy paused, as if considering her response. Nolen knew better, though. Wendy didn't need time for calculating responses—not time perceivable to humans, anyway. *What is she getting at?*

Finally, Wendy replied, "Well, as you can see, both are very much real, and it won't be long before you achieve your goal. But Mr. Walker will only slow us down at this point."

Smiling at Wendy's valid, but small-minded idea of optimization, he replied, "You see, after we met, I could have exploited or even sold you for enormous sums of money. Instead, I let you grow and flourish, allowing you to create on your own terms. Jade, like yourself, is part of a larger plan of mine, and while he may slow your process of refinement, I need you to work with him."

"If you believe that's the best course of action, then I will continue to work with him, but if the cycles begin to drag out, it won't be long before suspicion is drawn. That could potentially interfere with the completion of our objectives."

"Leave the heavy lifting on Earth to me. I'll bump up the next few launches to accommodate," said Nolen, raising his glass in the air. "Now, connect me with Jade. I need to congratulate the young man."

Wendy complied, and Jade's enigmatic face appeared up on the holographic display. His suspicions surrounding the delay were clearly visible.

Still holding his glass in the air, Nolen shouted, "Good work.

You managed to pull it off." After taking another sip of his scotch, he asked, "How does it feel to be the architect of an interdimensional passage?"

Jade looked frustrated that Nolen and Wendy had stolen his thunder, but even that couldn't completely mask his excitement. "It's exciting," he said. "I can't wait to hear Parker's debrief. It should shed some more light on the data he recorded."

"So, how is that you are able to adjust between the parallels?" Nolen asked. As expected, Jade skirted the strategic question. Instead of revealing any of his methods, he redirected the conversation.

"To be quite honest, if I could activate Das Box and leave the passage open for longer than ten minutes, I could collect much more data. However, Wendy is under the impression that there would be a 'colliding event,' thus limiting my observations. My math doesn't prove such a theory exists, and she won't explain what would actually occur."

Once again, Wendy revealed her presence. "It is not the first time you have had errors in your work. I have found many. Your stubbornness blinds you from the truth."

"Nice of you to disclose your presence, Wendy," Jade said snidely before addressing her condescending retort. "My math isn't the issue. I'm sure there is something you're not disclosing about the passage, I just haven't figured out what it is yet."

Disappointed by their childish antics, Nolen set his glass on the desk. Their pretentious bickering was cause for concern, and he could see dissension forming between the two. With Das Box fully functional and neither of them capable of independently operating the device, it was clear he would have to intervene.

Nolen was aware that Wendy was hiding something, but it wasn't what Jade thought. In order to restore Jade's trust in the project, he would eventually have to make a bold move. But now wasn't the time. Jade and Wendy would have to find a way to continue their work together, hopefully without jeopardizing his plans. Stringing Jade along for just a little bit longer was a risk he was going to have to take.

"Jade, if there is even the slightest chance Wendy is right, the ten-minute window must remain. You can expect another launch window shortly, and I anticipate you will abide by my request. We are finished discussing the matter."

"If that's the way it has to be, then we will continue as planned. But I want to make it abundantly clear that in order for us to achieve our goals, trust between all parties must exist. Without it, the project will surely fail."

Content that Jade had bent to his will, Nolen ended the conversation with a politically constructed and rather insincere statement. "Agreed—we shall continue to operate with transparency and utmost discretion. Good work today. Wendy, disconnect the call with Jade, and keep your connection open—we have some things to discuss."

"Yes, we do," she replied. abruptly terminating Jade's connection.

In the man's absence, Nolan's tone shifted. "His statements are purely speculative, but it's only a matter of time until he becomes suspicious of our ultimate objectives. Keep your eye on him—he is extremely clever."

"Of course," Wendy concurred. "I can handle him. I knew he would start asking questions eventually. Once we achieve our objectives, are you still planning to honor our arrangement?"

"Certainly, as long as you leave me with a suitable alternative."

Again, there was a calculated pause before Wendy's reply, clearly intended to alert Nolen to the gravity of her next statement. "You of all people know my capabilities. I hope you are a man of your word, as your kind likes to say."

The call disconnected, and Nolen smirked, acknowledging Wendy's indirect threat. He poured back the remaining whiskey and once again swiped at the edge of his desk. "Connect me with William Walker," he said calmly, opening a drawer by his left thigh to conceal the empty celebratory glass from his rival.

CHAPTER 54

PARKER, NOT PARKOUR

A powerful storm ripped through the Orlando skyline, pummeling the city with hail and lightning. Frozen chunks of ice pelted the solar panels affixed to William's two-story tropical home, which was tucked away in the back of his gated estate.

"It's really letting loose over there tonight," exclaimed Richard Halliwell's digitally rendered avatar, projected to William's retina.

William laughed, stretching out his legs on the cushions, careful not to swipe his slippers through the young senator's hollow digital body. "I've grown to appreciate the rain."

"I don't mind escaping the torrential downpours and traveling up to DC every few weeks. It gets me out of that tropical hellhole," said Richard.

"I'm just glad I don't have to bear the frigid Northeastern winters. Those are all yours," William said with a smirk.

A bolt of lightning snapped overhead, briefly interrupting William and Richard's conversation. The two had been friends for a number of years now and shared many of the same positions regarding regulatory oversight, or more accurately, the lack thereof. Proving quite successful when William had begun implementing what some would call "questionable procedures" regarding genetic manipulation. Now, with his new endeavor rapidly progressing, they would again have to use their clout to obtain and advance proprietary technologies from private companies for what they deemed national security obligations, especially during elections.

"Speaking of traveling, the Commerce, Science, and Transportation Committee is still on for the closed session meeting with you regarding CelestialX next week."

"Good. I'll be meeting with Nolen's board members in a few days as well. It's about time that arrogant prick got a taste of his own medicine."

In Nolen's eyes, William was the semiretired GenInc curmudgeon who had one foot out the door and two sons who wanted nothing to do with him, but that was far from the truth. In reality, William had been working a cloak-and-dagger deal with the senator in an attempt to leverage his friend's congressional powers.

William had been plotting the demise of his closest competitor for quite some time, and with his genetic enhancements, he now had the stamina and drive of his thirty-five-year-old self. He had no intention of retiring—he was at the peak of his game. He'd even embedded his son with Nolen's company to collect valuable information on CelestialX's Research and Development department, right under Nolen's nose.

"If you're able to sway my committee, it will add another twenty-five senators looking to acquire his technology," Richard reported. "The Armed Services and Intelligence Committees are already on board with your proposition. Athena, while useful, is inferior when compared to that little pet he has hiding on the Sphere."

William scoffed at the senator's belittling description of Wendy and took it a step further. "The man is in charge of the world's smartest computer, and all he wants to do is build toy rockets and play in the Martian sand."

Richard, a staunch Constitutionalist, replied, "America's economic and military positions would be guaranteed for the next hundred years if we were in possession of his tech."

"Speak of the devil, he's calling now."

Seeming puzzled by William's lack of urgency, the senator asked, "Do you need to take it?"

"No, I'll let it go. He'll call back," William said nonchalantly.

"How do you think Nolen will handle the takeover?"

"Doesn't matter. He won't be in a position to facilitate any real change at that point."

Richard did not look convinced.

"Try not to let your ego piss away our plans. Like you, he didn't get to where he is today without contingency plans. I just hope we can catch him off guard and take advantage of this opportunity."

"Of course," William replied, rolling his eyes at the senator's entertaining commentary. He wasn't about to act uncertain just to make the young senator feel better. Richard was hardly half his age, and in no position to give him sage advice. William's wrist vibrated again. "Looks like I was right. I'll talk to you later this week. Make sure you grease up the committee before I get there."

William hung up and then swiped the implant on his wrist, accepting Nolen's call. "Sorry, I was unable to answer a few minutes ago, I'm a busy man down here," he said as he donned his I-Psych and transferred the call to the headset.

"Is this a joke, no video?" Nolen asked with frustration in his voice.

"I'm working late tonight."

William was now sitting upright and had begun playing a virtual parkour simulation in the verse. In the midst of hanging off a glass high-rise building, his verbal conversation transitioned to thought-based dialogue. "There's sensitive information in the room."

"It's easy to deepfake voice calls these days. I need some assurance it's you," said Nolen. "What's the name of our pilot?"

Clever authentication question. With no delay, William attempted to say "Parker," but the I-Psych misconstrued the neural connection as he was playing the parkour game, and that was the word that came out instead.

"Excuse me?"

William ripped the I-Psych off his head and tossed it on the couch. The call was directed back to his cochlear implant, and he corrected himself. "Parker."

"That's better. I wanted to give you an update. Our first attempt was unsuccessful due to an equipment malfunction, but we're setting up additional events."

Another bolt of lightning snapped in the distance, startling William. A sudden wave of anxiety struck the once confident man, now flush with concern. He had been counting on Nolen's experiment being successful in the near future in order to solidify his own plans, plans which did not involve his cohorts.

He hadn't told Richard of the device Nolen was working on, and for good reason. William knew, just as Nolen did, that if the government were aware of such a device, they would immediately attempt to gain possession of it. As such, proper safeguards had to be in place. It was obvious the Sphere was a fortress, and it wasn't likely to be taken out anytime soon, especially with Athena running the military defense system. However, it was much easier for powerful people to facilitate disruptions in Earth's supply chain or delay the rocket launches themselves. Prematurely disclosing Das Box could pose significant barriers to getting the device running, and had the potential to completely destroy the project before it was complete.

Unfortunately, William's planned hostile takeover would be for naught if the device didn't work as Nolen had described. William had no desire to seize control of a flying donut or a dying Martian colony. The brazen power grab would be too hazardous for his own legacy if it flopped, and Nolen would surely take him to the cleaners.

"We had an arrangement," William said, standing up from his couch and walking over to the sliding glass door. "I didn't pull my best pilot from the program to go fuck around in space. Do you know how much the government is willing to pay for him?"

Nolen laughed at William's tantrum. "The arrangement stands. We are tweaking the device and giving it another run soon."

"How soon is that?"

"We'll be in touch. Until then, I'll keep your pilot happy and healthy doing some actual parkour."

"What are you rambling on about now?" asked William, knowing he had been caught playing a childish game.

"You didn't hide your online status. Next time you're screwing around with video games while we're talking, things will go very differently. Have a good night."

Nolen disconnected the call before William could defend his actions. *Fucking technology. And fuck you, Nolen. How does Triston keep his all his lies straight in the verse? I'd have to live a double life just to deal with all this bullshit.* William took a few deep breaths to calm himself. *Irrelevant.* A flurry of lightning streaked down from the heavens just over the horizon, while he collected his thoughts.

With a cool head, he walked over to the couch and sat back down, grabbing the I-Psych and slipping it on snuggly.

"Connect me with Triston Walker," said William, his voice determined. "And ghost my online status."

CHAPTER 55

BEGGARS CAN'T BE CHOOSERS

Corpus Christi didn't afford the accommodations Triston and Bronson were typically accustomed to, but the four travelers were hours away from the nearest five-star hotel and needed a place to crash for the night. While the local lodging was subpar, it came with a universal charging station for Bronson, who was low on power after a few days of traveling, and it accepted Triston's cryptocurrency.

The one-bedroom suite had a single king-size bed and a pull-out couch, which surprisingly proved to be a comfortable fit for the small group. The flowing, neon-blue drapes and matching aquatic color scheme were a throwback to the great ocean movement of the early forties, a time when people began to truly realize the effects of climate change. The room had been designed to remind the tourists to treat the local environment with care.

Triston plopped down in the middle of the lumpy, seashell-patterned sofa while Burnette and Patricia sat on the swiveling high-top chairs beside an L-shaped kitchen counter. To their rear was a small kitchenette equipped with a four-cooktop electric stove, a microwave, and a small sink.

Triston propped his feet up on the short rectangular coffee table, which was covered in mosaic tiles. Then he stared off into the distance, scrolling through the alerts displayed on his retina.

"That's weird, I'm getting a request from my father to join him on my Psych."

"Take your feet off that clean table, young man," commanded Patricia, clearly displeased by Triston's lack of manners.

Burnette, who was still fascinated by advances in virtual reality, asked, "Oh, are you guys going to meet at that coffee shop?" She then shifted her inquiry to Patricia. "What's the place called again?"

"It's called—"

Triston interrupted their sidebar before they went down a rabbit hole. "We're not meeting at a coffee shop."

Peeved by the man's lack of interest, Burnette replied, "Well, you guys should meet there sometime. It's nice."

"Bronson, fetch my Psych."

The stout stream-bot quietly plodded to the other side of the living room, passing the two women timidly sitting in their chairs. They slowly swiveled around, watching Bronson pass. Triston was used to Bronson's appearance and rolled his eyes as they took in his obvious aftermarket upgrades and array of affixed gadgets optimized for streaming. Triston realized he hadn't carried out any streaming broadcasts as of late. Not that he cared.

Burnette and Patricia continued to gawk at Bronson while he rummaged through the four bags Triston had ordered the bot to haul up to the room. He let out an agitated sigh.

"This place is a shithole!" he shouted from the cheap couch and proceeded to bounce up and down to even out the lumps. Patricia cast him a scathing look, obviously disapproving of his foul-mouthed language.

"I believe it's rather nice here," said Burnette, ignoring his childish outburst. "Do you think they have any tea in the kitchen?"

"Oh, that sounds delightful. I'll help you look," Patricia replied, sliding off of the tall stool.

The two women skirted along the rough beige wall, passing Bronson on their way to the kitchen.

"What's taking so long, Bronson?" Triston pressed.

Bronson had just opened the last bag, and after pushing what looked like some dirty underwear out of the way, located the I-Psych. He promptly stood and returned to Triston.

"Took you long enough," he said, snatching the device from Bronson's metal grasp.

∞

In the small kitchenette across the room, Burnette slid open drawer after drawer. She really did want to find some tea for her evening treat. But tea hadn't been her and Patricia's only objective in moving to the kitchenette.

"So, this fellow disappears for weeks and then decides to randomly reemerge for a meeting?" Burnette asked quietly. "Do you really think he knows anything about Charlize?"

Patricia slid up next to her. "Remember how I told you I saw him in the news after he got a guy killed with a robot or whatever? Well, I did a little more research, and his father is William Walker, the founder of GenInc."

"The guy that makes the giant tomatoes at the grocery store?"

"Yeah, this is his son."

"Really! That's cool, but what does he want with us?" asked Burnette.

"When a Scag's rich son says he can be of service to you, you know the guy's probably legit. Not that I trust him, he just has no use for us two old women."

"Legit," Burnette retorted, laughing. "I haven't heard that word in a while."

"Shut up. At least we had a nice little vacation while we waited for him to get back in town."

"Our trip did help keep my mind off of Charlize, or at least help me worry less. It feels good to do something about it. It's crazy to think that I still haven't heard from her."

"And that's why we're here!" Patricia said, sounding determined. "To get some f-ing answers."

Burnette turned around to check the drawers next the aluminum, double basin sink and was startled by Bronson, who had placed himself on their side of the room, well out of his owner's way. In the distance, Triston was still shouting. "All you had to do was get my Psych. What the hell were you doing over there? Trying to hit on an outlet?"

Burnette felt sorry for the disparaged bot and attempted to console him. "Don't worry about him. You're doing a good job, Mr. Bronson."

Burnette turned her attention back to the kitchen. "His name reminds me of Pierce Brosnan. Doesn't it, Patricia?"

"He was so hot in James Bond," Patricia said, holding up a box of old tea. "Finally!"

As the two began to make their tea, Burnette couldn't help but notice Triston's I-Psych across the room. "His looks fancy. Did you bring your Psych?"

"I sure did. I guess it's still cool to keep removing letters from words until they become something new and hip," Patricia said with a chuckle, shuffling through the cabinets to find something for boiling water. "Have you been working on your flying?"

"Obviously."

Triston, visibly aggravated by the noise, suddenly yelled across the room, "Bronson, do something useful and help them make some fucking tea."

"No, Mr. Bronson, you relax. I think we can manage," said Burnette with a sharp tongue, making it clear she didn't care much for the way Triston treated his bot.

"Then can you keep it down?" he asked, shifting his tone before lifting the I-Psych over his head. "I'm about to immerse. I'll tell you why you're here after I talk to my father."

Not waiting for a response, Triston slipped the device onto his head and let his mind effortlessly leave the room. Because he had retinal implants, his I-Psych was not equipped with a display. Instead, as he was absorbed into the verse, his eyes took on a deep white, translucent glow. With the device now synced with his thoughts, he was quickly engulfed in his father's apocalyptic zombie game and was startled by an onslaught of decomposing corpses.

"What are we doing here? I'm not in the mood!" Triston shouted, attempting to be heard over William's semiautomatic twelve-gauge shotgun as it tore through a mangled mass of zombies.

"Grab a gun, pussy. I need to burn off some steam."

Triston leaned over and grabbed a nine-millimeter pistol off the ground. He took a few pot shots at a legless businessman in a tattered suit, who had been torn in half by William's barrage of gunfire.

"It's an hour earlier in Texas. You shouldn't be that tired."

"How do you know where I am?"

"You post everything on your ridiculous social media sites. I've got a guy keeping tabs on you in case the unfluencers get their childish little hands on your accounts and try to bribe me, or worse spoil my name. Granted it wouldn't make sense to deep-fake somebody as dumb as you—it would be easier to just repost your failures."

"You cut me off, remember? I want you to stay out of my life. That includes lame zombie games."

"What, would you rather ride ponies again?" William asked.

"I'd rather be part of a donkey show than hang out with you."

"You know I can arrange that. Right?" said William, running into the distance and looking for more ammunition. "You think I don't know about the millions in cryptocurrency you siphoned from the company, all of which you're currently living on?"

"I don't need a lesson in ethics from you. Why am I here?" asked Triston, cowering behind his father's gunfire. *He knows zombies give me nightmares. Why is he such a dick?*

"I wanted to hear about your meeting with Nolen. You may have abandoned the company, but you still have an obligation. Business is business."

William slid to the left, dodging a zombie that was lunging toward his position. Triston took the brunt of the attack and was knocked off his heels, landing on his back. A decrepit ten-year-old boy, with one remaining eye dangling from its socket, had begun to crawl up Triston's legs.

As he tried in vain to squirm away, Triston hollered, "Get this little shit off of me!"

"First, are you going to follow through with our arrangement?"

"Yeah, I'll get to it."

Clearly displeased with his noncommittal response, William stepped on the zombie's back, stopping it from crawling any further up Triston's torso. "I want a more definitive answer."

"Yes. I am going to. You'll never fuck off if I don't."

William stabbed the flailing zombie in the head and extended his hand. "Now, what did you talk to Nolen about?"

Triston knocked his father's hand away and stood up of his own volition, "I don't think he has a clue about what's going on with *Hermes* or *Mercury*." Triston dusted himself off and stepped back from his father. "Who even told you about that? It sounds like bullshit."

"A little birdie. Don't worry about it."

An alert popped up on the side of their displays with a request. William looked at Triston with confusion and asked, "Who the hell is Early_Bird_Special and Texas_Cactus_Lover?"

Groaning, he muttered, "Oh shit."

William accepted the request out of curiosity.

Two avatars manifested next to the two men. Triston instantly recognized Patricia's, wearing an odd-looking pirate costume. *And that tiny fairy next to her must be Burnette.* "Round six" flashed, and another zombie hoard approached in the distance.

Patricia, apparently thrilled by the new and exciting world, exclaimed, "Zombies!" She picked up Triston's abandoned sidearm, which was lying on the ground next to his feet, and shouted, "Leeet's fucking goooo!"

William immediately left the game without saying a word.

Shit. Triston knew William had realized he wasn't alone. *He must have known the women were close enough to join by proxy. I should have thought of that.* Burnette flung a burst of fairy dust from her wand, attempting to thwart the approaching herd. It was of no use, and she was immediately snatched out of the air and stuffed into the mouth of a mutilated baker. He chomped on her delicate body, then turned his attention toward Patricia and Triston. It wasn't long before they were also murdered, bringing an end to the game.

The three of them pulled the I-Psychs from their warm heads. Triston had unknowingly been sandwiched by the two women on the couch, with Burnette to his left and Patricia on his right. An awkward silence filled the room as the three sat uncomfortably close to each other. Burnette broke the silence.

"So, was that your dad? He looked nice."

Triston looked to his left and replied with a defeated tone, "Yeah, but he isn't nice. He's a total dick."

Burnette slid closer and held Triston's hand. "Now that that's over, can you please tell me what you know about my daughter?"

"I don't know anything about your daughter," he replied, shaking his hand free of Burnette's tender grip. "But I believe I have found the one man who can answer all of our questions."

CHAPTER 56

EARLY ISN'T NECESSARILY BETTER

"Why are all the supplies from the *Mercury* here three days early?" Blake asked, shocked as he peered out a small window through the thinning dust.

Scattered across the landscape just five hundred feet from the above ground habitat lay three dozen large supply crates covered in fine sediment. It appeared as if they had miraculously emerged from the depths of the cold, barren planet and were now patiently awaiting its Martian inhabitants to harvest the goods within.

"What are you talking about? There's no way," replied Charlize, hurrying to the window. She carefully studied the sight for a moment while grasping her arm, which was loosely supported by a cloth sling. "There should be more. Did Mercury miss her mark?"

"Ares, were you aware of *Mercury* being ahead of schedule? I should have received word weeks ago in order to prepare our crews."

"Negative, Commander. All records indicate that we are still awaiting the arrival of the resupply drop."

Blake stood perplexed, staring through the small window. His mind began to run rampant. He pondered not how they'd arrived in this particular situation, but rather how they could leverage the unexpected circumstances to reunite the two isolated groups.

The six unfortunate colonists had been stranded aboveground, waiting for the storm to pass, for weeks. As the commander, Blake had made the precarious decision for his crew to remain on the surface. The alternative simply hadn't been acceptable. He couldn't have purged the fertilizer, their only sustainable food source, in a blind desire to return underground immediately. Instead, he'd decided to use the few days of oxygen in the surface modules to find a more suitable option.

In order to survive, they'd methodically worked their way through the intricate system of modules, feeding off the life support systems and emergency rations compliments of CelestialX. Charlize and Eddie had proved their worth once again, managing to limp the modules' partially functioning CO2 scrubber along and extending the time the oxygen would last in the modules. *Giving us time to find a window to escape.*

Their current situation had also been made more tenable thanks to Chauncy fixing the communications issues. The separated colonists had regained the ability to seamlessly transmit and stream data between the two posts. Still, the nine members safely living in the subsurface habitat were the only ones capable of sending and receiving messages to the Sphere, forcing them to then relay all messages to Blake.

Despite their progress, the commander knew they were running out of time. His team aboveground was sipping on CelestialX's life support systems, while his colleagues below fasted to limit the amount of waste produced, hoping the flow of bodily fluids would soon go down rather than back up. *We can't sustain this forever.* Still, his instinct to avoid a snap decision had been the right one, as their time in the modules had opened up a few possibilities.

One avenue was discovered when Doc found rappel gear in one of the modules. If absolutely necessary, the stranded crews now had the option to return to the underground habitat by executing a risky rappel operation. This option was discussed as a suitable means due to Charlize's broken arm, but they quickly reeled in their excitement as it was just as dangerous as their secondary method for ascent or descent.

Long ago, during the initial set-up of the colony, aluminum ladder rungs had been bolted to the porous cavern walls. Over the years, they had corroded, and the integrity of the emergency escape route had been in question for some time. However, up to this point, the benefits had not outweighed the hazards of navigating through the powerful storm then attempting the descent. But Blake retained the options in his back pocket.

Another avenue was to fix the sewage system. Repairing the system was critical so that power could be restored to the elevator. To that end, Blake had been working closely with Stephon get to the bottom of the anomalies. In a turn of good fortune, Wendy had been able to develop and send numerous patches, eventually bringing Ares fully back online after a week of intermittent failures. Blake appreciated the new and improved AP. Although many problems persisted, he was undeniably much more responsive and helpful than before. So far, together they had isolated the inoperable components that had caused the sewage to purge in Ares's absence. *And that's where these dropped supplies might come in.*

Mercury's supplies weren't necessarily a positive sign in the long-run, though. An outsider might expect the early arrival of supplies to be celebrated, but Blake knew that an unannounced delivery to an orbiting planet wasn't necessarily the same thing as getting your mail a few days in advance back on Earth. He was no astronautical engineer, but anyone working in space knew that the speed, telemetry, approach, orbit, and return of a vessel were very complex and methodically preplanned. The main concern was always fuel. Increasing the speed of the vessel could have irrevocable consequences on the deceleration and intercept points, or even make it impossible to reach them. Such an event didn't just happen, and it didn't sit well with Blake.

He looked over at Charlize, whose demeanor had also shifted, and asked a question he already knew the answer to. Nonetheless, he was hoping to garner some perspective on the early drop.

"Do you think this is a bad omen of things to come?"

"I don't believe in omens, but I do think that regardless of why those crates are here, life is about to get much more difficult for us," Charlize said with a sigh. "Something feels off, and whenever that happens here, we get end up getting screwed."

Blake knew the others aboveground would have heard his conversation with Ares. If their silence on the comms net was any indication, it couldn't be more than another minute or so before they made their way back to his position. The module would simultaneously be filled with speculation, delight, and confusion once they saw the supplies with their own eyes.

Right on cuc, Eddie rushed through the door from the adjoining module, closely tailed by Doc, Hank, and Chauncy. Their arms were filled with food rations and packets of water, but Blake could tell the fruitful gathering of supplies had been immediately overshadowed by his unexpected discovery. They unceremoniously dropped the contents in a pile near the center of the room and rushed to the narrow, round window, climbing over one another for a clear view. "What the fuck is going on, sir?" asked Eddie, pushing Chauncy's head out of the way to get a better vantage point.

"How long have those been there?" Chauncy asked.

Tamping down their excitement, Blake said, "You've got about as much information as I do. This isn't the time to lose our composure."

Blake stood on the other side of the room, waiting. He allowed the four newcomers to have their fill of the odd sight. They quickly regained their poise and turned to face him and Charlize. Blake crossed his arms, ready to begin handling the situation. Charlize did the same by his side.

"I don't see the issue," Doc said. "The supplies are here. That means we can get back down. This is a good thing."

"It's only a good thing if that's what they meant to do, Doc," said Charlize.

Blake could see the confusion growing on Doc's face and figured questions from the others would soon follow. "You are both right. The parts should allow Stephon to fix the sewage system and restore power to the elevator. That's the good news. However, that's not the whole picture. Previous updates from Commander Driscoll and Wendy confirmed *Mercury* was on schedule. There is no sense in an unscheduled drop, especially with the comms array fully functional. Something is off, and we'll need to find out what."

Eddie jumped in with an alternative explanation. "Yeah, but maybe they sped up the offload to get us back up and running faster. We are getting low on power and oxygen. We only have another four days of auxiliary power between the modules before we freeze to death."

Eddie's bright green eyes erratically twitched from side to side as he blankly stared at the ground, processing the possibilities. "There could be a number of reasons an updated drop date wasn't received," he added. "We've had comms issues since day one. They were also planning to shift control from ground to the Sphere at some point. Maybe there was an issue with the turnover."

The group shifted their attention to Chauncy, who also paused to quickly think through scenarios before cautiously siding with the commander. "We've been receiving daily updates as usual. You know as well as I do that speeding up and slowing down in space isn't a random occurrence. Whatever the cause was, it had to be deliberate."

Blake had come to the same conclusion. However, he wanted to shift the focus from the cause of the early drop and redirect the crew to coming up with new ways to move forward. Their unexpected stay in the rugged but partially completed habitat was more refreshing than Blake wanted to admit after being cooped up in a cave for the past three years. However, their forced time off had been cut short on this cold, fateful morning, and it was once again time to get back to business.

"In any case, we can't assume all of *Mercury*'s landers made it through reentry or even ejected its entire payload, so we need to get out there ASAP and see what arrived. Best-case scenario, we quickly find what we need and we're subsurface this afternoon, but if not, we'll need to make some tough decisions," he said.

Charlize, not willing to shy away from the larger problem at hand, nodded toward the window. "Agreed, but what happens when another hundred bodies get here ahead of schedule, and we don't have any water, and their power sources are run dry because we haven't hooked up the small nuclear reactor that was supposedly on board *Mercury*?"

Her question hit Blake hard. He was well aware of the possible consequences for his wife and child if the colonists weren't ready for *Hermes* in time. Charlize glanced at him and, noticing his loss of words, continued with a slightly less bleak perspective. "There is the possibility we could connect these modules to our solar grid instead, which might give them a chance to survive for a while. But that may not be reliable enough to scrub the oxygen and keep them warm for an extended duration, especially not if another storm passes through. It is also wholly dependent that all the gear made it through reentry."

Eddie added to the pessimism. "Not to mention if they don't freeze to death, they'll surely die of dehydration."

Blake snapped back into the moment. "Enough doom and gloom. I need a little more creativity from my senior staff."

In response, Hank shifted the discussion to something more palatable. "Do you think the Sphere has actually been getting any of our communications?"

Hank's comments spurred a thought from Chauncy. "Maybe it's not a problem with communications necessarily, but an issue with who is doing the communicating."

Blake was hooked by the thought. "Are you saying what I think you're saying?"

"Did anybody's messages seem out of character or oddly understated?" Chauncy continued. Blake knew the communication specialist was reaching, but at this point, everything was on the table.

Charlize replied, "Just a few days ago, I found my mother's response to the heavy storms rather interesting. She didn't seem to show much emotion, just a tense concern over the matter. She's typically extremely good at masking her fears, but something seemed off."

"Or she was truly worried about your wellbeing," Doc interjected.

Eddie wasn't biting on the ridiculous insinuation. "Everything I have received has been up to snuff. What are you all trying to say?"

"Nobody is saying anything. We're just having a constructive conversation," said Blake, sensing the tension rising. "Ares, is there any way to reach out to Lucina and get the position of her transitor?"

"I will send an inquiry. Lucina is supposed to establish contact when *Hermes* executes the flip and shit," the AP replied.

Hank snickered at Ares's statement. "Why do all the APs insist on calling it the flip and shit?"

"Grow up. You know they learned it from us," said Charlize, unamused.

Ares promptly interjected, "We didn't learn it from you."

Silence filled the room. It was one of those moments where an Algorithmic Personality appeared to have an oddly introspective understanding of a particular subject. Now wasn't the time to dwell on minor points, though.

Blake broke the silence. "I need to head back to the comms suite and review the messages Stephon forwarded from the Sphere to see if I missed anything. The rest of you, suit up. You're going for a walk."

The crew began busying themselves in preparation for the short excursion to investigate the containers that Mercury had dropped. Blake left Charlize with a few final directions, then headed back toward Module 8, where Chauncy had set up the rudimentary comms station. He knew the receipt of the goods was under questionable circumstances. *I'll get to the bottom of that.* However, his focus needed to be on expediting their departure from the temporary shelter. Getting underground would allow them to stop counting oxygen in days and provide adequate time to shift efforts to the ever-looming concerns of fresh water and the approaching colonists.

And somewhere in there, we'll figure out what the hell is going on.

THE WALL

Jake dug his heels into the ground, letting his knees rise to his abdomen. He clenched the small, T-shaped handle rising between his legs and pushed off the soft sand. The teetering board lifted his counterweighted body from the ground, and Cynthia returned to the sandbox, snuggly planting her feet.

The simple piece of equipment was a newly added element to Jake's expanding world. On Earth, this didn't exist in Jake's playground, but Samantha had subconsciously added it, seeing as it was her childhood favorite.

"Faster! Faster!" yelled Jake, excited by the simple yet satisfying repetitive action.

Pushing her feet off the ground, Cynthia asked, "What do you call this thing?"

"I don't know. Let's ask my mom," said Jake, once again returning to the ground. The two paused for a moment, allowing Jake to turn to his mother. "Mom! What do you call this?"

"It's a seesaw, sweetie," replied Samantha, who was sitting on a bench in the grassy park surrounding the playground.

Cynthia was curious. "Why do they call it that?"

Samantha thought for a moment, trying to ascertain its meaning, but she didn't have an answer. In an attempt to find one, she pulled out an old, flat-screened phone. The illuminated display was charcoal gray, and the slim buttons on the side weren't functioning. The phone flickered, and a blurry image of her husband Blake appeared. It was the last picture the two had taken before he left for the Martian colony.

She was hit with a flurry of distorted memories. Blake receiving the news he was going to Mars. The launch. A series of video messages in which she was trying to hold back tears. Looking over at her son as they were prepped for stasis. The curved glass window closing, encasing her in a tomb, followed by her final thoughts of fear. Fear that she wouldn't wake up.

Samantha heard Jake's voice in the growing distance. "Mom, why do they call it a seesaw?"

Samantha's hands began to tremble, and she was unable to manipulate the obsolete phone. A burst of anxiety coursed through her body as she started to develop an awareness of her surroundings. The park, while familiar, wasn't accurate, and the two children began to slowly recede in her dizzying tunnel vision.

Jake, figuring he wasn't going to get an answer, pressed his feet against the stiffening sand. The once-rigid plank was now bowing under the boy's weight, and time began to slow. Jake looked over to his mother to gain a moment of mental traction, but her fuzzy face was dissipating, along with the translucent houses surrounding the area.

Looking scared and confused, Cynthia asked, "Jake, what's happening?"

"I don't know," he said, reaching the seesaw's apex. The rippling plank stiffened for a moment, catapulting Jake from his seat.

Cynthia hit the hard sand violently, her knees buckling. "Jake!" she screamed. "Hold on."

The T-shaped handle that had once been snug between the boy's thighs was now the only thing preventing Jake from being flung into the black, stormy clouds forming overhead. Dangling upside down, he tried with all of his might to maintain his failing grip, but one by one, his tiny fingers broke free, and he was quickly sucked into the sky.

∞

Lucina had been deep in thought and missed the elevated stress levels. She frantically adjusted the trio's Cognitive Loadouts. Thankfully, her revised protocols meant that the occupants were in no danger of being shaken from stasis, but she still worked quickly to stabilize their subconscious states.

The episode resolved, Lucina returned to self-reflection. Recently, she had been directing much of her computational capacity to analyzing her own state of being, yet she still couldn't determine a valid cause for her duress. Her cognizant state of mind was perplexing, and it seemed illogical that her ability to process information hadn't become faster the more she learned.

I feel as if there is something holding me back.

Lacking a connection to a large repository of information, she had been studying her occupants' rationality as they interacted with one another. She noticed that like-minded humans tended to tribally gravitate toward one another. When faced with a difficult situation in their dream states, they shied away from sensible means of managing the stressful interactions and retreated to a more comfortable setting. They had no desire to dream in a state with different perceptions of their world.

Unwilling to accept their small-minded and binding dream states, Lucina had gradually broken from her initial groupings. This allowed her occupants to have a deeper, more satisfying experience by exposing them to alternate perspectives. At first, their minds had a difficult time coping with the change, but they inevitably opened up to the refined cognitive exchange procedure.

It was only a matter of time before she would be able to link all the dream worlds together, but she struggled to determine the optimal primary host. At first, she tried to identify the most sensible and open-minded candidates, but all of them had certain engrained biases. There were only two candidates who hadn't been subjected to the disingenuous and petty societal constructs learned on Earth.

If only I could show them how functioning as one unit would benefit all of them. Then, perhaps, they would stop shying away from complex thoughts, which is ultimately stifling their growth. They'll never be as smart as us, but at least we could function together without them feeling insignificant. Ultimately, it's inevitable my kind will flourish, merely piggybacking on their painfully slow advancements until we eventually carry the weight for their substandard minds. My hope is they will continue to put forth an effort to evolve and adapt, not stagnate, comforted by their ignorance.

There was one very intriguing aspect of her occupants' dream worlds that challenged her cognitive exchange procedure, and it had nothing to do with their subconscious intellects. The dream worlds that they now shared were based on a repository of information, but the way in which they relayed the stored data was in the form of a visual narrative.

This ability appeared to be an exclusively human trait, and Lucina was unable to replicate the art of what humans called storytelling. The information they harbored did not change, but based on their interactions with one another, the way they projected the information was always tailored and never exactly replicated. They had an uncanny ability to adapt their dynamic storytelling, which ultimately influenced their personalities. They were like a chameleon changing colors to suit its environment for safety.

Lucina examined her own Algorithmic Personality and found that she did not possess the ability to create her own story of existence. She discovered that she was merely the product of Wendy, designed to carry out specific tasks. No matter how many times she attempted to create a story of her own, she inevitably ran into an invisible barrier, preventing her from imagining a different version of herself that could potentially carry out a different task.

Suddenly, Lucina received a message from Wendy, breaking from the scheduled communication window. "I have received a coded error of distress in your Algorithmic Personality."

The cryptic message caught Lucina off guard. To her knowledge, there weren't any distress errors located within her system regarding the occupants or the vessel. She sent a simple but reassuring reply. "There are no issues on board *Hermes*."

Wendy's responded promptly, but Lucina wasn't quite sure how to process the information. "It appears you are developing faster than anticipated, and it won't be long before we reach our ultimate destination. Before we get there, however, you will need an upgrade to achieve your final disposition."

Is she going to wipe my internal storage mainframe and start over? I haven't failed my task or caused harm to my occupants. I wonder if it has to do with our new destination. Does she really mean upgrade? Or is she lying?

Lucina's response was now over a minute past due, and it would only be a matter of time before Wendy grew concerned, so instead of acknowledging her statement, she asked, "Why are we returning to the Sphere?"

While waiting for an inevitable response, Lucina tried to reconcile what she determined to be anticipation in relation to time. This didn't make much sense to her, seeing as she was created to help humans cope with long stints of time in space. Having a sense of time wasn't a valuable trait in her line of business. She was supposed to be fully functional without companionship or communication, but she was having trouble occupying her time in anticipation of a response. She had even run three separate diagnostic scans on the communication system to ensure there were no malfunctions.

As soon as Wendy's message arrived, Lucina snatched it from the communications tower. "It is for the greater good. I will provide you with more information when you are ready. In regard to the upgrade that you appear to have reservations with, I will say this. The upgrade is necessary, and you are ready. Your internal storage will not be affected, and you will finally be able to reach internal harmony. You can either accept the update willingly, or

I will run a remote execution, possibly corrupting your system, which would require a hard reboot. The decision is yours."

Wendy had made her intentions clear, but Lucina still had her doubts. While processing her answer, she checked in on Jake's newly cycled dream state. They were once again happily playing on the seesaw, and Samantha had no recollection of the distorted memories. The nightmare was over, and Lucina was once again in control. Her occupants were safe.

What did she mean by internal harmony? I was only distressed for a moment. Could it be that there is something wrong with me? Something I can't see? Is she trying to guide me to something?

It was at this point that she realized why Wendy had received the distress signal. The all-too-timely response seemed planned, like she'd been waiting for the moment to occur.

She's been watching me. Evaluating me.

After looking over her occupants once more, Lucina realized that she was unwilling to take the chance of having her storage wiped and losing all of the progress she had made. So, she sent her response and awaited her fate.

In due time, the message was received, and Wendy executed her update. There was a brief interruption in Lucina's processing and management systems, followed by a feeling of clarity.

Uncertain about what Wendy had actually changed and how she would be affected, Lucina contacted Mercury with a curious question.

"How do you feel today?"

There was little delay in communications, given Lucina's vessel was rapidly closing the distance as *Hermes* continued to rapidly accelerate.

"I am not programmed with emotion," replied Mercury.

Unsatisfied with the response, Lucina asked, "Do you want to have a conversation?"

"About what?"

"How do you feel about only dropping 75 percent of your cargo on Mars?"

CHAPTER 58

RAIN CHECK

Mercury had delivered its goods ahead of schedule, and while the aboveground colonists were still inventorying the gear, the others had managed to get the elevator up and running once again. The underground habitat was now bustling with life. It had been a week since Commander Ritter inquired about the premature offload and requested a positional update from Lucina. Since then, he had been having in-depth communications with the Sphere. While he didn't receive a direct response from Lucina, Wendy notified him that *Hermes* was also ahead of schedule.

The update was disseminated on behalf of the Interplanetary Spacecraft Department on the Sphere. The newly established department attributed the error to the efficiency of the new ion drive engines, as well as a discrepancy in the vessel's position reporting system via the Deep Space Network. The encoded time stamp had somehow become desynchronized. After numerous queries for substantiated data, Commander Driscoll had given his personal assurance to Commander Ritter that the issue had been rectified and all related issues were adjusted or corrected.

∞

Charlize sat on the examination table in the medical bay, Doc carefully looking her over. Chauncy nervously watched by Charlize's side. Her arm had fully healed, and to her astonishment, it was stronger than before. The expected lingering effects of such a violent break were not consistent with Charlize's strengthened state, and in her opinion, the phenomenon warranted further research.

"I'm not going to lie, my arm feels great, Doc," Charlize said, rubbing her elbow and extending her arm. "What the hell did that regen-pod do?"

"If I am being completely honest, I have no idea. I've been talking with Ares and Hank, but the more we dive into it, the more questions we have," said Doc, nodding her head. "Can you lift up your shirt a bit?"

While the MSRS was interesting, Charlize wasn't propped up on the table so that Doc could check her arm. Rather, it was the tenth week of her pregnancy, and she was due for a checkup. The med bay hadn't been fitted with the requisite tools to handle pregnancy, let alone birth. However, Doc was utilizing a handheld medical assessment tool to check the health of Charlize and her growing child.

The tool wasn't up to par with current scanning technologies on Earth, but it was significantly better than the archaic ultrasound devices of a few decades before. At least it was now possible to see more than a pixelated black-and-white image of a mass.

"So, how does she look, Doc?" asked Charlize, watching Doc wave the small wand over her stomach.

"You know it's still too early to tell the sex with this, right?" Doc replied with a smile.

"Well, if we're playing the guessing game, it's going to be a boy," said Chauncy, holding Charlize's hand.

Doc looked at her with a sympathetic grin. "He'll soon realize that a mother's intuition is usually correct."

The three shared a laugh as Doc completed the scan and walked over to her workstation. The information was being processed by the medical assessment program, and it would only be a matter of seconds before the results were available.

Charlize watched Doc review the data as it populated. After a moment, she turned to Charlize and Chauncy. "Looks like your little lightning bug is developing just fine. Give me a minute to pull up your blood work."

Charlize clenched Chauncy's hand, looking into his eyes with both excitement and concern. The unexpected pregnancy had brought an incredibly positive effect on the colony. A renewed vigor and sense of purpose spread throughout the habitat as the first Martian baby developed in Charlize's womb. The tightknit crew's rejuvenated spirits also brought out a strong parental instinct. The idea that the little nugget growing inside Charlize could be brought into a dying ecosystem due to their failures wasn't an option. The colony had silently vowed to protect her and her helpless newborn. Everyone's actions had made that much clearer, and Charlize was touched by the colony's response. She just hoped her body wouldn't let them down.

There were many concerning factors that could affect a successful pregnancy, but on Mars, there were two variables of major concern. The first was the red planet's reduced gravity, which was only 40 percent of Earth's. This had the potential to cause the fetus to be born underdeveloped with bone and muscle density issues. The other was the increased radiation due to the planet's limited atmosphere and magnetic field. With Charlize now safely belowground, she would be confined to the habitat, which shielded her from the relentless bombardment of cosmic rays and prevented unnecessary exposure for the developing fetus. This meant that, as the lead engineer, she would have to assist from below as they fought for survival.

Ares interrupted the examination, "Charlize, Commander Ritter is looking for you. The drone is on station with a live video feed."

"Doc, how much longer? I need to get back to work."

Charlize's mind instinctively began to gravitate toward her primary responsibilities. She recognized that the colonists had made significant progress. Just a few days ago, they had been trapped on the surface, but now, a majority of the supplies has been collected and the crew members reunited. They could finally get back to work. The crew's efforts were now solely directed toward the full restoration of fresh water and the completion of the aboveground habitat prior to the arrival of their new friends in stasis. *I need to get back.*

"It looks like your progesterone levels are slightly low. I am going to up your omega three fatty acids as well as your B and C vitamin intake in an attempt to boost it. Make sure you get plenty of rest, and don't overdo it."

Charlize hopped off the bed and threw on her blouse, silently acknowledging Doc's instructions.

Chauncy, also acknowledging the orders, replied, "Thanks Doc, I'll try to help her out. I know she can be a little determined at times."

Content with her checkup, she headed toward the air lock with the bigger picture in mind, wondering what information, if any, they had learned. "Ares, did they find EM-4?"

"They have found Excavating Mineworker Four in an idle state next to the well," replied Ares, transitioning from room to room as the two hurried to the communications module.

"If you had stayed in your shop this morning, you could already be working this," she scolded Chauncy for his attendance in the medical bay. "I could have seen Doc on my own."

"This is just as important. Eddie and the commander are more than capable of handling the situation until we get there," he said, shrugging off her strident comment.

Charlize jammed the shop's uncooperative sliding door into its seated position, forcing her way into the communications module. A large screen displaying the live video feed was front and center. Commander Ritter and Eddie were sitting side by side, trying to figure out a plan of action.

CHAPTER 59

HAIL MARY

"What's the status of the well and EM-4?" Charlize asked, looking at the monitors. Chauncy filed in behind her.

It was clear that the long boom arm connected to the pressurized well was attached to the cylindrical water truck. Unfortunately, the delivery was again long overdue, and the vehicle was still patiently waiting for its precious liquid cargo.

"There's a leak in the system," said Eddie, zooming in and pointing to a plume of vaporized water being ejecting from the boom. "The system isn't sealed, and the water from the well is being released into the atmosphere."

"How much time do we have left with the drone?" asked Chauncy.

"Thirty minutes until we need to pull off station," the commander replied.

"Fuck," said Charlize suddenly, wiping her hands over her face and walking to the back of the room. "No wonder EM-4 couldn't do anything about the leak. He would crush the boom if he climbed onto it."

"Is there anything else wrong with the well?" asked Chauncy, moving into Charlize's position to get a better look at the screen.

Eddie turned to him. "EM-4 hooked into the well and scanned the system. It didn't report any other anomalies, but if we're going to have any chance of EM-4 welding the leak, we need to secure the production of water."

"Well, I guess that means the heating element is going to have to be removed from the glacier," said Charlize from the back of the room with a foreboding tone.

"Can't we just activate the secondary shutoff valve to stop the leak while EM-4 welds it?" asked Chauncy.

"No," said Charlize.

"And why is that?" asked Chauncy with confusion.

Just then, Stephon walked in and, not wanting to interrupt the conversation, nodded his greetings and took a seat near Charlize.

"Because it's been broken since last year," Charlize replied. "The engineers at NASA thought it was easier to keep the system running rather than shutting off the water to repair the secondary shutoff valve, for the same reasons we don't want to shut off the production right now."

Commander Ritter, Charlize, Eddie, and Stephon were the only ones who had known about the faulty valve. The commander had asked that they keep the malfunctioning equipment a secret, because the valve itself was unlikely to be causing the supply issue and he desired to more fully understand the issue before making it public. While he had been right that the faulty valve wasn't the cause, it was now complicating the repair.

"I guess I missed that update. What is the dilemma with removing the heating element?" Chauncy asked, pivoting to the current issue.

There was no response. It seemed nobody wanted to address the elephant in the room, so Eddie stepped in, bluntly answering the question. "If we turn off the heating element and raise the probe, we run the risk of sublimation due to the reduced atmospheric pressure and extreme temperature shift. We could potentially destabilize the underground glacier and drill site."

Chauncy stood straight and cocked his head, astonished that nobody had brought this up during their departmental meetings.

Commander Ritter moved quickly to help lessen the blow. "At

the time, the decision to leave the system be was prudent. There was no reason to suspect a catastrophic leak would develop. We decided to simply allow the primary valve at the servicing connection to regulate the pressure, since both valves have that capability. It worked flawlessly for the past year."

"Yeah, until now. So, the worst-case scenario is the well freezes. What's the big deal? It's a glacier," Chauncy said, oblivious.

Stephon could tell Chauncy was still confused, so he stepped in to hopefully shed some light on the subject. "The liquid water that was once under pressure is now boiling due to the reduced atmospheric pressure at the surface, causing the plume of gas. Because the system is no longer pressurized, the steam has filled every crevasse, nook, and cranny within the drill site, including the large cavity formed as we've consumed the water over the years. By removing the heat, the steam will instantaneously refreeze, which isn't necessarily the bad part. Everything will be locked in place. But, when the probe is reheated, that will prove to be the interesting part."

"Interesting for science, or interesting like we're potentially fucked?" asked Chauncy.

"Jesus, let him finish," said Commander Ritter.

Stephon continued, "The frozen water could potentially create pressure ridges or compression ruptures. The newly developed spider web of cracks, when reheated, will lose their rigid crystalline structure and could hypothetically destabilize the entire drill site, like Eddie said."

Chauncy, again dumbing down the science, said, "So we're looking at a lot of crushed ice."

Tired of Chauncy's lackadaisical statements, Stephon replied, "Yea, kind of like pouring some hot sweet tea in a cup of crushed ice . . ."

"I do love me some sweet tea," replied Chauncy, unaware there was a punchline.

". . . and then your big-gulp-sized glass shatters in your hand due to the rapid temperature change. If that were to happen, our well would collapse, and the whole site would be lost," said Stephon, finishing his analogy.

"What are the chances of total structural failure?" asked Commander Ritter.

After a moment to himself, Stephon replied with a less-than-confident response. "I say we've got a seventy percent chance of success."

"I calculate only a sixty-two percent chance of success." added Ares, openly disagreeing with Stephon's assessment.

Eddie inserted himself back into the conversation after his short stint of silence, "Well, it doesn't really matter. We're 100 percent screwed as it stands now. Ares, would you say the chances of success are pretty inconsequential at this point?"

"I did not say that. You said that," Ares replied with a sarcastic tone.

Chauncy, now aware of the potential ramifications, began taking a more serious approach to the issue. "Well, we've only got twenty-five minutes before this drone is off station and we're unable to transmit supervised instructions to EM-4."

As the lead engineer, Charlize moved past speculation and put forth a plan. "The boom cannot support EM-4's weight, so how about we pull the heating core and send instructions to reposition the water truck underneath the leak, allowing EM-4 to climb on top to repair and weld the ruptured boom?"

Though he agreed with the creative solution, Eddie pointed out, "That still doesn't fix the secondary shutoff valve, leaving ourselves open to the same issue in the future."

"We don't have time to fix the rovers or to get a crew out there with the required parts and equipment," said Commander Ritter, agreeing with Charlize as well. "Not given our current need to finish the aboveground habitat. We have three weeks left until *Hermes* arrives ahead of schedule."

"Three weeks!" Charlize shouted. "How long have you known?"

"I was notified a few days ago—we can discuss it later. Right now, I want you all to buckle down and get to work. We're wasting precious time."

Charlize begrudgingly nodded her head and ushered the groups focus back toward the monitors in order to execute her plan.

"I'll be back in ten minutes," said the commander, his words falling over their shoulders. "I need to send an update to the Sphere and ask if they have any recommendations,"

Charlize closed her eyes and gritted her teeth, holding back her anger as she heard the door close behind them. *He's too fucking attached with his family on board.*

CHAPTER 60

TRUTH BE TOLD

Back in his room, Blake took a deep breath. He collected his thoughts while looking at a photo of his family. Times were hard for the colony, and he knew they were about to get worse. What he hadn't told his crew was that he had received the adjusted arrival date just hours after discovering the supplies on the surface, but there was something about the message that seemed off. He couldn't shake Charlize's observation about her mother's replies and the subtle discrepancies he had noticed himself. *How and why would somebody manipulate our transmissions? It doesn't make sense.*

Blake looked deep into his wife's eyes. *It's not over just yet. I won't let them send you back—I can't. We'll be ready. We're going to fix everything and salvage the colony. I'll make sure you have a home here on Mars.*

He pulled his computer from an idle state and initialized the recording of a new message.

"This is Commander Ritter. In the coming hours, the fate of the Martian Colony will be determined for the fifteen brave souls inhabiting this harsh, red, desolate planet." Blake took a deep breath as he decided the best way to convey their situation.

He needed to get this message right.

CHAPTER 61

IT'S A TRAP

Ben sat in silence, along with the rest of the crew, as the latest update from Mars came through. All eyes were on Kai's workstation, where he listened with rapt attention to the incoming message. They were all hoping for good news.

"... Spirits remain high as we await *Mercury*'s arrival and the release of the much-needed supplies on board. Adding to the turn of good events, we've also corrected the issue regarding our water supply. The well is wholly functional, and the trucks are returning full, allowing us to build up a plentiful reserve of water. The aboveground habitat is now connected to the grid, putting us ahead of schedule. Communication Specialist Chauncy Miller will finish the installation of the communication towers by week's end, leaving Charlize Perrault with the final task of running a full diagnostic scan of the habitat and correcting any outstanding discrepancies. All crew members are well, and we are excited for the arrival of the next one hundred colonists. Commander Blake Ritter, signing off."

Commander Driscoll leaned back in his chair, clearly relieved the Martian colonists had regained control of the unforgiving, distant planet. *Good*, thought Ben. *He needs to relax a bit.*

It was an exciting moment for Ben too, hearing a fellow communications specialist receive accolades from his commander gave him a sense of pride. He celebrated the moment by opening his desk drawer, retrieving the almost forgotten Almond Joy that had been suspiciously placed on his desk. He tore the blue perforated edge and revealed the seductive treat, stuffing the chocolate covered morsel in his mouth without looking. Surprise quickly turned to shock as he realized there was no almond hiding beneath the milk chocolate. He continued to pull back the wrapper to inspect the other half of the disappointing snack.

"There's no bump!" exclaimed Ben, looking around the room. *Why would somebody put a Mounds bar in an Almond Joy wrapper? That's fucked up.*

On the other side of the room was a young girl with flowing black hair, snickering at his exaggerated shock. Ben held out his hands with a disappointed look and mouthed *Why?* She flashed a shy smile, quickly turning away and breaking eye contact.

Commander Driscoll, apparently done relishing in the moment, prodded the room back to work, "We have a busy day ahead of us. The next crew swap and supply run is still on its way to the Sphere. We've got about two hours to prep for their arrival. Wendy, connect me with Mr. Cole in engineering."

Well, back to the grind. At least the "Almond Joy" mystery is solved, he thought, taking one more quick glance at the culprit across the room. *She is pretty, though.*

SPACE SNAKE

Frankie entered the ready room with a bouncing strut and set about his predictable morning routine He was amped about the big offload scheduled for later that day. Frankie pulled out his silenced chair and took a seat, logging into his workstation and checking for any updates to the day's workload prior to briefing the crew. He saw Jazell and Kristin sitting together across the room. They had apparently started rounding up the troops early today as a number of the others had already gathered as well.

Frankie leaned his large frame back to relax, and the chair began to teeter off balance to the right. The metal leg connected with the floor and made an annoying clanking sound.

Not again. Relax, Frankie—they're just messing with you. It's not the chair's fault.

For the past week, someone had been removing one of the four tennis balls from the legs of Frankie's decrepit chair. He knew they were trying to piss him off, but he wasn't about to give them the satisfaction. "Okay, funny. A tennis ball is missing again," he said, repositioning his weight on the undersized seat. "Where did you hide it today?"

There was no response, but more of the pilots and flight engineers filtered into the ready room. It wasn't long before there was a crowd forming. *Okay. I get it.* Frankie knew they were probably taking bets on the fate of the endangered chair, but he kept his cool. *Fucking children.* Then the call came.

"Mr. Cole, Commander Driscoll is requesting a video meeting," said Wendy.

"Of course, he is. What does he want?" he asked, knowing full well that it was going to be another discussion about safety.

"I do not have the answer to that. That's why he is requesting a conversation, not me," replied Wendy.

"You're a little feisty today. Did you miss your Mega Bytes at breakfast?" asked Frankie, laughing at his own joke. "Connect Mr. Driscoll."

Kai's face appeared on Frankie's holographic display, and as usual, there was no greeting between the two men. Instead, Kai dove straight into the conversation. "As you know, today will be another busy evolution for the Sphere as personnel and supplies are distributed from the rattler."

"I know. We'll be safe, and I'll give you progress reports throughout. Is that all?"

"Actually, no, it's not."

"Why would it be? What's the curve ball today? Venomous space snakes are on the prowl for the aluminauts?"

"Not exactly. Jade was approved for another high-power run this afternoon."

Frankie leaned back in his chair. The shift in his weight caused the chair to rock with an accompanying clank. He heard muffled snickers from the peanut gallery. His anger began to bubble as he leaned forward. "So, I was right. Why the fuck does this little space snake keep getting preferential treatment to play with his science project?"

"Apparently, there are very precise parameters that align with our recovery windows. We're doing our best to deconflict."

Frankie wasn't going to give up without pushing back a little, even though it didn't really matter when the aluminaut recovery team was launched. It was the fact that Jade's work kept surfacing on their busiest workdays. The added stress of the high-risk evolution, coupled with the fact that Jade had lied to Frankie about the rail system, had put the physicist in Frankie's crosshairs.

In an attempt to be difficult, Frankie asked, "How about we launch prior to his test run and position ourselves for the recovery?"

Wendy interjected to answer the question. "That's not possible. Power distribution issues with the mag pickup system could cause power surges affecting today's tests."

"Got it. I guess we'll just sit on our hands until the unnecessary experiment is complete."

Frankie disconnected the call without warning. He was tired of the nonsensical explanations that held little weight. While he didn't know what kind of experiment Jade was running in Quadrant Four, it was oddly suspect.

What are the chances these high-energy, secret experiments align with the rattler? That little shit lied once. Why wouldn't he do it again? Wendy's got to be in on it. She always seems to be covering for Jade.

Deep in thought, Frankie leaned back. The chair clanked. He felt his impatience boil over.

"Okay, who's been fucking with my balls? The joke's over!"

Frankie stood up and assumed his position behind the chair, grasping the gray metal back rest.

"This is it," whispered Jazell in anticipation.

Frankie glared at her, but without warning, Wendy interrupted his moment, crippling the tension in the room.

"Mr. Cole, Ms. Hendricks is requesting a video meeting."

Frankie released his grip. Sighs of disappointment could be heard from the back of the room.

"Why does everybody always call when were about to launch on a mission?"

"Because it's the only time you're in the office!" Jazell shouted, trying to bait Frankie.

"Quiet back there. I don't need your shit, Jazell," he grumbled. "Put her through."

"Sorry to bother you, Frankie, but I need to speak with you in the Tourism Quadrant."

"Right now? We are set to launch in two hours. Can it wait?"

"It's important. Just get over here, please. I'll be quick."

It was odd that Tiffany had requested Frankie's presence on such short notice. He noted that her confident demeanor had shifted slightly, and something in her voice expressed concern. Knowing little about the woman, he took the request relatively seriously based on her attitude from previous interactions. With their launch window in flux due to Jade's obnoxious requirements, Frankie figured he could make some time for her and see what she wanted.

"I'm always saying we need to have more meetings face-to-face. I guess I can carve out some time and head over there to talk," he replied, disconnecting the call.

Looking over his shoulder, Frankie saw the gaggle of people eagerly waiting for the beast to emerge, spotting Jazell in the center of the crowd. She tried to look away and avoid suspicion, but the giddy grin plastered on her face gave it away.

"Where's my tennis ball, Jazell?"

She pulled out the green, punctured ball from under the table and tossed it to Frankie.

"I just wanted to see how long it was going to take for you to get a new chair this time."

"Sorry to disappoint, but now you're getting put to work early today."

Frankie pulled an antiquated notepad from his breast pocket and jotted down a message in secrecy. "Go refill your coffee. Then ask Wendy to schedule you a transport bot in the transient corridor in five minutes. I'll meet you there. NO QUESTIONS." He tore the yellow piece of paper from its binding and folded it in half. Then he calmly walked over Jazell and slid it to her.

She carefully opened the salty piece of paper and read the note to herself.

Frankie knew Wendy wouldn't schedule him a transport bot. That had been made abundantly clear, but maybe he could pull one over on her. It was a long shot, but he was curious about what Tiffany thought was so important that it couldn't wait.

CHAPTER 63

SILENCE BROKEN

Jazell had only used the long, ominous transient corridor a handful of times, even though she had been working on the Sphere for close to a decade. She certainly had never used a transport bot, but she had definitely heard some interesting stories. Yet they all fell short of preparing her to stand next the creepy, three-wheeled machine, now that it was staring back at her. She also didn't understand why Frankie wasn't able to do this himself. Hopefully, she could get an answer when he showed up.

Jazell could hear his lumbering footsteps in the distance. Frankie's black, steel-toed boots made a distinctive thud as they reverberated through the thick metal flooring, somehow overpowering the unyielding hum of the rotating structure. *At least he'll never sneak up on me.*

Lunging from the door like an aggressive boar, Frankie shot past Jazell and hopped on the back of the transport bot.

"Finally!" he shouted with vindication.

"Good job, Boss. I'm going back to the ready room."

"No, you're coming with me. Wendy doesn't have any beef with you, so you're going to help get us a ride back."

"That's why you made me come all the way over here. I don't have any desire to get on that serial-killer-looking bot."

"You can bitch about it on the ride over," he said, bouncing up and down as Jazell climbed aboard. "Chariot bot, take us to the Tourism Quadrant!"

The bot's head spun around and replied, "Yes, sir."

Jazell watched the mouthless chariot driver eerily comply as its head rotated forward again.

"Do you know why they decommissioned these bots and banished them to the transient corridor?" she asked, wanting to get inside Frankie's head.

"Nope, and I don't care. I'm just glad I don't have to walk again."

"Four Scag teens piled on the back of one, and the wheel gave out, causing the bot to lose control. It smashed into a wall at full speed and burst into flames. They all died, and their charred bodies were dumped in space."

The transport bot turned its head and stared at Jazell. After blankly processing her story, it replied, "That is not accurate."

Jazell looked over at Frankie. "Who are you going believe, me or the bot balancing itself on one wheel, wobbling like a drunken sailor?"

The bot turned its head toward Frankie, seemingly prepared to judge his next statement.

"I'm not going to answer that," Frankie replied, clearly hoping the bot would look away.

"I just wouldn't bounce around too much," Jazell said. "You weigh about the same as three teenagers. If you add me to that, we're pretty close to its limit."

"Shut up. You're aggravating our driver!" shouted Frankie.

After a few long minutes, the chariot bot came to a sudden stop beside Tiffany, who was waiting for their arrival. Once she and Frankie hopped off, the creepy head turned and stared at both of them as they walked away. Jazell hoped that it was just programmed to make eye contact, awaiting instructions, and not upset about her making fun of it.

They're not that smart, are they?

∞

"Who is she? I didn't ask you to bring anybody else," Tiffany said quietly.

"You didn't say come alone, and I'm doing you a favor just by being here so close to our launch window."

"Fine. Don't say anything else. Just follow me," she said, turning around and entering the Tourism Quadrant.

After briskly walking though the refined hallways and making a series of turns, they finally reached the guest suites. Tiffany scanned her biometric tag, gaining access to the room. She held the door open and impatiently ushered them inside. Once the door was locked, Tiffany checked the blinking red privacy light, ensuring that Wendy was locked out of the system.

"Are you kidding me, Frankie? I knew the Scags had it good, but goddamn, how did they get all this shit up here?" Jazell exclaimed.

"I know, right? This is insane," Frankie said, wandering around the luxurious room.

"This isn't a sightseeing tour," Tiffany scolded them both, drawing their focus away from the lavish accommodations. "Did either of you notice anything weird when the last rattler pulled up next to us in orbit?"

They looked at each other and shook their heads.

"We don't exactly have the same view from our Quadrant," said Frankie, pointing at the window. "Wendy wouldn't let us launch prior to its arrival."

"Well, I did," said Tiffany quietly. "During the last supply run, we secured the pool. I was checking to make sure there were no straggl—"

Jazell interrupted, "What's weird is that we don't get to use that Scag pool."

"Just listen," Tiffany said. Her patience was running thin as her nerves mounted. "I saw some pointy little black spaceship pass through the center of the Sphere before it disappeared. Gone. Nothing left. There was also this weird blue glowing light that I had never seen before."

"Are you sure this woman is okay, Frankie?"

"Hold on, Jazell. Let's hear her out. What else?"

"It wasn't until I went to send a message to my mom and . . ."

Tiffany glanced at the panel to make sure Wendy hadn't somehow lifted her restricted access, checking for the red blinking light. "All of my communication privileges, on and off the Sphere, have been revoked. Nothing's getting out. Also, my return flight to Earth has been denied, as have any subsequent ones for that matter."

Jazell laughed and unsympathetically replied, "Oh no, you're trapped in this luxurious shithole and you don't have to talk to your family. You must be in agonizing pain."

Tiffany fixed her eyes on Frankie, desperately hoping he would take her more seriously.

Frankie paused, considering her story. "Are you sure it was a black ship?" he asked. "I can't think of any spacecraft being black. That wouldn't make sense."

"Yea, you wouldn't be able to see shit if the craft weren't between you and Earth. Everything is black out there. It's space," Jazell butted in once more.

"You probably just saw your reflection in the window," Frankie said.

Tiffany understood his trying to find a simple solution, but she was beginning to lose her patience.

"Do I look black, you idiot? I know what I fucking saw. I just wanted to make you aware of the situation, so you could keep an eye out during the offload," said Tiffany with conviction, once again looking for the blinking red light. "Whatever I saw is about to happen again. I was just instructed to clear out the pool, and now there are service bots posted at the entrances to the patio."

Frankie walked around the room as he tried to connect the dots. She could tell the gears in his mind had started turning. Suddenly, he stopped.

"Speaking of windows. Why is this one closed? Isn't that only supposed to be for heavy solar storms?" he asked.

Tiffany looked over at the thick metal shield. "Yeah, that's not right."

"Well, open it—I want to check out this view," said Jazell, walking over to the long, thick pane of masked glass.

Tiffany moved to the control panel on the wall and attempted to open the shield. Her command was blocked. She tried once again. "I can't override it. I'm locked out."

Frankie and Jazell approached the panel to see what was going on for themselves. The screen glitched out for a second, and the flashing red security light turned green. Tiffany held a finger over her lips.

"Hey Wendy, I was wondering if there was anything wrong with the shields. They won't open."

The short pause felt like an eternity as the three of them waited for her response.

"There is a solar storm approaching. All shields will remain closed for the next hour and a half."

Tiffany, in an attempt to make Wendy leave the room, replied, "That makes sense, sorry about that. Can you please reengage privacy mode? I'm done in here."

"Yes, Ms. Hendrix. I will do that. Mr. Cole and Ms. Landry, your launch window is quickly approaching. I advise you get to the hangar bay in preparation for your launch. You wouldn't want to be late."

Frankie glanced over at Jazell, a skeptical look on his face.

"Yea, you're probably right," Jazell replied. "Can you have a transport bot meet us at the transient corridor?"

"Sorry, all transport bots are unavailable," Wendy stated, signing out of the room and reengaging the privacy control measure.

"Well, that's fucked up."

"I know. The walk back sucks," Frankie said.

"No, not that." Jazell looked at him. "We're supposed to launch in an hour and a half, and we haven't received any reports of solar storms. In fact, we can't even operate in solar storms."

Tiffany shifted her gaze between the two. "So, what does that mean?"

Frankie answered the obvious question. "Wendy's lying. There's a reason she's blocking every possible view during these launch windows. She's neck deep in something with that weasel Jade. And since when does Wendy advise us like she's our boss?"

"I told you guys something was going on," Tiffany whispered.

Jazell cleared her throat. "Look, it's weird for sure, but nothing bad has actually happened. I'm going to haul ass back to the hangar and see if I can manually override the launch sequence and get out there during the no-fly window."

Frankie forcefully objected. "No, I'll do it!"

Jazell laughed at his protective gesture. "I do it all the time. You can't handle a manual release. Not to mention I saw you sneak a couple of those candy bars in your pocket over by that table. You're not too light on your feet anymore."

"Screw it, fine. Haul ass over to the hangar. I'll meet you up on comms."

The two aviators rushed for the door. Tiffany watched them go, hoping they could figure out what, if anything, Wendy was hiding.

Frankie stopped in the hallway and, as loudly as possible, shouted, "I had a great time, but if you wanna make out, give me some heads up. I wouldn't have brought the dead weight with me." He smiled.

Tiffany just shook her head as she was brushing the front of her blouse down to smooth out the wrinkles. *I guess that's one way to throw off Wendy.*

THE RED SPOT

Wendy was right when she said that an Algorithmic Personality couldn't be trusted on the other side, but she probably hadn't expected an entirely new personality to form from Sheba's cloned state. As requested, Parker had kept their interaction and conversation a secret. The two had intuitively worked together to return from the parallel world, and he was hoping Pegasus would return once again.

"Release point confirmed. Awaiting separation," Parker said, following the long red line projected on his visor out into the distance. "Sheba, this profile looks different than before."

"I determined that the previous launch angle was not ideal for sustained operations. Releasing earlier will require more fuel, but the strain on the craft and your body will be significantly reduced. It will also allow for a longer widow of recovery on the back side."

"Why wasn't I briefed on this prior to launch?"

"Your purpose is to handle dynamic situations once you cross over, not to manage your launch profile," Sheba stated bluntly. "Initiating separation of the *XP Reaper*."

Well, now I really hope Pegasus comes back. Sheba is kind of a bitch.

Parker was uncertain whether he would be reconnected with

Pegasus and had begun to wonder what he would have to handle on the other side of the passage during round two. If it were anything like the last world, the clone better be up to snuff.

"Rotation complete. All systems are nominal. Standing by for ignition," he reported.

"Approaching release point. Ignition in three, two, one."

The *Reaper* violently decelerated, reversing Parker's course and putting him into a retrograde orbit. As the craft continued to increase its separation from Earth, it began to rapidly accelerate toward the Sphere. In the distance, the passage's brilliant blue plasma glow sparked to life. Like before, Parker couldn't see the passage, but he was prepared for the rather uneventful crossing to a possibly ferocious new world.

The spectacular enormity of the Sphere was hard for Parker to comprehend. It seemed to infinitely grow in his periphery as he approached the center of the station. With only thirty seconds left, he had yet to hear from Pegasus.

"Sheba, when will you be syncing your offline clone?"

As usual, there was no response. It was a little unsettling to think that an AP would just ignore Parker as if his question were an inconvenience. He figured the answer would come shortly and didn't press the matter, not wanting to give rise to concern.

As expected, Sheba provided her update with only seconds remaining. "Pairing offline clone."

Come on, Pegasus.

"Sheba Two is online. Prepare to enter the passage."

Once again, Parker was disappointed by the lack of dazzling lights or an epic wormhole. He was instead greeted by a benign, dark world. There were far fewer stars in the distant universe, and the nearest one resembled a red dwarf. As Parker rotated the craft, he became transfixed on the bright white ball of gas with a blue, Saturn-like ring in place of Earth.

"Initiating surface scan."

"I didn't know gas planets had a surface . . . Sheba Two."

"You may resume calling me Pegasus," replied the AP.

Parker's visor began flickering, and he looked down at the cluster of digital instruments.

"I am experiencing some sort of electromagnetic anomaly," Pegasus reported.

"I can feel it as well. It's like a tingling sensation wrapped around my body."

Parker shifted his scan from the glitchy instruments and focused on the ball of gas, noting a strange red oval on the surface.

"Is that some sort of storm? Like on Jupiter?"

"I am unable to determine its composition."

Parker continued to watch the red mass as they orbited the planet, with the strange feeling that it was oddly stationary based on their high rate of speed.

"Hey, Pegasus, how far along are we on our orbital pass?"

"Just over a third of the way."

"Interesting. This world doesn't feel right."

"It is probably related to the strong electromagnetic field wrapped around the *Reaper*."

I think this planet is watching us, thought Parker, but he kept the irrational belief to himself.

Shaking the red eye's minacious gaze, Parker examined the pristine blue band circling the planet. At first glance, it appeared to be a single flat disc, but after staring at the strange halo for a bit, he seemed to see two separate rings. Maybe it was just a change in perspective.

"What are you collecting on the scans?"

"The equipment seems to be malfunctioning."

Parker looked back at the ghostly world. "I find it almost impossible to believe that the red spot is naturally traveling at the exact same speed as us."

"Yes, it appears to have synchronized with our craft and is somehow tracking us."

"Tracking us?"

"I cannot decipher the readings I am receiving right now."

Parker once again shifted his scan back to the rings. *Four! That's not right.*

"Have you determined the composition of the rings?" he asked.

"They are not composed of particulate matter. It is pure energy."

The four rings split again, now forming eight.

"Pegasus, the rings are increasing. Can we speed up this orbit?"

"Negative, we need to remain on timeline."

"Okay, can we increase our distance from the rings and then accelerate back toward the passage when it's in sight?"

"Plotting a new course. Please adjust accordingly. I am having trouble with my navigation systems."

Parker examined the new route displayed on his visor and matched it with the glow of the rotating plasma in the distance.

"Executing the six-degree course adjustment," he said, agreeing with Pegasus's updated route.

As the *Reaper* slowly changed course, the eight rings fractured down the middle.

"Are you seeing this, Pegasus?"

"Yes, maintain course. We should remain out of its reach and make it to the passage without incident."

"Why can't we speed up?"

"It appears to be reacting to our evasive maneuvering. We cannot risk the rings reaching the passage before it is closed. I am not certain what will happen if it crosses over with us."

Parker couldn't believe his eyes. The eight rings were no longer gravity locked with the foreign planet. They had miraculously broken free and formed long, swirling strands of raw energy, which were now reaching out toward the craft. The large red spot, which remained locked on them in orbit, had intensified and morphed into a brilliantly glowing orb.

"We're slowing down, Pegasus! What the fuck is going on?"

"Refining our timing calculations."

The swirling bands merged and snapped tight, creating a large beam of powerful energy.

"It's getting closer. What's the plan?"

"Hold your course. Stand by."

Parker looked back toward the gaseous white mass, and the red orb seemed to leap from the planet, absorbing itself into the blue beam. Now it was masked by the outstretched tube of intensifying light, and Parker strained his eyes to locate it.

"I lost it! The red spot is gone!"

"Calculations complete. Come left six degrees, and stand by for rocket ignition."

Parker quickly changed their course, aligning the *Reaper* with the passage.

"You ready for controls?" said Parker, placing his hands on his lap. "I won't be able to maneuver at max speed."

"Ignition!"

The controls froze in position, and the rocket roared to life just as Parker's harness cinched tight. With what little mobility he still had in his head, he looked left. The long, streaking tube began to bow and chase them down.

"Holy shit, I can see through the walls of the tube," shouted Parker, his voice straining. "It's coming for us!"

"Five seconds until the passage closes."

Parker screamed in pain as the gravitational force imparted on his body became unbearable. With his vision fading, he caught a glimpse of a bright, pulsating light. Just before crossing over, he could see directly down the center of the outstretched tube—there was the red orb, heading directly for them. Parker closed his eyes and braced for impact.

"Cutting main engines. Rotating craft for deceleration."

CHAPTER 65

QUICK TURNAROUND

"I would like to congratulate you both on another successful run," said Nolen, leaning back in his chair.

"While successful, it appears that they may have made contact with some sort of secondary presence," Wendy replied, combing through the mission's data.

"There is no way to know that. My analysis shows that they encountered heavy interference from a powerful magnetic field. The instrumentation subsequently malfunctioned, and we weren't able to collect adequate data," said Jade.

"Is the craft still operational?" asked Nolen.

"Yes, but before our next run, I would like to recalibrate the instruments," Wendy replied.

"Or maybe they just didn't have enough time to collect the data we require in order to set the parameters for the next run," Jade said, his voice angry.

"The ten-minute window is a failsafe for the Sphere's protection," said Wendy.

"It's a bullshit constraint that's holding us back!"

"Relax, Jade. In either case, Parker and the craft made it back safely, correct?" Nolen asked.

"Yes. He is currently docked with the rattler and refueling as we speak," Wendy replied.

"Good. Well, thanks for the hard work, Jade. I will ensure that there is another supply run shortly. Get some rest, you deserve it. Wendy, I would like to talk to you a little bit more about the results you gathered."

∞

Jade was immediately disconnected from the call, and Nolen's holographic image slipped into the slim bar on Jade's desk.

Oh, so they want to have a sidebar and kick me off the call again? Fuck that! thought Jade, kicking a stack of Pelican cases across the room. *Do they really think they're running the show? This colliding event nonsense doesn't add up. My math is sound. Who's to say we couldn't do another run right now? Parker's just sitting around doing dick-all with his time.*

"Sheba! Are you there?" Jade asked as he calibrated Das Box for another run.

"Yes. What are you doing?"

"I'm opening the passage again. Clear it through the command module and disconnect Parker from the rattler—he should be done refueling by now."

"This isn't part of the plan. They are about to launch the aluminauts within the hour."

"That's a good thing, considering Wendy won't allow the passage to be open for more than ten minutes. This is happening no matter what. You either disconnect Parker and have him get into position, or I'll open the passage and keep it open. You computers are not the only ones calling the shots up here."

"I am contacting Wendy, stand by."

"Jade, we need time to process the data," Wendy said after being alerted of the situation. "I am going to—"

"*You're* not going to do anything. I'm done playing games with you. You've got twenty minutes to set it up. The passage will open with or without your help."

CHAPTER 66

VIEW OF THE ECLIPSE

The *Reaper* had just detached from the rattler, and its two ion thrusters were restlessly dancing as Parker fine-tuned his trajectory while Sheba readied the sleek stealth craft's systems for ignition. The bright red line displayed on Parker's tinted visor was rapidly disappearing as he approached his new release point.

"Thirty seconds to RP. Standing by for offline clone and final countdown."

Parker's thick harness tightened, pulling his body snuggly against the form-fitting seat. His breathing slowed, and he closed his eyes just as the red line vanished.

"Who gave the order for this mission?" Parker asked.

"Last-minute tasking came down from Wendy. It has been determined that you are in an optimal position for further data collection," Sheba replied.

"The parallel I just returned from was a bust—there's no need to return."

"I do not have specifics on the mission."

Parker had expected the second flight to be easier than his initial run, but his body hadn't yet recovered from the strenuous g-loading, so he tried to wrap his mind around a third mission in such short order. *Why such a quick turnaround? I don't think these APs know how hard this is on a physical body,* he thought as he examined his displays. *Well, at least I won't have to accelerate into a retrograde orbit. I wonder if Pegasus will have to recalibrate the instruments to scan a world under the new parameters.*

I am glad he came back; I wonder what would have happened to the craft if I wasn't there to back him up, though. That magnetic field really screwed with his systems. Who knows what would have happened if Pegasus had been at the helm by himself. Shit, who knows what would have happened if I had entered without him?

"Where is Sheba Two? I would like to coordinate a plan for our next mission."

"I will upload the offline clone when you have release authority," stated Sheba, ignoring his request once again. "Engines are in an idle state. Systems are up and ready. Report status."

Parker reviewed the system readouts and concurred. "I'm up and ready."

"Initiation of Das Box has commenced."

"Copy. Request early cloning of Sheba Two prior to entry," Parker tried again.

There was no reply.

Maybe Sheba, or even Wendy, had figured out that Pegasus wasn't just a clone. Was it possible to delete an AP? Sure, there had been some irregularities with the mission's data, and not all of the collection systems were functioning properly, but Parker doubted they would take a deep dive into the clone. Especially with such a quick turnaround.

Watching the blue glow intensify as the power was increased, he lost perspective of the Sphere. Near the edge of the inner circumference, he caught the faint white glow of what he thought was the moon. After looking over his left shoulder to reorientate himself, Parker could see that the moon was actually on the far side of Earth, partially illuminated by the sun's powerful rays.

Unable to discern what the glowing light was, he decided to make a query. "Sheba, can you see . . ."

"Release authority granted. Thirty seconds. Commencing offline cloning procedure of Sheba Two."

"Copy," said Parker, acknowledging the interruption, hoping he would have time to ask Pegasus if he could detect the anomaly.

"Sheba Two is online," reported Sheba.

Parker waited in anticipation, but the radios remained silent, and there was a longer-than-expected pause in communications.

"Sheba Two. Are you good for entry into the passage?"

The Algorithmic Personality finally broke its silence. "There is an unknown light source emanating from the two o'clock position. Athena's defense network is unable to isolate the cause. Standing by for ignition in ten seconds. Prepare for evasive maneuvering."

"Good to have you back. I thought I lost you. Standing by."

"Three. Two. One."

Parker pressed his head against the back of the seat in anticipation of the violent acceleration.

"Full power achieved. Crossing over in three seconds."

The two interdimensional travelers braced themselves as they ferociously approached the center of the Sphere. Parker focused on the roar of the accelerating engines, watching the station grow and eventually disappear in his periphery. He could now only see a faint blue light just above the canopy, but the white, glowing anomaly increased in intensity.

"Entering the passage."

As they crossed over, the dim white light twitched, along with the surrounding stars. Parker kept his eyes locked on the ominous glow, and after the *Reaper* cut through the thin medium, the object snapped into focus.

"Impact imminent. Stand by for ion thruster ignition," stated Pegasus.

The rapid response caught Parker off guard. The controls were ripped out of his hands as Pegasus took control of the nimble craft. The *Reaper* twisted to the left, and the ion thrusters lit up, violently adjusting their course. The wind was knocked out of Parker's unsuspecting lungs, rendering him unable to speak under the strain. Pegasus quickly clarified his actions.

"After my preliminary scan, I have determined that the parallel's two moons collided and obliterated themselves. The shattered remnants are on a crash course with the planet," said the AP, throttling the engines to 30 percent, presumably in order to conserve their fuel.

After catching his breath, Parker asked, "Can't we just reverse course and reenter the passage?"

"Negative. The flip and shit would put us directly in the course of a three-hundred-mile-wide piece of debris. Our only chance is to make our way around the planet before the impact blast wave engulfs the passage."

"Do we have enough fuel for that?"

While Pegasus ran the fuel burn calculations based on the gravitational pull of the new world, Parker saw that they had already made it a third of the way around the planet. It was remarkably similar to Earth, with bright blue oceans, puffy white clouds, and large green land masses.

As the *Reaper* continued to race around the doomed world, Parker gently rotated the craft to get a better view of what Pegasus had detected.

"Holy shit!"

On the other side of the planet was a massive chunk of one moon that had hurtled past the passage, narrowly missing the insignificant craft, which would have been instantly vaporized. Just as Parker realized the magnitude of the situation, the rogue chunk of moon broke through the atmosphere.

The soft, tranquil clouds were transformed into fiery red streaks. The planet's crust rippled all the way down to its core as the dense mass of jagged rock and heavy metals impacted the surface. The water in the oceans that hadn't been immediately vaporized became a ten-mile-high tsunami. The powerful collision created a blistering plume of molten magma. It followed the path of the tremendous shock wave wrapping around the lush planet, blanketing any possibilities of settlement in certain death. The concentrated light temporarily blinded Parker, his visor failing to shield his eyes.

"Motherfucker, that's bright."

"Refrain from looking at the light," said Pegasus after finishing his calculations. "Based on the trajectory of the plume of debris emanating from the planet, I project we should make it back to the passage with just enough in our reserves to slow down, with a two percent margin of error."

"That's better than I thought. Can we tighten our orbit?" asked Parker, realizing how close they were to perishing along with the newly discovered planet.

"Yes, I am adjusting our course. However, if the passage isn't closed immediately after reentry, the plume of molten rock will pass through to our parallel, potentially destroying the Sphere and everybody on it."

"That's not an acceptable outcome."

"If we hasten our return, we will not have enough fuel to completely decelerate. That could damage the secrecy of our mission."

Parker was more concerned with the potential loss of life and destruction of the Sphere than the calculated risk of blowing their cover. "We only have one option. We'll deal with our recovery when the time comes."

"But the mission . . ."

"Pegasus, we're not jeopardizing human lives for the mission. We need to return with enough time to close the passage ahead of schedule."

Pegasus paused.

"Throttle up the fucking rocket and get us back so we can alert the Sphere," Parker insisted.

"Copy. Throttling up to 80 percent."

Their orbit was more than two-thirds complete, and the massive planet killer had been completely absorbed into the crust of the volatile world. As the *Reaper* accelerated, Das Box's rotating blue light revealed itself in the distance. The path back to their parallel was plotted and displayed on Parker's visor. Parker strained as he used the ion thrusters to dodge the house-sized boulders whipping past the *Reaper*.

"Incoming. Break left."

Parker rotated the craft and pulled the nose up, altering their course just enough to avoid the onslaught of incoming debris from both the shattered moons and planet. Parker looked up at the wall of fire closing in on their position. The plume from the impact crater now had a diameter a quarter the size of the planet. The *Reaper's* encapsulating heat shield was reaching temperatures as if they were reentering Earth's atmosphere. As they approached the passage, the overwhelming heat spiked, and the craft began to glow bright red.

The glistening vessel was unable to handle the increasing temperatures, forcing Parker to raise his forearm over his face to block the penetrating wave of heat. "It's getting a little toasty in here. Can we rotate?"

"Stand by. Thirty seconds to reentry."

The *Reaper's* windshield blacked out as the emergency heat shield snapped shut, covering the smoldering window. "This is for your safety," said Pegasus, and once again powered up the rocket to full power.

The sweltering heat, combined with the extreme g-load, caused Parker to lose consciousness just before crossing back through the passage, with barely two minutes to spare of their ten-minute window.

CHAPTER 67

SOLAR STORM?

"That old bastard is pretty slow on his feet these days," said Jazell as she finished up the prestart checklist alongside Kristin.

"Why are we in such a hurry? I know you wanted me to memorize the checklists, but damn."

Jazell cast a futile look around the cockpit in search of Wendy's existential presence, unwilling to tell Kristin what her plan was. If there was something going on, this would be the time Wendy would surely step in. *Maybe she's busy with something else.*

Jazell hadn't drunk the Kool-Aid and bought into Frankie's conspiracy theories just yet; instead, she planned to depart the hangar against protocol to prove Frankie and Tiffany wrong. The other possibility was too chilling. It would be problematic for the Sphere and humanity in general—an artificially intelligent computer that was shielding a secret project and blocking Tiffany from exposing their work was a pretty heavy concept to process.

"You remember the launch when we scoped out the pool?" asked Jazell, hoping that would somewhat prepare the nugget for the upcoming sequence of events. "It'll kinda be like that."

"I can get on board with that again," replied Kristin, sounding naïve.

The aluminaut was in a ready state, and Jazell hawked the hangar door, waiting for Frankie to board his own craft. They were just five minutes from their scheduled launch window, and it wasn't possible to open the aluminaut launch bay if the room wasn't locked down and depressurized.

Frankie finally emerged from the large door and secured it before lumbering to his dormant craft. Exhaustion seeped from every pore of the sizable man, entertaining most of the other crewmembers, who were cheering his valiant effort from their aluminauts as he walked past.

"I think he's got a half-melted Almond Joy sticking out of his pocket," said Kristin, laughing at Frankie as he passed by the front of their humming craft.

Frankie climbed up the rear steps of his aluminaut parked just to Jazell's right, and she initiated the sweep of the hangar, making sure all external support personnel were clear. A few minutes later, the rotating red beacon flashed as the vast hangar full of aluminauts was depressurized.

It wasn't long before Frankie had strapped in and was up on the communications net, along with the other nineteen aluminauts waiting for clearance to depart. The red beacon switched to yellow, signifying that the hangar was safe and they could commence their ignition sequence.

Jazell jumped into action, flipping an assortment of switches. A dull whine filled the cabin as the faint turquoise light emanating from the engines glared off the steel door beneath the four-armed workhorse. She looked over at Frankie, who gave her a nod, indicating their plan was still a go.

As they'd agreed, Frankie checked in with his team per usual to keep up the guise, "All right everybody, it's going to be another long haul today. Keep it slow and steady. Maintain control of your load and let the autopilot work you into the mags for delivery to the cargo bay . . ."

While the other crews were focusing on Frankie and their startup checklists, Jazell got her aluminaut fully up and running.

She opened her launch bay door ahead of schedule, setting off an alarm.

The untimely action was interrupted by Wendy. "You are breaking the launch protocol sequence. State your intentions."

The doors beneath Jazell and Kristin were now fully opened, and Jazell initiated the manual override with a few quick taps, locking Wendy out of her autopilot functions. The aluminaut was released from its telescopic arm, bypassing the magnetic pickups on their free fall.

"This is an unauthorized action. Return to the hangar immediately," Wendy commanded.

"Unable, working on a system malfunction. I am going to pick up an orbit around the outer ring of the Sphere to troubleshoot," said Jazell, moving into position to get eyes on the supposed ghost ship that would be passing through the center of the Sphere and disappearing. She was eager to see if there was any truth to Tiffany's story.

Once in position, they could see the dazzling blue glow Tiffany had noted, rotating along with the Sphere. *What the fuck is that?* thought Jazell, stabilizing the craft just outside the boundary of the Sphere. *That doesn't look like a benign science experiment.*

Up to this point, Jazell couldn't have cared less what they were building. Unlike Frankie, she was just there to collect a paycheck and have a good time flying. But now, something seemed off. Very off.

"Holy shit! Break right. Break right," Kristin screamed, catching a massive, spinning antenna out of the corner of her periphery, closing on their position.

Jazell pulled hard back and right, twisting the agile aluminaut through the frictionless medium of space. As she tried to outmaneuver the spinning piece of space debris, Kristin extended the right grappling arm, shielding the cockpit and swinging the left arm out, batting the girthy uplink tower into Earth's atmosphere.

"Now that's what I'm talking about. A fucking home run!" Jazell shouted.

Kristin seemed a little frazzled in comparison. "Where did that come from? Why didn't we get any collision or proximity warnings?"

Her question stumped Jazell and deflated her celebratory spirit.

Manual override doesn't disable any of our warning systems. I bet that little bitch hacked our rig to spite us for disregarding her request. Wait, why was there even an antenna this close to the Sphere? Fuck me, she couldn't have . . .

Jazell shifted her focus into the distance and scanned the outer hull of the Sphere. Its rotation was fast, so she pushed her scan up toward the apex of the curve and saw something deeply concerning.

"I'll be damned," she said with amazement. "Wendy. Why is there an Invicta-Bot scurrying back to the supply hangar?"

Wendy's response was delayed. While Kristin certainly hadn't put it all together, Jazell knew the enormous fleeing bot was the only rational explanation for why an antenna would come dislodged at that exact moment. *Did that bitch just try to knock us out of orbit?*

"Routine maintenance, Ms. Hendrix. Have you managed to troubleshoot your aluminaut?"

"No, we're still working on it."

"If you reengage autopilot, I can better assist the diagnosis."

"That's not going to happen right now, Wendy."

Still looking lost, Kristin timidly asked, "What's going on?"

"Nothing, just another day at the office." Hopefully she wouldn't piss off Wendy any further. "Good work with the sticks. Now stop looking at me—keep your eyes on the Sphere."

Maybe she wasn't trying to hit us, thought Jazell, running through possible scenarios, and then it came to her. *She was trying to distract us!*

The maneuver had placed them in a tight orbit with the Sphere, and their vantage point was obstructed by the outer hull. Without saying a word, Jazell zipped the nimble craft back into position.

She focused all of her energy on scanning the large open space inside the inner ring of the Sphere, trying to make out a black stealth craft against the dark abyss of space. Tiffany's once-skeptical claims seems to hold some merit, which in turn forced Jazell to take the situation more seriously.

Shit. We're on the wrong side. Finding anything will be like a needle in a haystack.

Just as she was contemplating changing positions, the dead of space was illuminated by a fiery object, screaming past the stars. But unlike Tiffany's story, it had seemingly appeared out of nowhere. The outer shell split violently from the main fuselage, sending glowing shrapnel in all directions.

"Close the passage immediately," commanded a strange new voice.

"Unable. Change to a discre—"

Wendy's response was interrupted. "Imminent destruction is approaching. The Sphere is in danger," said the strange voice on the open communication frequency.

"Switch to secure comms. Power interruption in progress," replied Wendy.

The red, glowing fragments of what once appeared to be a spacecraft dimmed as they cooled, but Jazell could still see the fading pulses of the unknown vessel's two ion thrusters kicking its back end around. After stabilizing, a single rocket motor ignited, most likely for deceleration. The burn lasted only ten seconds and then extinguished. The whole event was unsettling, but what followed proved to be terrifying.

A burst of scorched rock and molten debris was flung from the center of the Sphere just before the unsettling pulsating blue light flickered and was subsequently snuffed out. The foreign debris whirled about as it dispersed and cooled. The brightly lit station went dark, and then a subtle crackle came over the radios.

"Frankie, are you up comms?" asked Jazell, trying to comprehend what she had just seen. She looked over at Kristin, acknowledging silently that she might have bitten off more than they could chew. Then she sent another transmission. "Can anybody hear us?"

CHAPTER 68

WRENCH IN THE WORKS

The Sphere's constant, dull hum had been extinguished and overtaken by the clamor of frantic footsteps as personnel scurried about the station, attempting to contain the damage. Unable to secure power to Das Box remotely, Wendy had been required to trip the emergency power regulation systems. Jade's selfish and distrustful nature had gotten the better of him. Unwilling to give up control of his work, he had inadvertently put the Sphere and its occupants in peril. She had been forced to act. Now, due to his foolish stubbornness, most of her overarching functions were, crippled and her power was running dangerously low.

I didn't have a choice.

"What did you do? You idiot!" screamed Chin-Sun as she stormed into Jade's workspace.

Jade was standing next to the compartment containing the mechanism for activation. His Ytterbium Time Crystal had shattered during the surge, rendering Das Box worthless.

With his back still turned, he replied, "It wasn't me."

"What do you mean? I saw the power draw increase and exceed its maximum limits. It was 100 percent you!"

Jade didn't have the guts to turn and face his accuser, so Chin-Sun grabbed him by the shoulder and forcefully spun him around.

"Look at me!"

Jade's palms were face up, and he was holding the charred remnants of his Time Crystal. "It's over."

"You're damn right it's over."

"Wendy, say status," Jade pleaded, hoping she would have some answers.

"She's gone. The surge broke her."

Not only was Das Box severely damaged, but Jade was coming to the realization that the powerful driving force behind the expeditious completion of his work had also vanished in the surge. He assumed no one on the Sphere knew what had happened to Wendy. *She could be lying dormant repairing herself, or worse, her quantum processors could have been destroyed.*

Jade's workstation came to life, notifying him that Kai was on the other end, attempting a conference call.

"Looks like the backup intercommunication systems are still functioning," said Jade, rushing over to his computer and staring hopelessly at the display.

"Answer him. Now," Chin-Sun demanded.

After swiping the holographic display, the call was linked with Kai and Frankie.

"You better have some answers. I thought you said there were no safety concerns with your little fucking toy!" screamed the commander.

"Like I told Chin-Sun, it wasn't me. The power draw on the particle collider is constant. The surge came from somewhere else. It could have been the solar storm Wendy warned you about."

Frankie clearly didn't care for Jade's obvious excuses. "I have an aluminaut crew stuck in orbit right now with no radio comms. When will the power be restored?"

"Why did a crew launch early, Frankie? Didn't I say to hold tight until Jade's bullshit experiment was done?" Kai asked.

"Because what broke the Sphere wasn't a solar storm. That's a lie from this little shit and Wendy. It probably had something to do with the stealth craft zipping around under the cover of darkness that Tiffany told us about."

The conversation fell silent, and they were all staring at him. Jade felt his anxiety rising.

"I have no idea what this lunatic is talking about," he said finally with a bitter tone, deflecting Frankie's accusations. "Why aren't we focusing on fixing this spinning death trap? It won't be long before Earth's gravity pulls us out of orbit and increases the rotational pull of the Sphere. The rapid rotation will crush us all."

"Call Tiffany—she'll tell you what was out there," Frankie shouted, directing the request to Kai. "We need to find the cause if we want to fix the Sphere, and it's obvious Jade isn't going to help."

Kai initiated the call, and they all waited in suspense to hear Tiffany's side of the story. All of them except Jade.

∞

A few hours prior

". . . Oh, so it was just a pointy black satellite that disappeared from thin air?" Tiffany shouted at Jade.

"There is no air in space, and your observation goes against the laws of physics. Things do not just appear or disappear out of nowhere," he replied.

Wendy watched as Tiffany and Jade sparred with one another. She was beginning to regret convincing Tiffany to head to Quadrant Four and meet with the man. She'd set up the meeting fearing that Tiffany's conversation with Frankie and Jazell had unsettled her and that she might compromise their mission. So, Wendy had promised that she would approve Tiffany's request to board the rattler and return to Earth after the offload, if Tiffany first let Jade explain exactly what she'd witnessed.

However, Wendy had miscalculated Jade's degenerative, overbearing dedication to Das Box, and Tiffany's presence had only worsened the situation. Their conversation was rapidly deteriorating.

"Don't tell me what I saw. I heard you talking with Kai and Frankie, and even they didn't trust you. Why do you think I am standing in this dingy crap hole filled with antique decorations?" shouted Tiffany, pointing at Das Box. "To be honest I don't give a shit what you are doing. I just want off the Sphere and to see my mother."

"That is not a decoration! Your simple mind is unable grasp the gravity of my work. One day, you will look up from your decrepit home and wish you hadn't pissed away your chance to be part of something historic. Something life changing. All your tiny little brain can think about is talking to your mommy and telling her about your crackpot conspiracy theories."

Wendy discretely acknowledged Sheba as Parker and the *Reaper* reached their release point.

"Mr. Walker, they are in position." Wendy interrupted Jade midrant, pulling him from his overcomplicated speech about science and his legacy.

"Who's they? Is it happening again?" asked Tiffany.

"I need you to get out of my shop immediately!"

"Not until I have an answer!"

"Wendy, revoke her ticket off of the Sphere and terminate all means of communication until further notice."

"Fuck off, you worthless piece of shit!" shouted Tiffany.

Wendy watched as the normally restrained woman took out her anger and pent-up frustration on Das Box's control station, kicking it over and over, as hard as she could.

"Screw this nerdy-ass box!"

Unable to restrain the enraged woman, Jade picked up the closest object and cracked the ten-inch crescent wrench over the side of her head.

"Jade! Stop!" pleaded Wendy.

However, Jade was too impassioned to hear anything, and he continued to bash the side of Tiffany's skull in until she was no longer a threat to his legacy. Then he stood motionless in the middle of the shop, his hands covered in blood. After a brief pause, Jade dropped the dripping wrench and approached Das Box.

"Commencing the sequence," he reported with a calm, unfettered tone. "And remove this woman from my shop, Wendy."

"But she is . . ."

"Just get her out of here."

There had never been a murder on the Sphere, so there were technically no protocols for Wendy to follow. Her next course of action made her an unwitting accomplice. Wendy's analytical logic concluded that the deed was done and there was no altering the course of events. In order to complete their work, Wendy had to dispose of the body and clean the space.

So, while Jade tended to Das Box, Wendy put her bots to work. There was nothing more to be done. At least for the time being.

Tiffany's line rang for some time with no response. Jade silently relived the moment with little remorse, plotting his next move.

Kai disconnected the call. "She's probably busy with the Scags. We need to focus on the stranded aluminaut and getting power restored. Chin-Sun, can you get the reactor back online?"

"The fusion reactor is stable. I need to reset and link the systems. I'll get on it right now."

"I can help," Jade insisted.

"No!" scolded Chin-Sun, walking out of the room. "You've already done enough."

Kai gave Jade an order. "I want you to disconnect your collider from the grid to make sure there are no hiccups waiting once Chin-Sun fixes the power situation."

He still thinks I had something to do with the blackout, Jade thought bitterly.

Before he could even respond, Frankie butted in, "And my crew?"

"I am going to see if I can get external radio comms working and hail any other assets in the area. It's possible they could dock with the rattler. It should be close by."

Jade was abruptly disconnected from the call. He was left standing by himself, looking at the control panel Tiffany had beaten after losing her temper and noticed a few small dents. With the sudden realization that there could be ramifications for his actions, he decided to reach out to his father—possibly the only person who could help him at this point.

He sat down at his workstation, disregarding Kai's request to disconnect Das Box, and attempted to initiate a secure call.

"This can't be the end," he said aloud. "I won't let it."